Iron & Blood

First published 2015 by Solaris
an imprint of Rebellion Publishing Ltd,
Riverside House, Osney Mead,
Oxford, OX2 0ES, UK

www.solarisbooks.com

US ISBN: 978 1 78108 311 6
UK ISBN: 978 1 78108 310 9

10 9 8 7 6 5 4 3 2 1

A CIP catalogue record for this book is available
from the British Library.

Designed & typeset by Rebellion Publishing

Printed in the UK

IRON & BLOOD

A Jake Desmet Adventure

GAIL Z. MARTIN
LARRY N. MARTIN

SOLARIS

To Kyrie, Chandler and Cody for encouraging us
and allowing us the time to make these books happen.

"THIS WOULD HAVE been simpler if we'd done it my way." The slender woman lifted her chin defiantly. Dark ringlets framed her face, and her violet eyes sparkled. Her black wool traveling suit was nipped in at the waist, making the bustle in the back more pronounced. Her voice was starting to rise.

"Your way involved dynamite. We wanted to remain discreet." Jake Desmet tugged at the collar of his suit coat and tried to look nonchalant.

"We'd have been done by now." Veronique LeClercq fixed Jake with a glare. "Rick's taking forever to make the deal."

Jake took a deep breath and counted backward from five. His cousin's impatience was nothing new, nor was her penchant for more adventure than he fancied. And the dynamite had been a joke—maybe. "Nicki, be patient! Rick's good at this sort of thing. We've got to be delicate about this."

Jake hoped that passersby would take them for spatting siblings. While their disagreement was real, it was no accident that they were standing where they could keep an eye on the corridor in each direction. Jake smoothed a wavy lock of brown hair out of his eyes. Much as he hated to admit it, Nicki was right. Rick was taking a long time, and the delay was likely to cause trouble.

"Remind me again why you and Rick didn't just steal the damn urn?" Nicki's voice had dropped. "It would have been better than standing here like targets."

"One: I've got no desire to see the inside of Queen Victoria's dungeons for theft."

"Oh, piffle. Queens don't have dungeons anymore," Nicki said with a dismissive gesture.

"Two: The urn is very valuable to our client. It might be dangerous. We don't need to take additional risks." Jake could see Nicki's faint smile, which meant she wasn't really hearing a word he was saying.

"Tsk. If the urn is that dangerous, why hasn't it harmed the fellow who thinks he owns it? Eaten him, maybe, or sucked out his soul?" She was clearly relishing the argument, a pattern that hadn't changed since childhood.

"Andreas impressed on us that it could be dangerous, but he didn't say how," Jake responded. "Rick and I take him seriously when he says things like that." Jake focused on keeping his breathing regular. He'd been awakened in the night by a nightmare, and had had a sickening feeling of impending doom ever since. He'd told Rick and Nicki, but couldn't give them more details, just a gut feeling. Unfortunately, Jake's gut feelings were right more often than not.

"Just because your client is a centuries-old vampire-witch with a tendency for drama doesn't mean he's always right."

Andreas isn't the only one with a fondness for drama, Jake thought. Just as he was about to respond, the door opened. Out stepped a good-looking, young blond man in an impeccably tailored Savile Row suit with a bulky bundle, wrapped in oil cloth and tied up with twine, under one arm. Rick Brand was smiling broadly, and shaking the hand of a man who was hidden to Jake by the door. Their pleasantries suggested a meeting gone well.

Jake let out a breath he hadn't realized he'd been holding as he saw his friend safely back with them. The door closed and the smile disappeared from Rick's face as he strode toward them. His mouth became a grim line, and his sky-blue eyes flashed a warning. "Let's make a quick exit before the seller changes his mind," he murmured as he passed Jake and Nicki, forcing them to keep up.

They strode three abreast down the corridor, as fast as they could go without breaking into a run. Their footsteps echoed on the tile, mocking their desire for stealth. A black carriage awaited them at the curb. Jake gave the driver a hard stare, assuring himself that no substitution had been made. He kept back a pace, watching the street for danger, as Nicki climbed into the carriage, surrounded by her voluminous skirts.

Just as Jake started toward the cab, he caught a glimpse of movement and alerted Rick. Three burly men rounded a corner on the right and headed toward them at a dead run, while from the left, four more brawny strangers stepped out of an alleyway and started in their direction.

"Get in, get in!" Rick gave Nicki an ungentlemanly shove. Her protest was muffled. Rick swung up, handing off the wrapped urn to Nicki as he ducked into the carriage. "Come on, Jake." Jake already had a Colt Peacemaker in his hand, and was not surprised to see Nicki withdraw a pearl-handled derringer from her purse.

"Go!" Jake shouted, jumping for the doorway of the carriage. His foot had barely landed on the running board before the carriage lurched forward and the horses took off like the start of the Royal Ascot.

A shot splintered the rear left corner of the carriage. "I thought you said this coach was bulletproof," Nicki snapped.

"Part of it is," Jake said, ducking out of the carriage door long enough to size up their pursuers and get off a warning shot. Jake saw more men entering a waiting carriage down a side street.

"Only part?" Nicki's voice rose a few notes.

Rick opened his door, clinging to the carriage frame as he squeezed off two shots from his Remington revolver. An answering shot zinged past, putting a hole in the door just above his head.

"The carriage body is steel-reinforced," Jake said, before repeating Rick's move on the opposite side of the vehicle. "About to the height of the top of your head."

Nicki ducked. "Why not all of it?"

"Trade off, weight and speed," Jake replied, getting off another shot through the narrowly opened carriage door.

The carriage careened onto two wheels, taking the corner at breakneck speed as the pursuing carriage struggled to keep pace. Several of their pursuers' shots missed their marks, clattering against the brick walls of the buildings lining the road. Pedestrians and carts scrambled to get out of the way of the two carriages. Their driver had long been in the employ of Rick's father, and was one of the best in London, having survived more than one run like this. Still, as the carriage bumped and jostled, throwing them from side to side, Jake could not help wishing he were already safely back home in New Pittsburgh.

"Nearly there," Rick muttered under his breath, and Jake wondered if his friend had been counting the turns. Another volley of gunfire sounded around them, but this time, it seemed to come from every direction. Jake threw Nicki to the floor on top of the urn and dove to cover her with his body as Rick sank as low as he could into the seat.

A bullet tore through the top of the carriage, just missing the edge of the steel reinforcement. Several more clanged against the body of the carriage, leaving depressions in the metal. The shots were near-misses, despite their driver's efforts to keep their pursuers at bay.

Pinned between his chest and the urn, Nicki was muttering curses in French. Jake met Rick's gaze. "Why do our buying trips always end like this?"

Rick shot him his best crooked grin. "Because our usual business isn't business as usual," he replied, looking as unruffled as if he had just finished a cricket match back at Eton.

Jake kept his head down. There was good reason why the import/export company owned by his father and Rick's father employed ex-military sharpshooters for its drivers and secured former cavalry horses for its carriages. This sort of thing happened far too often.

"I thought they weren't supposed to be able to follow us," Nicki grumbled.

"Obviously, they're not as stupid as we took them for," Jake returned.

"I rather prefer dimwitted henchmen," Nicki muttered. "And I'll thank the two of you to mind not to sit on me. It's hard enough to breathe in this corset."

A few more twists and turns through the narrow streets, and the carriage finally slowed to a more acceptable pace. Another hail of gunfire sounded close at hand, then silence.

"Do you think we've lost them?" Nicki asked.

Jake shrugged. "Either that, or they ran out of ammunition."

THE CARRIAGE SLOWED to a halt. Rick and Jake exchanged a wary glance, rising carefully, guns at the ready. A sharp rap came at the carriage door. "Safe to come out now, guv," a familiar voice said.

Jake cautiously peered around the edge of the battered door, the Peacemaker still in his hand. Behind him, Rick also had his gun at the ready, and Nicki was struggling with her mass of skirts as she climbed off of the carriage floor. Jake's heart was still pounding, but his gun hand was steady. They had arrived in a walled private garden, where they were hidden, at least for the moment, from prying eyes.

"We've got a fresh carriage and a change of horses," their driver said. "Throw them off the scent. Standard operating procedure." He gestured toward a small, elegant carriage that looked like something a fine lady might use for a day of shopping. "Don't you worry," the driver went on, at Jake's skeptical expression. "It's reinforced, like the other one. A bit faster and lighter too, just in case they pick up the trail." Jake cast a backward glance at their carriage. The passenger compartment was peppered with marks where bullets had struck.

The driver waved them on. "Hurry now and get in the new coach. Then we'll send this carriage on—in the other direction. That should get rid of the blighters, and keep them away from the warehouse. Wouldn't do for them to catch up to us, or know too much about what Brand and Desmet does."

Jake, Rick, and Nicki moved at a run to the new carriage, keeping the bundle with the precious urn safely between them. They climbed inside and the carriage took off, drawn by different colored horses than the original coach and with a driver wearing a brand new cloak and hat.

The next time the carriage stopped, it stood in the middle of a loading area for a large, featureless warehouse. At least a score of brawny men greeted the carriage, most holding shotguns that were agreeably pointed toward the ground.

"All clear," the driver announced.

"Thanks for that," Jake said, opening the door and swinging down. To his relief, the area around the warehouse did not appear to have been the scene of any recent fighting.

"Think nothing of it, Mr. Desmet," the driver said with a broad grin. He shifted, and his dark cape gave a tell-tale jingle. "I was glad of the metal plates in my cloak and hat, that's for certain."

"Good to know," said Jake with a laugh. Behind him, Rick helped Nicki down from the carriage as if they were alighting at the opera.

"Guess that 'gut feeling' of yours was right again, Jake," Nicki said. "Now can you get it to be more specific about when and where?" She paused, as her gaze swept over the large warehouse. "Is that building one of yours?"

The driver bowed low and made a sweeping gesture with his hat. "Another fine warehouse of Brand and Desmet, m'lady."

All across Europe—and increasingly throughout the United States—warehouses were emblazoned with the 'Brand and Desmet' name. George Brand and Thomas Desmet—fathers to Rick and Jake—had built their import/export firm into an amazing, if decorously low-key, success story. Discretion was a necessity, given their clientele. Museums on both sides of the Atlantic hired them to bring back the relics of antiquity for their collections. Aristocrats in Europe and the rising elite in the States retained the Brand and Desmet Company to outfit their country houses, or to buy back treasures sold off or gambled away. Hard-to-find antiquities, rare objects, valuable pieces with unusual provenance—Brand and Desmet had built its fortune by acquiring these items for clients for whom money was no object.

Jake had long ago gotten over being star-struck by the names of their clients: dukes, earls, and lords in Europe; Carnegies, Vanderbilts, Goulds, Morgans, and the like in America. But he had not yet grown completely comfortable with their other customers, the ones who came by night to arrange more 'unusual' requests, like the immortal for whom they had retrieved the ancient urn and nearly been killed for their trouble.

People say that everything has its price. Mostly, Jake found that to be true. But sometimes, when a piece's ownership or provenance was in dispute and a buyer was insistent, successful acquisition had more to do with having a fast airship, good aim, cash for bribes, and a monetary relationship with customs officials. Those were the situations in which Brand and Desmet had earned a solid, if hush-hush, word of mouth reputation in the highest society circles. The rest of the import/export business was a well-maintained cover story.

"It's rather plain, isn't it?" Nicki asked. At first, Jake thought she was talking about the urn, but then he realized that she was staring at the unmarked warehouse.

Rick chuckled, his blood still rushing from the fight. "There's a reason for that. It's not just a warehouse, Nicki. It's also a hangar. Best to keep a low profile."

There was a hiss of steam, a whir of gears, and the muffled clank of chains. The sloped roof of the warehouse opened like the lid of a box and a large steel door slid back in the side of the warehouse, revealing just a glimpse of the private airship inside and a flurry of activity. Jake thrust his hands into his pockets, enjoying the show that he and Rick had seen before, but which was leaving Nicki, for once, almost speechless.

"*Mon Dieu*!" Nicki murmured.

"I had your things brought from the hotel and stowed aboard, as you requested, sir," the driver said. "Looks to be a good idea, since there were sure to be more of those blighters watching your lodging."

"Very good," Rick said, as unruffled as if a valet had just brought him his riding horse. "We'd best get going before any more of our 'friends' catch up with us."

"Mr. Desmet!"

Jake looked toward the warehouse, where one of the office clerks was running toward them.

"Mr. Desmet!" The clerk was out of breath when he reached them and his suit was rumpled. "I'm glad I caught you before you got aboard. Mr. Cooper asked to see you. He said it was important."

Jake shot a puzzled glance toward Rick, who shrugged. "Don't look at me. I wasn't expecting anything."

That wasn't entirely true. That sixth sense Nicki joked about was right more often than not, and all day, the expectation of bad news had hung over Jake. He feared he was about to discover why.

"Maybe Harold caught wind of what happened in town," Rick said with a meaningful glance. A telegram certainly could have reached their London office manager while Jake and the others were making their wild escape.

"Or maybe he's got an update on our next appointment," Jake replied, making an effort to keep the worry out of his voice. "Our Paris contact may have needed a bit more time to get the artifact, and our man in Krakow doesn't run on a strict London-style schedule. There could be a delay there."

"No way to know until you go talk to Harold," Rick said. "But you know how he goes on a bit. We need to get into the air and out of here before our 'friends' show up."

"I'll make it brief—and warn him to watch out for trouble," Jake promised, striding off toward the office next to the warehouse.

The office building was a two-story Georgian-style affair, understated yet dignified. It was all that remained of an old city estate belonging to a minor aristocrat who had owned this land long before the property was parceled off for other uses. Though converted to business use, the offices still had the feel of a stately residence, with beautiful woodwork, embellished plaster ceilings, and fine furnishings. It was every bit as grand as the New York office, and it was the standard the New Pittsburgh office had been designed to emulate.

The office building was unusually quiet when Jake entered. The grand home's entranceway remained a foyer, with the rooms to either side of the sweeping stairway given over to the use of the clerks, and the upper floors reserved for a meeting room, storage, and the office of their London manager, Harold Cooper.

Usually, Jake enjoyed seeing Harold. Although he looked like the quintessential British accountant, he was quick with a joke and whip-smart when it came to business. A former officer in Her Majesty's Army, Harold could hold his own on the occasions, like today, when the work got dicey. But he was also just as comfortable lifting a pint at the pub over a game of darts as he was reviewing ledgers and contracts.

"Mr. Cooper's waiting for you upstairs," the receptionist said, but for once, she did not greet Jake with her usual smile. In fact, she seemed to take pains to avoid meeting his eyes.

A leaden feeling grew in Jake's stomach as he climbed the stairs. He knocked once at Harold's half-open door. "Come in," a voice called.

"Your clerk said you needed to see me," Jake said, popping his head around the door. "Can we make it quick? We had a rather rushed departure from town. It would be good to get on to Krakow as soon as we can lift off."

"I'm afraid there's been a change of plans," Harold said. The manager was ten years older than Jake, and while he was still in his mid-thirties, his dark hair had begun to gray at the temples, something he jokingly blamed on Jake and Rick. Now he looked somber, and Jake's sense of foreboding grew. Jake sat down slowly, and Harold reached across the desk, extending a folded paper toward Jake.

"This telegram came through an hour ago," Harold said. "I'm sorry."

Jake stared at the piece of paper in his hands, reading and re-reading it as if the words might change their meaning. It took a moment for him to find his voice, and he blinked as his vision swam, then he crumpled the paper in his fist. "Father's dead?" He met Harold's gaze. "How can George be sure it was murder?"

Harold shook his head, and Jake saw loss in his eyes. Harold had worked with Brand and Desmet for over a decade, and his loyalty was absolute. "George sent a second telegram to me with the news, and instructions to have your ship ready to return to New Pittsburgh immediately. I've got another crew preparing to go on to Paris and Krakow, and we've got your airship prepped to make the Atlantic crossing."

It was all too much for Jake to take in. Part of him wanted to believe that if he just discarded the crumpled paper in his hand, it would negate the message and return the world to its prior order. But the truth was, the world had changed, and he would never see his father again.

"Ruffians chased us through London," Jake said, focusing on the immediate danger to avoid thinking about his pain. His voice was constricted as he fought for control. "We don't dare linger—they could show up at any moment."

Harold nodded. "The airship is ready. Rick and Miss LeClercq should be onboard by now. I asked Brant to give them the news. I thought that might be a little easier on you." Brant Livingston was Harold's long-time secretary, a thoroughly capable man with an almost encyclopedic knowledge of art and, occasionally, a fondness for ribald humor.

"Then I'd better get going," Jake said, putting on a good front with effort. He met Harold's gaze. "Someone just tried to kill us, and now this. I'm going to get to the bottom of it."

"Just be careful, Jake," Harold cautioned. "Someone out there wants something badly enough to commit murder, and if they didn't get it from Thomas, they're going to keep coming after you and Rick."

Jake closed his fist around the telegram. "That's what I'm counting on."

Chapter TWO

"I CAN'T BELIEVE he's gone." Jake stood at the window of the observation deck as the airship rose above London. The Thames snaked below them, but the smoky air obscured London's best-known landmarks. Nicki laid a hand on his arm, her violet eyes searching his.

"I'm so sorry, Jake."

Jake glanced away. Nicki was his mother's niece, daughter to Jake's eldest aunt, and right now, seeing her was a painful reminder of what his mother must be enduring. He swallowed hard.

Rick pressed a glass of scotch into Jake's hand. "Drink this. You've had a hell of a day."

The hum of the airship's engines filled the silence. The *Allegheny Princess* was the largest airship of the company's fleet, designed for transatlantic trips and named after one of the three rivers of New Pittsburgh. Its pilot, Cullan Adair, was the best in the skies. The *Allegheny Princess* was outfitted as comfortably as any luxury ocean liner, but its passengers were an exclusive few, the family and operatives of Brand and Desmet.

Jake pushed away from the railing and crossed to one of the leather chairs in the airship's lounge. He dropped heavily into the seat, still numb with shock.

"How can George be certain Uncle Thomas was murdered?" Nicki asked as she sipped a gin and tonic.

Rick grimaced. "Considering our afternoon, and the fact that we were nearly all gunned down, it doesn't seem that outlandish, does it?" He swirled the cognac in his glass. "The real questions are: why were we attacked, who gave the orders, and is there any connection to our most recent acquisition?"

Jake looked down at the amber liquid in his glass. "Father was always afraid something like this would happen. Moving priceless antiques. It's too much of a temptation."

"I have a feeling that this time, it's different," Rick replied. "That attack in London was too planned, and had way too many men, for the usual profiteers. Andreas paid a small fortune for that urn, but I'm wondering if the attack wasn't about something else, something he and your father were mixed up in, and someone thinks we know too much."

"When we don't know anything at all," Nicki said with a sigh. She settled back in her chair.

Andreas Thalberg, their client, was a man of many secrets. Jake was certain Thomas Desmet had known why the urn was so important, and when Jake returned to New Pittsburgh, he intended to find out.

"Andreas warned us that it was going to be a dangerous buy," Rick said, leaning back in his armchair. "Apparently, the urn caught the eye of some collectors who are used to getting what they want by any means."

"He's sent us on dangerous purchases before, and no one got murdered," Jake grumbled. "We always expect an ambush. And we've run into obsessive collectors before, but no one's ever dared to make such an open attack." He looked at Rick. "I think we should assume that this isn't over. That means New Pittsburgh isn't a safe haven from whoever—or whatever—is after us."

"Did Andreas give you any hint about what's so important about the damn urn?" Nicki demanded. Nicki's American-born mother, Jake's aunt, had married a wealthy French textile manufacturer. Although raised in Paris and educated at an exclusive Parisian finishing school, Nicki was, Jake thought affectionately, completely American at heart.

"The London trip came up unexpectedly," Jake said, taking a sip of his scotch and letting it burn down his throat. It did nothing to numb his grief. "Cullan barely had time to get the airship ready before we had to leave." He smiled sadly at Nicki. "I don't think George expected you to be joining us for the return trip."

Nicki shrugged. "Ah well. Probably a good thing, given what's happened. Aunt Catherine will need an extra hand. I'll send a telegraph to let my family know about the change in plans."

Jake sighed. "I can't even imagine how Mother's taking all this."

"Your mother is one of the strongest, smartest women I know," Rick replied. "She'll get through this. We'll make certain of it."

"Back to Andreas," Jake said, steering the conversation toward safer territory. He felt his control wavering, and he had no desire to break down in front of his friends. Jake shifted, maneuvering to get comfortable in his chair. At just shy of six feet tall, Jake Desmet was a few inches shorter than Rick, with a lean, athletic build. Jake's wavy brown hair framed pleasantly angular features and intensely blue eyes that he suspected were his best feature. "What was so important about the urn that we had to scramble to get to London so quickly?"

Rick sat stiffly, his tension clear in his posture. "Father didn't have time for a thorough briefing. Andreas was quite agitated and didn't share more than that the whereabouts of the urn had just been discovered, and it had to be brought to him as soon as possible."

Like Jake, Rick was in his mid-twenties, with golden blond hair and pale blue eyes, and a muscled build honed on Eton's cricket fields. Rick and Jake had grown up together in New Pittsburgh, a result of their fathers' partnership. Like Thomas Desmet, George Brand was an Englishman who had emigrated to America to expand his fortune, and, together, the two men had succeeded. But where Thomas had come up the hard way and fully embraced the raw vitality of his adopted country, George and his wife never gave up their English home and connections. Hence George's insistence on sending their only son to school in England, and their dismay when Rick later demanded to return to the States.

"How bad does something have to be to worry a vampire-warlock?" Nicki asked.

"Witch," Jake corrected absently. "He prefers to be called a witch."

Nicki made a face. "He's scary powerful, whatever you call him. Exactly what scares *him?*"

Rick tossed off the last of his cognac, but from the look in his eyes, it did little to blunt the loss they both felt. "I don't know—and that scares me."

"Sorry I couldn't join you before this."

Startled by the voice, Jake turned to see Cullan Adair standing in the doorway to the lounge.

"Don't take this wrong, Cullan, but if you're down here, who's piloting the ship?" Rick asked.

Cullan grinned. "Tommy's got the controls."

Jake raised an eyebrow. "You're letting your automaton pilot the *Princess?*"

"He's the best there is—trained him myself," Cullan replied. He chuckled at their concern. "Don't worry. Mueller's up there with him." Eric Mueller, Cullan's first mate, was nearly as renowned a pilot as Cullan himself.

"Sorry about your dad," Cullan said, crossing to join the trio. "Harold let us know and told us about the change in plans before you reached the warehouse." He glanced toward Nicki and smiled. "Glad to see you with us, Miss LeClercq. A rose among thorns, as it were."

Cullan Adair's black Irish good looks and his quick wit had won him many a lady's favor—and many a husband's enduring enmity. He winked at Nicki, who grinned and gave him a broad wink in return. It was a game they had played for years, and Jake was almost certain there was nothing to it beyond good-natured flirting. Then again, with Cullan, nothing was ever guaranteed.

"We'll stop in Long Island to refuel, then on to New Pittsburgh," Cullan said. "Given the bit of trouble you had back in London, I thought it best to wait until we're nearly there to telegraph the port crew about our arrival—just in case."

"Good idea," Rick replied. "Since we don't know who's after us."

Cullan regarded his three passengers, and Jake guessed that they looked the worse for wear, after their chase. "Your bags are in your cabins," he said. "You've still got a couple of hours until dinner. Why not get some rest, freshen up? By then, we should be well over the Atlantic."

"Captain Adair." The voice sounded over the airship's speaking tube. "You'd better get up here. We've got company."

Cullan's smile vanished. "You might want to hang on," he said. "This could get bumpy."

Cullan sprinted for the bridge, while Jake and the others ran to the lounge's observation windows. Through the clouds, they could make out dark shapes, too big to be anything but pursuing craft.

"There!" Nicki cried, pointing. Jake caught a glimpse of a one-man dirigible, much smaller than the *Allegheny Princess*. Instead of a passenger compartment under the dirigible's balloon, the smaller craft had what appeared to be a gunner's seat. A second later, fire flashed from the pilot's underslung mount.

"What the hell was that?" Rick strained to see what was going on.

"Looks like a Gatling gun to me," Jake observed.

Rick ran to the other side of the lounge. "There are two more on this side, closing fast."

"I see one... no, *two* more behind this one," Nicki reported.

Jake frowned. "Those can't possibly have the range to follow us across the Atlantic. It's suicide for them to come after us. Their ships can't carry Tesla cells powerful enough to fuel them that far."

"They don't have to," Rick replied, his voice cold. "Not if they can dock with that." Jake and Nicki turned in time to glimpse a full-sized airship that was easily as big as the *Allegheny Princess*, partially hidden by the clouds.

The *Princess* lurched, and Jake nearly lost his footing, saving himself by grabbing the railing that ran along the windows. A bullet cracked against one of the windows, sparking against the aluminum frame. "Damn," Jake muttered. "That's too close for comfort."

"Get down!" Rick ordered as he pulled Nicki to the floor and Jake dropped. A shot embedded itself in the thick glass. New Pittsburgh was well known for its glass industry, supplying fine housewares that were the envy of the world. But the city's captains of industry invested in more practical products, like the bulletproof glass that had become all the rage since the Braddock riots a few years earlier.

Rick found himself tangled in Nicki's skirts as she turned and gave one of her dazzling smiles. "Rick... really you shouldn't have."

"Nicki! I..." Rick blustered as his face turned bright red. Fortunately he was saved by a lurch of the ship.

The hiss of steam and the hum of gears grew louder as the *Princess* pulled ahead, and Jake guessed Cullan was attempting to draw their pursuers out over the Atlantic, where there would be more room to maneuver, and fewer prying eyes. The deck beneath them began to vibrate, and from below, they could hear the whirr of cables and the clank of metal.

"What's Cullan doing?" Nicki shouted above the din. She had braced herself behind one of the large leather chairs, which were bolted to the floor. Rick and Jake had done the same, trying to avoid sliding across the lounge as the airship banked and turned.

"Just a guess, but I'm betting he's launching those," Rick said, pointing toward the windows. "Damn it, Adam... holding out on me again! I helped with the specs for those and he never told me he put them into production!"

Several brass and aluminum saucers hovered outside the windows. Gears and pulleys covered them like sinews, and Jake could make out the rounded domes of aluminum-shielded balloons. Each was as wide as the passenger compartment of a carriage, but only a few feet high, and slung under every one of the contraptions was the unmistakable barrel of a Gatling gun.

The saucers opened fire on their pursuers, pushing the attacking mini-dirigibles farther away as Cullan banked the *Princess* hard to port, and Jake felt the engines rev, picking up speed. What he dared glimpse from the windows looked like lightning sparking in the clouds as the smaller craft battled each other. With a brilliant flare, one of the small dirigibles burst into flames and dropped from the sky.

"They're gaining on us!" Rick yelped. The ship banked, and Rick began to slide across the floor until he caught hold of the leg of a table.

"It feels like Cullan's pulled out all the stops," Jake replied, holding on to avoid a similar slide. Nicki shot Jake a cavalier grin that seemed to suggest she was enjoying the adventure.

"Don't—I repeat, do *not*—tell your mother about this," Jake warned Nicki, imagining his aunt's reaction.

"Not a chance," Nicki replied with a wicked smile. "This is too much fun. Isn't it Rick?"

The sound of gunfire made all three of them duck before Rick could think of a response. Jake raised his head warily. One of the brass and aluminum drones had taken a hit and smashed against a large window pane. The bulletproof windows did not shatter, and the damaged drone was lodged in the reinforced glass for a moment before wiggling lose and wobbling off to rejoin the fight.

"Quite a firefight out there," Rick observed at the flashes of light beyond the windows.

Jake dared a glance over the railing, and paled. "That's not from the Gatlings," he murmured. "Cullan's steered us right into a lightning storm!"

"Is he daft?" Rick scrambled to join Jake by the window. The dark clouds and white streaks confirmed Jake's conclusion. "If we get hit by one of those, we'll go down just as surely as we'd have from the Gatling fire."

Pieces of one of the unlucky mini-dirigibles peppered the observation windows like aluminum hail. Bursts of lightning lit the sky like the flashes of a photographer's phosphorous lamp as they flattened themselves against the deck.

The whirr of the engine was drowned out by the sound of an explosion that lit up the sky, and the *Allegheny Princess* bobbed like cork on a wild sea. Jake felt his stomach lurch, threatening to send back his lunch. White light illuminated the lounge and the *Princess* began to drop so rapidly Jake thought he might come off the floor. Anything loose in the lounge, from their cocktail napkins to their forgotten glasses, became airborne. Jake was grateful that the furniture had been bolted to the deck, or they might have been bludgeoned with tables and chairs.

"Are we hit?" From the expression on Nicki's face, it was clear that their situation had suddenly ceased to be a game.

Cold fear seized Jake's heart. *Please don't let my mother lose Father and me on the same day*, he thought. He braced himself for impact as the airship fell, wondering how he would die: in the cold North Atlantic waters, or engulfed in flames.

Before he could decide, the *Princess* slowed its descent, and in a few more heartbeats, leveled out, reducing its speed to a sane pace.

"This is your captain speaking," Cullan's voice echoed from the speaking tube. "In case you weren't sure, we're still alive. I'll be down as soon as we get the last of this storm behind us." He paused. "And if you've been airsick, do try to mop up after yourselves."

Jake gave Nicki a hand, hauling her to her feet in an effective, if not decorous, way. Rick climbed to stand beside the table, and looked out over the wrecked lounge. One of the observation windows was cracked, a clouded mass of splinters held in place by the special bulletproof coating. Several of the panes on the port side bore scratches and nicks where the exploding mini-dirigibles had peppered them. Through the remaining windows, Jake could see the clouds growing lighter.

Henderson, the steward, ran into the lounge and looked around in a near-panic. "Sir, is everyone well? Anyone hurt or injured?"

Jake dusted off his jacket. He managed an encouraging smile, although he doubted that it fooled Henderson, who had been with them for years. "No, everyone's fine. Just a little clean-up for later. Thank you."

Henderson glanced around the ruined cabin and raised an eyebrow, but merely nodded in response. "Very well, sir. Ring if you need anything." He left almost as quickly as he had arrived.

Nicki sank into one of the armchairs. Her hands grasped the arm rests as if she was not quite ready to believe their ordeal was over. "We made it!" Now that they were safe, her eyes sparkled with excitement.

Jake was peering out the port side while Rick scanned the starboard skies. "I'll hand it to Cullan," Rick said. "He shook off our uninvited guests."

Jake gazed down at the gray water that rolled far beneath them. "If that big bang was the mothership, then I doubt any of the mini-craft could have made it back to land, even if the drones didn't knock them out. I'm guessing Cullan had us too far over the ocean by then for them to turn back."

A hard glint lit Rick's eyes. "All the better. Let whoever sent them wonder."

Jake collapsed into a chair. "But why? If it's the urn they want, they're remarkably persistent. And if it's related to Father's murder, then why are they after us? Whoever sent that airship after us has resources, and I'm betting we haven't seen the last of them."

"Maybe they don't want the urn," Nicki replied, staring at the ruined window. "Maybe they just wanted to make sure that we don't make it back to New Pittsburgh."

That sobering thought left them silently weighing the repercussions, until the door flew open and Cullan stepped inside, wearing an ear-to-ear grin. "Mighty fine flying, if I do say so myself!"

"You nearly killed us!" Nicki retorted.

Cullan feigned a hurt look. "Did our maneuvering scare you?"

"Out of a year of my life!" Nicki replied, then grinned. "But it'll make an amazing story someday for my grandchildren."

Jake and Rick congratulated Cullan with hearty backslapping, and Nicki favored him with a kiss on the cheek. Cullan was playing the daredevil, but Jake knew him well enough to see that the battle had given the pilot a run for his money.

"Any casualties?" Jake asked. It was exactly what his father would have done, worrying about the crew over the hardware.

Cullan shook his head. "Nothing worse than some bruises and cuts. Mueller's got a nice shiner from where he rapped himself on a speaking tube. It could have been worse."

"What were those... things you launched? The hovering metal disks with the guns?" Jake asked.

Cullan leaned against a walnut-paneled pillar and crossed his arms. "Another illicit invention, courtesy of Adam Farber and Tesla-Westinghouse labs. With some input from you as well, I hear," Cullan said, giving Rick a grin.

"Just another mechanical nightmare Adam and I cooked up in his lab," Rick replied. "Didn't even tell me they were ready," he muttered, still annoyed.

Cullan shook his head. "The real beauty of it is, those things don't need pilots. Whoever was after us had men in their mini-dirigibles; I'm quite certain of it. Made for nasty business. Farber's flying automatons let us even the score without putting any of our crew at risk."

"How did you make sure they were shooting in the right direction?" Jake asked. "They're too small to have a difference engine aboard."

Cullan laughed. "I don't think even Adam Farber would try putting a difference engine into one of those things—although," he mused, "it might not be a bad idea. I'll have to mention that next time I see him, if Rick doesn't beat me to it."

"Actually, it's ingenious," Rick jumped in. "Adam's been toying with the idea of a radio telegraph—a telegraph that can transmit through thin air, without wires. Cullan can control the disks from the bridge, with Adam's new contraption. He said it sends Morse code signals through aetheric waves."

"Adam's been burning the midnight oil again." Cullan shook his head. "That boy is brilliant. I'm glad he's on our side."

Cullan glanced around the lounge, seeming to notice the damage for the first time. "Damn," he muttered, then his gaze slid sideways to Nicki. "Sorry." He shook his head. "Those windows cost a small fortune apiece. On top of losing a couple of the drones, this is shaping up to be an expensive flight."

The fact that they could have ended up as flaming debris in the Atlantic went unsaid, but Jake could see the knowledge in his friends' eyes. "What about Long Island?" Focusing on the details of the trip kept Jake from dwelling on what awaited them when they arrived.

"We'll use the beacon when we get close enough for a visual signal," Cullan replied. "With luck, whoever our 'friends' were who sent the other airship won't also have men on the ground in Long Island waiting for us; but if they do, we'll handle it."

Prior to being in the employ of Brand and Desmet, Cullan Adair had been a supply pilot for the U.S. Army's airship corps, with a flair for side dealings that had earned him a questionable discharge, dealings he described as being a 'naval redistribution specialist'. Today's flight, Jake knew, was not Cullan's first close call.

"I don't know about the two of you," Rick said, "But I'm all in. I think I'll go back to my cabin and clean up before dinner—and maybe get my stomach out of my throat," he said with a sideways glance at Cullan.

"Go ahead," Cullan replied. "I dare say the galley is going to need some time to pull itself back together after that ride. We might not get more than tea and sandwiches, depending on how much the cook got bounced around. And we've got to make sure we didn't miss any holes from all those bullets flying. That would make our trip real short."

Rick paused by Jake and squeezed his shoulder. "I'm here for you Jake... and we'll get through this, just like we always do."

Jake could only nod in response. He turned to Nicki and lent her his arm as they followed Rick down the narrow passageway to the airship's sleeping quarters. The *Allegheny Princess* was outfitted like a small cruise ship, with the ability to sleep a large number of guests comfortably in addition to the crew. Jake saw Nicki to her quarters, and she threw her arms around him in a fierce hug.

"If you need to talk, I'm here to listen," she said.

"I can't—not yet," Jake said, feeling his throat tighten. "Later. But thanks." Nicki nodded and disappeared into her cabin.

Jake feared the wild ride might have tossed the contents of his cabin around the room, but he was pleased to see the clasps on his drawers and cabinets had done their job. He tried to lie down, but he was too restless. After putting his things in order, Jake crossed the hall to his father's private cabin.

The first thing that struck Jake was the faint smell of his father's cologne. The cabin bore the unmistakable mark of Thomas Desmet's presence. The built-in furnishings were finished in the dark wood Thomas favored, and the paintings on the walls were of England and Scotland. Jake was quite certain that the cabinet held his father's favorite after-dinner brandy, and that the desk held a supply of monogrammed stationery.

Jake sank into the tufted leather of the desk chair and opened the desk drawer. His father had taken the airship up to New York just the week before, had sat in this chair, working on ledgers and correspondence. There was a loose square of paper, the kind his father liked to carry in a shirt pocket for making notes. On it was a list of names, written in his father's handwriting: *Nocnitsa, Nowak, Dabrowski, Jasinski, Kozlowski, Bajek, Chomicki, Kubiak, Radwanski, Alekanovo, Marcin.*

Curiosity won out over grief. Jake took the paper and slipped it into his jacket pocket. *Who knows how long it's been in the drawer?* Jake thought. *It could have nothing to do with this job—or his murder.* But just in case, he decided that he would show it to George, and maybe to Andreas. Someone had killed Thomas Desmet and been willing to stop at nothing to kill them. As soon as he got back to New Pittsburgh, it was time to figure out why.

Alone for the first time since he had received the news of his father's death, Jake covered his face with his hands. He was glad that the cabins were nearly soundproof, muffling his sobs, though he was certain his friends would not begrudge him his mourning. Thomas Desmet had been a good father, a family man. His marriage to Catherine had been a love match, and even after decades, the affection between the two was obvious. Quiet and unassuming, content to work in the background, Thomas's genius lay in his ability to see opportunities others overlooked and build a network of sources unrivaled by competitors. Where Rick often butted heads with George, Jake and Thomas usually got along. Life—and business—without him was unthinkable.

I've got to be strong for Mother, Jake told himself, shaking with the effort to slow his shuddering breaths. *I'm going to be the one she'll need to rely on. Henry's got the empathy of a rhinoceros, so he won't be any good helping Mother pull things together. And besides, George and Henry will be focused on the business.* Henry, Jake's officious older brother, ran the New York office.

Oh dear Lord, if this means Henry is going to move back to New Pittsburgh, maybe I should have just let those assassins put me out of my misery. Jake sighed. *Henry won't want to travel—or get shot at. He'll still need me for acquisition trips. Mother won't let him fire me, and I won't strangle him for her sake.*

Jake sat in Thomas's cabin for a long while, unwilling to let go of the last vestige of his father's presence. Finally, he pulled himself together enough to return to his own cabin. He splashed cold water on his face to hide the tears, catching a glimpse of himself in the mirror. His eyes were red, and even the polite fiction of a smile did not reach his gaze. Jake felt disoriented, as if he had failed to wake from a bad dream. The smothering loss and grief would only get worse when he arrived home and Thomas's death became undeniably real.

Jake drew in another ragged breath. *I have some time to think, time to figure out what to do next. And I'll need every moment of it.*

At top speed, it would take three days to cross the Atlantic, if weather was on their side. Once they arrived in New Pittsburgh, there would be the funeral, and after that, business issues would have to be handled. Grief was a luxury that would have to wait until vengeance and justice were served.

Jake's thoughts strayed to the attack in London. The wild carriage chase and desperate aerial pursuit made it clear that someone had a big stake in either killing Jake and his friends or acquiring the urn by whatever means necessary. Neither reason made any sense to Jake. *We've hunted down priceless relics from all over the world, and no one's sent this much firepower after us before. There's something we're missing, something we don't know. And until we figure it out, we are sitting ducks.*

Jake felt as if he had aged a decade in a few hours. He doubted that either sleep or scotch would give him a reprieve. *Mother is probably beside herself with grief*, he thought. *And Henry will make it in from New York before I can get there. That can only make things worse.* Henry was five years older and insufferably by-the-book. *No matter that I'm twenty-six years old*, Jake thought.

Henry will treat me like I'm still in knickers. The business will go on. That was a good thing, though the thought was tinged with sorrow. *George could run Brand and Desmet single-handedly.* But it was more likely that Thomas Desmet had left his share of the business to his eldest son.

Bloody hell. Do I want to work for Henry? He's such a martinet. Maybe I can get George to assign me to the London office.

He took another deep breath and shook his head to clear his thoughts. *Time to prioritize.* The first challenge was to get home alive, and then, assuming he succeeded, the next was to find a murderer. Scuffles with Henry could wait.

A tentative knock sounded at his door. "Jake? It's me, Nicki. Please let me in."

Jake opened the door and his cousin stood before him, a look of concern on her face. She swept past him without a by-your-leave and sat down in the chair by the desk. "First things first," she said, and withdrew a silver flask from somewhere within her voluminous skirts.

"Drink this." Nicki thrust the flask at Jake. He unscrewed the cap and complied, knocking back a mouthful and letting it burn down his throat. He capped the flask and tried to hand it back to her, but Nicki waved him off.

"Keep it. At least until we get back to New Pittsburgh. You need it more than I do." She winked at him. "And I've got another one in my trunk.

"You know Rick is really hurting for you too," she added. "He just doesn't have a clue what to say. So expect to do a lot of manly drinking over the next couple days." She sat up primly and placed both palms on her knees. "Now. Talk to me."

Jake sighed. "I don't even know where to start."

Nicki gave him her craftiest smile, the look that had launched one ill-advised adventure after another in their childhood. "Come on, Jakey. No secrets. Remember? We pinky-swore."

Jake was forced into a half-smile. "No one has called me 'Jakey' since I stopped wearing knickers. And we pinky-swore when we were eight."

Nicki raised her chin. "A pinky-swear is forever. Everyone knows that. Now—spill."

Jake slumped onto his bunk. "I guess I haven't quite let it all sink in yet." His voice lacked its usual gusto. "I just can't imagine going back to New Pittsburgh and Father not being there. Not ever being there again." Despite himself, his voice broke.

Nicki came over to sit next to him and draped an arm around his shoulder. "Do you remember the time Uncle Thomas caught us digging up *maman*'s rosebushes?"

Jake chuckled sadly. "And he listened without even cracking a smile when we showed him the treasure map we had 'found' and why we had to dig up the 'gold' to rescue the Prince."

"He might have been willing to hear us out to find out where Rick was," Nicki said. "Since he got stuck being the Prince and we left him tied up all day in the garden shed pretending to sleep."

"It wasn't *all* day," Jake countered. "Just all morning. And you're the one who said he had to be a sleeping prince to be rescued."

"He got to be the hero the time before," Nicki sniffed. "And you were the pirate. Besides, I did 'kiss' him awake and we shared our cookies with him. Even if we were sent to our rooms for the afternoon."

"Yeah, it was worth it for the look on Rick's face. You're the only one who can stun him speechless. Father thought it was hysterical. But that's just it." Jake took another nip from the flask. "Father is—*was*—so reasonable. So level-headed. He and Mother are such a good team. And he even takes Henry in stride." He shook his head and covered his face with his hands. "I can't even use the past tense to describe him. I don't want to admit he's gone."

"Tell me a good story. Any story."

Jake sighed. "Do you remember the time Rick and I borrowed the carriage to set off fireworks down along the river, and the horses got loose?"

Nicki chuckled. "How could I forget? Especially when the horses bolted after the fireworks all went off at once because you weren't too good at that sort of thing, and the harbor patrol thought it was a signal flare from a sinking barge and a couple of vagrants thought it was the river pirates, and by the time your father got there you and Rick were hunkered down in a shoot-out between the homeless guys and the patrol, and they were both looking for a missing boat that didn't exist."

"We were grounded for a long time," Jake said wistfully. "But you know, even when he was giving us a talking-to about that, I had the feeling that, secretly, Father thought it was a grand romp." He fell silent, lost in memories.

Nicki regarded him sympathetically for a moment, and gave his shoulder a squeeze. "Do you remember when your dog Spratt got hit by a wagon?" she asked. Jake nodded.

"Your father never faulted you or Rick—or any of us—for crying about it," Nicki recalled quietly. "He told you that feeling sad meant we really loved Spratt, and it was okay to miss him."

"I remember," Jake said in a muffled voice.

"And do you remember how your father came home early from the office, and he helped us hold a proper funeral, and then he made us each talk about our favorite memories of Spratt? And then he told us that was what really mattered, those memories, and never forgetting him," she said, giving Jake a gentle nudge in the ribs.

When he said nothing, she continued. "I know there's a big difference between Spratt and your father. But Uncle Thomas was right about the memories. We'll get to the bottom of the murder, Jake, I promise you," Nicki swore. "But your father is more than his murder. Remember all of that, not just the end." She met his gaze. "And believe me—we will find the people who did this and make them pay. Count on it."

Chapter THREE

"It's a bloody mess, that's what it is." The police sergeant said with a grimace. "Barely enough left to tell it was a person, God rest his soul."

Drostan Fletcher looked down at what remained of the corpse. He had seen worse in Burma, when he had served with Her Majesty's Army, before coming to America. Those were not memories he wanted to recall.

Just a few feet away, the swift currents of the Allegheny River slipped by, swollen with the runoff from snows upstream. The namesake city of Allegheny was just across the river from New Pittsburgh, its larger and more prosperous neighbor. The air smelled of glue and pickles, a combination Fletcher no longer found odd given the number of factories that clustered along the riverbanks.

"D'ya think it mighta been a wight?" Sergeant Finian was still staring at the remains. His voice carried a heavy Irish brogue, just as Drostan was sure people heard the traces of Scotland in his own burr, though it had been years since he had left his native land.

"What on earth would make you think that?" Drostan replied.

Finian shrugged. "I heard tell the Indians called these parts the 'dark places', back in George Washington's day. They thought there was something evil here, and steered clear." He nodded toward the body. "Maybe they were on to something."

It was so like the English to ignore the cautions of those who knew the land best, Drostan thought with a sigh. That was a lesson the Brits didn't seem to learn, no matter where they roamed. Scotland, Ireland, the Colonies, India... so many warnings unheeded, and so many needless deaths.

"Hardly something you can put in your report, now, is it?" Drostan remarked.

Finian flushed. "Can't imagine the Captain going for it, no, that's God's honest truth for you," he said. "So what's your take, Fletcher? You don't have to report to the likes of Captain Boyle."

Drostan Fletcher sighed. Boyle wasn't a bad cop. He was smart and tough. But like a lot of cops, he had the imagination of a cabbage. Most of the time, that wasn't a bad thing. Cops dealt with hard facts, and too much imagination could get in the way. A good cop was methodical, detailed, unwilling to engage in suppositions that did not corroborate with evidence. But sometimes, closing a case took more than that.

"I don't have a 'take' yet," Drostan replied. "But I'm not happy to see another corpse, and certainly not on the same stretch of riverbank."

"That why the swells hired you? Bet it makes them nervous, bein' so close an' all," Finian said, with a nod of his head. Even though Drostan couldn't see the brownstone neighborhoods from here, he knew well enough what Finian meant. Allegheny was a strange mixture of industry and luxury, immigrants and wealth.

Tanneries and soap factories, packing houses, and pickle manufacturers lined the banks of the wide river. So many German immigrants crowded into the cheap rooming houses and inexpensive neighborhoods that folks called the area Deutschtown. But just a few blocks farther on Ridge Avenue and the Mexican War streets, rows of brownstone townhomes and impressive residences were home to some of New Pittsburgh's wealthiest families, the men who owned the factories and employed the immigrants. Finian didn't need to know that Drostan's employer wasn't from this part of town, and that his real concern didn't lie with the murdered vagrants.

"How will you make your report?" Drostan asked. Finian was scribbling in his notebook, and took a moment to finish before answering.

Finian grimaced. "Not much I can say except the what and the where of it, now is there? We've got no who or why, and there's little enough of the body left, I'm not even sure of the how." Finian eyed the uneasy patrolmen waiting a little ways off next to a morgue wagon. "Dr. Sheffield won't have much to work with."

Sheffield, the county coroner, already had his hands full, Drostan reflected. The bodies had started showing up a few months before, working their way up the Monongahela River from down near Richeyville until they finally reached the big city, then across the Point and now along the Allegheny River. The bodies were always found on the riverbanks, in deserted areas screened from view by warehouses and factories. Since the dead were vagrants, indentured servants, and poor immigrants, police authorities had taken little notice.

"Fella probably came down here for a smoke or to finish off a bottle of whiskey and got more than he bargained for," Finian replied, looking at the savaged corpse.

Drostan's mouth quirked into a mirthless smile. Padraig Finian had a good eye for detail, and a disciplined imagination. *If you keep your head down and your mouth shut, you might make captain yourself one day*, Drostan thought. Until then, Finian was a good man on the job and an even better man to raise a pint with.

"You got any leads on that last girl that got killed?" Finian asked. He nodded for the other officers to come closer with a stretcher and blankets, though they would be better served with a shovel and bucket. A few moments later, the policemen's curses suggested the body was disintegrating. Drostan pointedly looked away. He had seen carnage before, too much of it.

"No," Drostan replied. "And her name was Alice. Alice Hancock."

"Yeah, I remember," Finian said. "I just don't like using her name. Got a niece named Alice. Gives me chills thinkin' about it."

"If I hear anything about your murders that might be useful, I'll let you know," Drostan said, shutting his own notebook and slipping it into the pocket in the lining of his coat. Finian had helped him out more than once, and Drostan returned the favor whenever he could. Good relationships inside the police department made his job a little easier. But the real reason Drostan was here had to do with a hunch that, for reasons he didn't dare try to explain, the murder of a business owner over in New Pittsburgh just might have some connection to the string of unsolved murders along the rivers. And Drostan was almost certain the connection had to do with magic.

"Appreciate your help," Finian replied. "I'll stay in touch," he added with a nod. "And until we catch whoever—or whatever—did this, best we were all watching our backs."

Drostan glanced around. There were bystanders, watching the police silently from a distance. No reason to think any of them was the murderer, but perhaps they had seen something. The police gave them no notice, but Drostan could not escape their watchful gaze, staring at him as if daring him to take down their testimony. "Do you mind if I hang around for a bit?"

Finian looked out over the bleak, garbage-strewn strip of land and the dark, swift river beyond it. "That's up to you." He pulled his uniform coat closer around him against the wind. "Personally, I can't wait to get back to the station and get some hot coffee."

Drostan watched the police finish up and return to their wagons, waiting until the last of them had pulled away before he walked over to the small cluster of onlookers standing silently off to one side. It grew colder as he approached them, and he wished he had worn a heavier coat.

"If anyone saw anything, now would be a good time to mention it," Drostan said, looking from face to face. There was an old man, probably a vagrant, with a grizzled beard and sunken eyes, who smelled of whiskey and licorice. Next to him was a teenager, raw boned and pale, and from the Old World cut of his clothes, Drostan guessed he was a day laborer, fairly new to America. A dark-haired woman clutched her shawl around her over her bodice, which still showed more than a proper woman would reveal. Drostan figured she was a tavern waitress, maybe even a prostitute. A peddler stood sullenly off to one side, as if he did not wish to be associated with the others.

"Well? I'm waiting—and I'm cold. Anybody see what happened here?"

"'Twas the Night Hag." The woman lifted her head defiantly, as if Drostan might question her right to testify. Her accent bore traces of her native Polish. "I've seen her."

"Who is the Night Hag?" Drostan asked, his voice gentle so as not to frighten the woman. The immigrants who crowded Allegheny's and New Pittsburgh's working class neighborhoods did not always think well of the police, often for good reason.

"You don't have to talk to him." The teenager eyed Drostan warily. "You don't owe him anything."

The woman's eyes were fearful. She'd been through a lot, most of it bad, Drostan guessed.

"Please. It might help keep someone else from getting killed."

"I didn't meet the Night Hag myself, you understand," the woman said finally. "My bad luck was running into a good-for-nothing boyfriend, but that's an old story now. But I like this place, with the river and all, so I stay here. Only lately, *she's* started walking here." The woman wrapped her arms around herself. "I don't like her."

"You mean the Night Hag?"

The woman nodded. "Back in my country, we had a name for her. *Nocnitsa*, we called her," she said, and moved as if to spit on the ground. "She would come to people in the night and steal their breath, sit on their chests, make them die. Very bad."

"*Strega Cattiva,*" the peddler muttered. "Tales to frighten children."

"*Die hexe*," the teenager said. "Such things, bad witches, are real."

"Did you see her, the Night Hag, with the man who was killed?" Drostan asked.

The woman shuddered. "I saw a man walking alone. He seemed to be waiting for someone. He stepped into the shadows and then there was a scream."

"And after that?"

"I saw a figure that looked like a bent old woman. She was leaning over him. Then she disappeared."

Drostan looked at the others. "None of you saw anything?"

"I've seen the old woman before." It was the gray-haired vagrant who spoke. "I've seen her hunting. I stay clear of her, even now."

"Where did she come from?" Drostan asked. "The killings... like this one... they're new."

"There's strong magic in this city," the woman said. "Three rivers come together. Caves in the hillsides, and mines underneath the ground, stirring up what's been buried. Fires burn night and day," she said, with a nod toward where the smokestack flames of steel mills were visible for miles. "So many people from so many places... they bring their magic with them. I told the witch there'd be more killin's."

"Witch?" Drostan asked.

"From the old country, came nosing around a while back. Couldn't tell him no more than we told you. Haven't seen him since."

"I'll come back," Drostan promised. "If you see anything, please let me know."

The young man gave a cynical laugh. "There will always be killings in a place like this. You can't stop them all."

"Maybe not," Drostan said. He looked at each of them in turn. "But this wasn't an angry lover or a robbery or bad whiskey, or a deal gone wrong," he said, looking at the peddler. "This was a predator, and she'll kill again."

"You know where to find us," the old man said. "We'll be here. We'll always be here."

One by one, their forms shimmered, like dust in a moonbeam. Gradually, their outlines faded until nothing remained except the faint smell of licorice. Drostan turned and walked back to the road and the cold comfort of the single electric streetlamp.

Even with an eyewitness, it's nothing I can take to the police, Drostan thought, his mood bleak. *And if I turn up knowing too many details without a good explanation... well, we've been down that road before.* Falling under suspicion of being an accomplice to murder—even if never proven, even if wholly untrue—had finished his career with the Scottish police. New Pittsburgh was supposed to be a fresh start.

It would be so much easier if I could just ask the victim. Drostan sighed. That wasn't likely to happen soon. It took a while before the dead showed up as ghosts, if they were going to show up at all. So Drostan was on his own.

He walked back to his rented rooms on Second Avenue, not far from East Park, and pulled the collar of his overcoat up to shield his face and neck from the cold rain that had just started to fall. Rain or no rain, the bars on Ohio Street were doing a good business. Music and loud talk spilled into the streets, as did the occasional patron who had exceeded his tab.

German bars, Croat bars, Polish bars—the buildings looked much the same from the outside, but woe to the man who wandered into the wrong place unawares. In the tightly knit communities of Allegheny, as with the other neighborhoods that lined the area's steep hills, newcomers quickly learned where they belonged.

One of the new electric streetcars rattled by, briefly illuminating the sidewalk. Drostan had chosen his rooming house in part because it was near a trolley stop, and because Ohio Street had been outfitted with electric streetlights. Drostan had had his fill of dark alleys, and had the scars to prove it.

Here and there, you could still see tell-tale reminders of the Conflagration of 1868 and the Great Pittsburgh Flood of 1869, twin disasters that had done enormous damage, both to Allegheny and to the city across the river. Drostan had heard plenty of stories from old-timers about explosions from the severed gas lines and fires burning out of control in the debris floating on the flood waters. The wealthier areas had rebuilt right away. Poorer sections had taken longer, and some of the worst areas had never built up again. Places like where they found the body, down on River Avenue by the suspension bridge, still had blocks that were little more than rubble, where squatters scratched out a meager existence.

Drostan fought the urge to put his head down to duck the rain. It was growing dark, and lower Allegheny was no place to walk without your wits about you. Drostan had a stop to make. He ducked down a side street, counting the doors until he came to a run-down tenement. Under the dubious shelter of a corrugated metal awning, a half dozen young men held court, seated on overturned barrels. A table fashioned from a wide board atop two sawhorses provided ample space for an animated game of dice.

"Yes! Eight the hard way!" A young man with dark blond hair grinned and collected his winnings. A cloud of cigarette smoke hung in the air, trapped by the rain and the awning. The young men grew quiet as they saw Drostan approach.

"It's just Fletcher," the blond man said, when Drostan got close enough to identify.

"Still on your winning streak, Ralf?" Drostan asked, eying the small pile of coins in front of the blond man.

Ralf shrugged. "Lucky enough, I guess. You bring something for us?" Drostan eyed the other boys clustered around the table. He would guess they were in their late teens, though hard work and poverty had toughened their bodies and made them jaded. Boys like Ralf took work where they could get it, loading ships and train cars or other odd jobs, and stole or gambled for what they needed when jobs were scarce.

Drostan withdrew a pouch of tobacco and a packet of cigarette papers, showing them just long enough for Ralf and his friends to see what he had before they disappeared into the pocket of his coat. "I brought something for you—if you've got something for me." He leveled his gaze at Ralf, and the young man's pale blue eyes glinted in acknowledgement.

"Maybe," Ralf replied.

"Someone got cut up bad down by the river," Drostan said. "Real bad."

A dark-haired boy on Ralf's left glared at Drostan. "We didn't do it."

Drostan gave a mirthless chuckle. "No, you didn't. Whoever did do it had butchering skills." He described the body in sufficient detail that Ralf and his friends blanched.

"It's not the first we've found," Drostan added. "But I'd like to make it one of the last." He paused. "The police worry about murders out in the posh sections long before they make time to look into the bodies people find along the river. I'm not the police. I'd like to make the killing stop—but I need information."

The boys traded glances, uneasy about volunteering information. "We give you information, you give us the smokes?" Ralf eyed the pocket where Drostan kept the bribe.

In response, Drostan removed the tobacco and rolled himself a cigarette, striking the match against a dry patch of brick beneath the awning. He took a long drag and blew out the smoke. It was good tobacco, better than Ralf and his friends were likely to afford or easily steal.

"People say it's a *geist* what's done the killing," one of Ralf's friends ventured. He was the smallest of the group, with short, sandy-colored hair tucked into a cap.

Drostan gave the boy a skeptical look, though his heart beat faster at the comment. "Come on. Do you take me for a fool? There are no such things as ghosts."

"Don't know what else to call it," the boy said defiantly. "And I'm not the only one to get a look at it."

Grudgingly, Ralf and two of the other boys nodded. "We've seen something down by the river," Ralf said finally. "Sometimes it looks like a shadow, only the light's not bright enough for a real shadow. Other times, it's a bent old lady. It walks the riverside, right around dusk."

"Are you sure it's not just someone having a prank?"

Ralf shook his head. "That's what we thought, at first. But then dogs went missing, and some chickens. We thought someone was stealing them, or maybe a fox got loose, but that shadow, it's bigger than a fox." He paused. "It's got so most people won't go anywhere near the river once the sun is low. They're scared." He raised his head, as if to assure Drostan than he was not intimidated.

"When did people start seeing the old woman?" Drostan asked, keeping his excitement out of his voice.

The boys conferred. "A while ago," Ralf said finally. "After Christmas." It squared with what few facts Drostan had collected.

"Has anyone actually spoken to the old woman, or gotten close enough to know what she looks like?"

Ralf cursed in German. "No. Hell, no. Any time you see her, there's a bad feeling, like you should be somewhere else. People tried calling the priest to make her go away, but he won't come anymore. Some of the women wear a saint's medal, or carry a rosary, as if that would scare it off." From the look on Ralf's face, he clearly thought that whatever haunted the riverside was not going to be so easily dismissed.

"You ever seen the shadow—or the old woman—anywhere except down by the river?" Drostan asked, forcing himself to sound casual.

They shook their heads. "I ain't heard anyone tell of seeing the old woman 'cept by the river," Ralf said, "but I heard my mother talking with some of the other women. People been having bad nightmares, and a couple of babies died in their sleep, one right after the other. That, and they've had a run of bad luck down in the mines."

Drostan withdrew the tobacco and cigarette papers from his pocket and laid them on the table. "Thanks, boys. Keep your eyes open, and I'll bring more—if you've got good information."

"We've always got our eyes open, and our ears," Ralf said. "That's how we stay in one piece."

"Oh, one more thing," Drostan said, as if it had nearly slipped his mind to ask. "Have any of you seen a witch poking about recently?"

"A witch? No." Ralf replied. "We steer clear of hocuses."

"Let me know if you hear anything." Drostan made his way back to the street. The smell of sauerkraut wafted on the evening air from a nearby kitchen. Drostan smiled. New Pittsburgh's immigrants were good cooks. Just on North Avenue, Drostan could sample dishes from across Eastern and Western Europe in the pubs that lined the street, and hear nearly every language from the Continent in the mornings and evenings as workers trudged to and from their jobs. The jumble of accents, languages and cooking smells were a comfortable patchwork, making him feel at home in his adopted city.

Down at the corner, a crowd of men rallied around a man standing on a wooden box. The speaker was a florid-faced man with a strong Irish accent, and he was exhorting anyone in earshot to cast their votes for 'Dynamite' Danny Maguire, the construction business owner turned political boss who was the darling of New Pittsburgh's working men and their unions. Drostan paused to watch from a distance, just for entertainment, and then crossed the street and moved on, eager to be home.

Drostan still wasn't sure what—if anything—the killings along the rivers might have to do with Thomas Desmet's murder. *Maybe nothing*, he admitted to himself. But Brand and Desmet was a long-standing client, often hiring him to validate the background of an antique or the trustworthiness of a potential buyer. He had liked Thomas Desmet, so when George Brand asked him to help them solve the murder, he agreed without a second thought, even when Brand made it clear that they expected a connection to dark magic. That was something else Drostan liked about Brand and Desmet. They knew about his 'gift' and considered it an asset rather than a liability.

Drostan reached his doorway and shook off the worst of the rain. "Good evening, Inspector Fletcher." Mabel Mueller, Drostan's landlady, greeted him as he entered.

"Good evening, Mrs. Mueller. Whatever you're cooking smells good." Despite the evening's events, Drostan managed a genuine smile. Mabel Mueller, and her husband Otto, owned the home where Drostan rented his room. Part of his room and board included breakfast and dinner with the couple, and Mrs. Mueller's cooking was an inducement to avoid missing meals.

"I know you're partial to shepherd's pie," she said, smiling at Drostan as if he were an underfed boy. "Otto likes his German meals, but I get hungry for the foods I grew up on," she said, bustling to set the table. Mabel Mueller was in her middle years, with a figure best described as 'pillowy'. She ran the kitchen with military efficiency, and kept the house, and the rented rooms, clean and tidy.

"I think shepherd's pie will hit the spot," Drostan said, as Mrs. Mueller gestured for him to sit down. She brought him a generous helping, then served a smaller portion for herself and joined him.

"You're too thin," she said, offering him a roll with butter to go with the meal. "I should pack you a lunch."

Drostan chuckled. "I wouldn't want to put you to that trouble," he said, and paused to eat a few bites. "I eat when I can, but sometimes things get busy."

"We're lucky to have good men like you on the streets, looking out for us," she replied. "I can't complain about the officer who walks our beat. He's always pleasant, and he tips his hat to the ladies."

That would be Finian, Drostan thought. A charmer, but a bulldog underneath. It would be to Finian's advantage to win the favor of the neighborhood housewives. After all, the women were in the area all day, and likely to notice anything amiss. Drostan cleared his throat and took a sip of the hot tea Mrs. Mueller poured for him. "Have you noticed anything odd down near the river lately?"

Mrs. Mueller frowned. "I do my best to stay away from the river," she said, brushing crumbs from her skirt. "Bad area. No respectable person has business down there."

Inwardly, Drostan groaned. *You've offended her. Nice job*. "I'm sorry, I didn't mean to imply anything... I just wondered if you had seen anyone out of the ordinary heading down that way."

Mrs. Mueller tipped her head and looked at him as if studying a child with a questionable tale. "You want to know what people are saying about the Night Hag, don't you?"

The back of Drostan's neck prickled. "Who is the Night Hag?"

Mrs. Mueller shrugged. "No one knows. Maybe just people's imagination." But something in the way she spoke said she was not convinced.

"Tell me what people are saying, please. There've been some deaths."

Mrs. Mueller caught her breath. "Local people?"

Drostan grimaced. "We don't know yet. It was... bad."

Mrs. Mueller nodded, needing no further explanation. "There's been talk, at the marketplace," she said, and took a sip of her tea. "At first, I thought it was just silliness. Superstition. Some of the women come over here and bring the worst parts of the Old

Country with them." Her accent had gotten thicker, a sure sign that she was upset. Usually, he only heard her brogue on the rare occasions when she and Otto argued.

"Tell me," Drostan repeated. "However silly it may seem. Something's gone badly wrong."

Mrs. Mueller's expression was skeptical, then she gave a sigh of resignation. "The Poles were the ones who started the talk. Stories of nightmares and night hags—evil spirits that look like old women and steal souls." She shook her head. "Imagine! Such talk nowadays!"

Drostan smiled indulgently. "Something must have gotten them riled up."

Mrs. Mueller drank her tea, and, despite her protests, Drostan could see that something was upsetting her. "People have been having bad dreams," she said. "Not just the kind you wake up from and pull the covers over your head." She paused. "These people dreamed they were fighting off monsters, and woke up thrashing and screaming."

"Bad beer?" Drostan suggested. "Something they ate?"

Mrs. Mueller frowned. "Perhaps. Mrs. Schmidt at the laundry said her son woke up fighting so hard he tore the sheets, and there were scratches on his arms that weren't there when he went to bed."

"Maybe he damaged himself when he was dreaming?"

She shrugged. "It's possible. Mr. Miller said he'd had one of the dreams himself, and it was so real, he didn't stop shaking for an hour. He said that an old woman all dressed in black stalked him in his dream, getting closer and closer and coming faster and faster until he was running out of breath. Said it was the Night Hag, come to take him."

"How did he get away?" Drostan leaned forward, nearly spilling his tea.

Mrs. Mueller gave him an odd look, as if she was surprised he would take neighborhood gossip so seriously. "He said that he began kicking and hitting and shouting, and he woke up fighting with the sheets."

"So the stories are around the neighborhood. Are people frightened?"

Mrs. Mueller sighed. "Some are. But there are too many real things to be scared of, if you want to be scared. No need to lose sleep over tales."

Drostan poured them each another cup of tea from the pot in the center of the table. "Is there anyone missing? Anyone who didn't come home?"

"Those deaths you mentioned, you think they were murdered?"

Drostan grimaced. "Yes. The killings were... unusually violent. It's going to be hard to know who the victims were, unless someone's gone missing and there are family or friends to identify... what's left."

"That's going to be difficult in a place like this. People come and go with the work and the ships. Some folks keep to themselves, so no one might notice if they went missing. And some people don't trust the police. They might not say anything."

Drostan sighed. "I know. It's an uphill battle. I just don't like unfinished business."

Mrs. Mueller patted his hand. "Give it time. You never know what could turn up."

Drostan forced a smile. "You're right. I will." He looked for a change in subject. "How's your son?"

"Eric's doing very well," Mrs. Mueller said with a flush of motherly pride. "He's got a good job, on one of those transatlantic airships. He has a good boss, makes good money." She smiled. "He sends some home each month, to help out."

"I'm surprised he doesn't come home for dinner whenever he's in town," Drostan said with a chuckle. "He's crazy to pass up such good cooking."

Mrs. Mueller laughed, pleased at the compliment. "Ah well, young people. Perhaps he'll visit while you're staying with us."

Drostan smiled, feeling suddenly exhausted. "That would be nice."

Mrs. Mueller gave him a pitying look and shook her head. "You're tired. You should get some sleep. I'll have breakfast ready for you in the morning."

Drostan trudged up the steps, feeling bone weary. The old house's stairs squeaked with every step. While electricity powered the trolleys and the street lights, few homes other than those of the very wealthy had electric lighting. The warm glow of gas light illuminated Drostan's climb, its hiss a familiar constant.

Drostan opened the door to his room and turned the key in the gaslight, dispelling the shadows. He shouldered out of his coat and hung it on a chair. Across the room, a pretty blonde woman sat on the deep window seat, silently watching.

"Not a good day, I'm afraid," he said quietly. "I wish I could do more."

"You're doing all you can," she replied.

"It's never enough." He sat down on a chair by the small table he used as a desk, and combed through the newspaper clippings piled there. Tomorrow, the paper would report that a murdered man was found by the river, but further revelations were unlikely. Finian was diligent, but he was just one man in a big city, and the interest in clearing up a vagrant's death was minimal.

"Another murder?"

Drostan replied. "A bad one, as if they're not all bad."

"A man?"

He nodded. "Couldn't make out much more, I'm afraid."

"Did you get a look at his clothing? Ask the women. They'll notice what someone is wearing, even if they don't pay attention to much else."

Drostan chuckled. "Smart. I'll do that."

"Maybe he'll show up, and you can ask him." The woman shifted, and moonlight streamed through her. She wore a dress in the fashion popular a generation earlier, complete with a hoop skirt. She was the daughter of the home's previous owner, staying on after scarlet fever took her from among the living.

"I don't know, Olivia. I think there's something different with these deaths. Something that might have taken his soul along with his breath."

The woman's gaze grew sad. "That's a bad business. Be careful, Drostan. Stay alive."

"I'll do my best," he said, flipping absently through the clippings. "No promises."

Her laughter faded with her image, leaving him alone.

“NO MATTER HOW many times I fly over the city, the sight always takes my breath away,” Jake said, watching from the lounge windows as the skyline of New Pittsburgh came into view.

“It’s not the city that takes your breath, it’s Cullan’s flying,” Rick replied.

Cullan brought the ship in an arc over the heart of the city as he headed for the Brand and Desmet landing field at Rodgers’ Farm. Seeing the city from this perspective always gave Jake a sense of awe. He wondered what the view would look like without the haze of smoke from the steel mills that worked day and night, sending plumes of fire high into the sky.

New Pittsburgh expanded from the triangle of land where the Monongahela and Allegheny Rivers converged to form the Ohio River, which locals called the ‘Point’. A fourth underground river lay hidden deep beneath the three rivers, the product of ancient glaciers.

Pittsburgh had stood at the Point since the founding of a fort before the American Revolution. But *New* Pittsburgh sprang from the ashes of the Conflagration of 1868 and the Great Pittsburgh Flood of 1869. Those disasters leveled much of the city and led to riots and chaos, quelled only by the temporary imposition of martial law. The Quake of 1872, only a few years later, not only devastated the rebuilt city, but also caused a hundred-foot drop in the level of the Ohio River, creating the Weirton Falls. That lucky accident added Niagara-like hydropower to the region and opened up new natural gas and coal seams to feed the city’s relentless manufacturing. The city that climbed out of the wreckage and remade itself became New Pittsburgh, dominated by the genius—and the fortunes—of the men whose factories lined the swiftly flowing rivers.

Usually, Jake looked forward to coming home after a trip abroad. He liked the solitude of the Shadyside brownstone where he lived, conveniently down the street from his family but no longer a daily part of the household. His gaze dropped to the black armband on his left sleeve, showing that he was in mourning. Rick wore a similar band, and Nicki was dressed in her darkest traveling suit, which would be replaced by suitable black crepe as soon as they reached the city. It was a reminder that, regardless of the urn's secrets and the danger they had faced, their homecoming would plunge them into the complex social obligations required of grieving families.

"Has Cullan heard anything else from your family?" Nicki asked, laying a hand on Jake's arm.

Jake sighed. "There was just the telegram at Long Island from Henry, demanding we come home as fast as possible, and the one from George."

"Father sent his regards?" Rick asked.

"More than that. He asked me to meet him at the office before I go home. He was very clear that it be the first thing I do."

Rick tore his gaze away from the view as the airship banked and headed over farmland. "You're certain he meant for you to see him straightaway?"

Jake nodded. "Read it for yourself. I don't think there's any mistaking it—and he was unusually insistent about it." Jake withdrew the telegram from his pocket and handed it to Rick. Rick frowned as he read and re-read the paper, then handed it back.

"Don't you think that's unusual, especially coming from my father? I mean, we're talking about George Brand, the man who never misses a social nicety." Rick's voice held affection, with a hint of impatience with his father's British correctness.

"Actually, yes," Jake replied. "But it also suggests that Mother is holding up well, or Henry is holding her up, and that the sky hasn't fallen in."

"I'm certain that even in her grief, Aunt Catherine is a pillar of strength," Nicki said. "It's that resolute American spirit that baffles the Continentals. Your mother has it in spades."

Jake chuckled. "So you've heard Mother's stories about how our ancestors came out to this part of the country with Daniel Boone? I never had any trouble imagining my mother's forebears driving West in a Conestoga wagon."

"Don't let on to the ladies at the Carnegie Society," Rick laughed. "They think your mother is one of New Pittsburgh's doyennes."

"Don't let Mother hear you call her a 'doyenne'," Jake warned jokingly. "She only plays the part when she absolutely has to."

"As opposed to my mother, who was born into the role." Rick sighed.

"Seriously Jake, what do you think George wants to see you about that would be so important?" Nicki asked.

Jake made a face. "He's probably going to try to break it to me gently that Father left his interest in the business to Henry."

Nicki rolled her eyes. "Henry, the 'frozen chosen'. Sorry, Jake, but your brother makes a cigar store Indian seem like the life of the party." She shook her head. "On the other hand, maybe this means you'll do more of the European acquisition trips."

"If the alternative is having to work with Henry day-in and day-out, I'll be wearing out my passport," Jake replied.

"You mean 'we'!" Rick said, alarmed. "You're not about to abandon me and leave me to wade through Henry's bureaucracy while you go off and have fun."

The closer they got to Rodgers' Farm, the heavier Jake's heart grew. All too soon, his father's death—still just a notion—would become the grim reality of funerals, well-wishers and endless social obligations.

"By the way," Rick said, "Cullan stopped by my cabin—didn't want to disturb you, he said—and let me know that Harold Cooper in the London office was going to telegraph Father to make sure security was tight when we land."

Jake raised an eyebrow. "We're landing in the middle of an open airfield, miles outside the city. Since when have we needed 'security'? Please tell me they didn't call out the Pinkertons."

Rick shrugged. "Between the attacks in London and your father's death, I don't think it's wise to take risks."

Jake turned away. "Precautions I understand, but if Miska thinks I'm going to put up with a bodyguard everywhere I go, I've got news for him."

"Don't blame him," Rick said. "My father probably put him up to it."

Jake swore. "Between mourning etiquette and 'security', my life is beginning to look like house arrest."

"Wait until we land," Nicki soothed. "There's no use fretting until we see what we're dealing with."

The *Allegheny Princess* rumbled through the skies, slowing over a large, open field northeast of New Pittsburgh. There were signs of construction; a new railway spur was being added so the city's elite didn't have to rely on carriages to get to and from their airships. Jake felt the airship reduce speed and began to descend, dropping its guy ropes to the waiting handlers below. Jake's eyes widened as he saw a cordon of men stationed around the periphery of the landing field.

"What the hell is *that*?" he said, pointing.

"I suspect *that's* some of the security Father arranged," Rick replied drily.

"Or we're about to be arrested," Nicki quipped, but she looked a little nervous.

Jake fidgeted as the *Allegheny Princess* docked. As they headed down the gangplank, a man bounded up to meet them.

"Glad to see you made it home in one piece!" Mark Kovach said. He had a rifle slung over his shoulder, and a pistol on his belt. He sobered quickly. "Sorry about your father."

"Hello, Miska," Jake replied, clapping Kovach on the shoulder. "It's been a while. Let me guess: George sent you to escort us."

Kovach grinned. "How'd you guess? Oh, and my mother read about your loss in the paper, and she insisted I bring some of her goulash, for the family." He shrugged. "What can I say? Old customs die hard."

Mark Kovach—'Miska' to his friends—was Jake's height, with a fighter's build and dark brown hair. Black eyes glittered with intelligence, constantly wary. No matter how often he shaved, Kovach never lost his five o'clock shadow, although the thick black moustache came and went from time to time. He wore a battered army vest, a remnant of his days with the Western regiments, and beneath the open collar of his shirt, a saint's medal. From what little Kovach would say about his time in the Army, Jake gathered it hadn't ended well. Kovach's fame as a sharpshooter was well-deserved, and he was the best rifleman Jake had ever met. Even better than Rick, which was saying something. Jake relaxed, just a little, knowing that Kovach had their backs.

"Hello, Mark." Rick greeted him with mock formality.

"Hello, Rick. Flat-bat season over back in Merry Old England?"

Nicki barely concealed a laugh as Rick gave an aggrieved sigh. "That would be cricket," he said. "And yes, it ended in September."

"Shame you can't get rounded bats over there," Kovach continued, taking perverse glee at needling Rick. "Baseball's getting bigger every year. I could introduce you to the sport if you're interested."

Rick laughed and rolled his eyes and then muttered something under his breath. Their good-natured jibes made it feel, just for a moment, as if nothing had changed. Jake stepped to the fore and maneuvered between Rick and Kovach, something he had discovered long ago worked in everyone's best interest or their banter could go on for a while. "Have you been to the house?" Jake asked.

Kovach grew serious, and shook his head. "No. Mr. Brand told me to bring the men here and secure the airfield. Said you had some problems shoving off in London."

"You could say that," Rick replied.

Jake noticed that Kovach and all the guards wore black armbands, in mourning for Thomas Desmet. It was a stark reminder, and would be all too common for the next year. "We've got guards around the house, and the office," Kovach said. "They're discreet, but no one is likely to get by them without a fight." He paused.

"I'm just sorry we didn't have them in place before..." He didn't need to finish the sentence.

Jake sighed. "If Father had suspected he was in danger, he would have asked you to post a guard. It's possible he didn't know, or didn't think it would get this far."

A hard glint came into Kovach's eyes. "You find out who started this, and we'll finish it."

Jake did not doubt that. Private security forces—even small private armies—were not unknown in New Pittsburgh, though usually they were the province of the captains of industry, like the Carnegies and the Fricks. Kovach's reputation as a marksman very likely would have found him a spot, perhaps even a senior role, in any of the large forces. He had turned down those opportunities to head Brand and Desmet's security.

"You remember my cousin, Veronique LeClercq?" Jake said as Nicki took his arm.

Kovach gave a nod. "Ma'am."

"Pleased to see you again," Nicki replied.

Kovach eyed the workers tying off the airship. It would be a while before Cullan Adair had completed his post-flight check and was ready to leave. "We'll have men here to guard the *Princess*," Kovach said, as several of his guards came to escort Jake and the others to the black carriages that awaited them. "And we'll have guards riding with the carriages."

He looked to Jake. "The word I got said to bring Rick and Miss LeClercq directly to the house, and to take you to see Mr. Brand at the office."

Jake nodded. "That's what we were told. Do you know why?"

Kovach shook his head. "Mr. Brand didn't say. I didn't ask."

Jake saw Rick and Nicki to their carriage, pausing long enough to see a guard climb up beside the driver and another take position on the running board. With a sigh, Jake turned and climbed into his own carriage.

Kovach leaned in the door. "Just thought you might want to know. Henry's already at the house. Don't take this the wrong way, but are you sure he's your brother?"

Jake chuckled. "I wonder that every time I'm with him for more than five minutes, Miska. Thanks for the warning."

Kovach grinned. "That's the beauty of being one of ten kids. It's easier to avoid the ones that rub me the wrong way." He shut the door and joined the driver at the front, and the carriage started forward with a jerk.

They jostled over the rocky roads until they reached the newly paved highways, leading into the heart of New Pittsburgh. The familiar rise and fall of the land soothed Jake as he looked out at the steep hills that framed the city, their crests barely visible in the midday smoke. He wondered how different it would be to come home from the airfield on one of the new trains.

The clatter of cobblestones announced their arrival in the Strip District, the warehouse and wholesale area on the city side of the Allegheny River where Brand and Desmet had their headquarters. During the Civil War, the Fort Pitt Foundry had built and shipped cannons from the Strip to aid the Union war effort. The Conflagration and Great Quake leveled the foundry and many of the old manufacturing companies, and upstart merchants rose from the rubble, taking advantage of the nearness of the river and proximity to the city of Allegheny and its factories on the other side.

The quiet, mostly deserted streets contrasted with the morning hours when the Strip bustled with greengrocers and fishmongers, bakeries and grain merchants, and its docks were filled with cargo of every type. Just after dawn, stevedores pushed heavy carts laden with crates and barrels from the docks to the warehouses, and from the train station on Liberty Avenue to the wholesalers' markets. Tucked in between the warehouses, pushcart food vendors called out their wares to tempt dock hands and clerks with borsht and pierogies, sausages, and fried fish.

The carriage drew up to a large brick building on Smallman Street, in the shadow of the new St. Stanislaus Kostka cathedral, just up the street from where the Chatauqua Lake Ice Co. building was being rebuilt. The sun was low in the sky. Electric streetlamps blazed, but their efforts to dispel the gloom were sorely tested by the perpetual smoky haze from New Pittsburgh's factories. Down the street, a noisy group gathered around a shouting man on a soapbox, waving hand-printed signs for 'Dynamite' Danny Maguire.

"Not much changed since we were gone, I see," Jake observed. The man on the box was too far away for his words to be distinct. But it was clear from his tone and the way he repeatedly slammed his fist into his open palm that he was passionate about whatever battle Maguire had picked this week to fight against New Pittsburgh's big industries and the Oligarchy itself.

"Probably quieter where you were, even if you *were* being shot at," Kovach said, and Jake gave a skeptical snort. "Seriously—Maguire's got someone out agitating nearly every day. He's making a real nuisance of himself, like he's daring the powers-that-be to come after him." Kovach shook his head. "Never fails to get an audience."

The carriage pulled up in front of Brand and Desmet's offices. Jake stepped down and Kovach walked him to the door.

"I'll be waiting," Kovach said. "There'll be a man at each entrance, as well as the extra security we put in place after your father's death. Tell Mr. Brand we'll have a carriage ready for him when you're done."

Jake drew a deep breath as he turned the doorknob, preparing himself for what was to come. He squared his shoulders, and drew himself up to his full height. The urn, still wrapped in oilcloth, was under his arm. *If the urn is behind all this, Andreas is going to have some explaining to do.*

"Jake, please come in." George Brand stood in the lobby. He wore a black suit with a black armband and pocket handkerchief. "I am so very sorry about your father."

"I want to know what happened," Jake said, meeting George's gaze. "I want to know what got him killed."

"Let's go into my office," George said, gesturing down the hallway to an open door. Jake followed him down the familiar corridor, and felt his throat tighten as they passed the closed door to his father's office. No light shone through the frosted panel; Thomas had always worked well into the evening.

George Brand's office was testament to the success of Brand and Desmet. The building had electric lighting—something Thomas Desmet had been quite proud to announce. The walls were paneled in dark cherry, and an antique Aubusson carpet covered the oak plank floor. George's desk, like its twin in Thomas Desmet's office, was a massive mahogany piece. Two leather wing chairs sat in front of the desk, and behind it stood large bookshelves, holding mementos of George's life. Several framed photographs of George's wife and children graced the shelves, as well as items he had picked up on his travels around the world. To the right, above the fireplace, a mantle clock chimed the hour beneath an oil painting of the Yorkshire moors.

"I think you'll need this." George poured two glasses of scotch from a decanter and handed one to Jake. "Drink. It's not a pretty story." He paused. "But first, tell me what happened in London."

George sat silently while Jake recounted the ambush, the wild carriage chase, and the airship battle. "I have to admit, I was relieved to see Miska when we arrived," Jake ended his tale.

George nodded. "Harold Cooper telegraphed the bare bones of what occurred in London. Cullan hasn't given me his report yet, but from his telegraph I knew you'd run into problems."

Jake let out a long breath and took a sip of the Laphroaig. "What happened to Father?"

George sat down in the tufted leather chair behind his desk.

"Hold that question a moment," George said. He held up a hand to forestall Jake's objections. "I know it's important. But there's something I need to talk about with you first." He met Jake's gaze. "Your father named you partner in the business, should anything happen to him."

Jake choked on his scotch. "Me? Are you sure he didn't mean Henry?"

The corners of George's lips quirked as if he were hiding a sad smile. "Your brother Henry is a good businessman, and well-suited to handling the New York office. But he lacks a certain level of imagination and expertise that your father thought to be essential to the future of this company."

"You mean, Henry doesn't believe in the 'shadow trade' and he's lousy in a fight."

"That's part of it," George replied. The 'shadow trade' was what Jake and Rick had dubbed the acquisitions they made skirting the bounds of legality. Sometimes, this involved stealing back an object that already had been stolen. In other cases, it meant liberating an artifact from an owner with dubious claim for a well-paying buyer who could convey the legitimacy of museum status. Many of the antiquities had been passed back and forth between kings, rogues, emperors, and ne'er-do-wells for so long that legal title was hopelessly muddled. In those cases, attempts to purchase the pieces, even for a museum, might be mired in scandal or politics, so discretion—and haste—were necessary.

Brand and Desmet specialized in acquiring desirable objects for collectors and museums, items that were usually of suspicious provenance and dubious ownership, and on rare occasions, pieces whose owners did not part with them knowingly or willingly. Being in the business of obtaining valuable things and discreetly transporting them meant it was often best to avoid attention, especially from the governments or local authorities.

Two of their frequent clients were Andreas Thalberg, and Dr. Konrad Nils, an antiquarian in the employ of Andrew Carnegie and the chief curator of Carnegie's growing collections.

"Henry is an excellent office manager," George said. "But when it comes to thinking on his feet under pressure—"

"Or under gunfire," Jake supplied,

George nodded. "Indeed. Let's just say Henry isn't ideally suited for the kind of... exploits you and Rick often handle."

Jake chuckled. "My dear brother has the soul of an accountant. I'm almost certain he's never even fired a gun, let alone swung a punch."

"Exactly." George leaned back, and considered the scotch in his glass for a moment. "The nature of the pieces our specialty business trades in are valuable because they're unique. Only one person can own them, and powerful people don't take disappointment well." George paused. "It was a good choice not only for the business but for my interests as well. Can't say I'm not pleased that you and Rick will continue the business... you keep him grounded, and get him out of at least as much mischief as you get him into."

Jake raised an eyebrow and sipped his drink. Over the past couple of years, he and Rick—and often Nicki—had retrieved a wide variety of antiques, curios, and oddities for some of New Pittsburgh's wealthiest collectors. Most had been straightforward—if expensive—acquisitions, but some of the pieces had a murky past, and others had been rumored to be cursed, or worse. A few of those adventures had included wild rides and close calls.

"So... how does this have anything to do with what happened to Father? Was it a robbery?"

George frowned. "Your father was known for working late. Four days ago, when he was nearly alone in the building, Thomas collapsed and died. Later that night, someone broke in and ransacked his office." He paused. "They also went through the shipping room looking for—something. We don't know what. None of the crates were missing. But someone expected something important to be here, and I believe they killed Thomas to get it."

That would have been close to the time I had that nightmare, Jake thought to himself as George took a sip of the scotch and continued.

"I came as soon as the janitor called me. He found the body. By the time I got here, I discovered Andreas Thalberg waiting for me in my office. He said he had come for a meeting with your father, and arrived too late to prevent his death. He also said that there was, as he put it, 'an imprint of dark magic' that clung to the body and the office."

George shrugged. "I'll admit, initially I was skeptical about magic. I'm Anglican, for God's sake! We stopped believing in that kind of thing back in Shakespeare's day." He let out a long breath. "Then I met Andreas. The man is what he claims to be. Over time, I've seen too much proof to doubt it. And Andreas is certain that magic was used to kill your father."

"You think Father was killed over the urn we picked up in London?" Jake felt his anger rise. "Because someone in London certainly wanted it very badly."

"The urn did not lead to your father's death."

Jake and George both started. Andreas Thalberg stood in the doorway. He was several inches taller than Jake, with a slender, strong build and an aristocratic manner. His dark brown hair was longer than the current fashion, but on Thalberg, Jake thought, it looked right. Thalberg looked to be in his early thirties, but his pale blue eyes gave a clue to his real age. They spoke of centuries, not decades. Jake wondered whether Thalberg's apparent youth was more a product of being a vampire or a witch—or both.

"How can you be sure?" Jake challenged. "Someone in London wanted that urn enough to try to kill us—twice."

"My regrets." Thalberg said, walking into the room. "That was... unfortunate and unforeseen. But I don't believe the would-be assassins had any connection to the urn, or I would have taken additional precautions."

"If the urn isn't behind Father's death, then what is?" Jake snapped. "And if it is, will whoever wants the urn stop trying to kill Rick and me once we've turned it over to you?"

To Jake's surprise, Andreas chuckled. He glanced toward George, and nodded. "Yes. I see why Thomas wanted this one as his heir. He has the spark, doesn't he?"

"Do you know who killed my father?" Jake asked, refusing to be sidetracked.

All traces of humor drained from Andreas's expression. "No. I do not. I assure you, I am making my own inquiries into the matter. But I do believe that Thomas Desmet's death was caused by magical means, and it is quite likely that whoever killed him did so not because of my urn, but because of something your company has handled recently—or that the killer feared you would handle soon."

George frowned. "To my knowledge, the urn is the only magical item we've handled lately."

An ironic smile touched Andreas's thin lips. "The urn is not magical. It has other value, but no magic. Do you assume that everything I commission is magic, and that none of your other cargo is? You would be mistaken on both counts."

Jake gave Andreas a hard stare. "The real question is—if it isn't the urn someone wanted, what were they after? Have there been any unusual purchases or shipments—even if they weren't magical?"

George and Andreas traded a look. "Likely, since whoever ransacked the office and shipping room was obviously looking for something," George said. "But other than a few shipping ledgers, nothing's missing, so odds are it wasn't here." He held up a sheet of paper. "I made a list of the most recent shipments and the people who commissioned them. We keep duplicates of all our ledgers, so we know which ones were taken. Andreas recognized a couple of people who may have been dealing in magical items. He will look into those. The others, I'd like you and Rick to check into, see what you can find out. Maybe something will lead us to Thomas's killer."

"Glad to do it," Jake said, reaching across the desk for the paper and tucking it into his jacket pocket.

"After the funeral," George continued, "I'm going to drop out of sight for a while. Mark Kovach thinks that's wise. We've had a couple more incidents, attempted break-ins, here at the office and it seems prudent to be careful. I've already sent the rest of the family over to the Continent to visit relatives. And as a precaution, I've moved our files about the 'special acquisitions' to the house where I'll be staying. That way, they're less vulnerable—and so am I." He sighed. "And as if we didn't have enough to deal with, those Department agents have been around again, trying to recruit us. Doesn't seem to matter how many times we tell them to go away, they still come back again."

Jake folded his arms. "Could the Oligarchy be involved?"

In the chaos after the Great Quake and the Conflagration, civil government had fallen into anarchy and the city's industrialists had used their private armies and the Pinkertons to take control and maintain order. Although the government was eventually restored, the industrialists had no intention of relinquishing their newfound power. It was well known, though not spoken of aloud, that the city had a shadow government, the Oligarchy, which influenced the city's leaders from behind the scenes.

"I don't know—yet." Andreas seemed to choose his next words carefully. "That's one of the reasons George engaged the services of that private investigator, Fletcher." His eyes narrowed. "Are you aware of the murders across the river, in Allegheny?"

Jake shook his head, but George nodded soberly. "Bad business, that," George replied. "But how would they be connected to Thomas?"

Andreas gazed out the window, looking out across the Allegheny River. "Perhaps they are not," he said quietly. "If we are lucky. But I find the coincidence disconcerting."

"I've been out of the country getting shot at," Jake interrupted. "I really don't know what's going on."

"There have been several rather gruesome murders over in Allegheny, and all along the rivers," George said. "The press is calling them 'Ripper-style' killings."

"Jack the Ripper was never caught," Andreas murmured.

"Speculation is running wild," George continued. "There are crazy stories about monsters, or evil spirits."

"Some superstitions arise from terrible truths," Andreas said. "For example, vampires." He smiled, showing the tips of his elongated eye-teeth. "Stories about my kind are told in every culture throughout time. Many consider us to be nothing more than superstition. And yet, here I am."

"You're saying that something supernatural killed these people?" Jake countered.

Andreas gave an eloquent shrug. "I don't yet know for certain. Something monstrous, certainly, to do that to a living person. Few humans are disturbed enough to commit this type of carnage."

"What does this have to do with Father? I don't see a connection."

"It's possible that an item was brought into New Pittsburgh that opened a doorway, so to speak, for such a monster to enter," Andreas said, steepling his fingers together. "Or that gave a weakened monster the power to strike." He paused. "Earlier on the day he died, your father met with Richard Thwaites. Thwaites is a business partner with Drogo Veles. Do either of those names sound familiar?"

Jake nodded. "Yes. But only by reputation. Thwaites is what Rick would call a toff. He's got more money than brains, likes to throw it around, has a bad reputation with women and a mean streak a mile wide. Veles, if I recall, is a wealthy man from Eastern Europe with a mysterious past, and has enough of a dramatic flair he doesn't mind rumors of magic."

"The rumors are true," Andreas replied. "Drogo Veles is a Romanian dark witch. I find it very disconcerting that someone connected to him was anywhere near your father on his last day."

"I didn't see Thwaites when he came in for his appointment, but it was several hours before Thomas died," George said.

Andreas shrugged. "If Veles intended to kill someone, he could arrange for it to happen once Thwaites was conveniently far away. Whatever they used to do it, like a cursed object, could have been retrieved during the break-in the night of your father's death."

They were silent for a moment as the ramifications of Andreas's statement sank in. Jake remembered the piece of paper he had taken from Thomas's cabin aboard the airship, and dug it out of his pocket. "I found this in Father's desk on the *Allegheny Princess*. It's his handwriting." He handed it to Andreas. "Does it mean anything to you?"

Andreas frowned as he read down the list. "A monster—and several powerful witches." He handed the paper back to Jake. "Interesting."

The clatter of carriage wheels on cobblestone and the shouts of Kovach's guards brought the conversation to an end. A flash illuminated the night sky. Jake sprang from his chair and was about to head across the hallway to an office with a view of the street when an explosion rocked the building, shattering glass and knocking them to the floor. Jake's ears rang and he lay still for a moment, fearing a hail of gunfire might follow through the empty windows.

"Are you hurt?" Andreas asked.

"Where's George?" Jake managed to sit up. Shards of glass littered the hallway outside of the office.

"I'm fine," George answered as he stood up from behind his desk.

Outside, Jake could hear Kovach shouting, a mixture of English and Hungarian. In the distance, sirens began to wail. A red glow from outside lit the hallway.

"It's best I leave before the police arrive," Andreas said, after he had helped Jake to his feet. "It's fortunate that you are both uninjured, but as you see, our enemy will not hesitate to play rough to get whatever it is he wants. He'll strike again, and harder. We must figure out his objective—and solve your father's murder—before whoever is behind this has a chance to better his luck."

Jake moved to respond, but in the time it took to turn his head, Andreas had disappeared.

"Get out of here, Jake." George nodded toward the door. "The fewer questions asked, the better. They'll wonder why you're here at such a late hour when you might be home consoling your family. I'll stay. With my partner newly dead, no one will wonder why I'm working late." He raised a hand to forestall Jake's protests. "Mark will make sure I have guards, and they'll see me home safely. Now go. Give my best to your mother, and tell her I'll come by when I can to call on the family."

Jake ran toward the lobby, only to run into Kovach coming his way. "We've got to get you out of here, now!" Miska said, grabbing Jake by the arm and nearly dragging him off his feet down to the street.

"Take care of George!" Jake protested as Miska shoved him into a waiting carriage and swung up to sit in the jump seat behind the main compartment. Miska shouted something in Hungarian to the two guards closest to the building, and the men nodded, then turned to go inside.

The carriage jolted into motion, clattering down Smallman Street. From the light of the fire, Jake glimpsed a crater and debris in the street near Brand and Desmet's building. The driver urged the horses on, and the carriage jarred every bone in Jake's body as it took a sharp left and then a right onto Liberty

Avenue. Police wagons rumbled past them headed the other direction, their bells clanging loudly, as the carriage slowed to a decorous pace, as if nothing at all had happened.

Chapter FIVE

"WHAT THE HELL were you thinking?" Drogo Veles paced the well-appointed parlor like a caged panther. "Your men were supposed to steal any record of Jasinski and make sure they didn't have that damned Polish witch's crates. That was all. Killing Thomas Desmet was not part of the plan."

Richard Thwaites leaned back in his flocked velvet armchair. His satin smoking jacket contrasted nicely with the upholstery. Like the furnishings, the jacket cost a small fortune. "There's no telling what Jasinski told Thomas Desmet, or what Desmet figured out on his own. 'No loose ends'—isn't that what you always tell me?" he asked with cultivated ennui, and puffed on his Cuban cigar.

"You used one of the medallions I gave you for emergencies," Veles growled. "You used my magic to kill him."

"And I made sure the medallion was retrieved," Thwaites replied with a shrug. "No fingerprints."

"Idiot!" Veles slammed his fist onto a Chippendale side table, so hard he splintered the wood. Thwaites winced. "A witch of any power—especially one like Andreas Thalberg—will know magic was used. Why didn't you just leave a calling card and be done with it?"

Thwaites gave Veles an annoyed glare but carefully avoided meeting the dark witch's gaze. "Has Andreas Thalberg come knocking on your door?" He asked. "No? Then it wasn't that obvious." He flicked the ash from his cigar. A stray ember dropped onto the Aubusson rug beside his chair and he extinguished it with the sole of his bespoke Italian shoe.

"It was reckless, and unnecessary. Thomas Desmet wasn't likely to be a threat. Giving his son a cause for vengeance could be dangerous." Veles's gaze was piercing, and although Thwaites did not meet his eyes, it made the social scion cringe.

"Our men in London are getting soft," Thwaites complained, taking a sip of his imported scotch. "They had two chances to eliminate the problem entirely and failed."

"Is that your idea of subtlety?" Veles asked. "A gun battle through London and an aerial shootout? Airships are not inexpensive!"

"We needed to keep Jake Desmet and Rick Brand from going to Poland. If they had picked up Jasinski's crate, our opportunity would have been ruined before we could contain the damage."

"But it didn't work, did it?"

"It may not have worked the way we planned it, but we don't think that the shipment ever got to Karl Jasinski—*or* to Brand and Desmet."

"Don't *think*? Don't think...You still don't know where it is." Veles tutted. "All that effort and blood, and we're no closer to laying our hand on those stones than we were when they were in Prague."

"I'm working on it. We'll find them."

Drogo Veles eyed his business partner. Richard Thwaites came from money, though the idea that any fortune in North America could be considered 'old' money was laughable. Thwaites was an asset, he reminded himself. Keeping that in mind lengthened Thwaites's life when he became insufferable. *Nouveau riche,* Veles thought. *He defines the term.*

Still, Thwaites was a born-and-bred American blue-blood, something Veles was not and never could be. With his blond hair, blue eyes and stage actor good looks, Thwaites looked the part of a successful American businessman, and his bona fides made him an inside member of New Pittsburgh's real ruling class, the Oligarchy. No matter how wealthy Veles was, or how powerful his magic, his Eastern European roots were not going to be overlooked by that esteemed crowd of WASP power-brokers. Not in any lifetime.

So he was stuck with Thwaites, at least until the Vesta Nine mine was tapped out. Perhaps longer, if Thwaites could be as useful as he was annoying. *He's got connections, and charisma. He can be helpful.*

"Relax," Thwaites said, stretching out his legs and crossing his ankles. "We'll find them. And Jasinski, too. Besides, the tourmaquartz vein is almost exposed. Pity this stuff is so hard to extract. A few more months, and we can forget the whole thing."

"Maybe." Veles stalked the length of the room, his hands clasped behind his back. He preferred a more somber look than Thwaites's dandyish tastes. Veles wore a slim-tailored black frock coat over dark slacks. The ensemble had a distinctly European cut that suggested a well-heeled Continental undertaker. It tended to make people unsettled, which suited Veles fine. *Machiavelli was right. 'Tis better to be feared than loved.*

"We've sold one small shipment of tourmaquartz to Spain, just enough to draw them in," Veles said. "They barely have a piece as big as my thumb, but it's enough to power an airship. The Chinese and the South Africans see the potential. They've made discreet inquiries."

"Of course they have," Thwaites said with a self-congratulatory note in his voice. "Tourmaquartz is a game-changer. Every arms dealer and inventor will be beating down our doors once word gets out."

"Don't fool yourself—the Department of Supernatural Investigations will get wind of it," Veles replied. "They'll move in big and even your connections won't be able to keep them from shutting us down. Remember how they covered up that downed airship in the Monongahela?" He shook his head. "We need to mine as much as we can as quickly as we can and get it to the highest bidders, then wash our hands of it before the whole thing goes bad."

"Drogo, Drogo. You worry too much," Thwaites said with a shake of his head. "It's a European condition—always focused on the problems instead of the potential." He took another puff of his stogie. "After all, this kind of thing happened in Russia a while back, the last time someone tried to mine tourmaquartz, right? And it all worked out."

"The *gessyan* escaped and slaughtered all the miners and the peasants in the village," Veles replied tonelessly. "Until those damnable witch-priests bottled them back up again."

"There you have it," Thwaites said with a shrug. "Once we have all the tourmaquartz we can mine, let someone find the witch-priests to shove the genie back in the bottle, as it were. We'll be so wealthy no one can touch us—and we'll control the most valuable resource for armaments and airships in the world. All the kings and despots and generals will have to pay our price. I'd say that's well worth a few dead miners, wouldn't you?

"Things are never that easy," Veles grumbled. "This problem with Desmet is a sign."

Thwaites made a dismissive gesture. "You and your 'signs'. Stories for old women."

"That's what you think of the Night Hag? A story for old women?"

Thwaites hesitated, but regained his bluster soon enough. "You knew about the *gessyan*. You knew that mining too deep could free them. You should have taken precautions. I thought you had magic for that kind of thing."

"'That kind of thing' is more complicated—and dangerous—than you want to bother your pretty little privileged head about," Veles shot back. "Your men on the police force won't be able to keep it quiet forever."

"A small price for the payoff we're going to have," Thwaites replied, grinning like a very full cat. "We'll be wealthy beyond compare."

"I have learned that it is best to count one's money only after it is well in hand and one is far from the scene of the crime. It's too early to make assumptions. For one thing, we've got to regain control of the *gessyan* and increase the number of workers in the deepest levels."

"That's why I brought in Dr. Tumblety and Dr. Brunrichter," Thwaites replied in an off-handed manner, as if discussing additional waiters for a garden party. "I have the utmost faith that they will solve the problem."

"We've had enough mad doctors around lately."

Thwaites chuckled and took a slug of his scotch. "Really, Drogo. The good doctors are committed to helping us with our labor problem. They've been dabbling in resurrectionist territory for years, and no one but Farber has come as close to working clockwork corpses as they have. Look how well the prototypes are working."

"They shamble and stink."

Thwaites clucked his tongue. "It's not as if they're serving canapés. When they wear out, we make new ones. Plenty of bodies to choose from. They don't snivel and scream like the miners we enslaved."

"At least they have their wits about them," Veles muttered. "Your clockwork corpses can barely lift and dig."

Thwaites shrugged. "That's all they need to do. Metal men would be better, of course; the *werkman* prototype we stole from the Department was a boon for Tumblety—he managed to put together a few copies rather well, don't you think?"

"I think it would be better if we just abducted Farber and had him build more of his wondrous *werkmen* himself."

"I'm working on it," Thwaites said. He stretched, then rose and poured himself another glass of scotch and took a second cigar from the rosewood humidor on his Hepplewhite desk. He took his time snipping off the end of the cigar and lighting it. He blew a smoke ring with a sigh of satisfaction and smiled indulgently at Veles.

"I've gotten quite cozy with Farber's bosses at Tesla-Westinghouse," Thwaites said. "Throwing sizeable sums of money at their pet projects seems rather to endear one to them," he added with a smirk. "I make sure to admire Farber's work, and inquire as to the good boy's health, suggesting that I might have a project or two coming his way."

"It would be easier to just snatch him and be done with it," Veles countered. "It's not like we can let him live when we're done with him."

"Leave the kid-gloves to me," Thwaites said. "Everyone knows Farber is brilliant, but flighty. We'll get what we want from him, then arrange an accident. You'll see." He narrowed his eyes. "Maybe you should be more worried about putting those poltergeists from the mine back in their place. I've lost four overseers in as many weeks."

He took another puff of his cigar and went to look out the windows. Thwaites's grand home on Ridge Avenue looked out onto a busy street. The streetlamps lit the sidewalk with a warm glow, and now and again, well-appointed carriages rolled by, heading for New Pittsburgh's Alvin Theatre and further downtown.

Veles knew his business partner considered himself American royalty. *What does he know of royalty? Upstart. A well-heeled braggart in a country too wet behind the ears to have any real history of its own. Toss him in with European nobility and even the ones who aren't vampires would eat him alive.* He took a deep breath. *Useful. Remember—useful.*

"I intend to 'put down those poltergeists', as you say, when we're done with the demonstration," Veles replied testily. "You're welcome to come along if you'd like to see for yourself."

"That's quite all right," Thwaites said, just a little too hurriedly. "I still don't know what's so important about a couple of old Russian stones with scratches on them and some Polish madman's book."

"The Alekanovo stones are artifacts of power," Veles replied. "They can channel and amplify magic. Marcin of Krakow's book recorded the ritual—the 'spell', if you like—that was used to bind the *gessyan* the last time they broke loose." He looked at Thwaites with annoyance. "I'll put it in language you can understand. Having the stones and the book is like having the proper tools and the instruction manual. You might be able to do without them, but it will take longer and is likely to end badly."

"That doesn't explain why my men couldn't get into that Polish witch's apartment," Thwaites grumbled. "They said it was like there was an invisible wall around the door. Couldn't even get close to it."

"That would be magic," Veles replied drily. "Jasinski knew someone was after him, or he wouldn't have disappeared. He set a powerful warding around his apartment and shop. One that even I can't cross."

"So Jasinski is a better witch than you?"

Veles ignored the impulse to throttle Thwaites. "It's not uncommon for one witch not to be able to dispel magic set by another. Jasinski would have expected a witch—perhaps me in particular—to want what he has. If he couldn't keep it, he made sure we couldn't get it."

"How do you know the Russian stones aren't in there?" Thwaites asked.

Veles shook his head. "Jasinski specializes in sending nasty spirits back where they came from. He does more exorcisms than the priests. And his power is real, there's no doubt about that. So of course he took the *gessyan* rising as a personal challenge. If he has the Alekanovo stones—and Marcin's book—he will try to bind the *gessyan*, and send the Night Hag back where she came from."

"And you're sure that's what is in the missing box, the one he hired Brand and Desmet to smuggle out of Poland?"

Veles nodded. "Jasinski has been in touch with witches all over Russia and Eastern Europe. He found what he was looking for, but it's difficult to get certain objects out of there these days. Brand and Desmet specialize in acquiring hard-to-find objects, without always worrying about the letter of the law. Of course he'd go to them to get what he needed."

"If he knows someone is after him, he's probably long gone," Thwaites replied.

That's what you'd do, Veles thought. *Then again, there's not an ounce of real commitment in your body.*

"Not Jasinski," Veles said. "I met him on a few occasions. He's like a bloodhound when something intrigues him. He's out there somewhere, trying to figure out where his pieces are, trying to make a plan for how to do what he set out to do. If we had the stones, I could be certain of controlling the *gessyan*," Veles continued. "Without them, it will be more difficult."

If Jasinski hadn't betrayed me, those stones would be in my possession by now, and we'd have the lid back on our own little hell. "I'm going to need those artifacts to pull the Night Hag and the wraiths and the hell hounds back into the mines," Veles added. "But in the meantime, I'll see what I can do about keeping the *gessyan* from eating all our workers."

"Frankly, I don't see the problem with the Night Hag," Thwaites said, swirling the amber liquid in his Baccarat Crystal glass and taking another puff of his cigar. "A good dose of fear keeps the rabble in at night, off the streets." He chuckled. "You know, they're actually talking about it being the Ripper at work?"

"The murder victims may not be members of your pricey Duquesne Club, but that doesn't mean they'll go unnoticed forever," Veles said. "Murders attract attention, and that's bad. Especially when it wouldn't take much for a clever policeman to trace the deaths back down the rivers all the way to Vestaburg."

"You're assuming one can find a 'clever' policeman in New Pittsburgh who isn't on my payroll," Thwaites replied. "I'm still surprised the spooks don't just prey on the miners. Why go out when there's good food at home? Seriously—why can't you just magic the tourmaquartz out? Save us time and money."

"First, because that's not the way magic works," Veles growled. "Even I don't have limitless power, and trying to control dozens of miners in the deep levels at all times would be suicidal. And second, because science is harder to track than magic. Every use of magic runs the risk of bringing the Department down on us. They have watchers who look for that kind of thing. Bad enough that we've used the magic I've already done for you. Fortunately wards and protections to keep the remaining *gessyan* in the mines don't make much of a ripple. Anything else, we might as well send up a flare."

"Pity," Thwaites said.

"It's my spells that are keeping them from devouring your miners on the upper levels," Veles said. "The overseers can't be helped. They go lower than the slave-workers, and I can't sustain wardings on a bigger area than I've already warded. Magic has its limits against old power like *gessyan*," he added. "And there aren't enough of your clockwork corpses and metal men to mine the tourmaquartz and the coal if the rest of the miners die or get so scared they won't come back."

"They won't strike," Thwaites replied. "Frick broke the union's back. The Homestead Strike put a nail in that coffin."

Veles considered pointing out a number of instances when peasants had indeed had enough of their masters despite the cost and risen up, with disastrous results for men like Thwaites. *His kind is doomed to repeat history,* Veles thought. *They consider themselves above it.* Magic had extended Veles's lifespan long enough for him to know the meaning of caution. Witches of his power could live a century and a half or more. Not as long as a vampire, but more than sufficient to inform his perspective.

"Don't think yourself so smart," Veles growled. "There's always someone. Or one of those muckraking journalists like that Ida Tarbell woman sniffing around for a story. And how they'd love to find a pretty little heir to a local fortune hip-deep in the muck," he said, raising an eyebrow.

"We're in this together," Thwaites shot back. "And I've got enough lawyers on retainer to take care of Tarbell and her ilk. You handle the magic; I'll handle the media."

"I FAIL TO SEE why you've brought us to the middle of nowhere." The Spanish nobleman leaned back in his chair and crossed his arms. He and the other passengers of the well-appointed, private passenger car looked out at the empty land on either side of the railroad tracks and then returned to glowering at Veles and Thwaites.

"Gentlemen! All will be made clear very soon," Veles promised.

Their guests were a volatile mix of personalities. A Spanish nobleman with financial interests dependent on Spain winning its conflict with the United States, an Italian anarchist, a leader of the Greek nationalist movement and a wealthy Sudanese tribal chief. All had come here for a demonstration of what Veles had promised would be a 'game changer' in pursuing their varied political interests.

"All of you depend on steam-powered machines—either for weapons or for transportation," Veles said. "But coal is bulky and dirty. It's difficult to transport and large endeavors require an unwieldy amount. What if you could power an airship with something no larger than my finger?" he asked. He had their full attention now.

"What if you could create powerful weapons with a sliver of this substance, making them smaller and easier to transport?" he asked, withdrawing a piece of tourmaquartz from one pocket. "This," he said, holding the crystal between thumb and forefinger, "is the equivalent of four cases of dynamite."

"Unbelievable," the Spaniard said with a dismissive gesture. "Do you take us for fools?"

"A pretty fantasy," the Italian added. "Prove it."

Veles signaled to the *werkman* who until now had stood silent at the end of the passenger car. The mechanical man came forward, and Veles inserted the sliver of tourmaquartz into a small opening in the *werkman*'s chest. "Leave the rail car," he ordered. "Go three hundred paces east. Then stop."

Obediently, the *werkman* did as he was told, and stopped within sight of the windows of the train. Veles's guests moved to look out the windows.

"Observe." Veles lifted a detonator. "An aetheric wave transmitter, attuned to the same frequency as the electrical system of the *werkman*," he said, pressing the button. "When a high voltage charge goes through the tourmaquartz—" The resulting explosion was spectacular enough he did not need to finish his sentence.

The excited buzz of exclamations and questions rose to a din before Veles raised his hand. "I'm sure that what you've seen gives you some ideas," he said with a smug half-smile.

"How do we know it's not a trick?" The Greek glowered at Veles. "Perhaps your mechanical man was filled with dynamite. The stone might not have had anything to do with the explosion."

Veles shrugged. "A reasonable question," he said magnanimously. "And I will set your concern to rest in just a moment. But I'd like to direct your attention to the rear of the car." The shades on the windows in the last third of the railcar were drawn, making it fairly dark. Veles walked a few paces to pull down a white screen, and returned to where he had been standing. A Théâtre Optique praxinoscope sat on a rolling cart in the middle of the car. Veles lit the lantern and spun the wheel.

Images appeared on the screen, and Veles's guests leaned forward to watch them unfold. A man held up a piece of tourmaquartz not much larger than the one Veles had displayed. He set it on a wooden crate and connected two wires to the crystal, then spooled out the wire and took shelter behind a thick stone wall. When the crystal detonated, the explosion hurled rock and bits of crate high into the air and left a crater several feet deep.

"Think of the possibilities," Veles urged. He turned off the lantern and moved the cart aside. "And now, if you'll follow me to the engine of this train, I have something else to show you."

The guests murmured among themselves as they followed Veles forward. He opened the door of the coal car, nearest the engine, to reveal an empty shell. As they exclaimed in surprise, Veles led them to the engine itself. Where there should have been a furnace filled with coal, a sliver of tourmaquartz glowed incandescently behind a mica glass window, and the heat radiating from the customized chamber was clearly enough to power the boilers that drove the train.

"You'll note the locomotive engine emits a cloud of steam, but no coal smoke," Veles said, gesturing skyward as his potential investors craned their necks to see. Everyone began to talk at once.

"Gentlemen, please," Veles said. "Let's discuss this in a more comfortable setting."

When they returned to the passenger car, a kingly repast of delicacies had been set out on a dining cart, complete with fine liquor. Another *werkman*, dressed as a waiter, made certain everyone was served before withdrawing discreetly to the back of the car. Richard Thwaites had taken a seat at the front, and now that Veles had made the presentation, Thwaites was at home pouring drinks and talking about money.

"Quantities of tourmaquartz are naturally limited," Thwaites said, leaning back in his chair. "In fact, the vein we've discovered is the only known source in the world not under the control of the government. We're prospecting for more, but as it stands, the production of our mine is all the tourmaquartz available to investors such as yourselves."

"We've already committed to several orders," Veles added nonchalantly, "so some of the production is spoken for. But there is some tourmaquartz still remaining, and it can be yours—if you have the cash to pay for it."

"The bidding starts at a million dollars a pound," Thwaites said with a smile.

DROGO VELES WAS in a foul mood as his carriage jostled back and forth. Two days had passed since the railway excursion with investors, and he had returned to New Pittsburgh tired and out of sorts. His carriage had left the comparatively better roads of New Pittsburgh proper a while back, and the roadways leading to the Vesta Nine mine were as shoddy and patched together as the run-down little company houses that lined them. His conversation with Thwaites had not helped his mood, but then again, it seldom did.

I doubt Thwaites likes my company any better than I like his, Veles thought. *But we are valuable to each other, and it's far too late to turn back now.*

The carriage was expensive, a handbuilt chariot d'Orsay with the Thwaites's family crest painted in an emblem on its side and back. It was ostentatious for a visit to a coal mine, but Thwaites insisted he take it, and Veles preferred using one of Thwaites's carriages to one of his own. *If it goes badly, let them remember seeing him and not me,* Veles thought, leaning back against the tufted velvet cushions.

"Wait here." Veles did not bother looking up at the coachman as he stepped out of the carriage, and he had the impression that the driver was glad to comply. *Nothing like a reputation as a dark witch to keep conversation to a minimum.*

He looked out over the sprawling Vesta Nine complex. Everything in New Pittsburgh seemed to be built on a scale the Old World only glimpsed with the pyramids and the Louvre, or perhaps Russia's Winter Palace. Steel mills rose like the tarnished palaces of sooty gods, taking up vast swaths of the riverbanks, belching smoke and spewing fire. The mines, with their tipples and myriad larger-than-life buildings, looted the treasuries of the Underworld and turned coal into gold.

Here, Veles's penchant for dark clothing served him well. He had no intention of being seen and remembered. The coachman would be easy enough to take care of, once he returned to the city. A bit of magic, and memory became unreliable. But magicking the memories of hundreds—thousands—of miners was another matter entirely. And despite Thwaites's blithe dismissal, Veles was certain that even the wretched brutes who worked in the depths of the Vesta Nine knew something was gravely wrong.

He had survived uprisings on the Continent. Unlike Thwaites, Veles understood that peasants could only be pushed so far before they rebelled, even against impossible odds. *Enough peasants with pitchforks—or miners with pickaxes—can overcome any hired army or Pinkerton strongmen,* Veles thought. *Bought loyalty only goes so far.* The situation was even more of a powder keg than Veles acknowledged to his partner. If the miners got balky, some kind of investigation was sure to follow, and Thwaites's payroll was unlikely to cover everyone likely to be poking noses into the affair.

He did not fear the night's work, not exactly, although an ancient, powerful supernatural hive could never be approached lightly. Yet over the long years, Veles had learned to focus, and had trained himself to discipline his fears with preparation. He had rested and made ready, gathered his amulets and talismans to protect himself and amplify his power. The time and day, even the phase of the moon, were auspicious. Without the Russian stones supposedly in that damned crate from Poland, it was the best he could do.

Despite himself, his heartbeat picked up its pace. The night air was cool, and the sky overhead obscured by the ubiquitous Pittsburgh smoke. He moved quickly, in the shadows. Well-timed flickers of magic distracted guards or gave them something else to remember. This part was easy.

It was the middle of the night shift, but even so, Veles avoided the main entrance to Vesta Nine. He had memorized the layout of the massive complex, and that exercise served him well. Even at a distance, he could sense the strain against the wardings he had set in place. His was powerful magic, but not omnipotent. *Gessyan* were well feared by reasonable people back where Veles came from. There were reasons Eastern Europe was thought to be a dark, forbidding place. Wolves were not the only predators long banished from the West that thrived in the East. Other creatures, red of tooth and claw, made the forests and caverns of the less populous Eastern kingdoms their homes. *We understand these things.*

He closed his eyes, opening up his magic. He could see his old wardings like gossamer strands forming a grid all around the mine. He had not been able to contain the most powerful *gessyan*, like the Night Hag, the wraiths and the hell hounds. They had fled the mine as soon as the deep places were violated and the ancient spells broken, screaming out into the night, ready for a harvest of blood.

Even they have learned not to destroy all the miners, at least, not all at once, Veles thought. *The* Logonje *taught them that lesson the hard way. They'll hunt farther afield if they can, and the hunting here is likely very good indeed.*

It irked him that even with all his power, he had not been able to force the Night Hag and her fellow spirits back into the deep places. He had settled for bottling up the lesser creatures, and forcing those with more strength to leave the mine, avoiding workers on the higher levels. It was a choice with consequences. By keeping certain *gessyan* imprisoned, he reduced the slaughter outside the mine, buying them time to complete the tourmaquartz extraction. But he could not seal the *gessyan* away completely, not without the Russian artifacts, nor could he recall the powerful *gessyan* that had escaped. And now that he knew about the *gessyan* and their power, he was not certain that he wanted to bottle them up, if he might be able to control such potentially useful creatures.

All this for a bit of rock. Not even gold. Yet he, even more than Thwaites, understood the true value of tourmaquartz. Thwaites saw everything in terms of money and social status. Veles had enough of both to last several lifetimes. The real prize was power—power enough to have prime ministers and madmen at his beck and call. Power to change the destiny of nations, unseat kings, nudge history's course to a path of his own choosing. Dabblers like Thwaites would never grasp that power was far more valuable than money. Money could be seized or destroyed. Power endured. And the power that came from control of a substance that could keep airships flying or energize the weapons of armies was rich indeed. It could be nearly unstoppable. The thought made Veles's lips quirk in the barest suggestion of a smile.

Few people in New Pittsburgh understood the nexus of power that surrounded them. Three rivers converged, and a fourth, hidden aquifer beneath the ground was the mightiest of all. Seams of rich minerals veined these hills. Countless tunnels ran through them, conduits for magic power. Even now, no one knew exactly how many tunnels there were or where they all ran. New Pittsburgh was like a magical kettle on a hot stove, ready to boil over. Even the original inhabitants, the people settlers ignorantly called 'Indians', knew that the swift, deep rivers were places where strong magic ran. It was a most volatile mixture.

Magic springs from the earth and the sky and the stars. Science is a pale competitor, trying to explain away what small minds can't comprehend. The Gloomy Dane was right; there are far more things in Heaven and Earth than are dreamt of by philosophers—or scientists.

In the shadows, Veles used salt and iron shavings to set a warded circle. He wore protective amulets of tin and aluminum, and carried a polished quartz disk in his pocket. Veles spoke his spells in Romanian, his native language, closest to his heart. The working required a few drops of his blood, shed with an obsidian blade, mixed with iron and lead. All of the clockworks and mechanisms in the mines seemed to resist his magic, as if in even the smallest of ways, the tension between new and old was ever present.

As Veles said the words of invocation, he felt a cold chill run down his spine and he shivered. All around the mine, the shadows came alive, and Veles sensed that he was being watched by beings both hungry and malicious. It was a struggle to raise his magic, even within the warded circle, as if something were pressing back against him. The magic stank of age and death, like an old grave. It was earth magic, the magic of the creatures of caves and hollows, crypts and wells, of stone and dirt, minerals and gems. Veles much preferred the magic of blood and fire: vital, fickle, and alive.

He had the same feeling that he often got walking past a disused cemetery or the ruins of an old house. *As you are now, so once were we. As we are now, so you will be,* the old tombstone rhyme came to mind. *Fire is fleeting. Sooner or later, everything comes under the ground.*

Veles gave a muted cry as he harnessed his power. A rush of magic flowed out from him toward the mine, an invisible wave imbued with his intentions. Veles felt drained, as if he had done a hard day's labor. Even for a witch of his considerable experience and natural strength, such a large, complex working strained his limits. *Thwaites has no idea*, he thought as he climbed back into the carriage. He knocked on the frame, and the driver moved on. Veles collapsed against the seat cushions, utterly spent.

I am going to find Karl Jasinski and get those damned stones from him if I have to move all Hell to do it, Veles swore to himself. *And since that cretin Thwaites has already opened Pandora's Box with the Desmets, we'll have to finish what we started.*

Chapter SIX

THE CARRIAGE DREW up in front of the Desmet home as the bells from the new Shadyside Presbyterian Church rang out the ninth hour. Kovach opened the door for Jake. His face was smudged with soot and pale grit dusted his dark hair. Kovach's clothing was streaked with dirt and speckled with what might have been blood, though Kovach himself appeared uninjured.

"Yeah, I don't look too pretty, but that's not much of a surprise now, is it?" Kovach said with a grin. "I've got a security detail all around the house. Henry threw a fit, but the guards are either dressed as house staff or in street clothes, so they don't stick out too much." He and Jake headed for the door, and Jake looked around, spotting a number of men 'working' around the outside of the house who were not usually present.

"As soon as I clean up, I'll be back. Don't want to upset Mrs. Desmet." He gave Jake a broad wink. "Mr. Brand didn't think it safe for you to return to your house, so he had me gather up some of your things and move them into your old room here. Don't worry—I've got men watching your place. It's taking a risk, having everyone in the same place like this, but it's just easier to make sure you're all safe if the family is in one spot. And George has moved me into the loft above the carriage house—he figured things would get messy."

"You don't think the rifle will upset Mother?" Jake asked. "Henry is sure to have a stroke when he sees it."

"Promise?" Kovach asked with a wicked grin. "Sorry. But I couldn't resist."

"No offense taken," Jake assured him. "At least, not by me."

Kovach went around to the rear of the house while the carriage driver took the coach further down the driveway. Jake drew a deep breath and squared his shoulders, stalling for time.

The Desmet home was modest by comparison with some of the grandest homes on Shadyside's Fifth Avenue. It was a stately house in the Second Empire style, with a mansard roof capping its third floor, edged with a decorative iron trim. The home was made of stone, with paired columns around the entrance and sweeping stone stairs. A short brick and stone wall, waist high, separated the semi-circular coach drive from Fifth Avenue's sidewalk.

Jake had always thought the house looked more light-hearted than its larger, more expensive and more imposing neighbors, but now, even the house was in mourning. A large boxwood wreath festooned with black crepe hung on the door. A large black ribbon adorned the door knob and knocker, reminding visitors to knock softly. The windows were open, but the curtains were drawn, making the house seem more still and dark than Jake could ever recall.

A chill settled over him as he climbed the steps. Usually, he looked forward to returning home, either to his parents' house or to his own smaller brownstone on one of Shadyside's pleasant side streets. Now he felt nothing but dread.

The door opened at his first knock. Wilfred, the family's long-time butler, opened the door. When it came to Wilfred, Jake always thought that the term 'butler' did not really fit. Wilfred was the glue that made the center hold, as discreet as a diplomat, and as efficient as a general.

"Welcome home, Mr. Desmet."

Jake swallowed hard. "Thank you, Wilfred."

"My condolences on your loss." Wilfred's voice had the impassivity of a professional butler, but there was a note of real grief behind his words, an emotion unmistakable in his eyes. Wilfred had been with the family since before Jake's birth, and, in their own way, Wilfred and Jake's father had been closer friends than their roles might suggest.

"Thank you," Jake replied. Down the hallway, the soft buzz of conversation from the parlor stopped, and quick footsteps came their way.

Henry barreled down the hall, annoyance clear on his face. "Where the hell have you been, Jake?" he snapped, barely keeping his voice down.

Henry Desmet was five years older than Jake, but several inches shorter. He took after their mother's side of the family in looks and build, unlike Jake, who was an echo of his father. Jake had always attributed his brother's controlling ways to his short stature, like Napoleon.

With effort, Jake kept his temper leashed. "You know damn well where I've been."

"You couldn't be home sooner?"

Jake took a deep breath. "I can't control how long it takes to cross the Atlantic. We got here as quickly as we could."

"No, Rick and Nicki got here quickly. You took your time."

Jake was about to reply when another voice carried down the hallway. "Jake? Is that you?"

"I'll be right there, Mother," Jake replied. He went to step around Henry, but Henry grabbed his arm.

"I don't know how you persuaded George to do it, but it's not fair!" Henry protested.

Jake shook off his hold and straightened his suit coat. "I didn't 'persuade' George to do anything," he replied sotto voce. "And it wasn't George's decision—it was Father's. George just broke the news."

"I could challenge you in court."

Jake met Henry's gaze. "Get over yourself, Henry. Father chose what he thought would be best for the business—you in New York, and me in the crosshairs. I'm not whining about getting shot at; stop complaining about getting to sit in a nice, safe Laight Street office."

"You'd better not louse up the big contract I've got pending," Henry said with a glower. "Richard Thwaites. New Pittsburgh money, spends a lot of time in New York, very interested in using our services."

Jake leveled a hard glance at Henry. "Really? With everything that's been going on, all you can think about is a business deal?"

"Is there a problem, Jake?" Kovach stood just outside the servant's entrance to the kitchen. He had changed his clothes, and now wore a long duster over fresh pants and a shirt. Jake would have bet money that there was a rifle beneath the duster, and probably a Colt Peacemaker or two in his belt.

Henry muttered a curse. "I'll let this go—for now—out of deference to Mother. But I'm not going to go away."

Jake shouldered past Henry and gave a nod to Kovach. Wilfred, who had witnessed the entire exchange without reaction, led Jake into the parlor.

Rick rose to greet Jake as he entered, a questioning look on his face. Jake gave him the briefest of smiles, just enough to let Rick know everything was as right as it could be. They'd been friends long enough that they could almost read each other's thoughts, useful in negotiations when they couldn't speak. Jake surreptitiously passed off the list of names George had given him and whispered, "Nicki," before turning to take in the room.

The argument with Henry had distracted Jake from the changes inside the house, but there was no mistaking the alterations to the parlor. Black cloth was draped over the large mirror, and on photographs and paintings, to keep the spirit of the deceased from being caught in a reflection. Other photographs had been laid face down, to protect those pictured from the angel of death. The clock on the mantel had been stopped at the precise time of Thomas Desmet's death. Jake caught a whiff of embalmer's fluid even over the profusion of lilies and bouquets that filled one side of the room.

Thomas Desmet's body lay in an oak casket atop a cooling board at the eastern end of the room. A wealth of flowers surrounded the casket. Jake caught his breath as he faced the unavoidable truth.

"Jake!" Catherine Desmet rose to greet him as Jake crossed the floor in two quick strides and swept his mother up in his arms. Rick stepped aside and rejoined Nicki in hushed conversation. Catherine was dressed in full mourning: a somber dress of Henrietta cloth with lawn cuffs and collar, trimmed in crepe with jet buttons. Her strawberry-blonde hair was pinned up in a severe knot covered with a widow's cap. Her mourning bonnet, weeping veil, gloves and kerchief lay nearby, should callers outside the closest circle of family and friends arrive.

"I'm so sorry," Jake murmured in her ear. He kissed her cheek, and swallowed a lump in his throat.

Catherine took a deep breath and squared her shoulders, taking a step back. "I'm sorry your homecoming had to be on such a dark occasion." She looked to have aged years just in the few weeks Jake had been gone.

Catherine led Jake to sit beside her on a high-backed sofa. Rick and Nicki sat across from them, and Jake realized that both had changed into proper mourning attire. Rick's suit was full black, with a black armband and pocket handkerchief. Nicki's gown was a somber echo of the dress Catherine wore, trimmed in lawn and crepe.

"Henry made arrangements for the funeral to take place tomorrow," Catherine said. Her voice was strong, but there was an uncharacteristic rasp to it. "The servants and I have been taking turns sitting up with Thomas," she said, avoiding a glance toward the casket. "Our friends have been so good about stopping by," she added.

"Adam Farber's been by, asking for you," Rick said with a pointed glance at Jake. "I dare say Cullan will stop in tomorrow, once he's gotten the *Princess* safely berthed and the repairs underway. Renate Thalberg also stopped by. We took a walk around the gardens."

Meaning that Renate put a warding on the perimeter, Jake thought. *I wouldn't be surprised if she put down salt or smudged sage. Best if Mother doesn't know.* Though Renate's magic might run afoul of Jake's Presbyterian upbringing, he found comfort in her actions, and relief that, if his father's killer had used magic, Renate's wardings might add another layer of protection.

"She also left a gift for your mother," Rick said. He gestured to a black velvet pouch on a side table. On it lay a jet amulet in the shape of a triquetra, an overlapping triangular knot. Catherine and others would see a symbol of the Trinity; both Rick and Jake recognized it as a much older symbol of protection.

"That was very kind of her," Jake said.

Catherine laid her hand over Jake's. "You'll be home now for a bit at least, won't you?"

"It depends on the business, but I'll do my best," he said, wondering if either George or Henry had given her the news of his promotion.

She squeezed his hand. "It's a comfort that you and Henry can be here with me." Catherine glanced toward the doorway, where Henry was chastising one of the servants about some imagined slight. "And I trust that you'll use all due caution finding the person responsible for the curse that killed your father," she said, dropping her voice.

Jake choked. Rick's eyes widened and Nicki barely repressed a gasp. Catherine regarded them all with a raised eyebrow.

"You know?" Jake managed when he regained his voice.

"Of course I know." Catherine sat up, her back ramrod straight. "George was your father's public business partner. I have always been a silent partner." Given that it had been money from Catherine's inheritance that had helped to fund Desmet's portion of Brand and Desmet, that made sense, Jake thought. Her family made their money from the sale of corn whiskey in the years after the Whiskey Rebellion.

"So you also know... about Henry?"

A faint smile touched the corners of Catherine's lips. "Yes, indeed. Your father and I discussed succession plans at length, before sharing them with George." She paused, seeming to enjoy his surprise. "That goes for the more specialized acquisitions as well."

Jake felt winded. Rick appeared at a loss for words. Nicki, the family's most vocal supporter for women's suffrage, attempted to look both decorously somber and gleeful at the same time.

"Andreas came by late on the night Thomas died," Catherine went on, keeping one eye on Henry to make certain he was preoccupied. "Wilfred helped him place protective wards around the house. He was quite worried about the family. Renate has since reinforced those wards."

Jake felt as if the world had tilted. He had known his parents were close, but had never imagined that their confidences ran to the details of the business or otherworldly connections.

"I've been on the edge of my seat since Harold's telegram," Catherine added. "I'm glad you're back safely."

"Harold sent a telegram to you?" Jake barely kept his voice down, and looked quickly to make sure Henry had not heard him.

"Really, Jake. He's a second cousin, on my mother's side. Who do you think recommended him for the London office?"

"There was another attack on the office, just before we came over," Jake said. "George is going into hiding after the funeral. Maybe you should consider—"

"Absolutely not," Catherine replied, lifting her chin defiantly. "I will not be run out of my own home."

Henry finished chastising the servant and began to walk toward them. Catherine cleared her throat, and for Henry's benefit suddenly looked distraught and frail. "Reverend McDonald will be coming by tonight for a private service," Catherine informed him. "Since Nicki and I can't be at the funeral tomorrow."

Jake wondered if his mother's sudden stringent propriety had more to do with remaining within Andreas's wardings than with the easily offended sensibilities of their Shadyside neighbors. Among New Pittsburgh's elite, it was not unheard of for women to attend the funeral service itself, though some of the older women kept to the more rigid British customs and remained home. Jake had no doubt that Catherine was doing exactly as she pleased, and that she had her reasons for doing so.

"I've made all the arrangements," Henry said, giving Jake a look as if to dare him to argue. "I've hired the best funeral company in the city to handle the procession from the church to Homewood Cemetery. It'll be a proper affair," he said, looking quite satisfied. "We'll have their nicest hearse and horses, plus their best carriage for us to follow the hearse."

"I left it up to Mark to hire the mutes," Catherine added offhandedly. "He's taken care of it, and assured me we'll have quite a few, as befitted Thomas's position." Jake and Rick exchanged a knowing look. Mutes were professional mourners, retained to help set the mood and add pomp to the procession. If Kovach had been responsible for hiring them, Jake was willing to bet they'd be riflemen in disguise.

"All the details are in place, right down to the funeral biscuits," Henry declared. "I think Father would have been pleased."

Father would have been appalled, Jake thought, knowing how much his father detested conspicuous displays of affluence. He did not doubt that Henry had made his plans to win the approval of his high-society friends in New York City.

"Did I mention that my dear friend Ida telegraphed to let me know she will be here next week?" Catherine mentioned, making small talk for Henry's sake since they could say little of consequence with Jake's older brother in earshot. "She'll be back from Paris by then. We've known each other since our university days—longer than I care to think about. It will be a comfort to have her visit."

The knock at the door startled them all. Jake heard Wilfred go to receive the caller, and heard a muffled sound suspiciously like a shotgun round being chambered. Jake tensed, and saw that Rick was ready to spring from his seat.

"Reverend McDonald," Wilfred said in a voice loud enough to carry. "Please come in."

Reverend Dennis McDonald was a tall man with a spare build, whose skinny legs and arms seemed too long for his body. His reddish-blond hair was thinning on top, and together with his spectacles, it gave him a scholarly look. To Jake's surprise, the minister held a large, wrapped floral arrangement.

"A man was having some difficulty with his horse near the gate," the minister said. "He asked me if I would bring this in to you."

Jake cleared a place on a nearby table, and Reverend McDonald set the arrangement down, making sure to set the glass vase atop a doily. Catherine carefully pulled back the protective paper wrapping to reveal the flowers inside, and gasped.

A profusion of monkshood and foxglove blossoms with a stalk of calla lily made up the center of the arrangement, surrounded by belladonna, nightshade, and larkspur. Caladium, bloodroot, and hemlock spilled from the edges of the vase.

There was a card attached to the base, which read, *Our wishes for the Desmet family.*

"Get that thing out of here," Catherine demanded. She had gone pale, and her voice shook. Nicki blanched, and stepped closer to take Catherine's arm.

"What's wrong?" Reverend McDonald asked, clearly flummoxed. "I don't know who sent them, but they're lovely."

"And every one of them is a deadly poison," Catherine replied. "It's a threat. That's the sender's wish for us. Death."

Chapter SEVEN

"Goodbye, Thomas," Catherine Desmet murmured as the pallbearers removed her husband's casket from the house.

"Make damn sure he's feet-first, mind you! I don't want talk in the neighborhood of haunts!" Henry fussed at the pallbearers.

"Don't tell me you actually believe in superstitions," Jake snapped. After an entire morning of Henry pitching a snit over every detail, Jake's patience was at an end.

Henry rounded on him. "It doesn't matter whether I personally believe it keeps the dead from returning. It's what the neighbors believe that matters, and whether they'll ever visit the house again."

Jake rolled his eyes. "I should have guessed. It's real estate values you're concerned about, not the afterlife."

"Now is *not* the time," Nicki grated. "You're upsetting your mother."

Jake took a deep breath and forced himself to relax. Even Henry had the good grace to look abashed. "Sorry," he said, though his eyes remained on the pallbearers.

Jake took his mother's hands. The loss in her eyes made his heart ache. "He'll have a good send-off, a proper service," Jake assured her. "And when we get back, I'll tell you everything."

Catherine met his gaze. "Thomas is gone. There's no changing that. But I don't want anything happening to the two of you. Be careful."

Jake nodded. "We will. And we'll get to the bottom of this—I promise."

It was time for Jake to take his place alongside Henry, processing toward where the hearse and carriage waited. True to his word,

Henry had spared no expense on the cortège. Six black horses were teamed to a large black hearse, through the glass sides of which the well-appointed casket would be seen. The hearse's corners were embellished with gold, and there was an ostentatious canopy of ostrich feathers, in the European tradition. Jake ground his teeth, biting back criticism, but Henry looked as pleased as circumstances permitted.

Neighbors and onlookers were already beginning to gather along the sidewalk, and men removed their hats as the casket was placed into the hearse. It was impossible not to notice the mutes. As professional mourners, the mutes stood silently with sad expressions, forming an honor guard on both sides of the street and down the steps of the house. Jake counted at least twenty men dressed in long dark coats, their top hats covered with black crepe, sporting huge crepe sashes that hung from shoulder to hip. Each carried a long pole or 'wand' that spread, fan-like, at the top, shrouded in crepe and tied with a bow. They looked to Jake rather like cloth-wrapped rakes, but given that Kovach had hired the mutes, he was willing to bet the wands were rifles and shotguns. On closer inspection, he was certain that he recognized several 'mutes' as being among the security men from the previous night.

"The mutes are a nice touch," Henry said in a brusque aside. "Adds a nice bit of pomp." Jake shook his head and gave silent thanks that Henry had not decided to employ professional wailers as well.

Kovach stood somberly beside the black carriage that awaited Jake and Henry. The carriage was as opulent as the hearse, and Jake was certain Henry had rented it from the mortician instead of using one of the company's vehicles. George and Rick would follow in a second, not quite so opulent, carriage. Jake was sure the driver was one of Kovach's men, as was the footman. Odd bulges beneath their cloaks suggested to Jake they were both well-armed.

"It's not quite what we had in London," Kovach murmured as he helped Jake step into the carriage. "You might wish to stay back from the windows."

"What the hell is he talking about?" Henry groused.

"We had especially lovely carriages on our last trip," Jake lied smoothly as he found a seat. "And the windows had curtains, for privacy." The answer pacified Henry, and Henry settled into his seat, taking up more than half, Jake noted.

Jake was mindful of the Peacemaker lodged in the waistband of his trousers as he seated himself. His sense of foreboding had come back this morning in full force; and while he thought it was probably from spending too much time around Henry, he wasn't taking chances. The procession started off at a stately pace, and Jake bet Henry had instructed the coachmen not to go too quickly, to make the spectacle last.

Thomas Desmet was not a famous politician or an actor, nor was he one of the true elite among New Pittsburgh's wealthiest men. So it was surprising to Jake that so many people thronged the sidewalks to gawk as the procession made its way toward Shadyside Presbyterian Church. Throughout it all, Henry sat with a satisfied half-smile, relishing the attention.

"Stop fidgeting," Henry admonished.

"We could have walked faster," Jake replied. "We could have walked faster even carrying the casket."

"Don't be disrespectful."

"You know how much Father hated ostentation," Jake returned. "He would have loathed this."

"It's good for business," Henry said, glancing out the window at the gathered onlookers. "Did you know these carriages and the hearse are actually nicer than the ones Congressman Brewer's family used a few years ago?"

Jake refrained from smacking his forehead in sheer frustration. He spared a glance from the carriage, but he was watching the mutes, not the spectators. Instead of trailing behind the hearse, most of Kovach's men walked beside the carriage, their wands held like rifles in a drill parade. Jake got a good look at the mute nearest the carriage and bit back a chuckle. The man had the squashed nose of a boxer and the thick-muscled neck of a pub brawler, his beefy arms straining the seams of his rented outfit.

Finally, the carriage pulled up in front of the stately church. Kovach rapped on the carriage door, and opened it to allow Jake and Henry to get out. The pallbearers unloaded the casket and started up the church's broad steps.

In the six years since its construction, Shadyside Presbyterian Church had already garnered notice as an outstanding example of Richardsonian Romanesque architecture. A central windowed tower—the lantern—was flanked by two transepts and a rounded tower on the side. Round-arched windows on the south transept and arched windows on the lantern gave the church a cathedral-like feeling, further increased by the carvings and grotesques around the main doorway.

The mutes were already in position, forming an honor guard flanking the steps. Even so, Jake and Rick kept a wary eye out as they climbed the steps. George kept his gaze straight ahead, as if resolved not to let Thomas's murder get the best of him. Henry seemed oblivious to everything except for the details of the procession itself.

The guests were already seated. Reverend McDonald, dressed formally in a Geneva robe and cassock, drew Henry aside and spoke in hushed tones. Rick walked over to stand beside Jake. Jake scanned the crowd. Most of the men, Jake could easily identify as his father's business associates, or friends of the family. A few he recognized as among New Pittsburgh's most powerful industrialists, come to pay their respects. The company's lawyer, banker, and accountant were in attendance, as were several of their Shadyside neighbors. All in all, he thought, it was a 'Who's Who' of the New Pittsburgh business community. *Henry must be bursting with pride*, he thought drily. *We might make the society column.*

One man stood out in the crowd. The stranger was tall with broad shoulders. He was bald and had a well-trimmed mustache. The cut of his suit looked expensive, and something about the man gave Jake the distinct impression that he was European.

"Who's that?" Jake whispered with a nudge to Rick.

"Don't know, but I'll find out." Rick went over to where George stood and whispered in his father's ear. A few moments later, he returned. "Drogo Veles. Father's as surprised as you are to see him here."

"Thwaites's business partner. And Thwaites was one of the last people to see Father alive," Jake muttered as the ushers seated the last of the mourners. "They're first in line when it comes to suspects, at least in my mind. I can't believe either one of them has the nerve to show up here."

Any reply Rick might have made was cut off as the organ began to play and the pallbearers carried the casket to the front. Ushers returned to seat first Jake and Henry, then George and Rick, in the pews reserved for family. As Jake made his way up the aisle, Veles watched him pass, and Jake could feel Veles's gaze on him even after he had been seated. The mutes filed in behind them, forming a line at the rear of the sanctuary. One look at the row of black-clad, brawny men standing at parade rest should have tipped off anyone that they were bodyguards rather than mourners, Jake thought, and wondered what the other attendees made of it.

A noise at the back of the church made Jake turn to glance over his shoulder. A man with the dark cassock and beard of an Orthodox Catholic priest entered. He seemed anxious to attract as little attention as possible, ducking into a back pew where he could observe without being seen. *What's a priest doing at Father's funeral?* Jake wondered, turning back around when Henry gave him a not-so-subtle jab in the ribs.

Jake's thoughts were a jumble throughout the short memorial service, and he heard little of the eulogy. Questions cycled in his mind. *Who killed Father—and why? What was it the killer wanted badly enough to continue his attacks?*

Jake realized how much his thoughts had wandered when the organ began to play the recessional and the congregation stood for the pallbearers to carry the casket to the hearse. Jake took the opportunity to scan the crowd once more, thinking about who was missing—and who was unaccountably present.

Andreas Thalberg had not attended because the funeral was held in daylight. Cullan Adair had slipped in at the last moment, his irrepressible good cheer dampened by the somber circumstances. He was sitting with Adam Farber, the genius inventor behind the airship's mechanical arsenal. In front of them sat a scholarly-looking man in his middle years. Jake recognized him as Dr. Konrad Nils, head of acquisitions for Andrew Carnegie's new museum.

The Catholic priest was gone.

Drostan Fletcher, the private investigator, sat in the back left corner of the sanctuary, a place that afforded the best view of the crowd. He was close to Jake's height, maybe six feet tall, with reddish-blond hair and a bushy red moustache. The suit he wore was an older style, a good tweed that had seen heavy use. Jake had never needed to work directly with Fletcher before, though he had seen him at the Brand and Desmet offices. Now Jake was glad George had the detective on the case.

Jake and Henry followed the casket, stopping at the front door of the church to form a receiving line. George and Rick joined them a moment later.

"So sorry about your father." One person after another murmured the same or similar words. Henry accepted their condolences with dramatic flair, as if he were barely holding on to his reserve. George stood to Jake's left, and after the first few well-wishers moved through the line, Jake realized George was greeting each by name and making a bit of revealing small talk for Jake's benefit, by way of introduction.

"I hear you'll be stepping into your father's role." The speaker was an elderly, white-haired man who stood straight-backed despite his age. He had a piercing gaze and the dour look of an undertaker or a banker, but given the fine gold watch at his waistcoat, Jake decided on the latter.

"I've been telling Mr. Mellon about you, Jake," George said. "I've assured him that you're well-versed with our European acquisitions."

"Yes, sir," Jake replied. "Of course, no one could replace Father—"

"Your father was an exceptional man," Thomas Mellon replied. "I expect you to be no less exceptional. In fact, I'm banking on it."

Henry nearly fell over himself to greet Mellon, but the elderly man favored Henry with only the briefest of nods before making his way down the stairs to a waiting carriage. Henry glowered at Jake, but said nothing.

Jake was still staring after the banker, so he did not see Veles approach until the man was already in the receiving line. Henry spotted him, and fawned over Veles until the man had to extract his hand from Henry's to move on. George gave Jake a nudge with his elbow to bring back his attention. "Mr. Veles," George said, added nothing to suggest the nature, if any, of Veles's relationship with Jake's father or the company.

"So you're the one who spends his time chasing shadows," Veles said in a quiet voice. He fixed Jake with a gaze that seemed to see down to his bones. "My condolences about your father. It's a dangerous business." Jake felt a sudden gut-level wariness, but saw no way to avoid shaking the man's hand. "I wish you good fortune working with the *powers*-that-be."

Henry opened his mouth to speak, but Veles gave him a cold, level stare that made him clamp his lips together and shrink back. Without another word, Veles swept down the steps toward one of the many black carriages below.

Out of the corner of his eye, Jake saw Fletcher slip out by a side door. *Curious.*

Richard Thwaites hustled through the receiving line like a man in a hurry to be elsewhere. New Pittsburgh's fair-haired boy, Thwaites was frequently in the society pages with a famous singer or actress on his arm, and just as frequently the topic of gossip when those liaisons went awry. Somehow, he managed to emerge from every scrape unscathed, though the trust fund his father's will had provided undoubtedly had something to do with it.

Henry greeted Thwaites like an old friend, and though Thwaites responded, there was a difference in enthusiasm that spoke volumes. *Leave it to my brother to be courting someone like Thwaites as a prospect,* Jake thought disdainfully.

After a long conversation with Henry that backed up the line, Thwaites finally moved on. His manner with George was decidedly more formal. "Sorry for your loss. Tricky business, what you do, isn't it?" Thwaites remarked, a comment that to Jake sounded suspiciously like he was blaming Thomas for his own murder.

"And you're the son who goes adventuring," Thwaites said, bypassing Rick without a word and eyeing Jake from head to toe. "Well, well." He gave a smile that did not reach his eyes. "Your father was quite the businessman. I hope his luck rubs off on you." He gave Jake a perfunctory handshake and strode out the door. *For a well-wisher, that had a rather threatening undertone,* Jake thought.

Several more business associates and neighbors shuffled through the line in a numbing parade. Finally, Cullan Adair and Adam Farber worked their way to the front.

"Sorry again about your dad," Cullan said, clapping Jake on the shoulder.

"So am I," Adam added. There was no mistaking Jake's friend as anything but an inventor. Adam stood several inches taller than Jake but probably weighed twenty pounds less, with straight, sandy brown hair that was always in his eyes and silver-rimmed spectacles that were constantly smudged.

"I know you've got a lot going on, with everything," Adam said uncomfortably, "but when things settle down, I've got a couple of new pieces in the lab to show you."

Cullan leaned in so that only Jake could hear his comment. "I've told Adam about the 'incident' on the way back from London, given him some ideas for improvements. Maybe even using a tourmaquartz crystal to power the Tesla cells, if we can get our hands on one. Probably a good thing for you and Rick to stop by sooner rather than later, if you know what I mean," he said with a wink.

It was time to follow the hearse to the cemetery. A light rain had begun to fall. The ostrich plumes atop the hearse and on each horse's bridle drooped, and the gray skies seemed utterly appropriate for a burial.

The rain deterred many of the attendees from following the hearse to Homewood Cemetery. Despite the weather, Henry insisted the procession take a roundabout route through the best neighborhoods to reach the memorial gardens. The carriages drove at a walking pace, and the mutes followed, maintaining their somber guard beside the two passenger carriages. Homewood was the newer of New Pittsburgh's large cemeteries. The sprawling lawns and gardens were quiet as the carriages rolled through the wrought-iron gates.

Jake felt his throat tighten at the sight of the canopy over the opened grave. Pastor McDonald was already awaiting them. Once more, the mutes lined up to form a cordon as the mourners alighted from their carriages. Only a handful of attendees besides Jake, Henry, George, and Rick followed to the graveside. Cullan and Adam were present, as was Dr. Zeigler, the Desmet family physician. Kovach stood to one side, as much on guard as paying his respects. Jake noted that neither Veles nor Thwaites were among those present. A movement to one side caught his attention, and he saw a figure in a dark cloak standing just close enough to be able to observe the proceeding, and realized it was Fletcher.

Kovach went over to speak quietly to two of his men. Jake watched as the pallbearers moved the casket beside the grave, laying it across two poles that would help them lower it into the earth. Nearby, covered by a tarpaulin, was the empty grave and the mound of dirt that would fill it in, along with a metal cage fashioned from iron spikes.

Henry followed his gaze. "Damn resurrectionists," he muttered. "Mortsafes like that aren't cheap, but it's a damn sight better than finding out the body's been stolen."

Jake looked around the rolling hills of the cemetery. It was a beautiful place, with tall trees and abundant plantings. He could understand why some families brought picnic lunches out to eat near the graves of their departed family members. The grounds had a quiet graciousness that made it a place of peace for the dead and of solace for the living.

Not far from where Thomas Desmet's casket lay, Jake could see one of the cemetery's newest landmarks, a giant white pyramid. It was a work in progress, not yet completed, but the outer walls of the pyramid were standing, topped by a large steel crane to move the massive stone blocks into place.

To their left, just far away enough to be out of earshot, another cluster of mourners hunched over a new grave. Their hearse and horses stood at right angles to the Desmet party, so that the back of the hearse opened toward Jake's group. Jake wondered who they mourned. This was the priciest section of the cemetery, earning it the name 'Millionaire's Row'. Jake frowned, trying to recall who among the circle of New Pittsburgh's elite had recently passed, aside from his father.

The domes of large black umbrellas formed a somber circle around his father's open grave. Kovach's guards kept up their guise as mutes, and had stationed themselves around the edges of the group, while Kovach himself stood just behind the mourners on a slope that afforded him a good view of the main approach. Cullan was nowhere to be seen, and Adam Farber had wandered off, deep in his own thoughts as usual, poking around the half-built pyramid.

Reverend McDonald cleared his throat and began to read Psalm Twenty-Three. The handful of mourners joined in, voicing the familiar words in a low rumble. Henry fidgeted, but whether it was out of grief or boredom, Jake could not tell. Jake recited the words, but he was distracted. His sixth sense told him that something was wrong.

Just then, the mourners at the nearby grave turned to face them. Dropping their umbrellas, they drew shotguns from beneath their cloaks and opened fire.

Henry cried out and dropped to his knees, clutching his shoulder, blood oozing from between his fingers.

"Stay down!" Jake commanded, dropping the umbrella and drawing his own gun. Another shot barely missed Reverend McDonald, ricocheting as it hit one of the nearby tombstones.

Reverend McDonald yelped as Rick grabbed him by the shoulders and pushed him into the open grave.

"Sorry," Rick said. "You'll be safer in there."

Kovach's men had shouldered their rifles, firing through the gauzy disguise of their 'wands'. Drostan Fletcher came running, a revolver already in hand, shooting at the attackers. The cemetery resounded with the fusillade, and all around them, Jake heard the ping of bullets and shot striking granite.

Under covering fire, four of their guards hustled George, Henry, and the handful of remaining guests to their carriages. There was no way for the guards to get to Jake and Rick without stepping directly in the line of fire. Giving a slap to the horses and a shout, the guards sent two of the carriages galloping away.

Jake and Rick had already taken up positions behind nearby markers, and were returning fire. Anger channeled Jake's grief, clearing his head and sharpening his aim. A shot grazed his left arm and he dropped and rolled behind a monument. Blood trickled from the wound, though the gash was not deep. Jake tied his kerchief around it to staunch the bleeding, cursing under his breath at losing a good suit. He scanned the land around them, but the tombstones and mausoleums provided far too many places to hide.

Jake took cover behind a tomb; larger than a headstone, smaller than a mausoleum, the grave had a solid base of carved stone blocks, with small obelisks on each corner, topped by a miniature Parthenon, crowned by a cornice and cupola.

Jake signaled to Rick and dodged from behind the monument to squeeze off shots at the nearest 'mourner' before moving to a better position. Rick and he had a well-established routine and Jake knew that his friend would cover him as he moved. Kovach's men and Fletcher had taken up positions surrounding Thomas Desmet's open grave.

The sham mourners' hearse flew open and more fighters poured out, even as additional men climbed from their hiding place inside the open grave around which the group had gathered. *Had they dug the grave themselves*, Jake wondered briefly, returning fire, *or commandeered a new grave dug on someone else's account*?

Gunfire echoed across the rolling hills. Jake could see Rick hunkered down behind a large basalt obelisk, methodically taking out assassins as they came within his sights. Jake poked his head around the edge of the tomb, and a shot cracked just above his head, sending stone chips into his hair. He was safe for the moment, but pinned down, and Rick appeared to be running low on ammunition.

By the look of it, their opponents were equal in firepower and forces, presenting the nasty likelihood of a bloody battle fought across Homewood's serene hills. From what Jake could see, one group of assassins was holding down the area near the pyramid, which sat between Jake's friends and their carriages. Another group had taken a position behind several graves on a slight rise, giving them an advantage. Scattered between the groups, Jake spotted several of Kovach's men, but Cullan and Adam were nowhere to be seen.

Jake swung out from his hiding place long enough to get in another shot; this time, he saw his bullet take a man through the chest.

"One more down," Jake muttered, reloading.

The rain was now a fine mist, casting a haze over the cemetery. Fog had rolled in, hanging in ghostly wisps low to the ground, making it even more difficult to see well enough to get a clean shot. On the other hand, Jake thought, it made it that much easier for his side to stay out of the line of fire.

A new noise sounded among the gunshots; a strange, high-pitched, ululating whine. Jake caught a glimpse of motion out of the corner of his eye. As he watched in amazement, a black-shrouded shape rose from the roof of one of the funeral carriages and hovered in the air, trailing its gauzy covering. Two more revenants joined the first, pausing for a moment before they fanned out.

Jake could hear shouts and curses from their assailants as the strange shapes moved in their direction, and several of the false mourners broke from cover, giving Jake the chance to squeeze off a few shots and fell one man as he ran from the apparition.

A low hum countered the high-pitched noise and grew rapidly louder. Jake could see Rick glancing around to find the source of the noise, as the whine reached an ear-splitting crescendo.

"What the hell is that?" Jake breathed. Sparks of blue light were running up and down the crane that stood poised over the pyramid.

At that moment, the ghostly things opened fire.

Fire blazed from the floating specters, sparking from what Jake could now see were the muzzles of Gatling guns. The gauzy coverings burned away in seconds, revealing the 'ghosts' to be three automated flying saucers, the same type that had saved their necks over the Atlantic. The Gatlings laid down a deadly spray of bullets. Emboldened by the sudden reprieve, Jake and Rick ran to new positions, the better to harry their opponents.

A crack like thunder rattled the glass in a nearby mausoleum. Jake turned to see a brilliant flare of blue-white light erupt from the tip of the crane. Ozone filled the air like the aftermath of a lightning strike.

The bolt touched down between the pyramid and a row of headstones. A blinding streak sizzled across the ground, leaving a scorched line in the grass. Three of the assassins were caught in the conflagration, screaming as the brilliant light cut through their bodies and left only charred remains.

The remaining assailants ran for their lives as a new volley of rifle shots from Kovach's men felled all but the swiftest runners. Jake saw Kovach signal several of his sharpshooters and take off on foot after the last of the assassins as the rest of the men, now divested of their guise as mutes, swiftly secured the area before giving the all-clear. Fletcher appeared to be searching the sham burial site for bodies and going through the pockets of the fallen attackers.

Warily, Jake rose from his hiding place, his revolver still at the ready. Rick carefully rose from his crouch, gun in hand. "What in the name of God was that about?" Rick asked.

"Did you see that?" Cullan Adair jumped down from behind one of the bullet-scarred carriages, beaming with victory. "Did you see those babies fly?"

"Were you trying to frighten the life out of us?" Rick looked as if he could not quite decide whether to be angry or relieved.

Cullan chuckled. "I really hadn't thought about what they might look like taking off when I put them on the tops of the carriages. I threw the cloth over them to keep them away from prying eyes. But did you see how well they flew?"

"We saw," Jake said, wiping his brow with the back of his hand. "And more importantly, they shot as well as they hovered."

"Is it over?" Adam Farber peered out of the doorway to the half-finished pyramid. His glasses were askew and his hair looked as if it had been standing on end.

"Appears so," Jake said, watching as Kovach's men began seeing to the casualties. A few of their guards were limping, and one or two were noticeably bloodied, but most looked none the worse for wear, considering.

"Is this the new project you were telling me about?" Rick's voice was awestruck as he stared at the crane above him.

A sly grin spread across Adam's face. "Yep. Although I never thought I'd use it quite like this." He sauntered down from the pyramid to join them, and let out a low whistle at the charred ground and incinerated bodies. "Wait until I tell Mr. Tesla about this."

"Or not," Jake said with a warning glance.

Adam frowned, then nodded. "Yeah. Or not."

"Something you whipped up in your spare time at Tesla-Westinghouse?" Jake asked.

Adam looked a bit thunderstruck by his creation's results. "Uh-huh. Cullan and Miska had asked if I could set up a distraction just in case anything went awry. It's got other uses, but when I heard the gunfire, I thought I might put the fear of the Almighty into whoever was out here." He paled. "I didn't mean to kill anyone. It's a prototype, fairly new, and we don't have the kinks worked out yet."

Jake clapped him on the shoulder. "You're a dangerous man, Adam. Remind me to watch your next invention from a safe distance—like several miles away."

"Adam, that has serious potential. You and I need to talk when this is all over." Rick eyed the wreckage, then turned to Jake. "Whoever did this, they had it all planned out. Want to bet the cemetery didn't dig that grave?" he said with a nod toward the open hole where their would-be assassins had gathered.

"They didn't try anything at the church service," Jake mused. "Too public? Too many big fish?"

"They probably bet it would only be close family here at the grave," Cullan said, his expression grim. "You, George, and Rick—which would have buried Brand and Desmet along with your father."

Jake let Cullan's statement sink in as his gaze followed the return of Kovach and his fighters. Kovach's anger was apparent in his brisk stride, and in the curses that carried in the still air.

"The rest got away from us," Kovach said. "They had a carriage waiting over the next ridge. We couldn't pursue them on foot."

"Any idea who they were?" Now that mortal fear had subsided, Jake's anger outweighed his grief for a moment.

"Offhand, I'd say they were someone who didn't like you much," Kovach said, running a hand back through his dark hair. "Otherwise, no idea—yet—about who hired them." He shook his head. "Unfortunately, they weren't amateurs."

"Nothing on the remaining bodies or hearse to give us a clue. But maybe your men will find something." Fletcher said as he joined them.

"Want to bet it's the same people who gave us a going-away party in London?" Rick asked.

"The question in both cases is, why?" Jake mused.

"Hello?" A faint voice quavered across the foggy air. "Is there anyone out there? Don't shoot—I'm a man of the cloth."

Reverend McDonald peered from the lip of Thomas Desmet's grave. Fresh dirt streaked his face and clumped in his hair, and his clerical collar was muddy and hanging at an odd angle.

"Oh, dear Lord, we left the reverend in the hole," Rick murmured as he and Jake headed at a run toward the befuddled and frightened cleric.

"You're the one who pushed him in," Jake muttered under his breath.

"Does it count against my immortal soul, do you think?"

Jake raised an eyebrow. "Worse. He's likely to tell Mother."

Chapter EIGHT

NICKI LECLERCQ MOVED as silently down the servants' stairway as her bustle would allow. She had intentionally chosen a time when the help would be busy cleaning up after breakfast, and her aunt would have retired to her room.

If she were caught, it would cause a scandal, she thought, and shivered. *Then I simply must not be caught.*

Her boots had the softest soles of any she owned, and she padded down the steps carefully, wincing at every creak and groan from the old stair treads. She breathed a sigh of relief when she reached the bottom.

Nicki peeked around the corner and saw no one in the back corridor, so she tiptoed to the servants' entrance. She had exchanged her deep mourning for a charcoal gray traveling suit that might have been acceptable for second mourning, but would cause a stir were she recognized as a close relative to the deceased. Yet it was worth the risk to gain information, news that would be all the more difficult for Rick or Jake to acquire given their sudden, unwelcome prominence.

"You'll be needing this." Wilfred's voice made Nicki jump and she gave a squeak. The butler stood just inside the vestibule. He held out an umbrella in a decorous shade of dove gray. "Madam said to remind you that the gentlemen will likely be home by noon, so you'll want to return before then."

"She knows?" Nicki's eyes widened.

The barest hint of a smile touched Wilfred's lips. "She strongly suspects."

"Is she... upset?"

"She said she'd have gone herself if she could have possibly arranged it."

Catherine Desmet's movements would be curtailed by social convention for the next year, as befitted her station and bereavement. Nicki, however, was neither as close to the deceased nor as well-known in New Pittsburgh.

Nicki gave Wilfred a broad grin. "Thanks," she said. "I'll keep a low profile."

The look in Wilfred's eye was skeptical.

Nicki let herself out the servants' door, glancing both ways before stepping into the back street. She made her way the length of the block before emerging onto Shadyside Avenue, where she caught the Squirrel Hill streetcar.

Nicki kept her head down until the streetcar was out of Shadyside, fearing she might run into one of the Desmets' neighbors. Rain kept many people indoors; all the better for her to move about unnoticed.

At the Squirrel Hill stop, Nicki alighted and glanced up and down Murray Avenue. Two other women and a man also got off the streetcar, but Nicki was relieved to see that none of them looked familiar. She drew her shawl around her shoulders against the cool wind, and hastened the few blocks it took to reach Woodland Road. It had become quite a popular address with many of New Pittsburgh's elite after the Civil War. Several grand mansions graced the street, but Nicki was looking for a smaller home tucked between two of its opulent neighbors.

The brick, neo-Renaissance house looked modest and circumspect in comparison, though Nicki knew property in this neighborhood was highly desirable and priced to match demand. She took another look around as she ascended the steps from the street and spotted a man farther down the block lighting a pipe. It was difficult to tell from the angle, but she was almost certain he had been on the streetcar with her.

The door opened at her first knock. A plump maid looked at Nicki with a bored expression. "May I help you?" she asked, her German accent unmistakable.

"I'm here to see Renate Thalberg," Nicki said, withdrawing a calling card from a silver case in her purse. She was careful to hold her purse so the maid would not glimpse the small derringer next to the card case.

"She's quite busy," the maid replied, glancing at the card. "Perhaps if you'll come back another day—"

"Priscilla? Who is it?" A woman's voice called out from down the hallway.

"A Miss Veronique LeClercq has come to call," Priscilla replied. "Are you—"

"Nicki!" A moment later, a slender young woman appeared in the hallway. Renate Thalberg was in her late twenties, slightly-built, with an ethereal appearance that even the bustles and mutton-leg sleeves of current fashion could not weigh down. Light brown hair in a loose chignon framed intelligent brown eyes and fine features just a bit too sharp to be conventionally pretty. "Priscilla, please see her in and bring us tea."

"Right away, ma'am." Priscilla eyed Nicki as if she did not relish the new assignment before stepping away to do as she was bid.

"It's so good to see you," Renate said, giving Nicki a hug and taking her by the arm to lead her to the sitting room. "I'm so sorry it's under such sad circumstances."

Nicki removed her shawl and sat in a wing-backed chair beside a small tea table across from Renate. For a few moments, until Priscilla returned with tea and a plate of shortbreads, they spoke of the weather and mutual acquaintances. When Priscilla drew the door shut behind her, Renate fixed Nicki with an inquisitive look.

"What brings you here on the day of the funeral, when you should be home in mourning?" Renate resembled Andreas enough to pass as his sister, but Nicki knew she was really his great-granddaughter.

Nicki sipped her tea and cringed. "I know it's not proper, but Jake and Rick will be too constrained, what with mourning and all, to make discreet inquiries, and I may be forgiven a little more freedom of movement since I'm not in the immediate family."

Renate gave a sharp laugh. "Discretion isn't usually your hallmark, Nicki. But Andreas told me you might call. I understand you had a bit of trouble bringing back his urn."

Nicki wrinkled her nose. "We were shot at, chased, pursued by an airship and shot at some more." She paused and sipped her tea. "Jake says Andreas doesn't think it was because of the urn."

Renate shook her head. "It wasn't."

"Why? If Andreas wanted the urn, maybe other people did, too. Maybe it's more valuable than he thought."

Renate sighed. "The urn itself is nice, but hardly a museum piece. Andreas wanted the urn because it contains the ashes of his fourth wife."

Nicki struggled to avoid choking on her tea. "Truly?"

Renate grimaced. "Truly. One of the prices of immortality is how frequently you outlive the mortals around you. Andreas is several centuries old. He outlived four wives before he decided to pull back from mortals. But the fourth wife, Elizabeth, was his favorite."

Nicki set her tea down and fixed Renate with a glare. "You mean to tell me we were nearly killed—several times—for ashes?"

Renate's eyes had a far-away look to them, and she frowned. "No," she said quietly, as if listening hard for a whisper Nicki could not hear. "Not the ashes. The danger comes from elsewhere. Not Jake... Thomas..." She seemed to come back to herself and shook her head as if to clear it. "Sorry."

"No, your visions are exactly why I've come," Nicki said. "Thomas Desmet was killed by magic; at least, that's what Andreas told Jake. Someone is trying very hard to use non-magical ways to kill Jake, and maybe Rick too. We've been lucky so far, but sooner or later luck runs out. We don't even know what the assassins are after." She took Renate's hand and met her gaze. "Please, will you do a seeing for me?"

Renate gave a faint smile. "I assumed that was what you came for. I've already set out everything I need."

Renate stood and crossed to a tea cart on which stood an absinthe fountain filled with ice water, a bottle of absinthe, a crystal reservoir glass, a silver plate with a pile of sugar cubes and an ornate silver absinthe spoon.

"It's quite the rage on the Continent," Nicki observed. "Especially with the poets and artists." She eyed the green liquor. "Do you think they glimpse what you see?"

Renate's smile was sad. "Not unless they possess magic like mine." Her hand touched the silver spoon gently. "This spoon has been in my family for many years. My mother and my grandmother were both absinthe witches like me. Both had the Sight, and both received their strongest visions with the aid of the 'green fairy'."

"What happens now?" Nicki asked, suddenly feeling a bit nervous. While she had heard Jake speak of Renate's ability, she had never witnessed a vision herself.

"Do you want to take the journey with me?" Renate's eyes sparkled.

"Can I?"

Renate reached for another glass and held it out to Nicki. "I can pull you in with me. You'll see what I see, but you won't be able to do anything—you'll just be an observer."

"How does it work?" Nicki was intrigued, but hesitant. "I've had absinthe many times, and I never saw visions—well, none that weren't accounted for by the absinthe itself!"

Renate chuckled. "That's how it is for most people. Different things trigger power for different witches. For me, it's absinthe and gemstones." She paused, then gestured to the room's couch. "We'll drink the absinthe, sit back on the couch, and the magic will show us what it shows us." She met Nicki's gaze. "No matter what happens, don't interrupt. My magic is strong enough to protect us in the world of the vision."

"Protect us from what?"

"Danger," Renate replied matter-of-factly. She closed her eyes and took a deep breath. When she opened her eyes again, it seemed to Nicki that Renate did not look quite herself. Motioning for Nicki to stay quiet, Renate began to chant, moving counter-clockwise along the edge of the round, braided rug beneath their feet.

Renate returned to the table, and poured a few ounces of bright green liquor into the reservoir glasses, and then placed the silver absinthe spoon over the top of each glass. She arranged a sugar cube in the center of each spoon, and let the crystal decanter drizzle the ice water over the sugar cube and into the absinthe. When the chilled water mingled with the bright green liquor, it created a milky louche. Renate spoke words Nicki did not quite catch over the mixture, and the liquid took on a faint, green glow as if it were filled with trapped fireflies. Then Renate removed the spoons and sugar cubes and gave Nicki her drink.

Renate seated herself on the couch and Nicki sat beside her. They sat in silence as they sipped their drinks, and when they were finished, Renate took Nicki's hand.

"What if Priscilla—"

"Priscilla is familiar with my visions," Renate replied. "She won't interfere."

Nicki was accustomed to the anise taste of absinthe. It was a potent drink, and the wormwood that was part of its distillation added a growing otherworldliness to her perception, as if everything had taken on a faint glow. So far, it was nothing beyond what she had felt on many a night out on the town with her bohemian friends back in Paris.

Nicki closed her eyes and leaned back, focusing her attention inward. She felt a tug, and it was as though she had been pulled through a curtained doorway into a place that existed somewhere very different from their cozy parlor.

In this in-between place, Nicki felt Renate's presence, and everything came into focus. Nicki hung back as Renate stepped away. The space around them was black, depthless. "Show me," Renate said, spreading her arms wide and letting her head fall back.

Images began to swirl around them. It felt to Nicki like being in the center of a zoetrope, surrounded by spinning, flickering images. The scenes blurred, although Nicki caught glimpses now and again that made sense. Thomas Desmet, writing in a leather-bound book, seated at his desk, appeared and then faded. In its place, a hazy image of a man dressed in a *żupan* and *delia* with a fur-trimmed hat and riding boots came into focus. The garb was old, perhaps medieval, Nicki thought, and Slavic... maybe Russian? This man had coal-black hair and bushy eyebrows over dark, piercing eyes and a carefully trimmed beard and moustache. In his arms, he cradled an elaborately-bound leather book. The man was partly turned away from them, as if hiding what he carried, but then he turned to face Renate, and his gaze met hers, as if to convey a warning.

The image blurred and faded. Another man appeared, dressed in present-day clothing. His dark hair was a little longer than the modern style, and his black eyes were haunted. He looked to Renate beseechingly and reached out a hand as if he wanted her to draw him from the abyss. Mist swirled around him, and the image vanished.

The darkness grew cold, and for the first time, Nicki felt dread. The air was heavy with the smell of moss and freshly turned dirt, and beneath the loam was the scent of decay. Red eyes peered through the darkness, and Nicki caught her breath and took a step back. A horrible screech filled the air.

The eyes grew closer, bright with the hunt. Nicki could make out a form in the gloom, the faint outline of a bent old woman in a long dress with a scarf tied over her head. The eyes seemed to bore into Nicki's soul, and a wave of overwhelming despair welled up from somewhere inside. Grief, for Thomas's death. Sadness for a host of disappointments. So much sorrow...

"Enough!" Renate's voice drowned out the monster's screech. She stood between Nicki and the red-eyed shadow, holding up what looked like a polished stone with a hole in the middle. "You have no power here!"

The screech became a howl of rage. The red eyes fixed on Renate, and the shadow surged forward.

"*Zostac*!" Renate shouted, and the red eyes narrowed, but the shadow came no closer. She shouted a longer command in a language Nicki did not recognize, and the shadow-thing drew back.

Renate took a step back. "Hold on," she said, never taking her gaze off the red eyes.

Nicki tightened her hold on Renate's hand. The darkness swirled like a cyclone, and for a moment, Renate and Nicki stood at the center of a powerful storm. Then, nothing.

Nicki's eyes snapped open, and she found herself staring at the ceiling in Renate's parlor. She pressed her palms against the brocade couch to assure herself that she was back safely. The sofa was reassuringly solid, and Nicki relaxed with a sharp exhale. "What was that nightmare thing?"

"The Night Hag," Renate replied. "*Nocnitsa*, the Poles call her. And unfortunately, she's not a nightmare. She's real." Renate rose from the couch and rang the bell pull. "Priscilla will bring us some more tea. I think we could both use some."

"That's the last time I drink absinthe," Nicki said.

Renate chuckled. "I told you: unless you drink it with me, it's just another cocktail. I'd hate to put a crimp in your social life."

Priscilla brought them a steaming pot of tea and two porcelain cups, along with cream, sugar and a plate of sandwiches. Renate watched as Nicki put a few extra cubes into her tea and took two of the small sandwiches.

"You feel drained," Renate observed.

Nicki gulped her tea and nodded. "I'm so hungry, I think I could eat all these sandwiches and ask for seconds!"

Renate nodded. "That's what the Night Hag does. She drains your life, your energy, and ultimately, your blood. She's the worst sort of vampire, a being that exists only to kill."

"I thought Andreas..."

Renate's eyes flashed. "Andreas is an immortal, but he is not anything like the Night Hag. Yes, he is a vampire. But he has a mind, and he chooses how to use his power."

Nicki held up a hand. "Please, I meant no offense." Nicki paused. "Those men I saw—did you see them too?"

Renate nodded. "One dressed like a Cossack, and the other man?" Nicki nodded. "From the clothing, I would say the first was Polish or Russian. The clothing looks like paintings I've seen from the 1600s. As for the other man, I know him. Karl Jasinski. He's one of us."

"A vampire?"

Renate laughed. "No... but he is a witch, and one of our coven."

Nicki leaned forward. "Jake gave me a list of names, some from the most recent shipments Brand and Desmet handled, others from a paper he found in Uncle Thomas's desk. Karl Jasinski's name was on that list. So was that word you called the Night Hag—*Nocnitsa*." She pulled the copy from her purse and showed it to Renate.

"That's interesting," Renate said. "I recognize some of these names. They're either witches, like Jasinski, or connected to the practice in some way." She frowned, thinking. "Do you know what Jasinski shipped? And when?"

Nicki shook her head. "Rick and George are going to go over the records after the funeral. Do you know where we can find Jasinski?"

"They call him the Witch of Pulawski Way," Renate replied. "At least, that's where he has his shop." She frowned, concerned. "Come to think of it, I haven't seen him around lately."

"Maybe he realizes things have gotten dangerous," Nicki said. "Does he have family in the area? There are bound to be plenty of Jasinskis in New Pittsburgh."

Renate smiled. "That's his 'practice' name, not his real name. Jasinski means 'one who works with ash trees'. The ash is a sacred, magical tree."

"Oh," Nicki said. "Then what's his real name?"

Renate shook her head. "I don't know. I wouldn't expect to know. Names have power. It's not wise to tell people outside your most intimate circle your true name. Knowing your true name gives a person power over you."

Nicki met her gaze. "So I'm guessing that Thalberg isn't your true name, or Andreas's either."

"You would be correct."

"Why did we see Uncle Thomas in the vision?" Nicki asked.

Renate looked thoughtful. "I don't know, but it's likely that the images have some relationship to each other. If we figure out the connection, it might tell us who killed Thomas—and why they're still after Jake and Rick."

After a little light conversation and profuse thanks, Renate began to walk Nicki out when a persistent knocking came at the front door. Renate closed her eyes for a moment, and when she opened them, she looked uneasy.

"Wait in here," she said to Nicki, steering her into a parlor. "Don't make any noise, and don't come out until I get you." With that, she shut the door just as Nicki saw Priscilla bustling up from the entrance to the house.

"Ma'am, there's a man here to see you, and he refuses to go away." Priscilla's voice carried.

Nicki pressed her ear against the door. She heard Renate's footsteps, then the door opening. "You aren't welcome here," Renate greeted the newcomer icily.

"Aren't you going to invite me in?" It was clear from the stranger's mocking tone that he did not expect an invitation. "I came to do you the courtesy of delivering a message from Mr. Veles." His voice had a heavy Eastern European accent.

"Nothing from your master comes into this house until it's been cleansed," Renate said, distaste clear in her voice. "Put it on the step. I'll deal with it."

"As you wish." The man's tone held a note of dark amusement that made Nicki grit her teeth.

"Now I'd like to return the favor and give you a message for your master," Renate continued. "Tell him that if he was involved in Thomas Desmet's death, there will be a reckoning."

Harsh laughter sounded. "You and Andreas have always thought so highly of yourselves. Perhaps you will be shown how mistaken you are."

The door slammed shut. Nicki moved quickly to the window, hoping to gain a glimpse of the stranger. He was a short, stooped man with dark hair. The messenger stopped, as if he knew he was being watched, and turned, looking directly to where Nicki stood concealed behind the curtain. An unpleasant smile touched his lips before he walked briskly toward the carriage waiting at the curb.

Nicki barely got back to her spot near the door before Renate opened it and motioned for Nicki to follow her back to the sitting room. "You should wait here for a while, to make sure he's really gone," she cautioned, ringing Priscilla for more tea.

"Who was that?" Nicki asked.

"One of Drogo Veles's lackeys," Renate replied uneasily. "Anytime Veles or his people show up, it means trouble. He's a dark witch, and he's got no compunctions about who gets hurt when he wants something."

"Do you really think he was involved in Uncle Thomas's murder?" Nicki asked, giving a nervous glance toward the window.

"Andreas does," Renate replied. "Or at least, Andreas believes Veles's magic had something to do with it. But the question is: why?"

"What message did he send you?" Nicki asked, curiosity trumping good manners.

Renate removed a sealed parchment from her pocket. "I made certain to check it for magical traps and cleanse it before I brought it into the house." The wax seal had been snapped, but the paper was still folded.

"Was it dangerous?" Nicki leaned forward to peer at the message as if it might spring up and bite her.

"Anything from Veles carries a taint," Renate said with a sniff. "He's not to be trusted. Fortunately, the message wasn't cursed, but it's best not to take chances. That's why I used magic to break the seal outside the house wardings, and I contained the energies." She smiled. "The front step is spelled to work as a holding area, if need be. Makes it handy to defuse things like this."

"Open it!" Nicki insisted, anxious to see what was inside.

Renate raised an eyebrow. "Honestly, Nicki! You did hear about that unfortunately curious cat, didn't you?"

"Piffle. I'm not worried. Now hurry up!"

Chuckling at Nicki's interest, Renate unfolded the parchment. Despite the fact that Renate had used her considerable magic to deactivate any dangerous sorcery, Nicki still drew back in her seat as the paper crackled open.

Anger flashed in Renate's eyes as she read the message. "'Mind your business, and you won't get hurt.'" With a curse, she balled up the paper; when she opened her hand, the parchment had turned to ashes.

"The nerve of that man!" Renate exclaimed. "What an arrogant ass! He's no older in the craft than Andreas, and rumor has it he's a pretender to the titles he claims. It's a good thing Drogo Veles didn't deliver this in person. I'd have been tempted to shrivel his... ego."

At that, Nicki nearly snorted her tea. But there was nothing funny about the threat, or about Veles himself. "He has to mean the matter of Uncle Thomas's death. Unless you have other business with him?"

Renate shook her head. "We go out of our way not to have any 'business' with Drogo Veles whatsoever. And I strongly doubt Karl Jasinski did, either—not willingly, anyhow."

"Do you think he's a threat to Jake and Aunt Catherine?"

Renate set her cup aside, dusted off the ashes from her hand into the saucer, and let out a long breath.

"Frankly? Yes, I do. Veles is ruthless, and he's used to getting what he wants. Most people in the magical community go well out of their way to avoid crossing him. Andreas is one of the few who could probably duel him and win—if Veles didn't cheat, which is unlikely." Renate's tone had an edge of bitterness. "There are stories about how he's eliminated enemies. They might have been exaggerated, but I doubt it. He's very dangerous."

"What are we going to do about it?" Nicki asked, raising her chin.

"We?"

Nicki gave her a look of pure stubbornness. "Yes. We. I've been chased and shot at, nearly blown out of the sky. And Thomas was my favorite uncle." Her eyes narrowed. "I've been known to harbor a grudge. Bad habit, but I'm not giving it up now."

Despite the seriousness of the situation, Renate chuckled. "I admire your courage. But please, leave Veles up to Andreas and me. I think Jake and Rick will need your help with the other, mortal, conspirators."

"I'm very good at research," Nicki countered. "And spying. Jake and Rick don't need me all the time."

Renate shook her head. "I'm serious, Nicki. Veles is a very dangerous witch. Other witches, even powerful ones, fear him. It's going to take a witch of Andreas's caliber to challenge him, and even then, Andreas will need to be careful. Please, let us handle him."

Nicki sighed. "Oh, all right," she said, pouting just a bit. "But I do so want to see Veles get his comeuppance!"

"You'll have to wait in a very long line," Renate promised. She got up and went to the window, then called to her maid and had her look out the door and up and down the street.

"No sign of Veles's henchman," Renate said. She closed her eyes for a moment, then opened them and nodded. "No sense of bad magic, either. I think it's safe if you want to head out."

"Thank you, I do have another errand to run before I return to the house. Promise you'll let us know if you find anything out?"

Renate took Nicki's hands. "I promise. Now, be careful. Not all the threats are magical, or from Veles. Keep your wits about you!"

Nicki slipped out of the house with a cautious glance in both directions. The rain had become a light drizzle, still enough to keep much of the normal foot traffic indoors. That made it easy to spot the man from the streetcar, who was lingering under his umbrella near a newspaper stand.

"No helping it; I'll just have to lose him later," Nicki muttered to herself, setting out at a brisk walk for her next destination. She made certain to remain on the opposite side of the street from her stalker, and used a purse mirror to check that he was keeping his distance.

Just a little ways further up Woodland Road stood an imposing brick and stone mansion replete with turrets, dormers trimmed in gingerbread molding, balconies, and bay windows. It had once been the home of a prominent banker. Now it housed the Pennsylvania College for Women. The very name made Nicki smile.

A glance in her mirror let her know that she had not lost the man shadowing her. She sighed, and hurried up the mansion's steps to ring the bell.

"I'm here to see Cady McDaniel," Nicki said to the housekeeper who answered the door.

The woman stepped aside, allowing Nicki to come in out of the rain. "And there's a man following me," Nicki said, hoping to give her best impression of a vulnerable young lady. "Thank you for letting me in; he's been behind me since I got off the trolley."

"Really? We can't have that. I'll get the gardener after him." The housekeeper chuckled. "John's put the fear of God into many a chap who overstepped his bounds. Don't you worry, miss." She paused. "Is Miss McDaniel expecting you? Whom shall I say is calling?"

Nicki dug out another calling card. "Please, tell her Nicki is here."

The housekeeper glanced at the card and nodded. "I'll do that. Wait here, please." She smiled. "And then I'll go talk to John."

Nicki fidgeted in the vestibule. She pulled back the lace curtains that hung at the windows, glancing out cautiously. The man waited across the street at a discreet distance, but there was no mistaking the fact that he was watching the building.

"Miss McDaniel will see you now," the housekeeper announced, and led Nicki down a long hallway to a comfortably appointed library. The room was as large as many a formal dining room, with a massive oak table that could have easily seated twenty people. Bookshelves lined the walls, and a cozy fire dispelled the chill. Nicki sighed and wished time allowed for her to find a book and settle into one of the chairs near the fire.

"Nicki!" Cady McDaniel, the college's head librarian, jumped from her chair and ran to greet Nicki with a hug. Just an inch shorter than Nicki, Cady still stood on tiptoe for the embrace. Her dark chestnut hair was pinned up in a prim bun, and a pair of eyeglasses framed her brilliant green eyes. Taken together with her modest shirt and suit, the hair and glasses toned down, but could not quite hide, Cady's pretty features and curvaceous figure. Nicki had seen Cady dressed for a ball, and knew that away from the library, she could easily turn heads when she wanted to do so.

"Hello, Cady," Nicki replied. "I couldn't pass up seeing you when I'm in town."

Cady gave her a skeptical look over top of her glasses. "You should be in mourning, unless I'm mistaken."

Nicki feigned wounded innocence for a moment, then smiled. "Yes, that's true," she confessed. "But there's a little bit of research I need your help with." She dropped her voice to a whisper. "It's quite literally a matter of life and death."

Cady flashed a grin. "Count me in." She reached up to pat her hair, assuring it was still tidy. "Sorry I'm so flustered," she said. "We have a famous person coming in to give a speech next week, and there are a million details to take care of!"

"Who? Tell me!" Nicki said excitedly. "Anyone I've heard of?"

"Ida Tarbell, the journalist," Cady said. "She's from these parts, you know. Born and raised in Titusville, first woman to graduate from Allegheny College, and now she's over in Paris, writing for *McClure's Magazine*. She's made quite a name for herself!"

Nicki looked thunderstruck. "*Mon Dieu*! That's my Aunt Catherine's friend! She just said an old friend from her college days was coming to town—from Paris."

Cady shrugged. "It wouldn't surprise me that Miss Tarbell knows Mrs. Desmet. We Association of University Women members stick together!"

"Hasn't she caused some fuss with her articles?" Nicki asked as Cady showed her the plans for the event. "She wrote about President Lincoln—and Emperor Napoleon!"

Cady nodded. "And she's had a few articles that were rather critical of powerful people, or about companies that aren't on the up-and-up. That put some noses out of joint, especially in society circles. I can't wait to meet her!"

Nicki looked at Cady's desk, neat and tidy despite her workload. She smiled as she saw one of the many code puzzles Cady adored. "Cady McDaniel! That's a page from the *Pall Mall Gazette*! It's a gentleman's magazine—what on earth are you doing with it?"

Cady tossed her head and made a dismissive gesture. "They run the best puzzles!" she said. "That's a nilhilist cryptogram by a Mr.

Schooling. He says no one can solve it—but I've worked it out and I intend to send in the answer and claim the prize."

Her defiance softened into an impish grin as she took Nicki's hands and led her to a chair by the fire. "Now, pray tell, what's going on?"

"I can only stay a minute," Nicki said. "I need to be back before the men get home from the funeral. But I'm hoping you can look into something for me. I need to know anything you can find out about a man named Karl Jasinski."

Cady raised an eyebrow. "A prospect?"

Nicki give her a dour look. "More like a suspect. You heard about Uncle Thomas's death?"

"Yes, of course. I'm so sorry."

Nicki nodded. "Thank you. But you don't understand; he was murdered."

Cady gasped. "I had heard it was his heart."

"That's the official story. But we have it on good authority that magic was involved. There have been other attempts on Rick and Jake—I was there." She met Cady's gaze. "I think there'll be more, unless we get to the bottom of this."

"And the police don't like dealing with magic," Cady said.

"Exactly. And there's something else I need, but it's a little strange."

Cady's bold grin returned. "I count on you to be a little strange, Nicki, and I mean that in the nicest possible way."

"What can you tell me about the Night Hag? Some might call her *Nocnitsa*."

Cady frowned. "'Night Hag'? Sounds like something out of a fairy tale." She thought for a moment. "It might be something our literature professor has heard of. I'll ask."

The clock on the mantle struck eleven. Nicki's eyes widened. "I've got to get going. Thank you so much—I knew I could count on you."

"You're staying with the Desmets?"

Nicki nodded. "Just send your card, and I'll know to come back when you've discovered something."

Cady made a dismissive gesture. "I can pay a call. That wouldn't be unusual."

Nicki leaned forward and took Cady's hand. "I'm quite sure the house is being watched. Please don't put yourself in danger."

Cady gave Nicki's hand a squeeze. "Don't worry about me. I can take care of myself."

When Nicki returned to the vestibule, there was no sign of the housekeeper. She looked out the window, but the dark-clad man was gone. Gathering her skirts and summoning her courage, Nicki grabbed her umbrella and started back toward the trolley stop.

A few blocks from Murray Avenue, a black carriage suddenly pulled out of an alleyway to block her path and a man lunged from the shadows to grab her wrist as the door to the carriage swung open.

"Get in if you know what's good for you."

Nicki took a swing at the man with her umbrella, rapping him smartly on the temple as she brought her boot down on his instep. With her right hand, she reached into her purse and grabbed the derringer, managing to squeeze off a shot through the fabric of her handbag. The bullet struck the man in the foot and he let out a cry that startled the horse.

"You shot me!"

Before anyone else could spring from the carriage to detain her, Nicki pivoted and ran across the busy street, barely avoiding being run over by a milk wagon. The wagon swerved, careening into the path of the carriage and overturning, spilling bottles onto the road that shattered in a spray of white. Behind the milk wagon was a grocer's cart loaded with produce, and the sound of smashing glass spooked the cart horse so that it bolted, strewing cabbages and potatoes in its wake. A crowd was gathering. Some pushed closer to the wreck, while others filled the street, picking up armfuls of spilled produce.

Nicki fled, dispensing with propriety and grabbing up her skirts to run without tripping. She tried to recall any identifying marks about the carriage; it might come in handy later. She dared another glance at the carriage, and saw a small crimson bird painted on the side of the coach, but then the crowd shifted, and she could not make out the symbol plainly.

Out of the corner of her eye, Nicki glimpsed the black-clad man once more. He was watching her, but the crowd was too thick for him to follow. She did not waste time staring at him. A trolley was coming, and with the crowd's attention still on the wreck, Nicki broke into a sprint before dropping her skirts and strolling the last little bit to board the trolley as decorously as if she had just gone out for a morning of shopping. As the bell clanged, she saw police running in the direction from which she had just come, but whether it was to clear the wreckage or see to the man she had shot, she did not know.

"I wonder what's going on down there?" the woman beside her whispered with a nudge and a nod of her head toward the chaos.

"I have absolutely no idea," Nicki replied, smiling as if she didn't have a care in the world.

Chapter NINE

RICK BRAND LOOKED up at the turreted front of the building most people called 'the Castle'. The massive Renaissance Revival/ Romanesque building looked more like a European manor house than the headquarters of a company founded on the brilliance of Nikola Tesla and George Westinghouse. The building's stone walls, turrets, and huge clock tower dominated the landscape of the town.

The Tesla-Westinghouse building never failed to amuse Rick, who had seen more than his share of real castles in Europe. Finding one here, in Wilmerding, housing one of the most innovative companies in America, seemed so completely out of place that it always made him chuckle and shake his head.

Just as he headed for the steps, a large black carriage drew up behind him, and the driver scrambled down to open the door for a well-dressed man in his middle years to alight. Rick was certain he had seen him before. It was difficult to overlook the expensive, bespoke suit, the imported shoes and the fine top hat crowning a head of blond, curly hair. Stocky and broad-shouldered, the man elbowed past Rick to be the first up the stairs to the front door.

"We'll have the carriage waiting, Mr. Thwaites." The man nodded curtly, his attention on other things.

Intrigued by the ostentation and annoyed at the man's rudeness, Rick climbed the steps and headed for the receptionist's desk. Thwaites waited impatiently to one side, tapping his foot as if whomever he was there to see should have been waiting for him. Rick bent over the receptionist's desk. "Can you please let Adam Farber know I'm coming?" he said quietly.

The receptionist looked up, alarmed. "You can't just—"

"He's expecting me," Rick said with a smile. "I know the way. Rick Brand—check your ledger; I'm listed."

And with that, Rick slipped out of the waiting room just as a man he recognized as the head of Tesla-Westinghouse's laboratories hustled in to greet the aggrieved Mr. Thwaites. Wishing he could have stayed to hear their conversation, Rick took the stairs to the basement before entering an elevator.

"Hello, Mr. Brand. Mr. Farber is waiting for you," Lars, the elevator operator, said. His voice had the scratchy quality of an Edison cylinder recording, making Rick glance up into his brass face as the mechanical man manipulated the buttons to send the elevator smoothly on its way.

"Good to see you, Lars," Rick said. One of Adam Farber's mechanical wonders, the metal man—dubbed a '*werkman*' by Farber—was someone Rick could count on to be unfailingly pleasant and polite. Lars was made that way.

The elevator buttons only showed the upper levels of the headquarters. Lars flipped open a concealed control panel, revealing the means to reach the subterranean levels that housed Tesla-Westinghouse's confidential and experimental projects. When the elevator doors opened, Lars swept out an arm toward the lab. "Enjoy your visit."

Adam Farber was waiting for Rick. He was dressed in a white lab coat that hung off his lanky frame like a scarecrow.

"Good to see you, Rick," Adam said, grinning broadly as he shook Rick's hand. "Glad you could come by, I've missed you. But I know you've got a lot going on. Sorry about all that."

Rick grimaced and shrugged. "Yeah. It hasn't been a good week. But you saved our butts at the cemetery. And I can't stand not knowing about your latest grand projects. Sorry I haven't been by sooner."

Adam ushered Rick into a wide expanse filled with tables covered with half-completed projects, strange metal casings and tangles of wires and tubes. Scattered throughout were empty coffee cups, Farber's fuel for the long hours he spent tinkering in the lab. Adam poured himself a fresh cup of coffee from a nearby urn as they passed by.

"Want a cup?" he asked, fairly vibrating from caffeine even before he downed the liquid in a gulp.

"No thanks, I'll pass," Rick said with a chuckle. He sobered, remembering the blond man in the waiting room. "I saw a guy named Thwaites up in the lobby. Pushy sort. He was at Thomas Desmet's funeral. Who is he?"

Adam's face fell. "Again?" He muttered a curse under his breath. "That's Richard Thwaites. Rich as Croesus, and used to getting his way."

"I figured as much," Rick said. "What's he here for?"

Adam sighed. "Me."

"Huh?"

Adam led Rick over to a large worktable and pulled out a chair, before collapsing into a second one. He set down his empty cup and reached out to grab another, half-finished cup from the table. "Thwaites wants to hire me to work on some kind of project for his new plaything, the Vesta Nine coal mine."

Rick raised an eyebrow. "Didn't look like the mining type to me."

Adam chuckled. "I doubt he's ever stepped out of his carriage onto the mine's property. But Vesta Nine is the largest coal mine in the world, and rumor has it, the deepest, too. You know guys like Thwaites—got to have the biggest toys. He's got a partner, but I don't know his name. Anyhow," he said, tossing off the cold coffee and looking around for another cup, "the last time Thwaites was here, he wanted to know whether I could build him enough *werkmen* to run the mine."

"Can you?"

Adam rolled his eyes. "Aside from the fact that it would take me years to construct them by myself, I doubt even Richard Thwaites is rich enough to pay for it. And besides, I don't trust him." He dropped his voice. "Fair bet he's Oligarchy."

Rick nodded. "I was thinking the same thing." He paused. "Think your boss will give in? Because we need you to work up some new pieces for us rather urgently, given what's been going on."

Adam reluctantly set aside his empty coffee cup. "I don't think my boss will give me up; at least, not just yet. But if Thwaites keeps asking, or if he goes high enough up the ladder, I won't have a choice."

"You can always come work for Brand and Desmet," Rick said. "Solid funding, private lab—pretty much free rein as long as we get first pick of the goodies you dream up." His tone was light, but Rick was serious. It was a discussion they had every time they met, and so far, Adam had managed to deflect a commitment. Now he looked as if he might be considering it.

"Let's leave that door open, shall we?" he said. "In the meantime, what did you have in mind?"

Rick grinned. "First off, we're all still in awe of the contraption you used at the cemetery. Kovach and I actually agreed on something, for once, and we're hoping you could make an even more portable version. He'd love to get his hands on something like that, if it could be toted around in a carriage instead of taking up a whole building." He gave Adam a conspiratorial glance. "And I expect Cullan Adair will want something he can use from up in an airship, too."

"Working on it," Adam said. "Power source is always a problem. The steam tanks take up enough room as it is; creating a furnace makes it unwieldy. The Tesla cells help store energy, but they've got their limitations, too." He stood up, swept the coffee cup to the side, and rummaged in the chaos of the worktable until he emerged with a small stone in his hand the side of a marble.

"Do you know what this is?" Adam asked, staring at the greenish, opaque stone as if it were gold. When Rick shook his head, Adam turned the stone in the light. "It's tourmaquartz. Very rare—and fabulously expensive. Most people have never heard of it. Can't find it many places, but here's what's special about it. A small shard of tourmaquartz, contained properly, can power a boiler as effectively as a whole hopper of coal."

Rick let out a low whistle. "Wow. And by 'fabulously'…?"

Adam shrugged. "Enough that for most purposes it's not worth it. The small shard still costs much, much more than the hopperful of coal."

"So it won't put the coal mines out of business any time soon. But I bet guys like Andrew Carnegie and Henry Frick could come up with some uses for it."

Adam nodded. "Believe me, they already have. But it's hard to get more than a few shards at a time. I had to pull some strings to get the bits I have—and I'd be grateful if you didn't mention it to anyone." He glanced around at the nearly empty lab. "We've had enough problems as it is."

"Oh?"

Adam hurried to fill another cup of coffee, drank half of it on the way back, and plunked down in his seat again. "A couple of shipments have gone missing, a few of them government projects. The Department of Supernatural Investigations is severely annoyed, to say the least."

"Seriously? The Department?" Rick said, shaking his head. "Those guys just don't give up. They've been trying to bring Brand and Desmet into their fold for years, get us to use our connections to spy for them. I don't trust them."

Adam nodded. "I like some of their people more than others, but I don't trust the Department itself farther than I can throw it. On the other hand, they're always asking me to build them strange stuff, and they pay well." He grinned. "Almost as strange as the stuff I build for you."

"Speaking of which," Rick said, "I've got a couple more things on my wish list and I'm hoping you can make them happen."

"Try me."

"All right. How about something that isn't much bigger than a shotgun, but that shoots something that doesn't create a spark? I don't know, maybe some kind of energy that pushes things away instead of shooting a hole in them. Jake and I have been in a couple of tight spots where we didn't want to shoot the place up or cause a fire, but we needed to be able to stop thugs at a distance."

Adam peered at Rick over his glasses. "You and Jake have an odd way of doing business."

"You don't know the half of it."

Adam pondered for a few moments, staring into space. "All right," he said. "I think I can come up with something. What else?"

"Could you come up with a pair of goggles that would help us see better in the dark? Sometimes, it would be handy not to need a light."

Adam looked thoughtful, drumming his fingers on the worktable as he thought. "Maybe. That's a little harder. On the bright side, I've been working on something similar for a while. Let me work on it some more, and see what I can come up with."

"Just let me know if you need money for materials," Rick said. "Beyond the regular budget."

"Will do."

Rick paused as something Adam had said earlier came back to him. "What you said about the shipment going missing—do you know where in the process the boxes went astray? I'm trying to track down some missing crates of our own. Now I wonder if there isn't something bigger going on."

Adam shrugged. "They left here just fine, on the right wagons. I saw to it myself," he said. "And our wagon men delivered the crates fine and dandy to the railway station. But DSI never got them. And no one on the train says they saw anything amiss."

"Let me know if you find out anything," Rick said. He patted his jacket pocket. "My father put together a list of shipments of ours that we're trying to chase down, to see if we can figure out what the people who killed Jake's dad were after when they broke into the warehouse."

"Your father doing all right?" Adam asked.

Rick sighed. "Yes—and no. Thomas was a lifelong friend as well as a business partner. Father's taking it pretty hard. Especially since someone keeps trying to kill the rest of us, and right now, we don't know why." He stood up. "Actually, I've got to go see him next. He's moved into another house with plenty of Miska's guards until all this blows over. But I'm helping him go through business records to see if we can figure out what was so important that someone would kill Thomas over it."

Adam stood as well. "Good luck. And let me know if you need to borrow some equipment."

Rick chuckled. "That's a dangerous offer—you know I'll take you up on it."

The whirr of the elevator interrupted them. Adam glanced over his shoulder in alarm. "Damn. That's probably Thwaites. You'd better get out of here. I think it best for you to stay out of his sight."

"How?"

"This way," Adam said. He led Rick through a pair of doors at the rear of the lab, down a wide corridor and to a service elevator.

"You don't need a key to open the door upstairs from this side," Adam said. "It's the freight entrance. I'll lock up after Thwaites leaves. Just use the lever to start and stop, and try not to jam it. It gets temperamental sometimes."

"Great," Rick muttered under his breath.

"Go!" Adam said, and in the distance, Rick could hear a man calling for the inventor. Adam pushed Rick into the elevator, reached in and shoved the lever down, and got his arm back before the cage doors shut. Before Rick could say a word, Adam was sprinting back toward the lab, his white coattails flapping as he ran.

Chapter TEN

"You sure you want to go out there, bub?" The man gave Drostan Fletcher a sidelong look. "The place is full of nutters, you know."

"Going to visit an unfortunate acquaintance," Drostan lied, with a half-smile he hoped was convincing.

The wagon driver shook his head. "I'll take your coin to drive you there, but I don't want nothing to do with that place myself. Folks say it's haunted, as if it those poor, damned souls needed any more problems."

Drostan climbed up to the passenger side of the buckboard wagon, and watched the countryside go past as they headed out. He had taken the trolley line as far as it would go, then hired a wagon to take him the rest of the way. All the way out to Kilbuck County, to the Department of the Insane. Local folks called the place 'Dix Mountain', or just 'Dixmont', after the reformer, Dorothea Dix. Some just called it 'Nutter Hill'.

It took a lot for Drostan not to nod off, despite the bumpy road. His dreams had been troubled, and he was tired enough that memory and dreams tended to blur. Scotland was heavy on his mind. He'd seen butchered bodies in the alleys of Edinburgh and Glasgow from murderers who fancied themselves the next Ripper. Crimes like that could break men, and it did, sending many of Drostan's colleagues to drink or the madhouse, or early death. And unlike Drostan, they couldn't see the ghosts the slayers left behind.

The wagon driver did not try to keep up a conversation, for which Drostan was grateful, and a generous tip assured that the man would be back to return Drostan to the trolley station in two hours. But despite the pay, the driver would go no closer than the end of the gravel driveway leading to the insane asylum.

With a sigh, Drostan hefted his rucksack over one shoulder and started up the long carriageway, watching as the huge, brooding complex that was Dix Mountain came into view. Nearly two thousand poor souls were housed in the sprawling brick buildings that spread across the hillside. The main building loomed high, four stories tall with a cupola on top, with granite pillars framing the entrance and long windows, the better to take in the breezes from the valley.

"Dr. Haverton is expecting you, Mr. Fletcher," the receptionist said when Drostan gave his name at the front desk. "Just have a seat and he'll be with you shortly."

Drostan was too antsy to sit. The foyer was large and scrubbed clean, smelling of antiseptic and lemon. Uniformed orderlies and nurses in starched dresses with pristine caps bustled through doors and exited into other corridors. Most people felt uncomfortable in hospitals or asylums, and did not know why. Drostan knew, and the knowledge did not make him feel any better. *The only place with more ghosts than a hospital or an asylum is a cemetery,* Drostan thought. *And none of them rest easy.*

"Mr. Fletcher! To what do we owe your call?" Dr. Haverton was a tall, spare man in his middle years, graying at the temples, with a gold pince-nez framing intelligent gray eyes.

"Good to see you again, Doc," Drostan replied. "I stopped by to see an old friend. Eli Carmody."

Haverton gave Drostan a skeptical look. "Just happened to be in Kilbuck County and thought you'd drop in for a chat, did you?"

Drostan gave him the kind of easy smile that he used on suspects in the interrogation room. "Something like that." He grew serious. "I don't imagine Eli gets a lot of visitors way out here."

Haverton's expression made it clear that he doubted Drostan was telling the whole truth, but he relented with a sigh. "No, he doesn't. Most of our residents don't. Families are just as glad to have these folks out of their hands and beyond the gossip of the neighbors. We're the antechamber to the Great Beyond. But you knew that."

Drostan fell into step beside Haverton as they walked down the long, tiled corridor. A guard walked several steps behind them. As they walked, Drostan looked around him. Walls, windows, and floors were pristine, but in the distance, Drostan could hear the moans and chattering of men whose minds had failed them, and as they walked down the hallway, hollow-eyed ghosts watched them pass with reproach. Dix Mountain was a far cry from the cramped, squalid dungeons where madmen had been kept in years gone by, but it was still drenched in tears and tragedy, its residents written out of the world long before their deaths.

"I don't remember quite so many guards around, the last time I visited." Drostan had counted two armed men on the front steps and two more in the lobby; and in the corridor, burly orderlies or uniformed guards were stationed at regular intervals.

Haverton shrugged. "Blame it on the full moon, or the way the planets align. Our patients have been restless, and we need to keep them from hurting themselves."

Or someone else, Drostan thought, eying the muscular guards. "I see you've built some new buildings," he said.

Haverton brightened. "Ah, yes. Dr. Hutchinson, our administrator, is quite energetic. There have been improvements to the grounds, and we've added a women's wing and expanded the kitchens. It's regrettable that the area has so many who need to be confined here, but at least they're entrusting the unfortunate folk to us instead of chaining them up in the attic or letting them wander the streets."

Better than those choices, but not something any decent person would wish upon another, Drostan thought. Even after death, these souls seemed to have nowhere else to go, unwanted by Heaven or Hell.

"Here's Mr. Carmody's room," Haverton said. "He's been quiet lately, and I don't think he'll give you any trouble, but I'll post a guard at the door in case you need anything." Haverton took a key from a pocket of his vest and unlocked the door. "Please don't upset him," he said with a stern glance. "It's inconvenient for everyone when patients become unruly."

"I'll do my best not to," Drostan said with a smile he hoped looked sincere.

"We've had some success with his medication. Sometimes, he's quite lucid, though lost in the past. He believes he's still on the force, and we let him believe that, most of the time. Relate to him like that, and you might get somewhere. Try to force him into the here and now and... you'll get nowhere."

Haverton bustled back toward his office while the guard stood to one side with an expression of complete disinterest. Drostan drew a deep breath, steeled himself, and knocked on the door.

"Eli? It's Drostan."

He heard shuffling on the other side of the door, and then the doorknob turned. The guard looked as if he were on alert should the patient make a break for the hallway, but when the door swung open, it revealed a frail old man in a dressing gown and worn, threadbare slippers.

"Drostan?" Eli Carmody croaked. "You can't be Drostan Fletcher. He's younger than you are."

Drostan chuckled. "Time passes for all of us, Eli. I'm not as young as I used to be."

Carmody scowled. "Well come in, why don't you? I don't have all day. No one told me you were coming. Damn that secretary of mine." He gestured for Drostan to enter, and then shut the door with a bang.

Carmody's narrow room had a cot, a window, and a small writing desk with a chair. Papers were strewn about, and it looked as if someone had given Carmody a worn-out satchel, because it sat on one side of his desk stuffed with more papers. Carmody sat down, moved the papers from one side of the desk to the other, and glowered at Drostan.

"Aren't you supposed to be on your beat?" he growled.

It was so like the Eli Carmody of old that Drostan's heart lurched. Captain Eli Carmody, New Pittsburgh Police, had been a force to reckon with in his prime. Drostan had been proud to serve under him, grateful as a new immigrant for the opportunity Carmody gave him despite Drostan's dismissal from the Scottish police. The mannerisms were pure Carmody, but a look in his eyes told Drostan that his old commander was not completely himself.

"Came in to make a report, sir," Drostan replied, falling into the old routine, hoping that wherever Carmody's mind strayed, he might tap into the memories he needed to learn more about the riverside killer, and maybe, about who killed Thomas Desmet.

"Well, get to it," Carmody snapped. "I've got things to do."

Drostan stood at parade rest in front of Carmody's desk, and tried not to see the withered old man in the hospital gown. "Got a bad one, sir," Drostan said, framing his words carefully. "Over in Allegheny."

"Allegheny? That's not your beat."

"No, sir. Got called in because they needed all hands. Another knife murder. Real nasty piece of work. The boys and I were wondering—do you think it could be like before?"

Carmody's eyes flashed. "You mean Tumblety? Good lord, I hope not." Francis Tumblety, snake-oil salesman, self-proclaimed physician, and suspect in the Ripper killings, had come through New Pittsburgh on Carmody's watch. There'd been a string of unexplained murders. Carmody had never been able to convict Tumblety, but he had never forgotten, or forgiven.

"You remember that case much better than I do, sir," Drostan said, hoping to spark Carmody's memories. "I was hoping you could help me put the pieces together."

For just a moment, Drostan saw the keen intellect in Carmody's eyes that had made him the most successful detective on the New Pittsburgh squad. "Lay it out for me, Fletcher, and let's see where the pieces fall."

Carmody listened intently as Drostan recounted the details of the killing on the river bank, omitting only the fact that the eyewitness testimony came from ghosts. "Doesn't sound like the Ripper," he said when Drostan had finished. "Sounds to me like what the new men are saying. About the shadow-killers."

"What new men?"

Carmody's eyes had lost the flinty look of a few moments ago. "Miners," he said. "Miners Forty-Niners. Got a whole batch of them, Poles and Slavs and Hungarians, locked up like loons—the ones who didn't die." He started to hum 'My Darling Clementine'.

"What about the shadow-killers?" Drostan asked.

"*In a cavern, in a coal mine, digging Vesta Number Nine, died the miners, ninety-niners when the shadows took their minds.*"

"Eli, help me," Drostan begged, but he could see his old friend struggling against the madness that gripped him.

"*They were bleeding, they were dying, down in Vesta Number Nine, when the* gessyan *killed the witches and the shadows took their minds.*"

"Eli, what are *gessyan*? I don't understand."

Reason had faded from Carmody's eyes, and his voice was a raspy sing-song. "*Dug to Hades, found the demons down in Vesta Number Nine, now they're hungry, red and bloody and the shadows took their minds.*"

For a few seconds, something close to sanity came back to Carmody's eyes. "Run," he said. "Before the *gessyan* get you."

Madness closed in again. "What the hell are you doing here!" Carmody raged, standing up so suddenly he overturned the table, sending papers flying. "Get back on your beat! Get back to the street and do your job! People are dying! You've got to stop the *gessyan*. They've gotten loose and you've got to stop them, stop them, stop them..."

He launched himself at Drostan, fists flying. Drostan held up both arms in front of his face to defend himself, knowing that he outweighed Carmody and was decades younger. Madness animated Carmody's frail body far past its normal strength, raining down blow after blow until the guard opened the door and two orderlies hustled in, wrestling Carmody off of Drostan and hauling him back, toward the bed.

"There'll be blood! Mark my words, there'll be blood, rivers of blood!" Carmody shouted, as Drostan got to his feet. And yet, despite the rage that had his old captain red in the face, spittle flecking his lips, there was a disturbing flicker of sanity in Carmody's eyes that made Drostan shiver with a cold that went to his bones.

He knows something, and he's trying to tell me, trying to get past the madness. But what's sane in what he's saying, and what's not?

The guard hustled Drostan out of the room as the orderlies restrained Carmody. "They'll make sure he's taken care of well, won't they?" Drostan asked as the guard closed the door behind him.

"He was doing much better before you got him stirred up," the guard said, hustling Drostan down the corridor.

"I'd heard a rumor that you've had several coal miners come in lately," Drostan said as they strode back toward the foyer.

The guard eyed him. "You want to get them all worked up, too?"

Drostan reached into a pocket and pulled out a twenty-dollar bill. Information was more valuable than the groceries he was going to buy, and he figured his friends would not let him starve. He passed the twenty to the guard. "Miners. New patients. What have you heard?"

The guard slowed his pace, and looked around to make sure no one was nearby. Drostan did the same, seeing no one but the ghosts that lined the hallway. "Got in ten guys from the Vesta mine, bunch of Polacks and Hunkies, you know?" the guard said. "Forgot most of the English they knew, if they ever knew it, raving in whatever-the-hell they speak over there, but one of the nurses caught a few words here and there. Goin' on about shadows and demons and monsters. Nonsense."

"How is it they all came in at once?"

The guard looked at him as if he had grown two heads. "What, you don't read the newspaper? Buncha miners died down in the deep shafts, musta been the blackdamp that took them." He shrugged. "It happens." Then the guard paused, frowning. "Only—"

"What?"

Again, the guard looked from side to side, and his voice fell to a whisper. "Usually, when they open up a shaft after there's blackdamp—bad air—they find the bodies. This time I hear they only found *pieces*, and not enough pieces at that."

They reached the foyer, and the guard opened the door. His expression hardened as the secretary looked up. "Probably good if you don't come back for a while," he said loudly for her benefit. "Let the old guy cool off."

Drostan nodded his goodbye to the receptionist and hurried down the steps, deep in thought as he headed for the end of the carriageway. He hoped the wagon driver would show up to take him back to the trolley.

"Have you talked to the witch?"

The voice made Drostan stop dead in his tracks. He looked around, but he saw no one nearby. Then the air shimmered, and he could make out the gray form of a stooped old lady, clad in a hospital gown with a scarf tied over her head like a babushka. "What did you say?" Drostan whispered, afraid someone might overhear.

Have you talked to the witch? This time, he heard the voice only in his mind.

Witch?

The old woman cursed in Polish. He caught only a few words of it, enough to know she had insulted both his hearing and his intelligence. *You want to know what killed those men? Ask the witch.*

I don't know any witches.

More cursing. *The witch of Pulawski Way. Tell him Irena Sokolowski sent you to him.*

What's his name? Who is he?

She looked at him as if he were stupid. *They call him the* czarodziej. *Ask. You'll find him.*

And with that, the old woman's ghost faded from his sight.

"Hey bub! You want a ride or not?" The wagon driver looked at him impatiently, and Drostan hurried toward the end of the driveway.

"You always stare into space like that?" the driver asked as Drostan climbed into the wagon. He shook his head. "Do that too much in a place like this, they don't let you leave."

"I'll keep that in mind," Drostan replied distractedly. He glanced at the driver. "Did you hear anything about problems at the Vesta mine?"

The driver gave a harsh laugh. "Which one? There're nine of them."

"Vesta Nine."

He shrugged. "Always problems with mines. That's why I won't have nothin' to do with them. My granddaddy and my daddy were miners, but I ran off when I was old enough and started working on the docks. Done all right for myself." He eyed Drostan. "Why?"

Drostan looked away. "Heard some men died. Wondered what happened."

"Men die in mines. If the blackdamp don't get you, the firedamp will, either suffocate you or blow you to bits," he said. "And that's if you don't get crushed or trampled or skin yourself up and get blood poison." He shook his head. "Bad places. Worse lately."

"Oh?"

Another shrug. "The *babas* say it's because the mines go too deep. Vesta Nine is the deepest of all their mines. The *babas* say the miners are disturbing things that shouldn't be woken." He gave a laugh that didn't reach his eyes. "Women. You know how they talk nonsense."

"Yeah," Drostan said. "Nonsense." He was quiet for a moment. "You ever hear the word *gessyan*?"

The wagon driver's face shut down. "I ain't got no more to say," he snapped. "And if you come back this way, I'm not your man. Keep your nose outta things ain't your concern."

Spooked him good, Drostan thought. *That's all right. He might not want to tell me, but I think I know someone who will.*

THE WAGON MASTER said nothing more the rest of the way to the station. Drostan rode the trolley back to New Pittsburgh deep in thought. The platform was nearly empty when he arrived, and he walked another two blocks to the dispatcher's station, stopping to pick up a bucket of beer on the way.

"You're out late, Drostan," the telegraph operator at the trolley dispatch office said as Drostan walked in.

"Business. You know how it is, Sam," Drostan replied. He hefted the bucket of beer. "Brought you something for after work."

Sam grinned. "Now that's something to look forward to." He leveled a glance at Drostan. "Guess this means you want me to send another telegraph for you?"

Drostan put the beer down in a safe, out of the way spot and nodded. "I'd be much obliged."

"You know the post offices are all closed. Whoever you're sending it to won't get it before tomorrow morning, probably later."

"Send it just like this—with this code at the beginning. It's a private receiver." Drostan said, writing out his note. Just a few words, '*gessyan* in deep mines.' Nothing that would make sense to anyone else. Drostan wasn't sure it made sense to him, either. But it was the most likely clue the night's work had turned up, and Jake Desmet had said he wanted to hear about anything and everything Drostan turned up.

Sam read it over and looked up. "Got a new case?"

"Keeping body and soul together."

"If you say so." The brass key flashed and blurred as Sam sent the telegraph.

"Thanks," Drostan said, taking the note back and holding it over the lamp flame, watching the paper burn to ashes.

"That's it? You're not going to wait around for a reply?"

Drostan shook his head. "None needed. Just checking in. Thanks, Sam. Enjoy the beer."

With that, he sauntered off, heading for Ohio Street and the room he rented at the boarding house. The ride back from the asylum had been a long one, and it was late. Mrs. Mueller would have left him a sandwich in the ice box, and if he was lucky, some ale to go with it. Even so, the smell of beer and bratwurst wafting from the taverns he passed made his stomach rumble.

The rush of workers heading home after a long day in the factories was over. Here and there, Drostan saw the glow of cigarettes where men sat on front stoops or leaned against walls, enjoying a smoke and watching the world go by.

Up ahead, a drunk lolled near the gutter, stinking of stale beer and old urine. Drostan gave him space, having no desire to show up at the boarding house with vomit on his shoes. He had just passed the drunk when the man spun suddenly, scissoring his legs, catching Drostan behind the knees and sending him to the pavement. A second blow caught Drostan in the jaw, making him see stars.

Moving far too quickly for a drunkard, the man sucker-punched Drostan in the side and got to his feet.

"Take my wallet!" Drostan gasped, but his right hand was already going for his shoulder holster.

"Don't want your money," a voice rasped as the vagrant pulled back hard on Drostan's collar. "Quit sticking your nose where it don't belong. Forget what you heard at the nut house. You might live longer."

Drostan kicked up sharply with his left foot, catching the vagrant in the shin. He rolled, and came up with his gun trained on the drunk's forehead. "And you might not live long at all unless you tell me who sent you."

Drostan saw the tip of a sawed-off shotgun start to rise from beneath the vagrant's tattered duster. He threw himself to one side as the blast kicked up concrete and filled the air with smoke. Buckshot peppered his shoulder, but he squeezed off a shot at the fleeing assailant, scrambling to his feet as the man turned around a corner and disappeared into an alley. Drostan had no desire to be around when—*if*—the police investigated. He ran into the alley, but the vagrant had disappeared.

Wary, gun still drawn, Drostan made his way down the alley to the next street and walked a couple of blocks out of his way before returning to Ohio Street. His jaw ached, his shoulder was bleeding, and he had a stitch in his side from where he had been punched. Drostan kept his gun in hand, hidden beneath his coat, but to his relief, no one approached him and the way to the boarding house was clear.

Mrs. Mueller had already gone to bed; the kitchen was dark when he let himself in. Drostan grabbed the sandwich out of the ice box and made his way upstairs, gun still in his hand, just in case.

The door to his room was ajar.

Drostan kicked the door fully open and dropped to a crouch, gun ready. Two figures waited for him, one in a chair in the center of the room, the other by the window.

"Put that down. It's not nice to shoot us."

Drostan recognized the voice. He swore and lowered the gun, pushing the door shut behind him and turning on the gas light. "What are you two doing here?"

Mitch Storm grinned. "We're the Department. We can do anything." A former Army sharpshooter, Mitch was a decade younger than Drostan, with short dark hair, an athlete's build and a permanent five o'clock shadow. He was every penny dreadful writer's cliché of a government agent.

The second man gave a loud harrumph. "He means we heard some chatter and happened to be in the neighborhood, so we caught a streetcar over," Jacob Drangosavich added. He was a big man with dark blond hair, a thin face and pale blue eyes, and he looked like he could fit right in with the Eastern European men who filed down to the mills and mines, day-in and day-out.

Drostan had crossed paths with Storm and Drangosavich more times than he wanted to remember. Sometimes, they were racing for the same prize. More often, they were at cross-purposes. And while Drostan grudgingly admitted that the two men were mostly trustworthy, his dislike of shadowy government organizations made him wary of them and of their employer.

Drostan put his sandwich down on the desk, holstered his gun, and gingerly shrugged off his ruined coat, then lit the other gas light. "No point sitting in the dark," he said.

"Who shot you?" Mitch asked, rising from the room's only chair as Drostan poured water from the pitcher into the wash basin and gingerly daubed the wound, grimacing at the red stain that quickly tinged the water.

"That's the question now, isn't it?" Drostan replied. "But since whoever-it-was warned me away from sticking my nose in places it doesn't belong, I've got to figure getting jumped had something to do with the case I'm working on." He glared at the two men. "Which has nothing to do with you, so you can go right back to where you came from."

"Sit down," Jacob said, pulling out a pocket knife and opening it to a slender blade, which he ran back and forth through the lamp's flame to sterilize it. "I've dug these out of Mitch's hide enough times, I should just pack it all in and become a sawbones."

Drostan glared at him, and Jacob sighed. "You want to explain a gunshot to the doctor at the hospital?" After a moment's resistance, Drostan nodded, although he didn't look happy about it.

Mitch slid the chair over, and Drostan sat down, pointedly looking away as Jacob began poking at his injured shoulder. He gritted his teeth, and a moment later a piece of lead shot hit the floor.

"What do you know about Vesta Nine?" Drostan said, trying to keep his mind off what Jacob was doing.

"Not much. Just that it's one of the biggest mines in the world and it's owned by Richard Thwaites and Drogo Veles," Mitch replied. "Between them, they're major investors in Carnegie Steel, Jones and Laughlin, H. C. Frick and Company—I could go on, but you get the gist." There was an edge to the agent's voice.

"So definite Oligarchy ties, at least for Thwaites," Drostan replied, trying to hide the strain in his voice as Jacob pried another couple of pieces of buckshot loose.

Mitch let out a harsh laugh. "Oligarchy ties? Thwaites's father formed the Oligarchy."

"I talked to Eli Carmody. Thought he'd remember bits of the old Tumblety case, see if that's who's behind the Ripper-style killings along the rivers," Drostan replied. "He didn't say much about Tumblety, but he got strange at the end, warned me about something he called *gessyan*, and told me to look for a witch." He had no intention of reporting his conversation with the ghost. Brand and Desmet knew about his abilities, and paid him a premium for his services because of it. Drostan suspected that the two Department agents knew that part of his record as well, but he had no intention of attracting government scrutiny by confirming rumors.

Mitch and Jacob exchanged a glance. "He said '*gessyan*'?" Mitch repeated.

Drostan nodded, then swore under his breath as Jacob dug the last of the shot out of his shoulder. "Aye. And when I mentioned the word to my wagon driver, he shut up tighter than a nun's knees."

"Carmody say anything else?" Mitch asked. "In his day, he was a good detective."

"He was the best, before something sent him round the bend," Drostan countered testily.

"Where do you keep your liquor?" Jacob asked.

"In the trunk at the foot of the bed," Drostan replied.

Jacob fetched the bottle of whiskey and a rag. "This is going to sting," he said bluntly, and proceeded to splash some of the dark liquid onto the rag and press it to Drostan's wounded arm.

"Son of a bitch!" Drostan yelped.

"Better than having it go sour," Mitch said as Jacob ignored Drostan's outburst and began to bind up his arm with strips of cloth from Drostan's ruined shirt.

"*Gessyan*," Drostan grated, his temper growing shorter as pain, hunger and tiredness took their toll. "What do you know?"

"Not as much as we'd like to," Mitch admitted, standing to pace the small room. "*Gessyan* are supernatural, live in deep dark places, and they're nasty predators. It's a blanket term for a bunch of spooky stuff—hell hounds, malicious ghosts, wraiths, and other things that prowl the shadows." He met Drostan's gaze. "Things like your Night Hag. Legends say the *gessyan* were all bound a long time ago so they couldn't come out to play."

"Bound how?" Drostan asked.

"Magic, if you believe in that sort of thing," Mitch replied offhandedly.

Drostan knew damn well that both Storm and Drangosavich—'Sturm und Drang' as they were known in the field—believed in the unbelievable. That was the whole point behind the Department, a secret organization that existed to find things that went bump in the night and make them disappear.

"Witches?"

Mitch shrugged. "Maybe. There are more witches than you can shake a stick at in New Pittsburgh—every *baba* and *nona* thinks she's got the Power. You'll have to be more specific."

"The Witch of Pulawski Way," Drostan snapped. He was growing tired of playing games, and his shoulder ached. He reached over and grabbed his sandwich, then poured a couple of fingers of whiskey into a glass before downing it in a gulp.

Again Mitch and Jacob exchanged a glance, and by now, Drostan had enough. "Say something useful or get the hell out," he muttered. "I gave you some information. Now it's your turn—and you haven't told me yet why you're here."

Mitch met his gaze. "We know who the Witch of Pulawski Way is. Guy name of Karl Jasinski. A Polish witch."

"*Czarodziej*," Drostan muttered.

Jacob winced. "Please," he said with a grimace, before correcting Drostan's pronunciation.

"What's so special about Jasinski?" Drostan asked. "And what does he have to do with coal mines and monsters in the dark?"

Mitch shrugged. "We don't know. That's the hell of it. But what we do know is that Jasinski seems to be nervous about something, and has gotten interested in those same killings you're investigating."

"Did he find anything?" Drostan pressed.

"Don't know," Jacob replied. "We haven't been able to contact him."

Drostan glared at the two men. "All right," he said, then gritted his teeth against the pain as he moved. "Now why are you here?"

Mitch clucked his tongue. "Really, Drostan. You sound bitter. We heard you were sniffing around, asking questions, and we thought we should drop in before you get yourself hurt."

"You're a little late for that."

"We also heard you were working for Brand and Desmet, and showing up in all the wrong places when it comes to inconvenient dead bodies by the river," Jacob added. "We wanted to have a chat before you become one of those bodies yourself."

"Is that a threat?" Drostan asked levelly.

Mitch shrugged and lit a cigarette. "Not from us. But the Department's interested in what's going on at the Vesta Nine for a lot of other reasons, and you're the mouse running through the elephant stampede. You could get squashed without anyone even noticing."

"Someone murdered Thomas Desmet using magic," Drostan replied. "I aim to find out who it was and why they did it."

Mitch and Jacob exchanged a glance. "Mitch and I are here looking into the river murders," Jacob said. "We also think Francis Tumblety might be involved—maybe Adolph Brunrichter too. Like a bad penny, those two just keep showing up."

Drostan remembered the names. He had helped Mitch and Jacob bust a bodysnatching and vivisection racket run by the two charlatan doctors, who'd escaped in the disastrous fire that destroyed their lab. Having them back in town made bad business worse. "Who are they working for?" Drostan asked.

Mitch shrugged. "We're not sure." He leaned forward. "But if it turns out that Carmody is right and there's some connection between the river murders and Vesta Nine, then my advice is for you to stay out of this. It's bigger than you realize."

"You know I can't do that," Drostan replied, meeting Mitch's gaze.

"Veles and Thwaites have something big and illegal going on over at the mine, and they will get rid of anyone—*anyone*—who gets in their way. You're outgunned."

"Wouldn't be the first time," Drostan replied with a shrug. "Do you know what the prize is?"

"We suspect," Jacob said. "Remember, Mitch and I aren't working on the Vesta Nine case. We just hear things. Something else to chew on: shipments from Tesla-Westinghouse have gone missing—shipments that were supposed to go to the Department. Find those shipments, and you might find the key to this whole mess."

"And if you find those shipments, call us," Mitch said. "Because you're going to need the back-up."

Drostan snorted. "Yeah. You backing me up. That's sweet. You mean, you want me to lead you to it, and then the Department swoops in and takes the spoils."

Another glance passed between Mitch and Jacob. For once, Mitch looked uncomfortable. "Jacob and I are not supposed to be anywhere near the Vesta Nine case," Mitch said finally.

"At the moment, we're sort of on probation and being considered for disciplinary review—again," Jacob said bluntly. "They think all the things that blow up and burn down when we're on a case attract too much attention and make the Department look bad."

"We got a tip that Tumblety and Brunrichter surfaced, and... let's just say that we've got a score to settle with them," Mitch said, and for once his usual cockiness was muted. "We're rogue on this. So we're not going to be reporting in and putting the Department wise to you, and frankly, it wouldn't do us any good if they knew we were sniffing around here."

"All your warnings—you were just blowing smoke to scare me off?" Drostan said indignantly.

Jacob shook his head. "Based on what we heard before we were put on probation and taken out of the loop, something big is going on with Vesta Nine. Big enough for the honchos at HQ to want to keep the whole thing under wraps, especially when rich, powerful men like Veles and Thwaites might be involved. So the warning was real." He sighed. "But right now, we're not *officially* included."

"And we'd appreciate your help," Mitch added. "Because while we were poking our noses into what the resurrectionists were doing, we stumbled into the same kind of connections you're finding—that lead right back to Vesta Nine. And that puts us in a bind. Catching Tumblety and Brunrichter could get us back in the boss's good graces if it's tied to the river murders. Mucking up the Vesta Nine investigation might get us Leavenworth."

"And if Thwaites is involved, you're not going to get much help from the New Pittsburgh police, because most of them are on the Oligarchy's take," Drostan said.

Jacob nodded. "Exactly. Odds are, it's all related."

"And the *gessyan*?" Drostan asked. "Are they under Veles's control?"

Jacob cursed in Croatian. "Pray God that they're not, or we've got even bigger problems."

Chapter ELEVEN

"WHERE DID YOU find the spy?" Veles asked sharply.

"Poking around the records," Thwaites replied. He had asked for a meeting with Veles in one of the private rooms at the Duquesne Club. Veles refused, wanting somewhere more discreet, and since Veles had no intention of having Thwaites intrude on his own home, he was obliged to come to Thwaites's brownstone again. Tonight, Thwaites looked scared.

"What did you learn?" Veles prodded. He leaned against the wall next to the parlor's massive fireplace.

"Not much." Thwaites said, wringing his hands. He began to pace, a fine sheen of sweat beading on his forehead. "He knew our men were going to kill him. There was no advantage to giving up information. They said it was clear he was a professional."

"Any identification?"

Thwaites shook his head. "Not on him—at least, nothing real. A phony union card, a few dollars. When we checked him out, the address he gave was a boarded-up store. My men asked around. Everyone said the guy was pretty new, but he asked a lot of questions."

"Anything else?" Veles asked, reining in his impatience. Thwaites was nervous, and slightly drunk on top of that.

"He's not local," Thwaites replied. "My men were sure of that. But we did find this." He held out his hand. In it was a small disk as large as a silver dollar and three times as thick. "They took it apart, and they think it's a listening device. Found two or three others just like it, hidden throughout the office. There's only one group likely to have something like this."

"The Department of Supernatural Investigations," Veles replied, his tone thick with contempt. "They're a constant thorn in my side."

"They can't be bought—at least, not the ones we've tried to bribe," Thwaites said. "Next thing you know, Storm and Drangosavich will be back in town." He looked up earnestly. "I swore to Tumblety and Brunrichter that we could keep those two well away from them this time. Tumblety has only barely grown back his hair after the fire, and Brunrichter has a nasty scar."

"What did you do with the body?" Veles asked.

"Gave it to Tumblety for his experiments," Thwaites said with a smirk, regaining some of his bravado. "The guy wanted answers. He'll get them now, all right. Too bad he won't be able to file a report."

Thwaites's casual cruelty and vindictiveness annoyed Veles. *He's made this personal,* Veles thought. *That leads to mistakes.* "Make sure if you turn him into one of their clockwork corpses that he's working deep enough no one ever sees him again. I don't want more questions," Veles snapped.

"What if he's already filed a report?" Thwaites replied, and though his voice never lost its bluster, it was clear the idea had him spooked. "What if they know?"

"If DSI knows anything, they'll need proof," Veles replied. "They'll poke around some more, send more people, tip their hand. We've got a little time—especially if your people in the city government can take their time with any official inquiries that come their way."

"That's a given," Thwaites replied.

"And the shipment—it went out on time?" Veles probed.

"There were... complications," Thwaites said. "We had to deal with the spy. Something got loose from your warding, and attacked my new overseer. Didn't leave much of him to identify. Not a lot of competition for that job. The men talk. They're restless."

"And what has that got to do with our shipment?" Veles's voice was low and dangerously quiet.

"You have no idea what kind of pressure I'm under!" Thwaites shot back.

Veles gestured sharply with his right hand and Thwaites was flung across the room, pinned a foot off the ground against the far wall. He wriggled in vain as Veles stalked across the parlor, taking his time to let the magnitude of his annoyance sink in. "If our buyers are disappointed, you will truly understand the meaning of the word *pressure*!"

"It's not my fault!"

Veles tightened his grip without touching Thwaites, and the pinned man gasped. "I have no patience for incompetence. And even less for outsiders meddling in our affairs. You are in this now up to your neck. Fix it!"

He gestured again and Thwaites fell to his knees. Veles ignored the glare of pure hatred Thwaites sent in his direction, purposefully turning his back as if to invite an attack—and another chance to put Thwaites firmly in his place. *Americans like to think they're all equal. Some of us are clearly superior. It's time he knows which of us is which.*

"I'll send word to have my men pick up the box tonight and bring it to the drop point," Thwaites said, getting to his feet and dusting off his pants. He adjusted his waistcoat and tie, then ran a hand over his hair to smooth it back into place. "You can let the buyer know the transaction will go as planned."

"It better," Veles replied. "Pietro Iannucco is not a patient man. His associates enjoy shooting at kneecaps, and the bosses in New York are even less patient. Magic, even powerful magic, only counts for so much against the 'family'. Disappoint him, and *malocchio* will be the least of your worries."

"We're keeping an eye on Desmet," Thwaites replied defiantly.

"And shooting up the mausoleums of dead millionaires too, from what I've heard," Veles said. "Do I need to define the term 'discreet' to you?"

"My men were plenty discreet tailing Desmet's cousin," Thwaites argued.

Veles sniffed. "My messenger spotted your carriage a block away, when he went to carry my warning to Renate Thalberg. Honestly, Richard, must you use carriages that advertise your presence? Do you even own a plain black carriage?"

"First the French girl goes to see Thalberg, then over to the women's college. What's her game?"

"I'm afraid I couldn't begin to guess her 'game'," Veles replied aloofly. "That is why we employ people to discover these things."

Thwaites gave him a petulant look. "Yeah, well we're not the only ones with 'people'. That Scottish investigator keeps showing up where he's got no business. Poking around the riverside where the Night Hag's been, and my sources say he's working for George Brand, investigating Thomas Desmet's murder. I don't like it."

Veles shrugged. "Drostan Fletcher? Surely your people know how to dig up dirt on that man. It's no secret he left Scotland under a cloud, an investigator who became a murder suspect. All kinds of aspersions to be cast there—wouldn't be hard to destroy his credibility." He sniffed. "Isn't that the kind of thing they taught you at boarding school?"

"I studied political science," Thwaites said huffily. "Maybe I'll run for Senate."

"You'll be running for your life if the Vesta Nine venture goes sour," Veles said. "What of the mad doctors? What do they report? Have they finished the new clockwork corpses?"

Thwaites muttered something obscene under his breath and turned away, then took his time pouring himself a whiskey—pointedly not offering one to Veles—before he answered. "They are making progress," he said. "I'm told these things are complicated. Delicate. They've finished several more and gotten them fully functional. Completed another *werkman*, too. They're making real progress."

He glared at Veles as if he expected him to quibble. "The last several clockwork corpses lasted much better, and could do more work. It's coming along."

"It would 'come along' much more quickly if you just snatched Adam Farber and put him to work for you," Veles observed. "Since you seem to love grand, dramatic gestures, why not just sweep him up in a speeding carriage one night and be done with it?"

"Because he hardly ever leaves his labs," Thwaites complained. "The man has no life aside from his tinkering. If he does step out, it's with Desmet and he's surrounded by bodyguards." He glared at Veles. "I have him under observation. In the meantime, his supervisor is fawning all over me for more research money. And I've gotten one of my men hired on as Farber's assistant. Once we know what projects the boy genius is working on, we'll have an even better idea of his worth to us."

"Just make sure you keep your priorities straight," Veles grated. "Mining the tourmaquartz is essential. Our clients do not take disappointment well."

DROGO VELES COULD be almost invisible, when it suited his purpose. He kept his head down, blending in with the late night trolley passengers. He had chosen to wear plain clothes that evening. Anyone who did give him a second look felt a gentle, subconscious pressure to glance away and remember nothing.

Men like Thwaites want to rule the world without having the slightest idea of how it works, he thought. Veles had seen plenty of Thwaites's kind back on the Continent: dilettante playboys with a keenly honed vindictiveness in place of ambition and the knowledge that their money and connections could rescue them from any misstep. He himself had never had the luxury of such foolishness.

His Romanian accent was authentic. The name to which he answered was a practice name, part of a witch's safety precautions. As for the title, it had become his long enough ago that anyone who might have challenged his legitimacy had long since passed. No one left to remember the unfortunate fire at a noble's manor and a switch of identities with the son of a lord to whom he bore more than a passing resemblance, since he was the boy's bastard brother. Even then, he was adept enough at magic to blur the memories of those around him, including the father who had wanted nothing to do with his illegitimate offspring.

Magic had extended his lifetime, and longevity was a good way to amass wealth. Now, firmly ensconced with his title, manor, power, and wealth, he moved easily among the upper levels of

European society. Those who opposed him found themselves deeply inconvenienced. He had deliberately cultivated a fearsome reputation and a sophisticated manner. Those of like mind, and there were many, took him on his own terms. He had no time or interest in those who did not, so long as they stayed out of his way.

He swung down from the trolley in an area of New Pittsburgh the locals called Polish Hill. Over the years, he had become fluent in many languages. Drogo listened to the conversations on the streets around him, which even at this late hour were busy with men coming home from the mills, or filling any of the numerous bars that lined the street.

He caught the word '*czarodziej*' more than once. 'Warlock'. It was said in a whisper, with a glance over the shoulder and a hand moving unconsciously to stroke a saint's medal The tone was worried, frightened. And in the block where Karl Jasinski—the missing Witch of Pulawski Way—had his shop, the pedestrians crossed the street and themselves.

For nearly an hour, Veles hung back in the shadows and watched the building. He did not expect to find Jasinski. The Polish witch knew that they were after him. He was in hiding, but Veles doubted very much that Jasinski had left New Pittsburgh. Jasinski had a mission to accomplish, one that had gotten Thomas Desmet killed and was likely to result in more deaths before things were settled.

Veles had been a few steps behind Jasinski for months, closing in only after the crafty witch had slipped the noose. Jasinski had sought counsel from other witches in Europe. Nowak, Dabrowski, Jasinski, Kozlowski, Bajek, Chomicki, Kubiak, Radwanski... the names replayed like a chant in Veles's mind. Some of the witches Jasinski had consulted had gone into hiding themselves, and the ones who had not, Veles had killed, but only after they had revealed what they told the Witch of Pulawski Way.

Now, Veles had more pieces of the puzzle he needed in order to force the *gessyan* to do his bidding. For now, he wished to force them back into the depths until the tourmaquartz had been mined. Afterwards, he could use his control over them to wield them as a weapon—but not until Veles found the artifacts Jasinski had gotten Brand and Desmet to acquire.

When the streets were quiet, Veles made his move. Jasinski had a shop on the first floor of the old rooming house where he told fortunes and set or removed curses. Above that was his apartment, and in the back of the building was an apartment that belonged to the landlady. At this hour, no lights glimmered in the back windows.

It should have been an easy thing to break in, ransack the place, and remove whatever notes or artifacts Jasinski had acquired. Except that it wasn't. Not with the wardings the witch had set. Thwaites had tried sending his men, but they had been unable to enter. Veles's prior attempt had gotten him nowhere, and he had been wary of attracting attention. He doubted that the landlady would have any special ability to get past Jasinski's wards, even if his men strongarmed her. That meant it was up to him to make another attempt.

The last time, he had tripped a magical alarm that set up a huge racket and caused brilliant white lights to go off all around the building. Simple, but effective—and it took skill to make such a warding undetectable. Veles had not stuck around to see what happened next, and had grudgingly upgraded his estimation of Jasinski's abilities.

Now, Veles walked in a slow circle around the building, a small dagger hidden in the palm of his left hand as his *athame*. Even at a distance, he could feel Jasinski's wards like a tension pushing outward from the building. Veles was sure he could get up to the rooming house, maybe even enter the landlady's apartment. But so far, the wards had repulsed any attempts to enter Jasinski's shop or apartment.

Veles stepped over the warded circle. A distinct uneasiness washed over him, the sense that he was not welcome and should leave. That alone would have been enough to send most regular people away. Taking advantage of the temporarily quiet street, Veles moved closer, fighting a growing sense of discomfort that escalated with every step.

By the time he reached the front door of the shop, his palms were sweating and his heart was racing. Yet while he was uncomfortable, nothing had physically prevented him from advancing. He had gotten this far before, only to fail when he had reached for the doorknob and been driven back by a burst of most unpleasant power.

This time he was better prepared. From a pocket, he withdrew a withered, blackened hand. From another, he took a candle, made according to strict specifications that would enable its light to be seen only by him. The hand itself had been difficult to acquire, even more difficult to imbue with the magic that would turn it from the severed hand of a hanged man into a true Hand of Glory, capable of opening any lock.

As he reached toward the knob with the Hand of Glory, he chanted under his breath in Romanian, gathering power from the rivers and coal seams, the valleys and cliffs. He sent the magic into the withered hand, felt the power swell, and reached for the door.

An invisible force crashed down on him, like being crushed beneath an ocean wave and swept out to sea. He found himself several feet away from the house, at the inside limit of the warding circle he had drawn, feeling as if he were being pressed by a heavy weight.

Veles sent a blast of his own power to counter the attack. His effort only made the force more difficult to resist, making it hard to breathe, almost impossible to move. He was pinned on his back in a public place. Jasinski's intent—to both repel and humiliate—was abundantly clear.

Veles lashed back with his own magic, shredding the force that attacked him. He stood up, brushing the dust from his clothing, and looked around. No one was in sight, but that did not preclude the neighbors from having seen him from their windows. Gritting his teeth in frustration, he hurled a bolt of power at the building, strong enough to blow the clapboard house apart. The energy hit Jasinski's warding and dissipated in a brief, golden glow, succeeding only in bowling over a couple of nearby garbage cans.

The defensive magic had the distinct 'aftertaste' he had come to associate with Jasinski's power. But this time, Veles sensed something else besides the magical signature of the Polish witch. Although he could not exactly say why, he felt certain Jasinski had warded the house specifically against him. That meant that any power Veles sent against the protections would generate increasingly dangerous repercussions.

Damn him, Veles thought, berating himself for losing control and using his magic in a loud and useless attack. *He knew it would be difficult for me to find another witch powerful enough to try to break his wardings. Andreas and Renate Thalberg are the only witches of sufficient skill, and they're on his side.*

Swearing under his breath, Veles strode off, sure that if the clatter of the metal cans hadn't drawn the attention of the neighborhood, his sorcery had. He had judged Jasinski's abilities as a witch to be powerful, but lesser than his own. *That might be, yet he's used his power cleverly. He's more of a problem than I expected.*

Returning would do no good. Another witch might be able to slip past the wardings, but only a massive strike from Veles might do the trick—one that would be sure to destroy the building and bring the attention of authorities. And while Veles was sure that the Alekanovo stones themselves were not in the house, he was equally certain whatever papers or journals Jasinski might have kept, that he was so desperate to guard, would be of use.

I don't have time to play games, he thought darkly as he strode away, eager to be gone before anyone investigated the noise he had caused.

He had not gone far when he felt the chill of old, fell power. The street around him had fallen unnaturally silent. A warning prickled at the back of his neck, and he called up his magic, ready for an attack.

The wraith sprang from the shadows of an alleyway. It swept toward Veles in a billowing wave, growing larger as it neared so that Veles could see nothing of the street behind it. The wraith's magic stank of decay as its shadows formed themselves into long, grasping fingers and bony, grabbing hands.

Veles stood his ground. "Go no farther!" he commanded, repeating the instruction in Romanian. He raised his right hand and held it palm out, summoning his power and sending a strong blast of wind toward the roiling darkness.

The creature fell back a pace, before regaining its momentum. Veles brought both his hands together in a loud clap, and a streak of lightning sizzled from his fingers, passing right through the wraith without slowing it whatsoever.

Veles reached beneath his shirt and drew out a silver medallion on a black silken cord. It was an old medal, imprinted with the scaled shape of a balaur, and like the legendary dragon, the medal was a powerful conduit of magic. A burst of midnight blue energy streamed from the medal, growing brighter and more powerful with Veles's chants. The wraith twisted and thrashed, and an unholy screech echoed in the night air.

The creature gave a desperate lunge, and its darkness tore at Veles's sleeves, ripping his coat and raising bloody scratches on his arms. He chanted even louder, holding the medallion white-knuckled, willing his power into it until the stream of energy was so bright he had to avert his face.

With a final, tortured scream the wraith slashed its claws across Veles's face before tumbling back into the darkness, dissipating like smoke on the wind. For another moment, Veles remained frozen in place, still gripping the medallion, though the blue light had winked out at the same time the wraith vanished. Slowly, warily, he lowered the medallion, but did not replace it beneath his shirt.

He stepped out of the street, into a doorway and took stock. His power was depleted, and he knew that he could not withstand another attack this night. He blinked blood from his eyes, and a glance in the window of a nearby store told him that the wraith had managed to inflict three long scratches across his left cheek. The sleeves of his coat looked as if someone had taken a razor to them, and while the scratches on his arms were not dangerously deep, Veles would need to apply poultices and magical herbs to his injuries to keep them from going bad.

For a few heartbeats, his hands shook from the terror of the confrontation, and his heartbeat pounded in his ears. Long training enabled him to regain control of his body and emotions. *Anger is far more productive than fear. Once I get the Russian stones and the Polish witch's book, those creatures will be terrified of me.* Veles scanned the area around him and quickly moved away—knowing that watchers would arrive soon. If the attack on the house didn't get their attention, the fight with the *gessyan* was sure to.

Chapter TWELVE

"I TRUST THE trip to England was uneventful?" Dr. Konrad Nils turned away from the large desk where he had been examining an antique manuscript, and set down his monocle.

"We had a couple of ups and downs," Jake replied, adjusting his collar.

"Nothing important," Rick echoed.

Nils raised an eyebrow as if he suspected there was more to the tale, but let it go. "I wanted to let you know how very sorry I am about your father's death. I relied on your father, and on Brand and Desmet, to bring me many of the lovely items in Mr. Carnegie's collection.

Jake swallowed, and nodded. "We're all adjusting to the loss. But I wanted to assure you that Brand and Desmet will continue."

Nils nodded, and then poured cups of tea for Jake and Rick and himself, before settling in behind his massive, mahogany desk. "I'm certain that in this time of sorrow, you have more essential things to do than meet with clients. Which makes me wonder what the real purpose is for your call?"

Jake took a sip of tea as he framed his response. "First of all, we're attempting to follow up on recent shipments, to make sure they were received."

"Yes, the shipments came in. I've got the paperwork here somewhere. The items are in the receiving room; I haven't had a chance to go through them yet."

Jake smiled. "I'm wondering whether there might have been something... unusual about the objects that may have drawn unwanted attention to Father, or to Brand and Desmet."

Nils put down his tea cup. "You don't think his death was from natural causes?"

Jake shrugged. "Perhaps. But there've been a number of unusual incidents since then. Let's just say, we're trying to be thorough."

For a long moment, Nils stared out the window before he spoke. "What I'm going to tell you can't be repeated. If you quote me, I'll deny it. You can't be in the museum business for long without realizing that some things can't be explained by normal facts.

"We handle artifacts used in religious rituals; mementos of important events, things that people valued because of their emotional significance. Sometimes, objects people wanted enough to kill or die for."

Nils took a sip of tea and leaned back in his chair. "You won't hear many scientists or academics talk about ghosts or hauntings, but very few people would find it comfortable to spend the night in a large museum, surrounded by the collections." A rueful smile touched his lips. "Perhaps we lock the doors at night as much to keep things in as to keep people out."

"What kinds of things?"

Nils gave an eloquent shrug. "Things as old as human memory—maybe older."

"I'm not sure—"

"Some collectors in New Pittsburgh have been looking for certain objects for a very, very long time," Nils went on. "Lifetimes, in fact. If such a dedicated collector were to discover that a coveted object had been acquired by someone else, the reaction might be quite heated."

He knows about vampires, Jake thought, working to keep his face impassive. "We've often seen bidding wars, when pieces go up for auction," Rick replied. "The competition can get vicious."

"I've seen many things in the years I've been tending Mr. Carnegie's collections," Nils said. "And on more than one occasion, I've suspected that someone who wanted an object very badly was willing to go to any length to obtain it."

"That's what we think, too," Jake said. "But we don't know which object, or who wanted it. Whoever it is, they're persistent—

and dangerous. And we don't believe they have whatever it is they thought Father possessed."

Nils's expression was difficult to read. "You're on the right path. If you hadn't already started, I'd have suggested you look at the most recent orders and shipments your father handled—the official ones, and the ones that were off the books. I assume that is the reason for your visit? If so, I can assure you that none of our recent acquisitions would raise an eyebrow."

Nils paused. "But I will tell you this: you're not the only one asking questions lately. A couple of agents from the Department of Supernatural Investigations were by here just the other day. That kind of thing can be bad for business. Collectors are a nervous bunch. They don't want the government knowing too much about their treasures—especially when the provenance on some of their items might be a bit..."

"Hazy," Jake supplied.

Nils nodded. "Indeed."

"Do you know what the spook boys were looking for?" Rick asked.

"I assume it was related to that awful article in the newspaper," Nils said with a heavy sigh. "You know the one?"

Jake shook his head. "I'm afraid I don't. We were out of the country on an acquisition trip and then what with Father's death—"

"Of course. Forgive me." Nils took a sip of his tea and the fragrant mixture seemed to fortify him. "You've heard about the killings along the rivers?"

Jake and Rick nodded.

"One of those muckraking journalists," Nils said with distaste, "wrote a sensational article that speculated that perhaps our new exhibit, 'Totems and Idols', might be to blame. Ignorant peasant. But that kind of sensationalism sells. I suppose I shouldn't complain. Visits to the museum—and the new exhibit—jumped sky high."

"Good for business," Rick observed.

"The visits, yes," Nils replied. "But it brought out the unsavory elements as well. We've foiled two attempted break-ins, and the additional security eats into the profits from the extra ticket sales."

Rick and Jake traded knowing glance. "Did the break-ins happen after the article was published? Or after the exhibit opened?" Jake asked.

Nils toyed with his cup as if unsure just what to share. "To be frank, the exhibit has been a headache since it opened. And I was hoping it would be a jewel in the museum's crown. Mr. Carnegie is so proud of the pieces."

"A headache?" Rick pressed.

Nils nodded. "First, it was the museum's ghosts. Many of our pieces bring a little 'something extra' with them. Not surprising, given the objects' pasts, but still disconcerting. As I said before, museum people expect a bit of this, but since the exhibit opened, I'd have to say the spirits have been extremely restless, maybe even angry."

Nils poured himself another cup of tea with the same grim expression with which other men slosh gin into a glass. "The first break-in happened the week the exhibit started. Our security guards heard a commotion, and the ruffians ran off. Then a most persistent man tried to purchase the entire collection—"

"Anyone we know?" Rick asked.

Nils glanced toward the door to make sure it was shut. "Richard Thwaites. He's quite wealthy, and very used to getting what he wants. But not this time. Mr. Carnegie treasures the collection and is unwilling to part with it." He smiled. "You know what they say about Scotsmen and stubbornness; Mr. Thwaites was most disappointed. Then again, Mr. Carnegie might be the only man in town who can say 'no' to him and make it stick."

"You can count on us to be discreet," Rick said. "Was Mr. Thwaites interested in any items in particular?"

Nils closed his eyes and rubbed his temples as if to ward away a headache. "I'm afraid Mr. Thwaites might be listening to nonsense and rumors. He was looking for a book supposedly written by Marcin of Krakow, a Polish priest—and some mystical stones from Russia. He demanded to know whether they were part of our exhibit, and refused to believe me when I said they were not."

He waived his hand dismissively. "Sheer nonsense, of course. Historians can't even agree on whether or not Marcin of Krakow was real, let alone authenticate a book by him. And as for stones, well, there are probably enough 'mystical' stones to ballast a coal freighter, but in the end, they're just rocks people believe are special."

Nils seemed to miss the look that passed between Rick and Jake. *'Marcin' was a name on Father's list,* Jake thought. *That can't be a coincidence.*

"What's so special about Marcin of Krakow and his book—assuming he actually was a real person?" Rick asked.

Nils looked beleaguered, as if he wholeheartedly wished the two of them would disappear, but he took another sip of tea and regained his composure. "You understand that this is sheer rumor and probably myth, nothing that serious scholars can corroborate?"

Jake and Rick both nodded. "Absolutely," Jake said, with a mischievous grin. "Then again, in our business, rumor and myth make hard-to-find objects all the more prized—and valuable."

"Too true," Nils acknowledged. "But to your question: Marcin of Krakow was a mystic who might have lived back in the fifteenth century. I looked into the matter after Mr. Thwaites's insistent interest. People who believe Marcin was real, and that he actually wrote a book, contend that the book gave instructions for binding dark spirits." He chuckled. "He cataloged quite a variety of these dark spirits—wraiths, killer ghosts, big black phantom dogs, that sort of thing. Marcin of Krakow called these spirits *gessyan*, and he claimed to have had them under his control."

"*Gessyan*," Jake repeated. "That's an unusual term." *Another coincidence,* he thought. *I'd never heard of them before Drostan's report. Interesting.*

Nils stood, and gestured for Jake and Rick to follow him over to the bookshelves on the other side of his office. He took down an old, leather-bound book, and carefully turned the pages until he came to a large illustration of several menacing shadows. Some were in the shape of a man or a bent old woman, while others took the form of large, threatening dogs, and still more had misshapen, twisted bodies like images from a nightmare.

"An artistic interpretation of the *gessyan*," Nils said. "Something else I researched after Mr. Thwaites's visit. This is a copy of a manuscript originally found in an old, hard-to-reach Polish monastery."

Jake peered over Nils' shoulder. "What does it say about them?"

The illuminated manuscript was written in Polish, but it was clearly one of the languages Nils read fluently. "'Beware those who delve the deep places! Mankind was not ordained to dwell below. The deep realms belong to the Old Races, and are not for Mankind to trouble.'"

Nils paused, then went on. "'Woe to you, greedy miners! You who press on in lust for gold and gems and silver. Ruin awaits you, and trouble will plague your house.'"

"Yes, but what are bloody *gessyan*?" Jake muttered.

"I'm getting to that," Nils said with mild irritation.

"'Before the world began, the *gessyan* walked the dark places. And when the land and the waters were parted, so that life began, the *gessyan* sought the dark places below and made them their own.'"

He cleared his throat and went on. "'The *gessyan* came from the darkness, and they sought the darkness. Their hunger cannot be sated, and thirst cannot be quenched. Before long, they sought the blood of men, but they could not walk in the light. And so they preyed on men in the night, and fed on the marrow of those who came below, those who lusted for the treasures under the world.'"

He glanced up at Jake. "This is where it gets really interesting. 'Then Marcin of Krakow fasted and prayed, and he cursed the *gessyan*, binding them to the depths. Woe to those who break his wardings! Leave the deep places for the *gessyan*.'" Nils closed the book. "To my knowledge, this is the only text we have in our collection that describes *gessyan* in any detail," he said, replacing the tome on the shelf. "The name appears here and there in legends and oral traditions, always as a caution, always linked to warnings about caves and mines. The term is something of a catch-all, for a wide variety of dangerous supernatural creatures."

"Do you know anything else about Marcin of Krakow?" Jake asked.

Nils shook his head. "He's mentioned in a few old Polish and Russian manuscripts, but not in the formal Church documents."

"Maybe Marcin wasn't a priest," Jake said. "Maybe his power was... other?"

Nils raised an eyebrow. "A witch?"

Jake shrugged. "Perhaps."

Nils walked back to his desk and finished his cup of tea. "I'm afraid I haven't been much help, other than spinning tales." He gave both men a flinty look. "And I am counting on your discretion. I'd not like to hear that our conversation was repeated."

"You can count on us," Rick replied.

Nils hesitated for a moment, then turned to Jake. "I know you're in mourning, and I don't mean to be unseemly, but if you're interested in the 'Totems and Idols' exhibit, Mr. Carnegie is hosting a reception here next Wednesday for donors and influential patrons of the museum. Your fathers certainly qualify," he added. "I can have you added to the guest list, if you're interested and family obligations permit."

"Please do, and thank you," Jake said. "We would be very interested. Sorry to take up so much of your time. You've been very helpful."

Nils rose to see him out. "Of course, of course, Mr. Desmet. I counted your father as a friend. This is the least I can do. And the museum values its relationship with Brand and Desmet. You can expect the contract to be renewed. Please send my condolences to your mother and to Mr. Brand."

Jake and Rick headed for the door. "Mr. Desmet—" Nils called. "If you're really interested in *gessyan*, there is someone else you might want to speak with."

Jake turned. "Someone at the university?"

Nils shook his head. "Quite the contrary. He's someone we have consulted, informally, about Old World folklore. Mr. Eban Hodekin is the night foreman at the Edgar Thompson Works." Jake got the impression that the curator had qualms about connecting him to Hodekin. "I met him while I was compiling a book on superstitions from Eastern Europe. I think you'll find him knowledgeable."

"Thank you," Jake replied. "Should I tell him who sent me?"

Nils looked briefly uncomfortable. "That won't be necessary."

Jake and Rick left the office and walked down the wide stone stairway, through the open atrium that showcased the museum's new collections. Andrew Carnegie's fascination with natural history sent researchers and scholars scurrying to every corner of the globe to bring back treasures for the massive Beaux-Arts building on Forbes Avenue.

"Didn't you say Drostan's telegraph mentioned the mines?" Rick asked.

Jake nodded. "Mines—and *gessyan*. It's not the first time Thwaites's name has come up, either."

He glanced at the faces of the people they passed: museum workers, administrative staff, visitors. None of them looked familiar, but Jake viewed them all with caution. Kovach had stayed with the carriage to avoid calling attention to himself. Now Jake wished he had allowed him to wait outside Nils's door, as Kovach had wanted to do.

You're jumping at shadows, Jake chided himself, just before someone shoved him hard from behind.

"Jake!" he heard Rick cry as he lost his footing and tumbled headlong down the marble steps.

Jake curled into a tight ball as he fell. Patrons screamed and cursed as they jostled to get out of his way. One portly gentleman was not agile enough to avoid him, and ended up cushioning Jake's fall as he hit the landing.

Rick hurried to the bottom of the stairs as Jake staggered to his feet, aching all over as if he had taken a thorough beating. He glanced around, but his assailant was long gone. Jake bent to retrieve the gun that had fallen from his waistband, and reached down to help the portly man to his feet. He was rebuffed with a snort.

"You could have killed both of us!" the man huffed. "Watch where you're going!"

"Sorry," Jake said, before making as hasty an exit as he could manage. He did not allow himself to limp until he neared the carriage.

Kovach strode over to meet him. "What happened? You're bleeding." Jake put a hand up to the back of his head and his fingers came away bloody.

"Someone pushed him on the stairs," Rick said.

"Damn, I'll be sore tomorrow!" Jake added. He turned to Rick. "Did you get a look at who it was?"

Rick shook his head. "I was trying to hold on and not go tail over teacup. You created such a stir that whoever pushed you just melted into the crowd."

"I knew I should have gone in with you," Kovach groused.

"Hard to explain a bodyguard when I'm supposed to be mourning a natural death," Jake replied. One of Brand and Desmet's carriages awaited them, pulled by two black horses. The carriage driver was a *werkman*, a mechanical man from the laboratory of Adam Farber.

Just as Jake, Rick, and Kovach were heading for the carriage, a second coach pulled up behind them. Jake recognized it as his family's personal carriage, and although the velvet shades were drawn, he had a good idea of who was inside. He stopped, aware that his sixth sense was steering him away from the first carriage, nudging him toward the second.

"Go on ahead," he said to Kovach. "We'll ride with Nicki."

"Sorry, but I'm coming with you," Kovach said. "We have no idea who's really in that coach, and you just had someone push you down the stairs."

The door to the carriage opened just enough for Kovach to glimpse Nicki inside. "For heaven's sake, get in!" she hissed.

Kovach insisted on sticking his head inside the carriage to assure that there were no other, unwanted passengers, then stepped aside for Jake and Rick to enter. He waved the *werkman* and the first coach on ahead. "I'll be riding shotgun," he said, closing the door and swinging up beside the driver.

"Glad I caught you," Nicki said as the two men settled in. She eyed the blood on Jake's collar and handed him a kerchief. "God, you look awful. What did you do—fall down the steps?"

"I was pushed," Jake replied curtly, pressing the handkerchief against the cut on the back of his head.

"Which suggests we're on the right track," Nicki said with a satisfied smile.

"You don't have to sound so pleased about it," Jake groused.

"Aren't you supposed to be at home with Catherine?" Rick asked.

"Pish," Nicki said. "It's all good so long as no one knows—and the curtains of the carriage *are* drawn."

Jake closed his eyes and leaned back, fighting a monster headache. "My dear Nicki, when have you ever been discreet?"

"Today, actually," Nicki replied. "Cady McDaniel finished some research I'd asked her to do. I didn't think it could wait—especially since you were just talking to Dr. Nils. So I decided to meet you here."

The carriages turned onto Bellefield, heading for Fifth Avenue and home. They were heading along a sparsely developed stretch of land when a volley of gunfire erupted from behind a rocky outcropping. Before Jake could call out a warning to Kovach, he heard an explosion, close enough that it almost rocked the carriage off its wheels and sent the horses into a panic. The air was full of the smell of sulfur and charred wood.

Kovach's rifle sounded twice before their carriage took off at high speed, throwing them to the floor. They braced their legs against the seats and stayed low, as the coach careened up onto the curb and back down again.

Jake went to steal a glimpse out the window as Rick pulled back the curtain. Nicki grabbed Jake's collar and pulled him back, sending them both sprawling. "Stay down!"

"I'd like to know what's going on," he objected, jerking loose. He moved toward the window again, and once more the carriage veered, throwing him against the seat. The headache that already pounded in his temples threatened to blur his vision, and he felt blood begin to trickle down into his collar again.

"Hold on!" Kovach shouted.

"Now he tells us," Nicki muttered, gripping the seat cushions for dear life with her left hand, holding a derringer in her right.

Rick had also drawn a gun from beneath his jacket. The carriage bumped along the paving stones, taking one sharp corner after another. Nicki swore in French as the coach bounced them hard enough to lift them off the floor.

After a few more harrowing turns, the carriage slowed and finally came to a halt. Hoof beats sounded nearby, slowing from a full gallop to a stop. Jake was feeling every bounce and jostle in his aching bones. Nicki looked as if she had just gone riding, her face decorously flushed and her hair slightly mussed, while Rick looked ready for a fight.

"Are we safe?" Jake murmured, drawing his gun.

Nicki brandished her derringer and produced a pearl-handled shiv from one of the ridges of her corset. "I'm game to find out. How about you two?"

Jake sighed. "And to think, you went to boarding school."

"Where do you think I learned to shoot?"

"All clear," Jake heard Kovach call. A moment later, the carriage door opened in the coach port of the Desmet house. "Save the questions until I get you three inside," he said. All trace of levity was gone from his face. This was Miska Kovach the soldier, sharpshooter, Army assassin. Jake managed a tired smile, knowing they were in good hands.

"Lead the way," Rick said.

Kovach brought them into the Desmet house through the servants' entrance, the better to shield them from prying eyes. Despite the attempt at being discreet, Catherine Desmet was already waiting for them in the kitchen.

"Jake! Rick! Nicki! What happened?" Catherine looked from them to Kovach, with an expression Jake knew well from childhood that meant that his mother would not be denied the full truth.

Jake slumped into a chair as Rick went to the sink. He soaked a cloth in cold water and handed it to Jake. Nicki perched prettily on a high stool and smoothed her chignon, having hidden both the shiv and the derringer somewhere in her full skirts.

"I don't actually know," Jake admitted as he tried to wipe the blood from his neck and hair. "Rick and I got into Nicki's carriage and Miska rode with the driver, then *boom!* The rest is something of a blur," he said, reaching up gingerly to probe the rapidly swelling goose-egg on the back of his head.

Mrs. James, the family cook, took one look at Jake and bustled off to the ice box, returning with a hand-sized chunk of ice wrapped in a tea towel. "Put this against the lump. It'll take the swelling down," she advised, and took the bloodied cloth with disdain, before returning to her work as if nothing were awry.

"We had gone to see Dr. Nils at the museum," Rick said. "On our way out, someone pushed Jake on the stairs. I had a better grip on the railing," he said wryly.

"I don't know who's behind this—yet," Kovach said, and Jake heard simmering anger beneath his tone. "But I assure you, I'll find out."

"Start right before when things went boom," Nicki advised. "That's where it got a bit spotty."

Kovach grimaced. "We made the turn onto Bellefield. I swear no one was following us, but there's a lot of open ground. Sent a small mortar shell at the first carriage, blew it to bits."

"*Mon Dieu*!" Nicki gasped. "What of the *werkman*, and the horses?"

Kovach nodded. "The *werkman*'s fine, although he might have gotten some of his gears bent and a few scratches to show for it. Very glad I'd sent him; it would have killed a living man, no doubt about it."

"What happened then, Mark?" Catherine asked. She appeared completely unruffled, except for the deadly glint in her eyes. His mother came from sturdy stock.

"Well, there's likely to be a little talk about that," Kovach replied. "As if there wouldn't be, about a mortar hitting the carriage. I'd assigned *werkman* Charles as the driver—he's one of Farber's newer models. Able to run a more complex cipher when it comes to responses." He ran a hand back through his hair.

"Anyhow, Charles got up, shook himself off and started running after the horses, which were still harnessed to the remains of the carriage," Kovach continued. "He caught them, and rode what was left of the traces like a chariot. I told him to get the stable master to check over the horses, and then come join us here."

"You think he might have seen something you didn't?" Catherine asked, arching an eyebrow.

Kovach shrugged. "He's got a difference engine for brains, binoculars for eyes, and I don't imagine he broke out in a cold sweat, even when the carriage got shot out from under him. He might have recorded something important while the rest of us were focused on staying alive."

Mrs. Jones returned with a tray of tea and cookies. "I thought perhaps a brisk cup of tea might help to settle things," she said, and proceeded to pour for everyone as if such events were an everyday occurrence.

A knock at the door startled them. Charles the *werkman* stood in the doorway. "My presence was requested," he said in a mechanical monotone.

Charles was average height for a man, with a sturdy build. He was dressed as befitted his station, with a billed cap that hid the lack of hair. His bronze features were pleasant and regular, if expressionless, and he moved with the hum of gears meshing and servomotors toiling. Blue light glinted from his eyes. Gloves hid the mechanical hands. Unless someone were to look Charles straight in the face, no one would realize just from looking at him he was a *werkman*. Few would bother.

"Thanks for your quick thinking today," Jake said. "You saved the horses."

Charles touched the bill of his cap and ducked his head. "That's all right, sir. It's my job."

"We were rather distracted when everything was going on," Kovach said. "What did you see, right before the coach blew up?"

Charles was silent for a moment. It occurred to Jake that the cliché of 'watching the wheels turn' was never more apt. "How much detail would you like, sir?"

"Start with everything, and we'll pare it down from there," Kovach instructed.

"As you like, sir." He cleared his throat, an uncannily human sound. "Four squirrels, two rabbits and fourteen birds were in the vacant lot—"

"You noticed that?" Nicki asked, eyes wide.

"I notice everything, ma'am," Charles replied.

"Skip the wildlife," Kovach instructed. "I want to know about people, weapons, and anything else dangerous."

"Very well," Charles said, and paused again, sifting through reams of information to retrieve the requested details.

"There were six people in sight at the time of the explosion," Charles said. "And two mechanicals."

"Stop," Jake said, sitting forward despite his pounding head. "There were mechanicals? Where?"

"Driving one of the coaches coming from the other direction," Charles replied.

Jake looked at Kovach. "Damn. I thought we had the only ones Farber supplied."

"They weren't my kin," Charles said, "The first one's gears sounded wrong. And the other was mostly flesh, with metal parts."

Rick and Jake exchanged a glance. "You mean, a living man with a metal hand or arm?" Rick asked.

Charles shook his head. "No, sir. A dead man with gears and motors to make him move."

Nicki muttered a curse under her breath and Catherine covered her mouth in horror. "Are such things even possible?" Catherine asked, appalled.

Rick made a face. "Theoretically, yes. Adam helped a couple of Department agents who were hurt in a bomb blast by fixing them up with mechanical replacement parts—jaw, arm, that sort of thing. He calls them his 'Midas Men', after the myth where a man turned people to gold. But that's just a better version of a wooden leg. Those men were still alive."

"Clockwork dead men," Jake mused. "Like mechanical zombies."

"Adam would never be involved with anything like that," Rick argued.

"Add that to the list of things to look into," Nicki said. "Who else is building mechanicals—metal or otherwise—and who are they supplying?"

"Go on," Kovach instructed. "What happened to the *werkmen*, after the explosion?"

"They drove off, straightaway, without a second glance," Charles replied.

"Rather cold-blooded after there had been an explosion, but then *werkmen* don't have emotions," Catherine observed.

"Could you see where the explosion originated?" Kovach asked.

Again, Charles paused. "It was in the general direction of the other carriage, but it did not come from inside the carriage. The carriage was intact when it pulled away."

"Which is more than we can say for ours," Kovach replied with a grimace.

"Could the carriage have been shielding someone with a weapon?" Jake asked. It hurt to think. Sound and light made his temples throb. But there was too much at stake for him to leave the conversation, though he desperately wanted a slug of scotch and a soft pillow.

"It's possible," Charles said. "Regrettably, I cannot see through solid objects."

Remind me to point that out to Farber as a possible improvement, Jake thought.

"Is there anything else that you might have noticed, anything at all related to the explosion?" Rick said.

This time, Charles hesitated just a bit longer. "There was one thing, sir. But I'm not sure what to make of it."

"Tell us, and we'll figure out whether it's important or not," Kovach replied.

"Well sir, just before the explosion, I detected an unusual energy signature coming from inside the swale," Charles said.

"What kind of energy?" Rick asked.

Charles shook his head. "That's just it, sir. It wasn't anything on the electro-magnetic spectrum with which I'm acquainted. It was—other."

"Magic," Nicki said, looking up. "Which is what I came to warn you about in the first place."

"That will be all, Charles," Kovach said. "Go have the mechanic check you over. Thank you for your service today."

"Pleased to do it, sir," Charles said with a nod, and left the kitchen. When he had gone, Jake and Rick took turns filling the others in on what Nils had said.

"I'm not surprised at all."

Everyone's attention shifted to Nicki.

"Well?" Jake asked.

Nicki gave a dramatic sigh, barely hiding a grin. "As I was about to tell you, before I was rudely interrupted by that awful explosion—Cady McDaniel let me know she had completed the research that I commissioned."

"And?" Jake prodded, gesturing for her to speed it up.

"I asked Cady to look into the Night Hag—*Nocnitsa*—and Karl Jasinski. And she came through for me." She grinned. "You can always count on a librarian when it comes to digging up dirt."

"That's why you were out in the carriage," Jake said. "You'd slipped out to see Cady?"

Nicki nodded. "I was going crazy shut up in the house." She smoothed a lock of hair back into place. "Everything Cady found supports what Renate saw in the vision I told you about. Add to that the fact that Renate recognized the name 'Marcin' on your father's list, and that one of Drogo Veles's men showed up to tell her to mind her own business—well, I think some of the pieces are starting to come together."

She took a sip of water before continuing. "Look. Karl Jasinski hasn't been seen in a while, by the people in his neighborhood, or by Renate's coven. So is he lying low—or did he disappear?" Nicki met Jake's gaze. "I think he's important. Find him, and we might know why someone keeps trying to kill us."

Chapter THIRTEEN

"NOT MUCH LEFT, is there?" Sergeant Finian observed.

Finian and Drostan stared down at the body. "You're sure it was a woman?" Drostan asked. From what remained, it was difficult to tell.

"Think so. Might have been a young man, but he was fine-boned if that's the case. The coroner will figure it out," Finian replied.

They stood in the carriage lot behind the Highland Club in Evergreen Hamlet, upriver from the previous murder scene. The club, a 'gentleman's establishment', did its best to detract from any respectability Evergreen Hamlet attempted to earn. Forty years ago, the old tavern had been a stop on the Underground Railroad. Rumor had it that a secret trap door beneath the bar led into a cavern where runaway slaves gathered, and an old tunnel up to the hillside beyond. Nowadays, if the cave and tunnels were still used, Fletcher suspected it was to hide philandering husbands from their angry wives.

"You think it was someone at the bar?" Finian mused.

Drostan grimaced as he thought. "Those sots come to see women without their hosiery and ogle a bit of leg. Hard to imagine them doing more than throwing a punch or two."

Finian nodded. "My thoughts, too."

"Looks more to me like the unfortunate we found down by the river," Drostan added, "and all the other ones, all the way down the Mon to Vestaburg."

"Dammit, Finian! That's twelve dead so far, all savaged almost beyond recognition, and the only things they've got in common were that they were out along one of the rivers late at night."

Drostan shook his head. "It's got to mean something. Why have all the bodies been found between here and the Vestaburg docks? If these were just the usual knifings, I'd figure the killer was traveling on barges up and down the rivers. But there's nothing 'usual' about these murders." He sighed. "I don't know what to think."

"I agree, but the brass at the station aren't having any of it," Finian said. "They don't want to hear about Ripper-killers or patterns. Want to treat each one by itself, just some poor nobody got cut up for a wallet or purse, and sweep it under the rug quick as possible."

"They're scared," Drostan said. He had seen the signs before, back in Scotland. Then, police too frightened to accept a supernatural threat turned to a more believable possibility: a corrupt investigator.

"Yeah." Finian did not have to point out that he was the only cop assigned to the corpse. Here, behind a seedy drinking club, no one downtown cared who the killer or the victim was so long as they stayed away from the swells in the better neighborhoods.

"I talked to Carmody," Drostan said. He was trying not to look too hard at the body. Whoever he—or she—was, no one deserved that. The murderer would kill again, and whether or not the victims mattered to the higher-ups, it bothered him. He knew he wouldn't leave well enough alone.

"Get anything?" Finian was nearly done jotting notes in a report no one would read.

"He's gone round the bend, that's for sure," Drostan admitted. "At the end, he started talking about mad miners and Vesta Nine."

Finian froze. "You're sure he said Vesta Nine?"

"Sure as I breathe," Drostan replied.

"Now that's odd," Finian said. "We've had some trouble out that way. Not my beat, you know, but I hear things."

"Like what?"

Finian snapped his notebook closed and put it back in his jacket. "Like more miners than usual been dying." He made a dismissive gesture. "Oh, they're saying it's bad air—blackdamp and all—but the truth is the mine superintendents don't know, and don't care so long as it doesn't shut down work."

"I hear Vesta Nine is the deepest mine around—maybe in the whole country," Drostan ventured.

"Wouldn't know. What are you getting at?"

"Maybe nothing. But it isn't natural, men being down so far underground. We haven't explored much, down there. How do we know there aren't things there no one's seen before, things that shouldn't get loose?"

Finian raised an eyebrow. "You keep talking like that, I'm going to sleep with a lamp burning. Next, you'll be telling ghost stories."

"You ever heard of *gessyan*?"

Finian snorted. "Is that some fancy word for a spook? I'm willing to believe we've got a Ripper killer loose, maybe even Tumblety back for a second try. But ghosts and goblins? That's stretching it too far." He peered at Drostan skeptically. "Did Carmody actually mention ghosts?"

"Uh-huh. Well, *gessyan* specifically. And when I did some asking around after the last killing, people started talking about the Night Hag, *Nocnitsa*," Drostan said.

Finian shrugged. "Easier I guess to believe in boogey-men than to think one of your neighbors might have done the killing."

Drostan was quiet for a moment. "What if there's something to it?" he said finally. "Not boogey-men, but something that's gotten loose that shouldn't be out, something that kills like a beast."

"Mighty smart animal to only pick poor folks the brass won't bother with."

"No smarter than a lion sizing up a herd of antelope and picking out the sick and the old. It's pretty certain that the victims were alone when they were killed, or we'd have more than one corpse. Wealthy people don't usually wander the city alone, not in deserted areas like the riverside."

"We're not on the riverside now," Finian pointed out.

"No, but there's not a lot of traffic out this way, and not much light, either." Drostan nodded toward the ravine that ran behind the club. "Got a ditch back there that goes on a ways. High grass. Good hiding place. And we're not that far from the riverside. I bet half the alley cats in Allegheny have been this way and back."

"Maybe," Finian agreed grudgingly. "And I have to say, I'd rather be tracking one killer instead of several. But no one is going to believe either theory—a new Ripper *or* some kind of monster."

"I'll keep digging. You done?"

"Almost. I'll have to put the body in the back of the paddy wagon," Finian said, disgust clear on his face. "Damn. I hope it doesn't come apart like the last one."

Drostan helped Finian roll the corpse onto a piece of oilcloth and heave the remains into the back of the wagon.

"I hate driving around with a dead body," Finian admitted. "Not that I'm scared. It's just... unnatural."

Drostan chuckled. "I don't envy you. How 'bout this? You give me a ride back to Ohio Street, and then you've got company for half the trip."

"Sounds good."

Drostan carefully climbed up beside Finian on the driver's seat. "Hey, before I forget—you hear anything about someone named Karl Jasinski?"

Finian looked over at him. "You get around, don't you? What's the interest in Jasinski?"

"Carmody mentioned him."

Finian's eyes grew skeptical. "How's that? Carmody's been out at Nutter Hill since before this whole mess began."

Drostan shrugged. "If I had an answer, I wouldn't be out here in the middle of the night hauling dead bodies around."

Finian drove a few blocks in silence. "Folks say Jasinski's a witch. Warlock. Whatever you want to call it. The Witch of Pulawski Way. That's over on Polish Hill."

"Is he? A witch, I mean."

Finian snorted. "You're scaring me, Drostan. First ghosts and Jack the Ripper, now witches. Watch who you talk to, or you'll end up on Nutter Hill, too."

I'm well aware of that. "I meant, what do the people on Pulawski Way think of him?"

Finian looked away. "There's what they tell me when I'm in uniform, and what they say when I'm at the tavern with some of my friends. I talked a buddy of mine, Stan Rutkoski, into taking me over there one night. Did a little asking around. Folks were scared of Jasinski. Not because he was a tough guy; because they thought he could put the evil eye on them."

"Interesting."

Finian shook his head. "You know how it is, Fletcher. People bring the old ways over with them. Superstition. Ignorance."

"So you don't believe in the *Dearg-Dur*?"

Finian crossed himself. "All right, all right. Maybe there's something to some of the old stories."

"You were telling me about Jasinski."

"I heard that people ask him to set curses or lift them. He has a pretty good track record: folks seem to think he has the Power."

"Anyone seen him lately?"

Finian scowled. "No. He's missing—or at least he's not where people think he ought to be. Maybe someone he cursed caught up to him. Or maybe he's a charlatan and he figured he'd get out of town while the getting was good."

They had turned toward town, and the stretch of road was desolate. All of the houses were dark, since it was long past the hour where decent people were awake. Even the taverns were closed. The gas street lights gave a dim, orange glow, but on a moonless night, they only served to chase back the darkest shadows.

Ghosts wandered along the sides of the road. This was an old trail, long used. Before the modern road went in, the way had been a plank road, and before that, a footpath used by traders, settlers and native scouts. Death was no stranger here. Highwaymen and robbers had frequented the road throughout its history. Accidents and illness had claimed other lives. Drostan was certain that if everyone could see the spirits that lingered throughout the city's streets they would shut themselves up in their homes and not come out.

Most of the time, the ghosts regarded Drostan with curiosity, if they acknowledged him at all. As the police carriage clattered down the road, several of the ghosts met his gaze and slowly shook their heads. One by one, the ghosts winked out, before the carriage could reach them.

Drostan felt a chill run down his spine. Overhead, the gas lights wavered. The night air grew unseasonably cold, and gooseflesh rose on his arms.

"We need to get out of here. Now," Drostan warned.

Finian looked at him as if he had lost his mind. "There's no one about. What's the hurry?"

"We're in danger. I feel it," Drostan said, and chanced a look over his shoulder. The shadows seemed to press in on them, darker than the night had a right to be. And then Drostan realized something.

The shadows blotted out any glimpse of what lay behind them.

"Something's coming!" Drostan hissed.

"I don't hear any hoofbeats," Finian countered. "And I don't think too many ruffians are willing to run down a police wagon."

Drostan looked behind them again. A curtain of darkness was rolling toward them like a wave, swiftly gaining on the carriage.

"For God's sake, Finian, look!"

As the policeman turned, the color drained from his face, and his eyes went wide.

"Sweet Mother Mary. What is that?"

"Nothing good. Get us out of here!"

Finian flicked the reins, and the horses surged ahead, as if they had been chafing for permission to run for their lives.

"It's gaining on us!" Drostan said, holding on as they skidded around a bend. The wagon was built for rugged use, but not for comfort. Drostan felt as if his teeth would shatter as his jaws snapped shut when they jolted over bumps in the road. He marveled that Finian kept his seat.

The ghosts had all disappeared. All that remained was the pursuing darkness. The wagon sped down the road, the gas lights winking out as the wagon reached them. The shadows were darker than night and hungry as the grave.

"What in the name of Heaven is chasing us?" Finian shouted.

"Nothing that has anything to do with Heaven," Drostan replied. "Those things you said were boogey-men and fairy tales? They're gaining on us."

The horses were flecked with sweat. Finian shouted to the team for speed, and though their hooves pounded down the empty street, the shadows seemed to swallow all sound.

"What happens if it catches us?" Finian asked.

"I don't want to know."

"How do we lose a shadow?" Finian's face was pale with fear. He was a good man and an honest cop, a veteran of the streets. None of that prepared him for the silent terror behind them.

"Watch out!" Drostan shouted.

The road took a sharp left turn beneath a railroad trestle. Finian reined the horses in hard, and the carriage tottered up onto two wheels, threatening to roll over. Finian jerked the reins again, and the panicked horses bolted. The carriage swayed crazily, and the traces snapped, sending the wagon with Finian and Drostan off the road and into a hedgerow.

We're dead men, Drostan thought, climbing out of the brambles, steeling himself for whatever horror the shadows brought with them. Finian scrambled to his feet, and the two men stood shoulder to shoulder, resolved to await death head on. Finian drew his service revolver, but his hand wavered as he saw nowhere to shoot.

Drostan blinked, and a man appeared in the middle of the road, standing between them and the writhing shadows. He had dark brown hair and a neatly trimmed beard, and he wore the black cassock of an orthodox priest, with a crimson sash and a black rope belt.

"Get out of there!" Drostan shouted. "Run!"

The stranger did not turn. Shadows rushed toward him.

"Are you crazy? Run!"

Instead, the stranger lifted a golden box—a reliquary, Drostan guessed—and began to chant. The chanting grew louder, and the priest lifted the box high before bringing it down to chest level.

Drostan looked wildly about, but there was nowhere to hide. The horses had fled, and the ruined police wagon lay smashed in a ditch. He and Finian were bloodied and bruised, in no condition to run, even if there had been anywhere to run to. The shadows would be on them in seconds. They, and the black-robed stranger, were going to die.

"I banish you, in the name of all that is holy!" the stranger cried out, repeating the command in the language he had used before. The reliquary flared with light, and a piercing beam burned from its center, striking the heart of the boiling darkness.

Drostan braced himself, but the shadows abruptly stopped. The brilliant white light bored a hole in the darkness, tearing it open. Drostan glimpsed stars through the gap. He watched, speechless, as the light burned away at the shadows, like fire consuming paper, until the last of the unnatural night became a black mist and disappeared.

When Drostan looked back to thank the priest, the man was gone.

Finian crossed himself, then he reached beneath his shirt for a saint's medallion, kissed it, and closed his eyes in prayer. Drostan stared at the empty road and willed himself to stop shaking.

"What the hell was that?" Finian asked when he had gathered his wits.

"I have no idea," Drostan said.

"Those shadows—were they *gessyan*?"

Drostan shook his head. "Maybe. I don't know. I've heard tell of them, but have never come across an accurate description."

"Where did that priest come from—and how'd he get away so fast?"

Drostan spread his hands wide. "You're asking good questions, but I don't know. Never saw him before."

Finian looked at the ruined wagon. "Damn. If that corpse wasn't already in pieces, it can't be in good shape now. And the Captain will have my ass over this." He sighed. "No one is going to believe me."

Drostan took pity on the cop. He laid a hand on Finian's shoulder. "No, they won't. And if you try to explain what happened, they'll hang you out to dry."

"What's my choice?"

"Tell them a story they'll believe."

Finian glared at him. "You want me to lie?"

"You want to keep your job?"

Finian gave a snort. "Like I have a chance of that, after what happened to the wagon and horses." He smacked his forehead and grimaced. "Sweet Brigid and Mary! The horses! If they've gone lame or we can't find them, they'll take them out of my pay; I'll be in debtors' prison for sure."

"I'll help you find the horses," Drostan said, cursing himself for making the night longer than it already had been. "But what will you tell your Captain? What would he believe?"

Finian was a smart guy, Drostan knew. He had come up the hard way, and this probably wasn't the first time he had shaded the truth. His conscience likely kept him from doing it too often. But Drostan could see Finian's mind working, thinking through the choices.

"We were heading back from the Highland Club, and got chased by a pack of wild dogs," Finian said. "Spooked the horses. I kept control as long as I could, but the horses didn't make the turn. The dogs came after us again, and I fired my revolver. They scattered."

Drostan nodded. "All right. That's good. Better fire your gun."

"What? Oh, yeah." Finian drew his pistol, aimed at the ground a ways off, and fired.

"I'd appreciate it if you kept me out of it, but if you need corroboration, I'll back you," Drostan said.

Finian gave a crooked grin. "Somehow, admitting I was with you doesn't seem likely to keep me out of trouble."

Drostan chuckled tiredly. "Let's go. We've got horses to find."

Hours later, Drostan headed back to the rooming house. Finian got lucky: the horses somehow made it back to the station house safely, and were waiting for them. Drostan had helped Finian check the horses over. Nothing worse than some bruises and a few superficial cuts—easily fixed with a little salve and a couple of apples to appease the skittish geldings.

Drostan felt the evening's work in every muscle, bone and sinew. "I'm getting too old for this kind of thing," he muttered to himself. He was jumpy as hell, flinching at every noise. In the distance, he heard hoots and shouts, and guessed that the pack of boys he had befriended, his informants, were having a late night, playing dice and drinking stolen ale. The sidewalks were deserted. Drostan walked quickly, forcing himself to be alert, unwilling to end the night the victim of a petty thief.

We got lucky. Tonight could have gone wrong in a hundred different ways.

A man in an overcoat came out of a side street and strode toward Drostan. The brim of his hat shadowed his face and he kept his gaze averted. Long habit made Drostan pay attention. The man was built solidly, dressed in the dark clothing of a manservant: curious attire for this part of town.

Just as Drostan moved to cross the street, the stranger moved lightning quick, seizing Drostan's arm with a steel grip. The man's head came up, revealing a face that was half-human, half-machine, with a mechanical eye and exposed gears.

"Come with me," the clockwork man said. Drostan struggled, but the vise-like grip would have broken bone before it released, and reluctantly, he gave in, knowing that he was in no shape for a fight.

The stranger steered him towards the next alley. Drostan tried to reach his gun, but his captor bumped his hand out of the way. "You won't be needing that," he said in a voice oddly reminiscent of a recording cylinder. The clockwork man looked alive, at least the flesh-and-blood parts of him did.

Drostan and the stranger started down the darkened alley, and Drostan expected to feel a blackjack against his skull at any moment. Instead, the clockwork man stopped about halfway in, far enough from the street that they were unlikely to be disturbed.

Two figures stepped out of the shadows. "We heard you had a busy night, Drostan." Jacob Drangosavich and Mitch Storm stood in the half-light. "Thank you, Hans. That will be all. I think we can count on the detective not to run away at this point. Please see that we're not interrupted."

Hans nodded and retreated to just inside the entrance of the alley.

"I thought you were working to keep a low profile?" Drostan snapped, still rubbing his wrist. "Why the metal thug?"

"We figured you'd be a little trigger-happy after what happened, and we didn't want to surprise you in your room again," Mitch replied.

"If you were watching me, I could have used some backup. We nearly got killed."

"But you didn't," Mitch said.

Drostan wished he could wipe the smirk off Mitch's face. "It was close enough. Look, I'm tired. What do you want?"

"We made sure the horses got back safely," Mitch said. "You could be nicer."

Drostan checked his temper with effort. "Thank you," he said in a strained voice. "Finian is a good cop—and a good source. I don't want him to get in trouble."

"He won't," Jacob said. "The Department will make sure the report gets 'lost', and the wagon won't be a problem."

Drostan eyed him skeptically. "I thought you were not acting officially."

Mitch shrugged. "We're not assigned to the case. But I told you—the Department is very interested in what's happening out at Vesta Nine. If they have any suspicion that the river deaths have a connection to the mine, they'll cover up anything strange." He shrugged. "Jacob and I just want to nail Tumblety and Brunrichter for good."

He paused. "And before you ask—no one from the Department is saying a word about any of this, which is pretty strange. When we've been in trouble before, my sources have kept me updated on everything. This time, they're dry as a bone. Someone high-up is keeping this very quiet."

"All right," Drostan conceded. "What do I owe you for corralling the horses?"

"We want to know what you saw," Mitch replied.

"I thought you were tailing me. If you saw me, you saw what happened."

"We heard about the incident from a third party," Jacob said.

"The priest."

Jacob shrugged. Drostan felt his temper rise. "I'll tell you what I saw, but I want to know who the priest was. Dammit! I can't do my job if I don't know what's going on."

"One thing at a time," Mitch said. "Tell your story, and we'll tell ours."

Drostan glared, but recounted the evening's adventure from the time he and Finian examined the body behind the Highland Club.

"You didn't see any kind of witchy objects around the body?" Jacob prodded.

"No. And no one flew by on a broom, either," Drostan said. "I saw a savaged corpse, and not enough blood on the ground for what was done. I saw shadows that didn't come from any natural thing. And I saw a priest appear out of nowhere and dispel what I can best describe as a demon."

Mitch and Jacob exchanged a glance. "It wasn't a demon," Mitch said "But it might have been a *gessyan*."

"Tell me something I hadn't figured out for myself."

"All right," Jacob said. "The priest who rescued you was Father Matija. He's with the *Logonje*."

"What are they, some kind of Slavic community group?"

Jacob managed a half-smile. "A secret society of priests committed to banishing evil spirits."

Drostan was silent for a moment. "Well, damn. How'd he know where we were?"

Mitch shrugged. "That's what he does. We don't control him. He answers to a higher authority."

"Who, God?"

"The President's secret cabinet," Jacob said drolly. "Seriously. The *Logonje* have a higher security clearance even than the Department."

"But you know each other?"

Mitch nodded. "Sure. We all know each other. Whether or not we tell each other anything—that's the rub. But in this case, we're in luck. Matija is one of the good guys. He plays fair with us, even when the brass is mum."

"Tell him thank you for me," Drostan said, forcing down his bruised ego. "I really thought Finian and I were dead men."

"You would have been, if he hadn't gotten there in time," Mitch replied. "He's pretty sure that it was a *gessyan* that attacked you, but the truth is, we just don't know much about them. And to our knowledge, this was the first sighting of this particular type of *gessyàn*, since all prior reports have been of the Night Hag. That's why we need your help."

Drostan gave him a quizzical glare. "You're the high-falutin' Department. I'm a lousy private investigator. And you want *me* to help *you*?"

"A partnership, then," Jacob said. "Since I speak the language of a lot of the miners over at the Vesta mines who might or might not have seen something."

"And who definitely won't say anything to anyone who looks like they're official," Mitch added.

"I think Vesta Nine dug too deep and let something out," Drostan said, deciding that the night had already gone seriously cock-eyed, and one more crazy statement couldn't hurt.

"We think so, too," Jacob said. "But we've got no proof."

"So we've got a supernatural force that just might be something loosed from the deep regions, and we're flying blind," Mitch added. "And we've got sightings that say Tumblety and Brunrichter are back in the area, but how they're connected, we don't know yet. And while we dither around, people keep dying."

"About that—" began Drostan.

"I'm afraid that if anyone goes looking, what's left of the police wagon and the body will be gone," Jacob said. "That's how the Department works, especially if they want to keep something secret. They'll get to people, pull strings. The police won't bother about the killing, because their records will say that it didn't exist. The horses are safe. The dead man was a vagrant, so there won't be a family inquiring. Only you and Finian—and a few others—will know differently."

"I just wish someone would give that poor dead blighter an honest burial," Drostan said wearily. "I don't know who stirred up the Night Hag and the *gessyan*, or what they want, but I can't imagine that a drunk in a carriage lot had aught to do with any of it."

"That's just it," Jacob said. "None of us know much about it either. And there will be more casualties—like the miners at Vesta Nine, and like the dead vagabonds—unless we find out."

"Father Matija doesn't know?"

Mitch shook his head. "He's an ally, not an investigator. Matija has other responsibilities. He doesn't kick demon ass full-time."

"On the other hand, I'm already in too far to back out, is that it?" Drostan grumbled. He was tired and he hurt, and right now, he wanted nothing more than his own bed.

"You said it," Jacob said with a shrug. "But I don't think you want to walk away from this. Not when you still haven't figured out what all this has to do with Thomas Desmet's murder."

"All right," Drostan said after a moment. "But I want something in return. If there's anything—*anything*—you can do to help me find out who killed Thomas Desmet, I want your word that you'll do it."

Mitch and Jacob exchanged glances. "Fair enough," Storm said finally.

"Anything else?" Drostan asked. "Because I've had a rough day, and I could use some shut-eye."

"I'll send you a mecha-pigeon," Mitch said.

"A what?"

Mitch grinned. "A clockwork carrier pigeon. He'll roost near your window, until you need him. When you want to get us a message, just slip it in the capsule on his leg. It's a bit more discreet than blasting out a telegram."

Drostan nodded. "When and if I find out anything—I'll let you know. Now if you'll excuse me—" He pushed past Mitch and headed for the street. "I could really use some sleep."

Neither of the agents tried to detain Drostan as he headed resolutely toward the boarding house.

The night was far spent, and it would be dawn soon. Mrs. Mueller was fast asleep as Drostan trudged up the steps toward his room, trying to tread quietly so as not to wake her. He was relieved to find no surprises waiting for him when he opened the door to his room. Instead. Olivia the ghost girl paced by the window.

"I haven't seen you in a while," Drostan said quietly.

I was worried about you, Olivia replied. *Bad things happened tonight.*

Drostan tried to shrug it off. "I'm an investigator. It's a rough business."

Olivia turned toward him. *Ghosts talk among themselves. The ghosts out there, they're afraid. Not much scares the dead.*

"Talk to me," he whispered. "Because I'm missing pieces in all this." Drostan took off his battered overcoat, stained with grass and mud from the night's adventures, and pulled off his shoes. Then he sat down in his chair and waited for Olivia to speak.

There are more miners than usual among us, she said. *Always a lot of them. Dangerous business. But now—something's killing them. Something that lives in the shadows.*

"What? *Gessyan*?"

Olivia gave an eloquent shrug. *I don't know everything just because I'm dead. But these new ghosts are in a bad way. Something ate them—took their energy. No one should die like that.*

Drostan was so tired that he was having difficulty keeping his eyes open, and he wondered if, when he woke, he would decide that this was all a dream. "What can I do to help?"

Find the witch. The Witch of Pulawski Way. Find him and you'll find answers.

"What if he's dead?" Drostan asked. "What then?"

Olivia's turned away sadly. *Then more people will die. Maybe everyone.*

Chapter FOURTEEN

"EVERY TIME I see this place, I can hardly believe it's real, it's so big." Miska Kovach craned his neck to see the tops of the huge chimneys at the Edgar Thomson Works in Braddock. The massive plant—created to make Bessemer rails for the railroad—took up over sixty acres and had its own wharf on the Monongahela River.

"They say the Edgar Thomson makes a million tons of steel a year," Jake said. The huge steel mill was like a man-made mountain, belching smoke, steam and, from the highest peaks, jets of flame. Railcars laden with steel or filled with raw materials clanked into and out of the yard at all hours of the day and night.

"It's impressive in daylight. It's monstrous at night," Rick observed. The flames from the burn-off cast the night in a hellish glow. Although the plant, a modern marvel, had electric lights around the perimeter, there were large, dark gaps between the light posts where anything might lurk.

"Let's see what's so special about Eban Hodekin," Jake said, taking a deep breath to banish his jitters.

"Makes you wonder, doesn't it, why a man like Dr. Nils knows the night shift supervisor at a steel mill?" Kovach mused. "Wouldn't think they'd exactly go to the same dinner parties, if you know what I mean."

Jake had been mulling over the same incongruity, without coming to any conclusion. "He said Hodekin was a source for a folklore book. Maybe that's true, maybe it isn't. One thing's for sure: if Nils thinks Hodekin might know something about what killed Father, I don't care how they know each other. Let's get going."

The night guard eyed them suspiciously when they approached the gate. "Hey! Turn around! Factory's closed for the night unless you work here. Don't look like you do."

Jake suspected the steel mill did not get a large number of gentleman callers with bodyguards arriving in the middle of the night. "We're here to see Mr. Eban Hodekin."

The guard frowned. "Mr. Hodekin's busy. He didn't leave no word he was expecting anyone."

"We need to speak with him," Jake replied. "It's important."

"Gettin' the steel rolled into rails, that's important. Talkin' ain't."

"Just tell Hodekin we're here to see him," Rick said.

The guard glowered at him, then called over to one of three other security men who were warming themselves around a barrel fire. "Hey, Miller! Go tell Hodekin he's got visitors."

Miller shuffled off toward the main factory building, in no particular hurry. Jake, Rick, and Kovach waited impatiently for what seemed like forever until Miller trudged back.

"Boss says to send them in," he reported with a shrug.

The guard glowered at them. "All right. Get on with you. No trouble, you hear?"

"Where exactly do we find Mr. Hodekin?" Jake asked. Kovach had grown testy with the guard's attitude, and had moved close enough to loom over the man. If the guard suspected that the bulge beneath Kovach's left arm was a gun, he did not scare easily.

"Take the first door, up the steps, go to the right. You'll see a sign that says 'office'. That's the place—if he's not out on the shop floor like he's supposed to be. But you can't just walk in there. I'll have to send an escort. Wait here." The guard's expression made it clear that he did not appreciate the extra work. He walked a few paces to speak with one of the security guards, and both men leveled a suspicious glance in their direction. After a bit more muted discussion, the two men walked back.

"Come with me," the guard said grudgingly.

Kovach said something in Hungarian beneath his breath. Jake did not recognize the phrase, but from the way the guard stiffened, he assumed that it was not complimentary.

"Try not to annoy the natives," Jake murmured as they walked away. "I've got no desire to have a ladle of hot steel dumped down my back."

"Maybe we should have brought Charles with us," Rick said. "I wouldn't mind the extra muscle."

"I didn't want to explain a *werkman*," Jake replied. "And I wasn't sure how well he'd fare with the heat and smoke at the mill." The smell of the coke fires filled the air, and dozens of other materials added their tang. Jake resisted the urge to hold his nose, and wondered how the men who toiled in the huge mill managed to cope.

"He'd be handy in a fight," Kovach added.

"I'm hoping to get out of tonight without a fight, thank you very much," Jake replied.

"What fun is that?" Rick replied with a lopsided smile.

The guard opened the door to the mill, and a blast of air hit them, so hot it made Jake take a step back, thinking they had nearly entered the furnace instead. The guard gave a nasty chuckle.

The heat was unlike anything Jake had ever felt. Even the scorching heat of the Egyptian desert was different. There, the heat was natural. Here, the heat was contained within a cavernous building, where the air was foul with the smell of coal smoke and machine oil and unwashed bodies. Jake felt sweat bead his forehead, and by the time they were halfway across the room, rivulets were running down his back, so that his shirt clung to his skin. His eyes burned and teared. The clank of the chains and the bang of tools and molds was deafening, enough to make him feel as if his head were inside a ringing bell.

How do they do it? he wondered, watching the red-faced men who toiled at the machinery. It was common knowledge that the workers of New Pittsburgh's steel mills worked twelve-hour days, seven days a week, save for the Fourth of July. *Not a wonder few live to old age.*

They approached the office door, and the guard rapped once, then turned the knob. "Mr. Hodekin? These are the men here to see you."

"Send them in," a gravelly voice replied.

"Thank you, Mr. Hodekin," Jake replied, pushing past the reluctant guard. "This truly is a matter of life or death."

Hodekin muttered something under his breath while the guard eyed them warily, ready to escort them out. "All right," Hodekin replied grudgingly. "But make it quick. I've got work to do." The guard stepped back, making it clear that he would wait outside to escort them back out of the mill.

Jake glanced around the room, and the dim light revealed little except a battered desk piled with papers. He had to look twice to spot the top of a man's head nearly hidden by the stacks of documents.

"Mr. Hodekin. I'm Jake Desmet."

"Desmet. Any relation to Brand and Desmet?" Hodekin replied, not stirring from where he sat.

"Thomas Desmet was my father," Jake said. "I've stepped up as one of the managing partners in the firm since his death. Rick Brand," he added with a nod toward his friend, "is one of my business partners." He let Kovach go unannounced, which was how his bodyguard preferred things, but Hodekin could probably figure out his reason for being present.

Jake heard shuffling and the creak of a chair. A short man bustled around the desk, barely standing taller than Jake's waist. Eban Hodekin was a stooped old man with wisps of gray hair straying from his mottled scalp. His eyes were wide-set and large, with a jutting jaw and a crooked nose that seemed out of proportion to his face. Hodekin had a barrel chest and muscular, bowed legs. His hands were calloused from hard work and scarred from dangerous jobs. Jake thought he looked more like a gremlin than a mine foreman.

"What do you want?" Hodekin demanded in a thick German accent.

To Jake's surprise, Kovach's face drained of color, and he reached for his gun.

"Don't," Hodekin said, fixing Kovach with a glare. "You can't hurt me. And so long as you follow the rules, I won't hurt you."

He turned his attention back to Jake and Rick. "I'll ask you again. What do you want?"

Jake had no idea what had just transpired between Kovach and Hodekin, but this wasn't the time to ask. "We understand that you are an expert on folklore, and we were hoping you might be able to help us. We're trying to find out more about *gessyan*," he added, watching Hodekin carefully for a reaction. "We were told by a mutual acquaintance you might know something about them."

"Why?" Hodekin demanded. "You're not telling me all. You want to know about something... very dangerous." He moved slowly around Jake, and Jake felt as if he were being sniffed by a wolf, a predator who could read him by his scent.

"We believe my father was murdered," Jake said with a sigh. "I'm trying to find out by whom. We think he was murdered because of an object—or objects—that somebody thought had come into the company's possession. And we think that whatever the object is, it has something to do with *gessyan*."

"Say on," Hodekin snapped.

"Rumor has it a wealthy patron is looking for an old Polish book and some magical Russian stones. The book was by Marcin of Krakow, about *gessyan*," Rick replied. "Such a collector, if he thought Jake's father had the book and some artifacts, might have wanted them badly enough to kill."

"So?" Hodekin demanded. "What's that got to do with me?"

"We were told that you might know something about *gessyan*, something from folklore or oral tradition that would give us some insight," Jake said. "I don't know if *gessyan* caused my father's death, but I'm going to chase every bit of information until I find out what actually happened."

Hodekin fixed him with an unsettlingly intense stare. "Pray that the *gessyan* have nothing to do with it."

"They're real, then?"

Hodekin paused, then nodded. "Ach. They're real."

"What are they?"

Hodekin's eyes narrowed. "They're an ancient evil. Do you remember your catechism?"

It had been a while, and Jake hadn't paid particular attention at the time, but he nodded. "Yes."

"'And the Earth was without form, and void. And darkness was upon the face of the deep,'" Hodekin quoted. "Sound familiar?"

Jake nodded. "What's that got to do—"

"Before the world was, the *gessyan* were," Hodekin snapped. "Eons passed between those sentences you read in Genesis. The *gessyan* moved across the face of the deep when it was dark. They like it like that," he hissed, leaning his misshapen face closer so that Jake could see his snaggled teeth. "No one knows how many of them there are. The *gessyan* move through the core of the world, going to and fro from place to place."

"What did they eat, without people to feed on?" Jake asked.

"The energy of the Earth itself. Blood is a tasty bonus," Hodekin replied in a tone that made Jake shiver.

"What happened to the *gessyan*? Why haven't they been around until now?" Rick asked.

Hodekin walked back around his stacks of paper and sat down heavily in his leather desk chair. "Oh, they've been around. They can travel through the core of the Earth, from deep place to deep place. They are legion, you know," Hodekin added. "They used to be able to walk among mankind in the night. But long ago, someone locked them in the deep places of the world. That 'someone' was Marcin of Krakow. I know. I was there when he bound them. And they stayed bound—until recently."

"What changed?"

Hodekin shook his head. "Don't know. Someone broke the spell? Destroyed the wards? Whatever it was, the deep mining woke things up that should have kept on sleeping. Seems that some of them got out." He fixed Jake with a pointed stare. "That's trouble."

"Why? Are they connected to the murders near the rivers? We've heard rumors of the Night Hag—some call her *Nocnitsa*. Is she *gessyan*?"

Hodekin smiled. "Oh, yes. She is one type of *gessyan*, though there are many. As for the deaths down by the rivers, they could have been done by *gessyan*."

Jake felt a chill down his back. "Surely they can't—"

"Did you come for information, or to argue?" Hodekin snapped. "A long, long time, they were bound. Centuries. And then about fifty years ago, again they were disturbed—in Russia, again they were bound. Since that time, they've been quiet. And now, since the Vesta Nine went deep, bloodshed." He paused. "Someone's got to seal them back up again, or there will be hell to pay."

"I'm just trying to find out how my father died."

"You're asking the wrong question," Hodekin said. "You should be asking *why* your father died. Who wanted him dead? What did he know—or what did someone think he knew? Who was he helping? And what did somebody powerful stand to lose?"

Jake stared at Hodekin, stunned. "I don't think—"

"No, you don't. Your father got into something over his head. Maybe there were forces at work he didn't understand." He leaned across the table, and Jake could smell his foul breath. "Or maybe, your father knew exactly what he was doing and was willing to die for it." He sat back down. "You won't know until you follow the threads."

"Where?" Jake pressed.

"Someone stood to profit. Figure out who, and you're on the right track."

"Can the *gessyan* be bound again?" Rick asked. "Could that be done? Or worse, could someone control the *gessyan* that got loose, make them do his will?"

"Maybe. It would take powerful magic," Hodekin said. "Old power doesn't recognize your new, steam-powered toys. There are things in this world much older than you realize. The old ones only respect power as old as they are."

Like vampires and witches, Jake thought. *It's time I had another talk with Andreas Thalberg.*

"I've told you all I know," Hodekin said roughly. "Leave."

No one spoke until they were out past the gates. "You saw something in there, when we first met Hodekin, something that made you go for your gun," Jake said. "What was it?"

Kovach looked more rattled than Jake had ever seen him. "Hodekin isn't human."

Rick gave him a sidelong glance. "I'll grant you that he's the ugliest man I've seen in a long while—"

Kovach shook his head. "No, Rick. You're not listening. He isn't human. We have stories about his kind, back where I come from. Kobolds."

"What the hell is a kobold?"

"Have you ever heard of a hobgoblin?"

Jake frowned. "Sure. Little guys who hide in gardens and play tricks on people."

"Is that what they tell children nowadays? It's a crime!" Kovach sighed. "That's a dishonest version, if that's what you've heard."

"Inform us," Jake replied.

"Where I come from, kobolds are spirits—and not particularly nice ones," Kovach said. "They live near water, and in caves and mines. Sometimes, they trick people just for spite. They like gold, and they can be bribed to do nasty things to people." He shook his head. "They're bad news. We tell children to stay away from them. They're a bloody danger."

"And you're saying that Hodekin is a kobold?" Rick asked. "If they trick people, how can we believe anything he told us?"

"I'm sure he's a kobold. As for whether or not he was lying, who knows? There'd be no love lost between them and the *gessyan*, and the kobolds would probably have more experience with *gessyan* than anyone else."

"He said he remembers Marcin of Krakow," Rick added. "That's got to be worth something."

Kovach nodded. "Something's afoot we really don't understand, something bigger than we thought. I think your father got in way over his head, and it killed him. My job is to keep the same thing from happening to you two."

They did not speak again until they were at their carriage, where Charles sat in the driver's seat, waiting for their return.

"And for the record, I don't like or trust Hodekin," Kovach said as he opened the door for Jake and Rick to enter the coach.

"Neither do I," Jake replied. "But it doesn't seem that he's working against us."

"Rough when we don't know who our enemies actually are," Rick said dryly.

"Or our friends," Kovach added, closing the door before he swung up to the seat next to Charles.

Even the darkness could not disguise the fact that Braddock was a rough town, an overgrown mill patch with dreams of greatness. Smoke hung low over the company houses, row upon row of identical, cheaply-built dwellings smudged with coal dust. Most looked hard-used, though Jake could see here and there where care had been taken, flowers planted.

Steel work was hard and dangerous, and the men who made their living in the mills played hard, too. It wasn't unusual for bar fights to spill out into the streets, or for lovers' quarrels to end up involving the neighbors in an outright brawl. Life was lived large and loud in the cramped quarters and narrow streets, because existence was an uncertain thing.

The carriage turned down a dark stretch of road. Old storefronts lined the streets, but in this section, the shops looked down on their luck. Awnings hung askew, with tattered canvas fluttering down, and here and there a broken window was boarded up. Stray dogs slunk along the walls, avoiding the drunks that curled up in the doorways of abandoned buildings. Most of the streetlights were broken.

Without warning, fire burst from an alley, along with the clatter of gunfire as Jake's carriage passed the shadowed mouth of the street. Shots fired, round after round, in the trademark rhythm of a Gatling gun, like quick drumbeats, striking the carriage. Jake and Rick dove for the floor. The shots clanged against the steel plates inside the carriage doors and cracked loudly against the bulletproof glass. Outside, Jake could hear Kovach and Charles returning fire as the horses took off at a full gallop through the empty streets. The fire continued to strike the back of the carriage as they tried to escape.

Someone's got to hear the gunfire and wonder, Jake thought, sliding into a squat on the floor facing Rick as the carriage bounced and jostled at high speed. Kovach had built some surprises into a few of the Brand and Desmet carriages that went beyond bulletproof doors and windows. Jake pulled down the tufted velvet upholstery of the front-facing seat to reveal a secret panel of controls.

He pressed a button. Gears whirred. The back panel of the carriage dropped away to reveal a Gatling gun turret of their own, its barrel protruding through a swiveling bubble of bulletproof glass and metal. Rick moved into position and laid down a blanket of cover fire behind them to deter their attackers from following. Stray shots hit a gas line in one of the street lamps and the explosion reverberated from the hills, sending a pillar of fire into the night.

Jake gave a cry of hell bent exultation as Rick's gunfire cut down several of the gunner crew. In response, the survivors sent a fresh hail of bullets streaming toward the carriage.

More shots rang out, this time from the front of the carriage. Someone had expected them to bolt, and decided to take no chances. Shots clanged against the door, and although the steel stopped them from penetrating, they rocked the carriage and made a deafening racket.

Kovach and Charles had fitted the horses with black steel armor that covered heads and body, almost like the knights of old. Impractical and too attention-getting during the day, the armor was almost impossible to see at night. Charles was fairly well-protected by his metal body, and Kovach had steel shields he called his 'duck blind' that pulled up to surround the drivers in an emergency. Even so, the carriage could only take so much punishment before horses were killed or the carriage's defenses were overwhelmed, and Jake feared that despite their efforts, they were rapidly reaching that point.

Abruptly, the Gatling gun behind them stopped firing. Men's screams carried on the night air. The exploded street lamp cast its bonfire light on the street, and Rick exclaimed and pointed as Jake saw the broken bodies of their attackers strewn about the street.

The gunfire from the second Gatling ceased. More screams echoed, then silence. Whatever had slaughtered their attackers now stood between the carriage and escape either from the front or the back. Charles might be able to take the carriage down a side street, but attempting any speed was suicidal in the crowded, trash-strewn alleys. Jake and the others were pinned, about to discover whether their rescuers were any less of a threat than the attackers they had stymied.

"Hold your fire!" The voice boomed with unnatural volume, and for a moment, Jake thought that the police had descended with their bullhorns. Instead, through the curved glass of the hidden gunner's mount, Jake saw dark-clad figures emerge one by one from the wreckage behind them.

These men wore no special protective gear, no uniforms or insignia, but they moved like predators: feral and wary. A sharp rap came at the carriage door.

"Jake Desmet, Rick Brand. You are safe. Open the door. I would have a word with you."

Jake recognized the voice and opened the carriage door to see Andreas Thalberg, standing in the rubble-strewn street as if it were the most natural thing in the world to find him in a mill town-turned-war zone.

"Why? How?" Jake asked warily as he and Rick climbed out of the carriage.

A ghost of a smile quirked at Andreas's mouth. "Why? Because I value our partnership. How?" He clucked his tongue. "My dear boy. Mortal guns matter little when one is fast and deathless."

In the gaslight flames, Jake took a closer look at their rescuer. Andreas's jacket and vest were streaked with blood. Bullet holes had torn his tailored suit to shreds in places, yet he stood before Jake seemingly unharmed.

"Did you know this was going to happen?" Rick asked, echoing Jake's thoughts.

"No," Andreas replied. "If I had, I would have sent my men on ahead to remove the problem." He shook his head. "I sent them to follow you, and to ensure you reached your home safely. It was unfortunate that they were unable to intervene before the unpleasantness erupted."

"Who were the men who attacked us?"

Andreas glanced toward the silenced Gatling gun behind them, even as his vampires used their speed and strength to gather up the dead and remove the large guns before the authorities arrived.

"Veles would be likely to use magic instead of force," Andreas replied. "But if Thwaites is involved, he's probably got a private army like most of New Pittsburgh's elite. I've confirmed that Thwaites and Veles are the owners of the Vesta Nine mine. And you were right—Thwaites is buying up magical objects. But as is often the case, answers yield more questions." He paused.

"And as you already know by now, someone is committed to making sure you two, and those helping you, stop asking those questions—permanently."

Chapter FIFTEEN

"It's a beauty, isn't it?" Adam Farber regarded his handiwork with pride as Rick turned the odd-looking weapon in his hands.

"What *exactly* does it do?" Rick asked.

Adam grinned and jerked his head to flip a stray lock of lank sandy-brown hair out of his eyes. "Just what you asked. It uses manipulated energy to push objects or people away with a cold wave of force. Actually, depending on how high you have it turned up, it's the difference between shoving someone and throwing them across the room."

Rick chuckled. "That sounds perfect. What powers it?"

Adam pointed to a small chamber. "Tourmaquartz crystal—really, just a chip of one. But it's enough to superheat steam and contain the expansion, channeling it into the weapon—in other words, all that force comes out here, like being shoved by an invisible hand," he said, touching the muzzle.

"Does it have any unfortunate aftereffects?" Cullan Adair, Brand and Desmet's ace airship pilot, regarded the force gun suspiciously.

Adam looked skeptical. "Like what?"

"Oh, you know. Missing body parts. Large bloody holes. Ruptured hearts. That kind of thing," Rick replied, still gazing at the chunky gun with admiration.

"Nothing we've found so far," Adam replied. "Then again, we haven't wanted to try it out on a live subject just yet. It's still in prototype."

"How about showing me what it does?" Rick asked.

Adam grinned, always happy to show off his newest inventions. He gestured for Rick and Cullan to follow him deeper into the underground lab to where Adam had set up a test firing range. On the way, Adam grabbed a half-empty cup of black coffee and downed it without breaking pace, then set the cup aside at the next worktable.

Three dressmaker's dummies were set up on wheeled stands. On the floor beneath them, Rick could see paint marking off a scale in one-foot increments all the way to the far wall.

"All right," Adam said. "I designed this to fire like a rifle. You shoulder it, press the button to have the tourmaquartz engage—" A rising whistle interrupted him, painfully loud, and the crystal chamber glowed brightly. "And then you pull the trigger," Adam shouted, since Rick had his hands over his ears.

Whoosh. Two things happened at almost the same instant. The dressmaker's dummy was hurled backwards into the wall, so hard that a crack snaked up the plaster, and Adam was thrown in the opposite direction, skidding to a halt on his backside halfway across the lab. His eyes were wide with triumph.

"That. Was. Amazing!" Adam said with a look of utter wonder.

Rick ran to give Adam a hand-up, which the inventor accepted gratefully. "Well? What did you think?"

Rick chucked. "As you said, it still needs some work. But nothing caught on fire, and the wall will survive. Although the dummy isn't in good shape."

Adam gazed ruefully at the ruined dressmaker's dummy. The wire ribcage was flattened by the force, and the form hung drunkenly from its support post. "Yeah," Adam admitted. "But it's a tremendous improvement over the last time."

A nearby fire extinguisher and a flared pattern of scorch marks farther down the back wall gave Rick a sense of how the earlier tests had ended.

"Wow, what's this one? Looks deadly," Rick said as he picked up what looked like a cross between a cannon and a rifle. "The ammo must be huge!"

"That's not a weapon. Or rather it's not supposed to be—it's mine for emergencies. After the last unfortunate incident, I wanted something that would let me quickly shut down an invention if it was going badly. I call it a 'disrupter'. In layman's terms, it sends out a cone shaped burst of energy that shuts down mechanical or electrical devices." Adam carefully took the disrupter from Rick and placed it in the cabinet.

"Adam, not to scare you, but that's a hell of a weapon. If the government or military..."

"And that is why you need to forget you ever saw it," Adam interrupted, looking Rick directly in the eyes with a hand on his shoulder. "Please."

"Yeah, Cullan and I didn't see anything... so how soon do you think you can work out the bugs in the force gun?" Rick asked. "I have the feeling we're going to need several of these soon, given the way things are going."

Adam stared at the gun, deep in thought. "A couple of days, if I'm not interrupted. I've got some ideas." He sighed. "The real hitch is getting enough tourmaquartz. It's very rare. Only a few mines exist, and the price has skyrocketed since we've started finding uses for it."

"Just let me know what you need," Rick assured him. "I'll get you the money."

"Thanks. But most of the time it's not about cost—it's about availability. Even Mr. Tesla has difficulty getting a steady supply."

Cullan was looking at the force gun. "Do you think you could come up with something that would work in a gunner's mount on an airship?" he asked. "I like the idea of a gun without sparks. Sparks are an airman's worst enemy."

Adam nodded in agreement. "I think I can come up with something. You'd just want the engines to be at high enough power to overcome the recoil."

Cullan grinned. "Oh, the *Allegheny Princess* has power enough for that, I warrant. I'd love to have a couple of these for the fleet."

"Add it to my tab," Rick said drolly, slapping Adam on the back. "What else do you have for me?"

Adam walked over to his desk and lifted a leather airman's cap with an unusual pair of goggles attached. The goggles' lenses were thicker than usual, and had wires coming out of them, connecting to a small box on the back of the cap.

"I call these 'gadget glasses'," Adam said, pride tingeing his voice. "Thanks to another chip of tourmaquartz, these babies will let you see through the eyes of a *werkman* a short distance away. It uses aetheric waves to transmit."

He hefted the cap in his hands. "I'm working on making them smaller. Less bulky. But the point is, you could have a *werkman* scouting for you in a dangerous situation and see what he sees without putting yourself in the line of fire."

"Nice," Rick said. "I'd like to get a couple of those, as well as those remote transmitters you made for the Department, the ones that let you hear and speak to someone from a distance?"

Adam nodded. "I'm ahead of you. I've got a pair you can take with you."

"And Drostan asked for some of your signal markers," Rick added, as if rattling off a shopping list. "He wants a way to mark places or things so he can find them again if he needs to go back to them."

Adam took a bag out of a desk drawer, counted out a quantity of brass disks roughly the size of half-dollars but three times as thick. "I've got a dozen you can take with you."

"Drostan will be very happy about that," Rick replied, taking the pouch from Adam. "What else?"

Adam brightened. "Oh, I think you'll like this." He rummaged around on one of the work tables and withdrew a box the size of a notepad and as thick as a can of sardines. Indicators and a row of lights filled the front.

"What does it do?" Rick asked, puzzled.

"It's a Maxwell box. Measures the fluctuation in energy that accompanies the appearance of a supernatural entity," Adam answered, preoccupied with an errant wire on the box. "Your private investigator who can see spirits helped me do some preliminary tests. Set it on a low frequency, and you can actually attract ghosts. Turn it up too high, and, well, you get more than you bargained for," he admitted with an expression that suggested he had discovered the outcome the hard way.

"Once more, in English?" Cullan said.

Adam frowned then rolled his eyes. "For the non-scientist, I'll use small words," he replied with a side-long look at Rick, though his tone was good humored. "We—*scientists*—have noticed that whenever something spooky or woo-woo happens, there's a change in nearby electrical and magnetic fields. Usually, the shift starts out small, then rises as an appearance is about to happen."

"Thank you. Your small words were quite helpful. Or to say it another way, it's a ghost caller, or a ghost fishing net, depending on how you set it."

Adam's face twisted in an expression that told Rick the inventor was torn between precision and essential meaning. "Basically, yes. We think it may also help identify where magic is being used, but we haven't studied that part much. It's all still in the testing phase."

"Can you show us?"

Adam frowned, considering. "It's the middle of the day. There are a couple of ghosts here in the Castle, but they don't usually get active until late at night."

"Aw, come on. There's gotta be something."

Adam thought for a moment. "If we go back a block, there's an abandoned building that sits over some old graves from the French and Indian War. Whoever's buried there doesn't like it. Locals avoid the place, which is why it's abandoned; no one can stay in it for long. We could try there."

"Come on then!"

Adam headed for the back entrance, where the freight elevator led out into the alley.

"Miska's waiting at the front," Cullan pointed out. "Shouldn't you bring him along?"

Rick rolled his eyes. "Mark's got some Old World superstitions when it comes to ghosts. He'd probably rather stay where he is. Besides, what's he going to do? Shoot at shadows?"

Reluctantly, Cullan joined them as they stepped into the freight elevator and clanked to the top, slipping out the back entrance of the Castle. Kovach was nowhere to be seen. Adam gestured for them to follow him. Shouts and cheers sounded in the distance, and

Rick peeked around a corner to see a crowd gathering around one of Maguire's agitators. Some of the crowd held hand-lettered signs aloft on wooden poles, while others waved their handkerchiefs to and fro in solidarity with the speaker, who looked like he was just warming to his topic.

"Maguire's folks, again," he muttered when the others gave him questioning looks. Skirting the crowd, Adam led them down a back alley toward a decrepit building. A name had been painted over the door, but it was faded with age, most of the letters illegible. Trash and dry leaves crowded the stoop, and the place looked forlorn and bleak.

"This is it," Adam said, as a shutter banged on one of the upstairs windows.

"Can't say it's the kind of place I'd choose to be a ghost," Cullan observed. "Personally, if I'm going to haunt somewhere, it had better be a pub!"

Despite Cullan's humor, Rick repressed a shiver. Just being near the old building made the hairs on the back of his neck stand up. Rick had glimpsed a few ghosts on some of the acquisition runs he and Jake had made, and he did not relish repeating the experience.

A low moan came from the direction of the abandoned building, though the wind was still. Boards covered the door and the first-floor windows, but some of the second floor windows were uncovered, grimy and dark. Rick looked up, and for an instant, thought he glimpsed a pale face. When he blinked, it was gone.

"On second thoughts, maybe I can take your word for it on that box," Cullan said with a nervous glance at the derelict structure.

Adam withdrew the Maxwell box from under his arm and switched it on. The box lit up and began to hum as Adam calibrated it, turning knobs and watching the needles and colored lights with rapt attention.

"Give me a second, and I may have a ghost to show you," Adam said. "The settings are touchy. If you turn it up too high, it creates some problems."

"Like what?" Rick wanted to know.

But before Adam could answer, two armed men emerged from around the side of the building. "Stay where you are," the taller of the two gunmen ordered.

Rick had a gun tucked into the back of his waistband, but he wouldn't be able to draw it before one of the gunmen got off a shot. He did not know whether Cullan was armed, but he was sure the airman at least had a shiv in his boot. Adam was likely to be a liability in a fight, Rick conceded. *Best to watch for an opening,* he thought, raising his hands in surrender, as did Cullan.

"Hey, you in the white coat!" the second gunman said. "Drop that box and put your hands up!"

Adam gave the knob on the front of the Maxwell box a hard twist and laid it on the ground pointed toward the house. A faint, high-pitched squeal began to build as Adam stepped away from the box.

The first gunman came a few steps closer. "We can do this real civilized. All we want is the guy in the white coat. No one needs to get hurt. Our boss just needs him for a project." He gave a snaggle-toothed smile that was patently insincere. "Just come with us, and there won't be trouble."

Bang. Bang. Bang. The shutters on the old building's second floor began to slap against the weathered boards and windows as if flung by a hurricane. Green lights flickered in the blackened interior, and the low moan grew to a loud wail.

"What the hell did you do?" the first gunman said to Adam, moving forward to grab the inventor by the arm.

A swirl of gray mist gathered around the upstairs window where Rick had seen the face, and streaked toward the men in the street below. The temperature plummeted around the abandoned house, and new tendrils of gray mist began to slink from other openings as the box emitted an ever more piercing squeal.

The gray ghosts threw the gunmen off guard, and Rick whipped his revolver out from behind his back, drawing down on the second thug. Adam rammed a bony elbow into the gut of the gunman holding him and twisted away, just as Cullan kicked out, knocking the gun from the attacker's hand.

Kovach and three guards ran into view around the corner, guns drawn, then skidded to a stop, dumbfounded by the scene in front of them.

The ghosts were angry and ready to visit their frustration on those who had dared disturb them, circling and diving at the living men locked in combat. Shrieks split the air. From inside the empty, abandoned building came a disquieting jumble of heavy footsteps, rattling window casements, banging shutters and heavy, thumping sounds. Green and blue orbs of light whirled and flitted in the darkness, visible through the grimy upstairs windows. The air was cold as winter, and a heavy sense of despair and vengeful fury hung over the area. The ghosts screeched toward the trapped mortals, and when the gray mist passed by, bloody claw marks appeared on arms and faces.

Adam focused on getting away from the thugs. Cullan tackled the man who had grabbed the engineer, taking both of them to the pavement as the ghosts howled around them. Rick squeezed off a shot, dropping the second thug with a hit to the knee as Cullan laid his opponent out cold with a right hook.

The ghosts did not take sides in the mortal fight. Their anger was focused on the living and their fury turned on Rick and the others. Kovach and his guards had nothing to shoot, and the ghosts quickly visited their frustration on them as well. Amid the cries and the futile attempts to run, Adam dove for the Maxwell box, like a baseball player sliding into home. The revenants tore at his skin and shredded his white coat, but Adam grabbed the box with bloody hands and spun the knob to zero.

The gray ghosts vanished. Just as abruptly, the old building fell silent, and the pulsing orbs of light winked out. In a heartbeat, the temperature returned to normal.

"What the hell just happened?" Kovach asked, wide-eyed and pale, as he and his guards moved with military precision to cuff the two thugs, who were nearly incoherent with terror. One of the attackers had soiled himself, and the other threw up on Kovach's shoes.

Everyone turned to look at Adam, who held the Maxwell box as if it were a container of nitroglycerin. He looked like he was in shock, and Rick moved behind him, putting his arm across his shoulders, ready to catch him if he passed out.

"It's the Maxwell box," Adam said, his voice reedy. "On lower settings, it just detects the anomalies in the electromagnetic field caused by supernatural manifestations—"

"In other words, it spots ghosts," Rick said.

Adam was too shaken to glare at Rick in response. "I'd never turned it all the way up, but I knew that the higher the setting, the more agitated the ghosts became. When we got jumped, I turned it on full blast. I thought it might provoke the ghosts into showing up, and that might help us get away. I never meant—" He spread his hands helplessly to indicate the bloody scratches and torn clothing.

"Humph," Kovach said, which seemed to cover his thoughts on the subject. He grabbed one of the thugs and hauled him to his feet. "First things first. Take out the trash, then get the rest of you back where you belong," he said with a pointed glance at Rick and Adam.

Two of Kovach's men hauled the wounded attackers away. Clawed and bloody, stinking of urine and vomit and petrified with fright, the thugs barely protested, as if they considered detainment preferable to their current situation.

Kovach and the other guard escorted Adam, Rick, and Cullan back to the rear door of Tesla-Westinghouse. "I can't let you out of my sight, apparently," Kovach muttered under his breath. Adam and Rick were subdued. Cullan still appeared badly rattled.

Adam headed back into the doorway, then turned. "Those guys followed us," Adam said, and his hands, still gripping the Maxwell box, were shaking. "They were watching the lab, waiting for me. And you can take them away, but whoever is behind this will send someone else. Sooner or later, you won't be here to help. Please—you've got to get me out of here."

Rick and Kovach traded a glance, and nodded. "Grab your stuff," Rick said. "Pack up whatever you can carry, and what we can fit in the carriage. You can come to my place for now. We'll come back tonight and get anything else that isn't nailed down."

"Really?" Adam looked up hopefully.

Rick placed a hand on his shoulder. "Yeah. We should have gotten you out before this. Jake and I meant what we said about a new lab for you—and I think we've got just the place for it. Now get your gear before anybody else comes along and takes a shot at us."

Chapter SIXTEEN

"Is he still out there?" Cady McDaniel asked as Nicki peered at the street from behind the velvet curtain in the parlor. "If we open the window, I can get him with the rifle."

"Pish posh," Nicki said. "If he were a little closer, I could probably get him with my derringer."

"No one is 'getting' anyone out my parlor window," Catherine Desmet said archly, although the hint of a smile softened her remonstrance.

"How about out of one of the bedroom windows, Aunt Catherine? The angle would be better from up there."

"Nicki—"

"You never let me have any fun!" Nicki said, stamping her foot.

"What if we sent one of the servants out with cookies—made with castor oil," Cady suggested.

"Heavens, no!" Catherine objected. "I won't have our cook's baking maligned."

"It was just an idea," Cady replied.

"Who do you think he is?" Nicki asked.

"A spy?" Cady suggested. "Sent here from a secretive foreign power—"

"I'd believe that, if he were dressed better," Nicki said, still hiding behind the curtain. "The overcoat doesn't fit well, and the hat is too big."

"What's the point of a disguise if you still look natty?" Cady asked, looking up from her stack of shipping rosters.

"I always look natty when I'm disguised," Nicki sniffed.

"Girls! A bit more attention to the matter at hand, please!" Catherine reproved, although her eyes were livelier than they had been since Thomas's death. Nicki smiled to herself, glad to have lightened Catherine's grief, if only for a moment or two.

Catherine sat with a stack of Thomas Desmet's journals and a well-used linen handkerchief. As she worked her way through her husband's day books, she alternated between sad smiles and dabbing tears from her eyes.

Cady applied her organizational skills to the records of Brand and Desmet's recent orders—both the ones on the official books, and the ones on the 'private' roster. Rick and George had already narrowed down the shipping receipts, manifests, and other paperwork, then turned the shortlist of missing or unusual shipments over to Cady for a second look, and to cross-check against the list Jake had found in Thomas's airship cabin. Her code-breaking talents came in handy as well, deciphering some of the cryptic notations. Meanwhile, Nicki put her knowledge of languages to good use working through correspondence, since Thomas Desmet's clientele came from all around the world.

Hours had passed, and they had found nothing to reveal a clue to Thomas's murder.

Just then, there was a sharp rap on the front door. The three women exchanged glances. Cady's hand strayed toward the Winchester rifle beneath the desk.

"I'll get the door," Nicki volunteered. "Keep an eye on our gentleman out front," she instructed Cady.

The housekeeper went to the door with a silver tray to receive calling cards. "Desmet residence, whom may I say is calling?" she asked archly. Nicki lurked in the shadows at the entrance to the hallway.

"I'm here to give my condolences to Mrs. Desmet," a man said. "I was an associate of her late husband's."

"I'll handle this," Nicki said, with a half-smile and a nod to the housekeeper. Nicki bustled up the hallway, drawing herself up to her full height, and affected the fragile, grief-stricken demeanor she had practiced in the mirror that morning.

"I'm afraid Mrs. Desmet isn't receiving callers at the moment," Nicki said. "I'm her niece, Veronique LeClercq. May I help you?"

The man who stood on the doorstep had the haircut of a soldier and the cocksure grin of one of the wastrel noble boys Nicki had left behind on the Continent. He had dark hair and a five o'clock shadow despite being clean shaven, with brown eyes and a solid, toned build that was attractive even beneath his off-the-rack suit.

"May I come in?" the stranger asked with a smile that was used to getting its way.

Nicki went for her best impression of an ill-tempered poodle and gave a withering stare. "I'm afraid I didn't catch your name?"

The look in the stranger's eyes said he knew a test of wills when he saw one. "Captain Mitch Storm. *Agent* Storm. Perhaps we should have this discussion somewhere more private?"

Nicki grabbed his arm and yanked him inside so quickly that Mitch stumbled on the carpet as she slammed the door behind him. "Let me see your badge, *Agent* Storm," she said.

Cady had come to the parlor doorway, Winchester rifle raised and ready. "Prove you're who you say you are," she demanded.

Mitch's eyes widened at the sight of the rifle. No one who saw Cady wield it would question whether or not she knew how to shoot. He stiffened when he heard Nicki pull back the hammer on her derringer behind him.

"Ladies. Please." He swallowed. "I swear, I mean you no harm."

"Is he the man you shot?" Cady asked. Nicki kept her derringer trained on Storm, and moved to the side enough to look at his feet.

"Don't think so. The other man was taller, heavier. And he'd never get those shoes on over the bandages."

"Hold out your badge," Cady demanded. "Or whatever papers you have." She looked at Nicki. "I'll cover you while you take them." She fixed her gaze on Mitch. "Don't try to grab her gun. Nicki's high-strung. It could go off. The last fellow who tried joined the women's choir."

Mitch swallowed hard, reached carefully into his jacket pocket with one hand while keeping the other well away from his body, and withdrew a leather flip-wallet. Nicki moved around to the side, remaining out of reach, her derringer pointed not at his face but at his groin.

"Throw the wallet over there," she said, indicating a spot on the carpet.

"Do you ladies do this a lot?" Mitch asked, his devil-may-care attitude severely crimped.

"More than you'd think," Nicki muttered. Cady covered her as she retrieved the wallet, and stepped back, still holding the derringer. With a flip of her wrist, she opened and studied the document.

"Agent Mitch Storm, Department of Supernatural Investigations." Nicki gave Storm the once-over. "If you're a government agent, why didn't you do something about the man outside? He's been watching the house for hours."

Storm met her gaze. "That's my partner. Agent Drangosavich."

Cady and Nicki exchanged glances. "I guess it's a good thing we didn't shoot him," Cady said, as if the topic came up every day.

"If you would please stop pointing your guns at me, I won't mention that it's a federal crime to shoot a government agent," Mitch said politely.

Nicki sniffed. "Only if they find the body."

"Do you ladies always greet visitors with loaded guns? Or have you been feeling threatened a lot lately?"

"If his credentials check out, please lower your guns and show him in." Catherine Desmet stood in the hallway, wearing a mourning cap and a heavy black veil that obscured her face.

Reluctantly, Cady and Nicki stepped back and allowed Mitch to pass, no longer keeping their guns leveled on him, but not putting them away, either. Mitch tried to look blasé as he walked ahead of them into the parlor.

"Mrs. Desmet. Please accept my apologies for bothering you at such a time," Mitch said.

Catherine eyed him stonily. "That depends, Mr. Storm, on why you've come." She gestured toward a chair. "Please. Sit." It was more imperative than request.

"Now," she said, smoothing her skirts. "What can possibly be so important that you've come to pay a business call, and placed a government agent outside my *house*, while we are in mourning?"

Mitch fidgeted in his chair. "Mrs. Desmet. I don't want to cause you further distress, but we are concerned that—"

"I'm not a shrinking violet, Agent Storm. If you're here to say something, say it plainly or leave."

Mitch took a deep breath and nodded. "Very well. We have reason to believe that your husband's death was not from natural causes."

"Ha," Nicki said with an unladylike snort of derision. "We'd already figured that out. Is that the best you can do?"

"How much did you know about your husband's business dealings, Mrs. Desmet?"

"I often helped him with his accounts. I would say that I was well-informed."

"We know that Brand and Desmet handled acquisitions for private clients. We think it might be possible that his death was related to one of these private deals."

Catherine drew herself up, sitting ram-rod straight. "Are you suggesting that there was anything improper about my husband's business dealings?"

Mitch held up his hands. "Of course not. But perhaps he was engaged to acquire an artifact of such interest to others that someone might be willing to kill in order to take possession of it—or stop someone else from possessing it."

"Once again, Mr. Storm, I must ask you to speak your mind or leave," Catherine said irritably. "I find myself quite tired these days. Do you mean to place me under arrest?

"Certainly not!" Mitch said, eyes widening. "We want to keep you safe."

"You're not doing such a good job," Cady drawled, and fixed Mitch with a look that made him shift in his seat.

"Mrs. Desmet," Mitch said. "Did your husband believe in the supernatural?"

"He was a life-long Presbyterian," Catherine replied.

Mitch cleared his throat. "That... wasn't exactly what I was referring to. I meant, did your husband believe in the occult?"

"Just what are you implying?" Catherine demanded. Right on cue, Wilfred the butler stepped into the parlor doorway.

"Is there a problem, madam?" he asked, with a pointed look in Mitch's direction.

"That's yet to be determined, Wilfred," Catherine replied.

"Ah, well then. I'll have the sharpshooters stand down then, ma'am." Wilfred gave a shallow bow and retreated.

"Are you always quite so... armed?" Mitch asked, alarmed.

"Only in response to a crisis or when people threaten my family," Catherine answered. "Now you were saying?"

Mitch looked as if he desperately wished he had sent his partner in to do the questioning and remained outside himself. Nicki concealed her glee.

"It's not my intention to imply anything at all, Mrs. Desmet," Mitch said in a placating tone. "But we think that items may have been brought to this country by Brand and Desmet that some believe have significant supernatural power."

"Relics?"

Mitch looked uncomfortable. "Ah, no. Something on the other side of the spectrum, actually."

"*Magique*," Nicki said, looking down her nose at Mitch. Her French accent was almost impenetrable now. She forced a derisive chuckle, and silently congratulated herself on her acting skills. "He thinks Uncle Thomas got a bad magical item."

Mitch reddened, both in embarrassment, Nicki bet, and in frustration. "There are forces at work beyond what most people care to notice," he said. "And people who take those forces seriously can be dangerous if they believe they have been crossed."

"I'm not aware of any 'magical' items among the last acquisitions my husband sought," Catherine replied. "But should I become aware of any, if you leave your calling card, I will let you know immediately."

Nicki was willing to bet Mitch knew he was being played. She saw a glint of stubbornness in his dark eyes. "Here's something you need to know, before you throw me out," he said. "The Department is looking into two other deaths similar to that of Thomas Desmet. Both men had recently done business with Brand and Desmet, with shipments from Eastern Europe. Pawel

Kozlowski and Eljasz Bajek." Both names were on the list Rick had given Nicki.

"Both men died suddenly, when they hadn't been known to be sick," Mitch continued. "In both cases, witnesses remembered a new object showing up right before the death, and vanishing afterwards. And both times, the men's place of business—and homes—were ransacked." He leaned forward, eyes narrowing. "I want to know why."

Wilfred returned to the doorway as if summoned telepathically and Mitch realized that he was being dismissed.

"Sorry to have troubled you, Mrs. Desmet, ladies," Mitch said with a nod. "I've left you my card. The reverse side has a special telegraph exchange. If you do hear—"

"This way, sir," Wilfred said with polite firmness. He escorted Mitch to the door. Nicki moved to her spot by the window.

"He's having a word with the dowdy one outside," Nicki reported a moment later. "It's a shame Agent Storm's with the government. He is rather dashing, don't you think?"

Cady sniffed. "Not really my type."

"Why do you think a government agent is involved?" Nicki mused, giving up watching the surveillance man and leaning back against the wall. "And do you think he really believes in magic?"

Catherine put the journal she had been reading back in her lap. "We should assume that he does believe. Thomas had encounters with the Department in the past. I don't know whether or not it was with the same agents... but if they're involved, this situation is bigger than we thought."

"It doesn't look like either Storm or his partner are leaving," Nicki reported, watching the street.

"Let them stay," Cady said. "Kovach has his men watching the agents while the agents watch you. The more the merrier."

Nicki returned to the writing desk and her stack of letters. Wilfred brought a tray with tea and fresh cookies, and the women worked through the afternoon. Finally, Catherine looked up. "I think I've found something," she said.

Cady and Nicki gathered around her. "This was Thomas's last journal," Catherine said. "His private notes, things he kept separate from official business." She paused. "The entry is dated a little more than a month ago."

Catherine's finger pointed to a passage in neat script. "'KJ came to see me. Wants a special job, a crate of books and a relic moved from Poland to New Pittsburgh, no questions asked. I pressed him about it, and after he explained further, I assured him we could assist him discreetly. My gut tells me this is important.'"

"*KJ*. Karl Jasinski," Nicki mused. "And now he's disappeared, either hiding out, kidnapped or dead. And we still don't know why." She looked at Catherine. "Does the journal say anything more about the books or the relic?"

Catherine frowned as she read down through the entry. "He says that shipping anything out of Poland and Russia is a headache, but 'KJ' had everything ready."

Cady leaned back in her chair and stared at the ceiling, fingers tented in front of her. "He wasn't wealthy... where would he have come up with the money to pay for it? And if someone killed Jasinski, or if he already feared for his life and had gone into hiding, then there would be no one to pick up the shipment when it came in. And if that same someone thought your Uncle Thomas knew what was in the shipment—"

"He might have killed him in order to get his hands on it," Nicki finished. "Or Jasinski didn't have the money and he double-crossed Uncle Thomas to take it..."

"Both of which could explain the break-in and bombing at the office," Catherine chimed in. "Either someone was trying to destroy the shipment, or frighten everyone out so they could get in."

"We've got a missing Polish witch and government agents," Cady said. "And a Night Hag—the timing can't be an accident."

Cady shrugged. "At the moment, the connection to Jasinski is just a hunch. But the Night Hag—*Nocnitsa*—had to come from somewhere."

"Which would mean someone called it, or opened a way for it to come," Nicki supplied.

Cady nodded. "It's not the Thalbergs—they're trying to figure this out like we are. And the names they recognized on Mr. Desmet's list were witches—two of whom the agents just confirmed are dead."

"If this Karl Jasinski was a witch, might he have somehow called the monster and then not known how to banish or control it?" Catherine mused. "Maybe he needed some other magical items, even relics, to get the monster back under control, or send it back where it came from? That would explain the items he wanted Thomas to smuggle out of Eastern Europe. The sightings and killings began long before he contacted Thomas."

"Maybe," Cady said. "Or perhaps someone else called it, and Jasinski was trying to figure out how to stop it, but didn't have what he needed to do the job." She sighed. "There are too many questions, and not enough answers."

A thought occurred to Nicki, and she leveled a questioning look at Cady. "Exactly how did you get the information about Jasinski?"

Cady brightened. "I gave a generous tip to the Polish woman who cleans the classrooms at the Women's College. She's often around when I'm finishing up at night, and she's a motherly type. I asked her if she knew a man named Karl Jasinski, and offered her a few more dollars if she could tell me something useful about him."

She grinned. "Money speaks every language. Mrs. Zukowski said she didn't know him herself, but she'd heard others speak of him. They call him 'the Witch of Pulawski Way'; people went to him to have fortunes told, bad luck reversed, curses put on people. But she said that he had gone away suddenly, and no one knew where he was or when he'd be back."

"Polish Hill isn't very far from Brand and Desmet's offices on Smallman Street," Catherine said. "And it's just across the river from where you said all the trouble is happening in Allegheny."

"Actually," Cady said, "there's been trouble in more places than just Allegheny. There's talk of bad things happening up the Mon and around the Point, like someone—or something—is following the rivers to hunt."

Catherine nodded. "Drostan Fletcher said the same thing. I asked him to use his contacts to see if he could pinpoint where the bodies have been found on a map."

Nicki sank down dramatically onto the divan. "My head hurts," she said, closing her eyes. "We've got a missing witch and a nasty monster—both Polish—and federal agents outside." She sighed. "We still don't know who the men were in the carriage with the red falcon; the ones who followed me and tried to kidnap me when I went to see Cady the first time."

Catherine blanched. "Did you say, 'red falcon'?"

Nicki nodded.

"I've seen that before," Catherine said. "It's Richard Thwaites's personal emblem. His name keeps coming up, doesn't it? That can't be a good thing."

"And we're no closer to solving Thomas's murder," Cady said. "Or knowing whether those boxes from Poland had anything to do with his death."

"What if the Night Hag, whatever it is, wasn't supposed to happen? What if it's an accident, and now someone's got to clean up the mess?" Nicki asked.

Cady nodded. "That's possible. Something that came over with a new batch of immigrants and no one knows how to make it go away? Or maybe a spell that Jasinski did for someone went wrong? Someone like Thwaites."

"I don't know which sounds worse, going up against an ancient monster, or taking on the Oligarchy," Catherine said. "Because Richard Thwaites is *very* well connected—and protected. He's got his own men, and rumor has it he's bought and paid for half of the New Pittsburgh police force."

There were male voices outside, loud enough to stop their conversation. "Hold on," Nicki went to the window.

"It's Jake. He's having a row with Agent Storm and the dowdy one."

Catherine rolled her eyes. "I'm really not obsessed with our reputation, but I would like the neighbors to keep speaking to us." She sighed.

"I don't think you have much to worry about." Nicki said. "There's no one else out there that I can see except some White Wings."

Three years earlier, New York City had initiated a campaign to smarten up its streets, employing legions of white-coated street cleaners, or 'White Wings'. Not to be left out, New Pittsburgh immediately did the same, deploying its own white-clad clean-up crews to rid the streets of horse dung and trash. They made their rounds armed with long-handled brooms and water wagons to hose off particularly stubborn grime. This crew had two wagons: the water wagon, hauled by a lugubrious horse that looked ready for the knacker's yard, and a second wagon to collect the trash.

Nicki frowned, and turned toward Catherine. "Aunt Catherine, what day do the White Wings come by?"

"Mondays, usually, and again on Thursdays," Catherine replied absently, having gone back to reading through one of the journals.

"But it's neither of those days. And this lot are wearing white, but their uniforms don't all match."

She gasped and yanked down the window sash. "Jake! Get down! Those aren't the real White Wings!"

Even as she spoke, one of the sweepers kicked the broom-head from its handle and leveled the shaft at Jake and the agents.

The gunshot reverberated, sending the china clinking in the cabinet and the pendants in the crystal chandelier swaying. Cady had the Winchester at her shoulder, and the attacking White Wing swayed on his feet, a neat hole in his forehead.

"Oh, my God," Catherine whispered. "Did you just shoot the street sweeper?"

A hail of gunfire sounded on Fifth Avenue. Mitch had pushed Jake to the ground and dragged him behind the low wall separating the Desmet house from the street, while he and Jacob returned fire. The false White Wings had dropped all pretense, rifle-brooms at the ready. There were at least twenty of them. Shots pinged off the wall; somewhere nearby, glass shattered.

Kovach's men came running, as the snipers on the roof picked off two targets. Cady swung out from the safety of the wall to fire another shot, catching an attacker in the shoulder. An assailant veered close to the house, coming into Nicki's range. Like Cady, Nicki was a crack shot, taking one of the enemy through the leg.

Wilfred ran into the room, alarm clear on his face. "Madam. I must insist that you and the young ladies retreat to safety."

Cady squeezed off another shot. "We've got a better angle than Jake does, and—with the trees blocking some of the upstairs windows and roofline—maybe even than the snipers do on the roof. Even with the two government agents, our sharpshooters are outnumbered. They need us."

The cleaners returned fire. Cady squealed and dropped to the floor as a bullet zinged through the top of the window, then rose to her feet and fired.

"Get out of here, Aunt Catherine. You're in mourning. You can't be shooting people," Nicki said, reloading. "It wouldn't be proper."

"We've got problems," Cady shouted.

"Did you just figure that out?" Nicki retorted.

"No, *bigger* problems." Cady pointed. "I don't think that water wagon is filled with water."

"*Doux Jésus*!" Nicki muttered. "Petrol."

"Charles!" Catherine shouted.

"He's already gone 'round to help Mr. Desmet," Wilfred said. "Please, let me get you to safety."

"My great-grandmother didn't leave the homestead when the Davey Lewis gang came through town," Catherine said. "My mother didn't run off when the Molly Maguires set to. And I'm not going anywhere, not as long as my son's out there and our home is at risk." A determined glint had come into Catherine's eyes. "Wilfred. Fetch me Thomas's Colt revolver." She headed for the stairs. "I'll be in my room."

Mitch, Jacob, and Jake were giving as good as they got from the deadly cleaning crew. Kovach's men waded in with guns and fists, but the numbers still favored the attackers. If Cady's fears about the water wagon were correct, firepower alone wasn't going to be enough.

"Go, Charles!" Nicki cheered as the *werkman* ran toward the water wagon with inhuman speed. Shots clanged off his metal body, but Charles never slowed.

Three of the false White Wings threw themselves at Charles, but the *werkman* tossed them aside with ease.

"They're going to set off the wagon!" Nicki shouted, loosing another shot amid a barrage of vulgar French.

"Let's see if I can get the driver," Cady said with a hard glint in her eye. She fired, but the bullet went astray, nicking the driver's bench. "Damn."

The wagon and its attackers were out of Nicki's range. Charles was doing his best to move the wagon backward—water tank, horses and all—but several of the false street sweepers were trying to drag him away.

Bam-bam-bam. Kovach's sharpshooters hit their targets. From the open parlor window, Nicki could hear cursing in Hungarian. The men restraining Charles dropped in their tracks. A fourth attacker who had wriggled along the ground toward Jake's hiding place jerked and went still as a bullet found its mark. From the angle of the shot, Nicki was pretty certain Catherine had pulled the trigger.

Charles brought a metal fist down, smashing the wagon tongue and freeing the horses, then he pushed the wagon toward an empty lot across the street. Kovach laid down covering fire so that none of the surviving attackers could get close. Nicki held her breath, watching as Charles put his mechanized muscle against the weight of the wagon. The wheels creaked over the curb, and the cart began to roll into the open field.

With a roar and a blinding flash, the tank exploded. Fire danced into the sky nearly as high as the two-story homes on either side of the empty lot. A plume of black smoke and the smell of burning gasoline filled the air. Charles was nowhere to be seen.

Sirens wailed, getting closer. Half a dozen of the surviving faux cleaners returned fire to cover their comrades, who dragged away the dead and wounded, then threw the bodies onto the remaining wagon and pulled a tarp over them before climbing aboard and heading away from the sirens.

"They're getting away!" Cady shouted, raising her rifle once more.

Nicki put a restraining hand on her shoulder. "Let them go. They're taking the dead and wounded. We won't have to explain the bodies to the police. And we've got to get Jake and the others to safety before awkward questions get asked."

Cady raised an eyebrow. "We've just had a Wild West shoot-out on Fifth Avenue—you don't think awkward questions are already being asked?"

"I think we have a much better chance of explaining it away if there isn't a wagonful of corpses in front of the house," Nicki said archly.

"And the burned-out wagon?" Cady asked.

Nicki smiled. "Spontaneous combustion. Darndest thing."

Their attackers headed off at full gallop. Miska Kovach was already down at street level, hustling Jake, Mitch, and Jacob from their hiding place and around to the back of the house. Cady slid the window closed.

Just as Jake and the others rounded the corner of the house, the police wagons came clattering up. Cady watched from the cover of the heavy parlor drapes. "Uh-oh. They're heading this way," she gave a murmured warning.

Brusque knocking sounded at the front door. Wilfred appeared in the hallway, forever unflappable, standing straight and tall with an unreadable expression. "I'll handle this," he said, making his way down the hallway without a hint of hurry.

Nicki had a view of the hallway from behind the parlor door. A florid-faced policeman stood in the entranceway.

"We had a report that shots were fired," the officer began abruptly, with a thick Irish brogue.

"We made no such report," Wilfred replied. His glance strayed to the conspicuous crepe wreath on the door. "And since the household is in mourning, I'll thank you to keep your voice low."

The officer looked abashed, and removed his hat. "Sorry for your loss," he mumbled. "But there are spent shell casings in the street from a variety of guns. They came from somewhere."

He pointed toward the still-burning wagon. "And there was an explosion. Surely you heard that!"

Wilfred turned his head toward the flames then back to the officer with a total lack of emotion. "Living in the city, one is accustomed to taking a variety of noises in one's stride. We do not rush to the windows like voyeurs."

"I don't know about voyagers," the cop replied. "And I'm sorry to bother you at a bad time, but what about the blood? There's blood on the street. What do you make of that?"

Wilfred affected an expression of boredom. "I don't 'make' anything of it. That is what we depend upon your illustrious department to discover. Now if you will excuse me, I must attend to my duties."

He shut the door in the officer's confused face. Nicki had to stifle a laugh. Once his back was turned, Wilfred allowed himself a hint of a smirk.

"With luck, he'll go bother the neighbors," Wilfred said, a gleam of wicked humor in his eyes.

"Won't they report what they've seen—shots traded, sharpshooters on the roof, all that?" Nicki asked.

Wilfred chuckled. "Even if they saw it, they wouldn't dare breathe a word. Might lower property values, or cause a scandal." He sighed. "Although Madame may find invitations to afternoon tea less forthcoming for a while."

"Pish posh," Nicki said with a dismissive wave. "Any neighbor who wouldn't have you over for tea for taking a few well-aimed shots at intruders isn't worth the bother."

"Indeed," Wilfred said.

Catherine descended the stairs, minus her mourning cap and veil. "Is it over? Where's Jake?"

Wilfred nodded toward the kitchen. "They were just coming in when that insufferable policeman came to the door."

Catherine gathered her black skirts and ran the length of the hallway, with Nicki and Cady close behind.

"Jake!" Catherine cried out, in a mixture of relief and alarm. Jake sat at the kitchen table with his shirt partly off. Blood streaked down his chest from a gash on his upper left arm. Mrs. James, the family's cook, was boiling water and fetching linen bandages, while the dowdy agent who had been keeping watch outside the house staunched the bleeding with a compress.

Agent Storm sat next to Jake, his shirt stained with blood from a bullet that had clipped him in the shoulder. Miska Kovach stood by the kitchen door, his face and shirt smudged with dirt and gunpowder, glaring at Mitch.

"There's hot water and iodine," Mrs. James said. "That should help you clean up properly."

"Much obliged," the dowdy agent replied. He was taller than Storm, with blond hair and blue eyes, and his voice carried a strong hint of a Croatian accent. As if he suddenly realized that he had not been introduced, the man looked up and gave a nod of acknowledgement.

"Agent Jacob Drangosavich," he said. "Sorry about the unpleasantness. We were afraid something like this might happen."

"And before you ask, I'll be fine, Mother." Jake managed a rueful smile. "It's just a cut, not even a bullet. I've had worse."

Agent Storm raised an eyebrow. "I didn't know the import business was so dangerous."

"You have no idea."

"Agent Storm," Catherine said. "Who were those men, and why were they here?"

Mitch shifted in his seat, and Nicki guessed that the wound pained him more than he wanted to let on. "Someone within the Oligarchy, would be my guess. Those weren't common hirelings—not the way they stood their ground, or the way they gathered their dead and wounded. They were well-trained."

"I caught a bit of what they were saying to each other," Kovach said. "Pretty sure it was Romanian they were speaking."

Romanian, Nicki thought. *Like Drogo Veles.* She saw a flicker of recognition in Jake's eyes, and made a mental note to ask him if he had someone in mind once their 'visitors' had gone.

"Good thing your *werkman* got that wagon out of the way," Mitch said as Jacob began to wash his wound. He gritted his teeth as his partner pried a bullet loose, but the iodine wrenched a choked cry from his lips. Jacob muttered something in Croatian, and kept right on binding Mitch's injury.

"Whoever sent that meant to do quite a bit of damage," Catherine observed. Nicki looked over to the corner of the kitchen where Charles sat on a wooden chair. His bronze skin was dented and scorched in places, and his clothing burned and torn, but the light in his eyes was bright and he looked to be fully functional.

Mitch gingerly pulled his shirt on over his bandages. "I don't know what game you folks think you're playing," he said. "But it's dangerous. We can help."

Jake and his mother exchanged glances. "We appreciate the concern, Agent Storm, but we will be fine," Catherine replied. "If you want to be of use, find out who killed my husband and why."

Mitch and Jacob collected their things and headed for the back door. "We will," Jacob replied. "But think about this: whoever sent those assassins today isn't content to have killed Thomas Desmet. Someone wants you all dead."

Chapter SEVENTEEN

LATE THE NEXT night, Jake and Rick took the long way toward their destination. They rode in the back of an unmarked delivery wagon rather than use one of their carriages. Kovach and a newly-mended Charles drove. Kovach had chosen the fastest horses for the night's work, and insisted on hastily reinforcing the sides of the wagon in case of an ambush. But he had gone with aluminum instead of heavy steel to keep the weight down, in case of a quick get-away. The real goal was to get in, haul away what Adam needed for his research, and get out without incident. Jake was skeptical that it would be that easy.

"Relax. It's not like it's the first time we've broken in somewhere," Rick said, and Jake could hear the excitement in his friend's voice.

"Maybe not," Jake admitted. "But it's the first time we've broken into Tesla-Westinghouse."

Rick clucked his tongue. "Actually, we're not really breaking in. We're just helping transport scientific equipment outside of normal working hours."

"Uh-huh. Equipment that hasn't been signed out, paid for or declassified."

Rick grinned. "That's what makes it interesting."

"Kind of scary that Adam doesn't trust his management anymore, but if they've gotten cozy with Thwaites, then Adam's not safe there and neither are his more useful inventions," Jake said.

"We sure don't want Thwaites getting his hands on everything Adam's invented—or on Adam himself. I think he's right to want to disappear," Rick added. He paused for a moment. "Did you find anything out about the shipment your father was importing for Jasinski?" Their wagon clattered over the bridge, crossing the Monongahela River to Wilmerding, to the headquarters of Tesla-Westinghouse.

"Only that it's missing," Jake replied tersely. At his mother's insistence, Jake had permitted the family's physician, Dr. Zeigler, to treat his arm once he had assurances that the doctor would not report the injury to authorities. Even with stitches and a poultice, the arm hurt like blazes, but Jake had refused any morphine, wanting to keep a clear head. The gash had not been deep enough to keep him from using his arm, which was all that mattered.

"Our shipments don't just disappear," Rick argued. "We have people and processes to make certain of that. And if what Agent Storm said is true, then a couple other people from Thomas's list shipped something with Brand and Desmet and died because of it."

Jake shrugged, then regretted it as pain lanced through his wounded arm. "I have a gut feeling that it's all related. And I don't think Jasinski's crates were just any shipment."

The carriage came to a stop in an alley behind the Castle. Kovach let Jake and Rick out of the wagon.

"I can't believe Adam nearly burned this place down with one of his experiments," Rick muttered as they got out of the carriage.

"Looks good as new to me," Jake replied.

Charles sat in the carriage driver's seat, in better shape from the exploits of the day before than Jake was. Kovach had worked on the mechanical man, repairing the damage and buffing out the worst of the scratches and dents.

"Don't spend too much time chatting with Farber," Kovach warned. "We doubled back several times, but I can't shake the feeling that someone was trying to follow us."

The three men approached the rear of the building, alert for patrolling security guards or attackers lurking in the shadows. As they neared the building, a door opened on the loading dock.

Adam Farber was waiting for them. "Rick! Jake! Miska! Great to see you!" he whispered, grinning. Before Jake could fend him off, Adam slapped Jake on the shoulder and Jake gasped in pain.

"Good to see you, too," Rick replied, trying and failing to keep a hint of amusement out of his voice as Jake grimaced. "Let's make this a quick visit, shall we?" Rick tapped Morse code into a Farber-made wristwatch that sent a wireless signal to Charles to let him know it was clear to proceed. A few minutes later, and the *werkmen* brought the black wagon up to the doorway.

"Absolutely. I wouldn't have come near this place again if it weren't so important... especially after those hired gorillas... well, anyway. Lars and I have been waiting for you," Adam said, indicating the clockwork man who stood to one side, wearing the uniform of an elevator operator.

Jake looked askance at Lars. "Won't he report back to management?"

Adam chuckled. "Who do you think programmed him? Let's get the first load into the carriage, and I'll go back for the second batch. Security isn't making its rounds tonight, but I could swear I saw something out there, not long before you came."

Jake and Rick stepped into the darkened stairwell. "How did you manage to get rid of security?" Jake asked.

"I sent them all 'updated' work schedules at the last minute, making sure none of them were on shift for tonight. And if anyone asks, they're signed and official." Adam's grin broadened. "I had Lars copy the signature of the temporary scheduler who just finished today. She won't be around to dispute it or take the blame. Perfect crime."

Jake shook his head in admiration. "Adam Farber, you're a dangerous man."

"Give us a couple of minutes, and we'll have the wagon loaded," Adam replied. "We'll go down the stairs so you can unload the service elevator. Send it back down to us when it's empty, and we'll reload it and ride back up." He gestured for Lars to follow him. They disappeared down the stairs to the Castle's lower levels, the secret underground labs where the geniuses of Tesla-Westinghouse created electro-mechanical marvels and tested the boundaries of known science.

After tense, silent minutes that seemed to stretch forever, Adam and Lars returned.

"Rick probably told you, I've been working on some really interesting things," Adam said, talking quickly and nearly twitching with excitement. Jake guessed his friend was running high on caffeine. "And after what happened, I'm glad you two could hide me and my projects somewhere safe."

With Kovach and Charles as sentries, Jake and Rick pitched in to help Adam and Lars load the wagon. Wooden boxes stuffed with small gadgets went in first, then crates with Farber's tools and equipment.

"Isn't anyone going to notice that all your stuff is missing?" Jake asked.

Adam chuckled. "No. They might think I cleaned the place up, but I've got duplicates of most of the tools, and plenty of half-made stuff that isn't dangerous, so the lab will look as cluttered as ever." He dropped his voice. "Although the pieces that were one-of-a-kind are what I'm trying to secure."

It took Lars and Charles together to move a large crate, which looked suspiciously like the weapon Adam had used during the fight at Jake's father's interment.

"You saw one of my special projects at the cemetery," Adam said as the workmen carried in the heavy box. "The Tesla ray served its purpose, but it was rough. I've been trying to refine the beam to make it a little less—unpredictable. And I think I'm close to making it more portable."

In other words, to make it more dangerous for the people in front of the contraption than for those behind the controls, Jake thought.

"It's technically an off-the-books project anyhow," Adam said. "Now and then, Mr. Tesla drops by late at night when I'm working alone down in the lab. He'll hand off some drawings, maybe a sketch he's made on a scrap of paper or an equation, and tell me to run with it, but keep it quiet." He laughed. "Why do you think I'm so happy to work odd hours?"

Lars and Charles returned from the back of the wagon, and Kovach handed Charles back his rifle.

"We've got one more load," Adam said.

"Make it quick," Kovach snapped. "We've been here too long already."

Adam and Lars headed back down in the elevator. When they returned, they had two more *werkmen* with them, but the mechanical men looked different from Charles and Lars. Adam spoke a few quiet words to his creations, and they lined up to enter the wagon, then stood, rigid as soldiers on review, with the rest of the cargo.

"Prototypes," Adam said. "They look alike on the outside, but inside, we've made a lot of improvements." He lifted up a bag and rattled it. "I've been doing a lot of radio telegraph experiments, like what's in the little pods I equipped your airship with. There's so much more that could be done."

"Save the chatter," Kovach prodded. "Let's get out of here before someone comes by."

Adam locked the door behind them, and he and Lars turned to follow the others to the wagon. Lars stopped suddenly, and looked back at the building.

"Dr. Farber," Lars said in a scratchy voice that sounded like a phonograph recording. "I detect the presence of nitric acid. Containment is advised."

"We've got problems," Adam said.

"Come on!" Kovach urged.

Adam shook his head. He pointed toward a stack of small wooden crates just a few feet away from the door they had just locked. "Those boxes shouldn't be there," Adam said. He turned to Lars. "Is that where you're detecting the nitric acid?"

"Yes, Dr. Farber."

"Is anyone else in the building?" Kovach asked.

"No. At least, no one is supposed to be," Adam replied.

"Then let's get the hell out of here."

"Lars," Adam said, ignoring Kovach. "Do you detect a mechanism in the boxes?"

"Yes, Dr. Farber."

"Does anyone know you were planning to be here tonight?" Kovach demanded.

"Everyone knows I'm here every night," Adam replied. "Go on ahead. Lars and I will defuse it."

"Hell, no," Jake said. "We need to get you—and us—out of here right now."

"Dr. Farber," Lars said in his flat, mechanical voice. "I have detected five more such boxes."

"Can you tell how much time we've got before the clockworks winds down?" Kovach asked.

"The mechanism is nearly spent," Lars replied.

"That does it," Kovach said, grabbing Farber by the arm. Jake seized him by the other. "We're getting out of here."

Charles was already in the driver's seat, and Jake guessed that he had no desire to be blown up twice in as many days. Rick and Jake pushed Adam into the back of the wagon, dragging Lars with them as Kovach slammed the back doors shut, leaving them in darkness.

"Move!" Kovach hissed to Charles as he ran for the driver's seat. The wagon lurched as the horses took off abruptly, making Jake, Rick, and Adam lose their balance and nearly toppling the *werkmen* onto them.

A deafening roar sounded behind them, then another and another. Thumps and thuds came as debris rained down on the carriage.

"The lab!" Adam cried out, lurching as if he meant to throw himself out of the wagon doors. Jake and Rick grabbed his arms and held on tightly.

"You're sure no one knew you were planning to move some of your projects tonight?" Rick asked, searching for a handhold as the wagon careened around a corner.

"I didn't tell anyone," Adam swore.

"Thaddeus." Lars's flat voice sounded in the darkness.

"Who's Thaddeus?" Jake lost his footing as the wagon took another sharp corner at high speed. He staggered, and landed against one of the *werkmen* prototypes, which caught him and kept him from falling. "Thanks," he muttered, managing to get his balance again.

"Thaddeus Hillard, my assistant," Adam replied. His voice was thin and reedy; Jake guessed the inventor was reeling from the bombing's implications. He turned towards Lars. "What made you think of Thaddeus?"

"He removes files for projects not assigned to him. He enters restricted areas." Lars replied tonelessly.

"Wait, what?" Adam said abruptly. "What do you mean, he enters restricted areas?"

"He leaves at night, and then returns. He goes to other labs and offices."

Adam frowned. "Why didn't you tell me about this before?"

"Your supervisor ordered me to give him access," Lars replied.

Adam swore under his breath. "Did my boss order you not to tell me?"

"No," Lars said. "But he did not order me *to* tell you. You did not ask. Thaddeus's clearance level was sufficient for what he was doing and where he was going. It was not relevant to speak of until now."

"Sounds like you've got a spy," Rick said. "But the real question is—is Thaddeus the one who planted the bomb, or is more than one enemy involved?"

"One is enough," Adam said, sagging to sit on the wagon floor. The horses had slowed their pace, even as the clang of fire alarms roused residents of Wilmerding from their beds and fire trucks rattled toward the Castle.

"Did you have any other problems, after what happened when Cullen and I were with you?" Rick asked.

"Little things that were off," Adam said, sounding tired and defeated. "My boss has always left me alone to tinker, but he started asking a lot of questions, trying to get a look at the projects that aren't ready to show anyone yet."

"Is that so strange?" Rick asked. "He *is* your boss."

"You don't understand," Adam said miserably. "Some of my projects come direct from Mr. Tesla. Those are off-limits, even from my boss. Other projects come from the government—like the Department—or private patrons—like Brand and Desmet.

They negotiate my time with my boss, but they provide the budget, and usually a very strict contract, so the projects themselves are on a need-to-know basis, and he usually doesn't need to know."

"Did either your boss or Thaddeus threaten you?" Jake asked.

"No," Adam replied. "I just felt… watched. I used to feel very safe at the Castle, but the last couple of weeks, it's been strange. Odd people in and out. Mr. Thwaites having a lot of meetings with my boss. I don't go upstairs much, but I have friends in the front office, and they were getting nervous."

"Nervous about what?" The wagon jolted them so hard Jake's teeth snapped together, and he bit back a cry of pain as he fell against his wounded arm. Blood trickled down his skin underneath his sleeve.

Adam took a deep breath. "I heard talk about strangers walking back and forth by the Castle, or sitting on a park bench nearby, watching the place. Then some shipments for the Department went missing." He sighed. "That's about the time my boss 'gave' me Thaddeus. Told me he would help me manage my hours, finish more projects in less time."

"You didn't ask for an assistant?'

"No. I like working alone. Thaddeus was nice enough, but he always seemed to be in the way."

A sudden suspicion nagged at the corners of Jake's mind. "You don't happen to know a guy named Mitch Storm, do you?"

"You've met him? Sure. Where do you think we get the money to do half of the stuff we do here?" He leaned forward and dropped his voice. "But we're always very careful to keep the best stuff for ourselves."

"Glad to hear it," Jake said. "What's your take on Storm and his partner?"

Adam shrugged. "They're all right, as government types go. Did I ever show you my clockwork homing pigeons?"

"Maybe another time," Rick said, trying to gently nudge Adam back on topic. "Are you working on anything that might make someone want to blow up the Castle?"

Adam was quiet for a moment. "Steal things? Yes. Kidnap me? I guess we know the answer to that one. Blow the place up? No."

"What were you afraid might get stolen?" Jake prodded.

"My *werkmen*. That's another reason why I wanted you to come and get me before it was too late. Lots of people have tried to make automatons. No one's are as good as mine." Adam's voice held no boasting, only a simple statement of fact.

"We have Charles," Jake said. "You've got Lars. You brought your prototypes with us. Does anyone else have one of your *werkmen*?"

"I've built a couple for the Department of Supernatural Investigations—Mitch Storm's outfit," Adam replied. "And they've also got Hans, the first flesh-and-blood man I outfitted with clockwork pieces to replace damaged body parts; my first Midas." Adam's voice regained its enthusiasm. "Imagine—no more war wounded! No more men crippled by industrial accidents!"

"You sound like you're veering a little close to resurrectionist territory," Rick replied with a worried tone. "Tell me you didn't do any grave robbing."

"Absolutely not! I've only made a couple of Midas men, and they are very much alive. I practiced on some cadavers, but the ones we used all came from verified sources."

"Unfortunately, I can think of a lot of shady types who would love to get their hands on that kind of equipment," Jake said. "And they'd be more than willing to steal it."

"Steal it, yes. But then why blow up the Castle?" Adam asked. "Do you think Kovach would go back—just close enough that we can see how bad the damage is?"

"No!" Both Jake and Rick spoke at once.

For a moment, they sat in silence. "We'll get you to the warehouse in the Strip District that we were renovating before Father died," Jake said finally. "Miska will post guards. You should have plenty of room there, and since the renovation's been halted indefinitely, there shouldn't be anyone in or out."

"Would anyone be overly distressed if you went missing?" Rick asked. "Because it could take a while for the police to figure out whether or not anyone got killed in the bombing. You could disappear, let things cool off, maybe throw the thugs off your trail until we figure out what's going on."

"I don't have any close family, or romantic interests—at least, not right now. Some of the people at work might be worried, but they'll be just as glad when I show up again, so I think it will be all right."

"There's a tunnel that runs between the main Brand and Desmet building and the new warehouse," Jake said. "No one else should have a reason to use it. We can keep you supplied with food and materials without anyone seeing us coming and going."

"Suits me," Adam said. "After tonight, I don't want to poke my head outside until we know who set those bombs—and who sent the kidnappers."

The streets of New Pittsburgh were nearly empty. Charles slowed the wagon to a decorous pace that was unlikely to draw attention. Finally, the horses came to a stop, and Jake's hand fell to the Colt revolver in his holster, just in case.

The doors opened and Kovach stood framed in the dim glow of the gas lamps. "We're here," he said. "Step lively."

Charles brought the wagon up to the side entrance of the warehouse, close to the big doors to the building's basement. Adam rallied his *werkmen*, and they made short work of carrying in the heavy boxes and crates, filing in with orderly precision.

In another hour or two, Smallman Street would be bustling with greengrocers and fruit merchants, fishmongers, and bakers. But right now, in the wee hours just before dawn, Jake saw few people; and those who were awake were going about their business with insomniac intensity, paying them no attention.

"What do you think?" Jake asked. "Will it do?" The large basement had narrow frosted glass windows at sidewalk level, covered with iron bars, assuring privacy and security.

"Oh, my," Adam said, turning to take in the huge, empty space. Overhead, bare Edison bulbs glowed, illuminating the laboratory's new home. "This is perfect."

"You've got water and electricity," Jake said. "There won't be anyone up above to be bothered by noise, and as long as you don't blow the place sky high, the din on Smallman Street during the day is enough that no one should hear anything you're doing."

"Thank you," Adam stammered, overwhelmed. "I was afraid I'd end up with all the *werkmen* stuffed into my landlady's attic and me tinkering in the garden shed."

Rick chuckled. "I think we can do a bit better than that. And if you like it, we can work out a more permanent arrangement," he added off-handedly.

"Absolutely," Jake said. "We can talk about adding security, a special entrance, an apartment for when you work late, whatever you need. There's also a sub-basement that hasn't been reclaimed; it may come in handy." He met Adam's gaze. "Think about it. Here, you can work on your private contracts and special projects away from the prying eyes of Tesla-Westinghouse. And if they insist, you can always keep your projects for them over at the Castle."

"If the Castle still stands. I feel awful that I was the cause of all that." Adam sighed. "And it wasn't even an experiment gone wrong this time."

"You didn't cause the blast," Rick said. "Someone else planted those bombs. The real question is—which of your projects were they trying to stop?"

"Or, was it Adam himself they were trying to stop?" Jake asked. "We need to seriously consider whether he was the target, not just his inventions, especially if someone knew you keep late hours and were likely to be there when the blast went off."

Adam paled and sat down on a pallet of two-by-fours, looking as if he might pass out. He stared wide-eyed at Jake and Rick. "It's one thing to be kidnapped. Do you really think someone is trying to kill me?"

"I think we need to err on the safe side, until we figure out what is actually going on," Rick replied. "Drostan Fletcher's due to report in, and that might shed some light. Tomorrow, we'll find out how much damage was done to the Castle. You'll go 'missing', Adam, at least until we know who the enemy is."

"But my projects for Tesla-Westinghouse—and my patron-projects. What about them?" Adam asked.

"They'd come to a permanent halt if you were really dead," Rick said. "Think how happy they'll be to find out that you're still alive. A little delay won't seem so bad. And when it's safe to bring you back, we'll just say you got hit on the head and wandered off and took a while to come back to your senses."

"How likely is it that Tesla-Westinghouse could hire someone else to take over your work?" Jake asked. "Like Thaddeus, for example."

Adam thought for a moment. "Thaddeus is good at taking direction, but I haven't seen him come up with anything on his own. I'm sure there are people they could find who could build from plans I've left behind—although the Tesla weapon technology is experimental. They're not going to find many people with that kind of experience. As for the new stuff..." He shook his head. "I made sure to bring my notes and drawings with me, as well as the prototypes. And most of it was still up here," he said, tapping his forehead. "Anyone else would have to start from scratch."

Just then, Jake heard distant pounding, as if someone were hammering on the first-floor door. He pressed a button, plunging them all into darkness. They waited in silence until Jake heard a voice from the top of the stairs.

"Jake?" Kovach called. "We've got a situation up here. There's a very angry plumber, and he's demanding to see you."

Cautiously, Jake turned on the lights again.

"What on earth is a plumber doing here at this hour?" Rick said.

"We'll find out," Jake said with a shrug, leaving Adam and the others behind as he sprinted up the steps.

At the warehouse's front door, Jake could see a heavy-set man arguing loudly with Kovach, who stood, arms-crossed. Behind the stranger was a cluster of a dozen men in tradesmen's clothing, milling about and muttering angrily. Farther down the street, near the main Brand and Desmet building, another knot of men had formed a cordon around the basement doors.

As Jake drew closer, he caught bits of the angry man's diatribe.

"Unpardonable! ...violation of contract. We won't stand for it! ...ignoring Union rules—"

"What seems to be the problem?" Jake asked, joining the two men. By the light of the streetlamp, he could make out the stocky man's features enough to recognize 'Big' Joe Doheimer, one of the senior plumbers Brand and Desmet retained to keep their buildings running, and the president of the New Pittsburgh Plumber's Union #407.

Doheimer straightened to meet Jake's gaze, flushed in the face from his argument with Kovach. "We're onto you," he said, wagging a finger in Jake's face. "We know your secret. And we demand something be done about it, before someone gets hurt."

Jake felt his stomach knot. "I'm afraid I have no idea what you're talking about."

Doheimer took a step closer, so that his florid face was nearly nose-to-nose with Jake. "Don't deny it! Brand and Desmet is using scab plumbers to get around Union wages."

Jake looked at Doheimer, and his mind raced, trying to figure out what in the world the angry plumber was raging about. "Scab plumbers?"

"Don't deny it! We've got you dead to rights."

Jake spread his hands. "I think there's been a misunderstanding. I came here to oversee a late shipment. It's got nothing to do with plumbers."

"Then how do you explain the men over at your other building? The ones working on the pipes in the basement? One of my men saw them carrying pipes and fittings a couple of hours ago, sneaking around after dark so no one would know Brand and Desmet hires scabs!"

"Brand and Desmet does *not* hire scabs," Jake retorted. As aggravating as Doheimer and his accusations were, the notion forming in Jake's mind was much worse. "Show me these scabs. They're no one we've hired."

"So you say," Doheimer grunted.

Kovach placed Charles on guard at the doors to the lab before he and Jake set off at a brisk pace behind Doheimer, following to the main building.

"It just so happened that Hank was coming back from the pub, and he walked past," Doheimer said, giving Jake an accusing look. "He saw men carrying toolboxes and pipes into the basement, skulking around in the night so no one would know you're cheating the honest Union workmen of New Pittsburgh!"

Doheimer paused to wipe a sheen of sweat from his forehead. "Hank came around to my place, because he figured right that I'd want to know. When I heard what he saw, I roused a couple dozen of the boys and we figured we'd catch those scabs in the act and have them here to face you with the evidence in the morning."

"So they're still here?" Jake said, glancing at the non-descript utility wagon parked behind the main Brand and Desmet building.

Doheimer gave a sage nod. "Aye, though they put up quite a struggle. But my boys had their Irish up, and they were mighty steamed about scabs cutting into one of our big jobs. So when push came to shove and the fists started to fly, my boys came out ahead. Your scabs are worse for the wear, tied up neat as a Christmas present, proof that you've broken our contract. Bad enough you use those steam engineers for your airships instead of regular working plumbers. But this is going too far."

"I haven't hired any plumbers—scab or Union—to do night work at the main building," Jake said. "And if George had hired them, Rick or I'd know." He looked Doheimer straight in the eyes. "Those aren't my men. So if they're here, they're up to no good."

"Did anyone go into the basement to see what they were working on?" Kovach interrupted.

Doheimer shook his head. "Didn't need to, because they told us right out they were fixing the pipes on your boiler."

Oh God, Jake thought. *Another bomb.*

"I can't get my men here fast enough," Kovach said with a worried look; he'd evidently come to the same conclusion. "And we have no idea when they've set it to blow."

Jake turned to Doheimer. "Those men aren't plumbers. They're anarchists," he said, fudging the truth for ease of explanation. "And if they were working on our boiler, it was to set it to blow up."

"Anarchists?" Doheimer repeated. "Here in New Pittsburgh?"

"Where are the men you captured?" Jake asked. Rick had come up behind them, close enough to hear what was being said, and Jake was sure Adam was hanging back in the shadows, out of sight but within earshot.

"I'll show you," Doheimer said, still looking skeptical. "Don't expect my boys to give you a warm welcome."

"We don't have time for that," Jake snapped, "not if the building is going to blow. Bring the men you captured and get your own people away from the building. Hurry!"

Doheimer headed toward the crowd, shouting orders. Boos and catcalls greeted Jake, Rick, and Kovach. Kovach and Charlie made a quick check to clear the area, but found no one else. A dozen or so plumbers moved to the relative safety of a spot across the street and down a block, then swarmed around them, chanting Union slogans. Jake paid them no heed, and focused on the sullen prisoners, who were tied with strips of the cotton duck cloth used by plumbers to wrap the joints of their pipes.

"Here're yer scabs." A tall plumber with a cabbie hat jammed down over his wild dark hair gave the nearest prisoner a kick before stepping back as Doheimer and the others approached.

The three men sat bound hand and foot on the sidewalk. They had the rough look of hired muscle, dressed in dark colors to blend into the night. Scars marked their faces from old fights, and one of the men was missing part of an ear.

"Who do you work for?" Jake demanded.

The man with the missing ear looked up and gave him a sly grin. "Brand and Desmet, guv. Just here to do a job on the cheap."

The plumbers howled their anger, and began their chants again. Doheimer silenced them with an ear-splitting whistle.

"Now what do you say?" Doheimer demanded. He turned to face Jake with his hands on his hips, ready for a fight.

Jake ignored him and moved down the line to the second prisoner. "That your story too?"

The second man glared at him. "I don't got nothin' to say."

"You hired us, and now you don't want no one to know about it, so how 'bout you let us go and pay us our money?" the third man shouted at Jake. Beneath the bluster and the subterfuge, Jake heard a note of fear and realized none of the saboteurs had bargained on being close to the building when their handiwork went off.

"I had guards patrolling the building," Kovach said, and the tone of his voice made the plumbers quiet down. "What did you do to them?"

"You mean the drunk guys out back?" one of the plumbers yelled. "We found three big oxes sleepin' like babies with an empty bottle of vodka."

"My men don't drink on duty," Kovach grated. He grabbed One-Ear by the shirt and dragged him to his feet. "What did you do to them?"

One-Ear smirked. "Just helped them get a good night's sleep, that's all." Kovach threw him to the sidewalk, cursing under his breath in Hungarian.

The plumbers began to shout once more, threatening everything from personal violence against Jake and Rick to organizing a tradesmen's boycott of Brand and Desmet.

"These men are burglars and anarchists," Jake yelled above the noise. "They didn't come here to fix anything. They came to plant a bomb!"

"Who are you kidding, bub?" one of the plumbers shouted back. "Yer just duckin' the charge so we don't picket yer building."

Jake turned back to the three prisoners. "How about we all wait here together until daybreak?" he said, looking from one of the bound saboteurs to another. "How long will it take for the pressure in the boiler to build up? Maybe we should move you three into the basement and we can all wait for the explosion together?"

One-Ear licked his lips nervously. "We just do what we're told, guv. Nothin' personal."

"I ain't going back in there!" the third prisoner said. He was the youngest of the three, with a dirty, pock-marked face and a nose crooked and flattened from fighting. Beneath the dirt that streaked his face, he had gone pale. "I'll tell you what you want to know, but don't put us down there to die!"

His outburst silenced the plumbers, and Doheimer stepped forward, bending over to go nose-to-nose with the man. "What did you do and why did you do it?"

"Shut up, Dave!" One-Ear said.

"I don't want to die either!" the second man said. He had the beat-down look of a man who had tried and failed at everything, with a sallow complexion and basset eyes. Jake stepped closer to him, catching a whiff of tobacco and cheap gin.

Doheimer gave Dave the pox-faced man a shake. "What did you do?"

"They said we'd be clean gone by the time it went off," Dave said, panic clear in his voice. "Just a quick job. Break in to a building, mess up the boiler, and be across the river before it blows. Then we'd get paid. Now we ain't gettin' paid and you're going to get us all killed."

"I'm going in there," Jake said. "We're wasting time. If there's a way to undo what's been done, we've got to get to it."

"You don't know a thing about boilers," Rick argued.

"But you do," Jake retorted, "so help me! And for that matter, I've helped Cullan more than once with the boilers on the *Allegheny Princess*."

"You're all scabs," Doheimer said, throwing Dave to the sidewalk and landing a kick to One-Ear's rump in the same movement. "Don't know a boiler from a horse's ass."

"So you'll go in with us?" Jake challenged. Doheimer looked like he was about to decline, but he did not have the chance to say anything before they were interrupted.

"I'll go. I know more about boilers than either of you."

Jake turned to find Adam Farber behind him, his face hidden by the up-turned collar of a rain slicker. Lars the *werkman* was behind him, a dirty jacket thrown over his elevator operator's uniform.

"You ain't a plumber," Doheimer challenged. "And I bet you ain't Union, either."

"Actually," Adam said, "I am. International Union of Operating Engineers, Local #06."

"Now we're talkin'," Doheimer said, and broke into a grin. "Hey fellas! We got a Union brother!" Adam looked uncomfortable as a cheer went up from the plumbers.

"The question is, do you have his back?" Jake asked. "Or did you forget that there's a boiler set to blow?"

Doheimer's expression hardened. "I'll go in with you. Nothin' against engineers, but they ain't plumbers." He turned toward the others. "Boys! Listen up! These three sa-bot-eers messed with a boiler in that building. Eddie! Sam! Haul these sons of bitches out of the way and keep an eye on them. Don't let them go nowhere. The rest of yunz clear out the area and block off the streets around here. Keep the rubberneckers away." He turned back to Adam, Rick, and Jake with a curt nod. "Let's go."

"We're coming with you," Jake and Rick said in unison.

Kovach grabbed Jake by the arm. "No, you're not," he said, holding Jake back.

"Here," Adam said, shoving something into Rick's hand. "One of you, put these on." Then Adam, Lars, and Doheimer headed into the open basement door of the Brand and Desmet headquarters.

"Let them do what they're good at. We'd only be in the way," Rick said.

Jake shook off Kovach's hand, but did not move to follow. He and Rick withdrew to a safe distance down the block while Kovach went looking for his missing men. Before long, he showed up with one man slung over his shoulder.

"Here," he grunted, unloading the man like a sack of flour onto the sidewalk. "That's one of them. Looks like they're all drugged. Don't go anywhere." He took off at a run. Jake dragged the unconscious man out of the middle of the sidewalk and propped him against the wall of the building down the block and out of harm's way. Kovach returned in a few minutes with the second man, and headed after the third.

"I hope they're all right," Jake said, staring at the darkened windows of the Brand and Desmet headquarters.

"Nothing's blown up yet," Rick replied.

Once Kovach had retrieved the last of his men, he walked over to One-Ear and hauled him to his feet, pushing him hard up against the wall. "What did you use on my men? Because I know damn well they didn't get drunk."

"Why should I tell you?"

In response, Kovach put One-Ear in a headlock and began to drag the bound man back toward the Brand and Desmet building.

"All right!" One-Ear cried, and Kovach stopped. "We shot 'em with darts."

"What was on the darts?"

"Don't know," One-Ear replied, and howled when Kovach kicked him in the leg. "God's truth, honest! The guy who hired us gave us a bottle of some kind of liquid, told us to put it on the dart tips but not get any on ourselves. That's all I know. Worked like a charm."

Swearing in Hungarian, Kovach dragged One-Ear back to the sidewalk. He drew his revolver, and stood where he had a clean shot at all three saboteurs. "I wouldn't mind some target practice right now to let off some steam," he warned. "Don't give me a reason."

A short way off, Rick pressed the goggles into Jake's hand. "Here, you can do the honors."

Jake looked down at the goggles. The thick frame that encased the lenses was filled with wires and small, intricate gears, while the lenses themselves glittered with a strange iridescence. "Those are the gadget glasses Adam showed me," Rick said excitedly. "He must have gotten them working!"

"Never saw a pair of glasses with a switch," Jake said, turning them on and lifting them to his face. "Well what do you know? I see what Lars sees."

Rick moved to stand beside him, as if to see what he was looking at.

"They're working their way toward the boiler," Jake said. "Looks like One-Ear and his buddies trashed the place. All right. They're at the boiler. Not good. I don't have to hear what they're saying. Lars can see the gauges. If they can't bring down the pressure real quick, that boiler's going to blow."

"Can they do it?" Rick asked, his voice taut.

"I don't know," Jake replied, squinting. One-Ear and his men had added some kind of infernal mechanism to the boiler.

Jake could see Doheimer shouting at Adam as they both bent to the work of undoing the damage the saboteurs had done. "The emergency release valve has been badly damaged, welded shut—they can't budge it. And there's a timer mechanism attached to the side." Jake watched as Doheimer and Adam strained to turn valves and knobs with wrenches. Lars lent his mechanical strength but was also thwarted.

"They can't turn down the pressure. And the boiler looks like it's straining at the seams." Through Lars's eyes, Jake could read the gauges. Every one of the gauges was in the red zone.

"They're not going to make it. It's going up any second. Everyone pull back!" The group moved another block down the street, dragging the saboteurs and unconscious guards with them; still within sight but, with luck, out of the range of flying debris.

Jake's field of vision changed so quickly it nearly made him lose his balance. Rick put a hand on his shoulder to steady him as the scene blurred, and when the images cleared, Lars was on the other side of the boiler.

"Oh, no," Jake murmured, knowing what the *werkman* intended an instant before Lars's metal fist slammed through the emergency release valve.

Caught up in the vision, Jake reeled as scalding water burst from the ruptured valve, dousing the *werkman* and spraying the room behind him. Clouds of super-heated steam billowed from the tank, hot enough to sear skin and lungs. A muted bang rumbled across Smallman Street, and Doheimer's plumbers cried out in alarm.

"Adam and Doheimer?" Rick pressed.

"I can't see them," Jake said. "I can't see much at all."

Steam clouded Jake's vision even as the *werkman* tried to back out of the way. His metal skin and clockwork mechanisms protected him beyond the limits of fragile skin and bone, but Jake knew as the image flickered and faltered that the damage was done. Lars looked down at the fist that had ruptured the damaged release valve, and the metal was melted and misshapen, fingers fused together.

Lights flickered at the edge of Jake's vision, warning signals from the difference engine in Lars's mechanical brain alerting him to critical data. Perhaps with forethought, Adam could build a *werkman* especially suited for the conditions of the ruined boiler room, but Lars had been intended as an elevator operator, not meant for extreme conditions.

"He's dying," Jake said.

"Who? Adam?" Rick's worry was clear in his voice.

"No, Lars," Jake replied. "He's shutting down."

The warning lights from the difference engine were dimming. The point of view did not move—perhaps, Jake thought, Lars' legs were fused, like the fingers of his hand, by the superheated steam. The images in the gadget glasses flickered, obliterated by bursts of static. Colors faded. The lenses went dark.

"He's gone." Jake swallowed down the lump in his throat. *He's mechanical*, Jake told himself. *Adam can fix him, build another one.* Still, he couldn't shake the feeling of loss.

"Jake." Rick shook his shoulder. "Jake. Take the glasses off. Look. Adam and Doheimer. They're coming out of the cellar. They're alive!"

Jake removed the gadget glasses and tucked them into a pocket of his jacket. He saw Adam's loping figure next to Doheimer's squat, bustling form. "They made it," he said, relief flooding him. "It didn't blow up the building."

The plumbers sent up a cheer as Doheimer and Adam crossed the street to rejoin them, crowding around and shouting in triumph. Jake left Kovach to mind the prisoners, and went to greet them.

Adam's glum face was in marked contrast to the celebratory mood of the plumbers gathered around Doheimer. "You saw?" he said, meeting Jake's gaze.

Jake nodded. "Yeah. What was that thing?"

Adam shook his head. "I didn't have time to study it. Some kind of detonator that would have magnified the blast, I'd guess. They'd welded the knobs. The only thing I could think to do was release the pressure, and Lars was the only way to do it in a hurry." He looked haggard. "Doheimer and I barely had a chance to find cover before I had to give Lars the order. I didn't go in there intending to destroy him."

"I'm sorry," Jake replied. "Can you fix him?"

Adam let out a long breath. "I can build a new body, but each *werkman* has his own quirks, little design flaws that make them individual. Once he's fixed, he'll function, but I don't know if he'll still be Lars."

"Someone meant to do you a world of harm." Doheimer stood in front of Jake, backed by his men. "Never thought I'd say it, but I'm mighty glad those guys were scabs. No Union man would do such a thing."

"Thank you," Jake said, extending his hand. Doheimer's roughened fingers closed around his in a bone-crushing shake. "You took a big risk."

"Sorry about your man," Doheimer said. "Don't know how he managed to do it, welded solid it was, but if he hadn't, we'd have all gone up along with the building."

Jake nodded. "We'll see to him." He looked up at the crowd of plumbers. "We're all right, then—misunderstanding straightened out, no boycott?"

Doheimer grinned. "Right as rain, son. Got no patience with anarchists. You want my boys to work them over, find out what they know?"

"That won't be necessary," Rick said. "But thank you."

"You sure?" Doheimer said, giving One-Eye a look that made the three saboteurs shrink back against the wall. "Stuff like this makes my guys real mad. Leaving those three in a bloody heap might send their bosses a message."

"Thanks, but no," Jake said. "We'll handle them."

"All right then, let's clear out!" Doheimer shouted to his plumbers. "'I'll be back first thing Monday morning and see what it'll take to replace that boiler and get things set right. I'll get you a good price." And with that, Doheimer and his men strode off down Smallman Street.

“What do you intend to do with them?” Kovach asked, raking the prisoners with a glare that made it clear he would not have minded taking Doheimer up on his offer.

“A slightly more elegant version of the same thing,” Jake said, feeling all the night’s danger, tension and loss turning into cold resolve. “I thought we’d take them to Andreas, let him find out what they know and make them forget it all.”

Kovach turned back to the prisoners. “You might want to beg those plumbers to come back and work you over,” he said with a nasty smile. “Because he’s going to turn you over to a vampire-witch.”

“And then what?” Rick asked quietly.

“Then we take what we find out, and figure out if the same people trying to kill Adam—and me—are the ones who killed my father,” Jake replied. “It’s time to settle the score.”

Chapter EIGHTEEN

"For someone who's supposed to be in mourning, you get around," Cady McDaniel said as Nicki slipped into the carriage a few blocks from the Desmet home.

"Extraordinary circumstances require a little rule bending, and besides, except for church, we spent all of yesterday cooped up," Nicki said offhandedly. While she was not wearing black or gray, her navy blue dress was suitably dark, and a conservative hat was strategically positioned to partially shadow her face.

"There are worse things than offending the guardians of fashion," Renate Thalberg observed, and knocked on the glass panel at the front of the carriage, signaling the driver to go.

"If he's gone missing, surely the police have been to Jasinski's apartment," Cady said.

"Doubtful," Renate said. "Folks on Polish Hill don't trust the cops much. And even if they did, why would the police bother? Karl was no one important to them."

The carriage jostled along the streets of New Pittsburgh, winding from the broad boulevards of Shadyside toward the more modest accommodations of Polish Hill. At Catherine's behest, the driver and his assistant were two of Miska Kovach's security men. Both were armed, as were the passengers in the carriage. Nicki had her derringer, Cady had a Colt Peacemaker tucked into her large purse, and Renate's protections were of an entirely different and magical sort.

"You still haven't explained how Cady and I are going to be able to recognize anything witchy on our own." Nicki tucked her hat pin back into place, trying to keep the large hat from listing as the carriage bumped over the cobblestone road.

Renate reached into a velvet bag that hung from her belt and withdrew a glass orb the size of an apple. "This is an oculus," she said, looking from Nicki to Cady. "When I activate it, I will see whatever is in front of the oculus. I'll see what you see."

"Great," said Cady. "But how will we know if we're looking at something important?"

Renate grinned. "Because I can send a flicker of magic through the oculus to signal you. Yellow means something is important enough to take with you. Red means danger—don't touch."

Nicki shrugged. "That seems simple enough."

Renate replaced the oculus in its pouch and handed the velvet bag to Cady. "Hopefully, it will be that simple."

"On the other hand, we have no idea who else might have been there ahead of us," Nicki said. "Including those two government agents."

"True," Renate conceded. "But they're not witches. And a lot of powerful magical items appear quite normal and unimportant to someone without magic."

"Hiding in plain sight," Cady said.

"Exactly," Renate said.

"How do we know Drogo Veles or some of his henchmen haven't beaten us to it?" Nicki asked.

Renate sighed. "We don't. But Karl knew Andreas and me. We were part of his coven. I thought he trusted us. I'm betting that if Karl spelled his place against witches, I might be able to bend his wardings a bit to allow you to enter." She smiled. "I have an amulet he made. It may have enough resonance of his power to do the trick." She paused. "Or he may have set his wardings so that his landlady's willing permission will allow a visitor to pass. There are a lot of ways to set a spell like this, if you expect the other side to use force."

"Mrs. Zukowski gave me a note for Karl Jasinski's landlady," Cady said, withdrawing a folded piece of paper. "It's in Polish. But Mrs. Zukowski says the landlady is a friend of hers, and if she vouches for us, the landlady will let us into Karl's shop."

"Let's hope the note doesn't say 'Call the police right now', in Polish," Nicki muttered. "You trust people more than I do."

Cady chuckled. "Not so much. I looked it up one word at a time in a Polish dictionary before I came."

"Suppose Karl was trying to stop the Night Hag," Nicki said. "What kind of things would he need? Other than whatever he was trying to ship to Brand and Desmet that never arrived."

"Notes—very possibly not in English," Renate replied. "Diagrams. Symbols or runes. Maps. Maybe some type of relic. Eastern Europe is very big on sacred objects of all kinds. Belief invests a lot of power into something like a relic. If you see items you think are odd, hold up the oculus, and I can tell you whether it's worth taking."

"You want us to steal things from Jasinski's shop?" Nicki asked, raising an eyebrow.

Renate met her gaze. "I don't think Karl abandoned his mission," she replied. "Either someone took him, or he's dead. In either case, nothing would please him more than for his work to go on, to succeed."

"Let's hope he was on the right track," Cady said. "Or we've got even bigger problems."

The late afternoon sun cast long shadows from the buildings on Pulawski Way. Rooming houses, homes, and shops with signs in both English and Polish lined the narrow streets. Washing hung from laundry lines and fire escape railings. Boys played marbles in the street and old men lounged on front stoops, talking in Polish and watching people pass by. Old women in head scarves and long black dresses, tired-looking women with babies on their hips, and workmen coming back from their shifts jostled for space on the cracked sidewalks. The smell of sausage and cabbage, tripe, and freshly baked bread wafted from open windows.

The carriage that Renate had acquired was plain, of a kind often hired by the hour; something no one would look twice at. The driver and his assistant were dressed plainly, and all three of the women had taken pains to choose clothing that would not stand out in this neighborhood of mill workers, tradesmen, and recent immigrants. Nicki had somehow acquired a half-mourning gown made of affordable bombazine, and her hat, while it had a veil that partially obscured her features, was far below Nicki's usual sartorial standards.

Their carriage parked around the corner from the address written on Cady's scrap of paper. "Time to activate the oculus," Renate said.

Renate took a silver cup from the small carpetbag on the seat next to her, and handed the cup to Cady. She handed a silver bowl to Nicki. Then Renate took out a silver absinthe spoon, the handle of which was in the shape of a pentacle, and a vial of green absinthe.

"Hold the cup still," Renate instructed. She placed the pentacle-spoon across the top and dripped thirteen drops of absinthe through its silver lattice. She stoppered the absinthe vial and withdrew another vial of water, adding a couple more drops into the silver cup and clouding the drink.

Renate cradled the oculus in her hands for a moment, then held it out over the bowl.

"Pour it over the orb," Renate said. Cady removed the pentacle-spoon and carefully poured most of the small amount of liquid over the orb as Renate began to chant. The globe went from translucent to a milky white glow. Renate lifted the bowl to her lips and drank the remaining liquid. She dried the orb with its velvet bag, then handed it to Nicki.

"As soon as you can, when you're in Karl's shop, take out the oculus," Renate instructed. "I will go into a trance here in the carriage, so I can see through the device. Move it slowly, and if you think something's important, bring the oculus as close to it as you can without touching it." She looked from Nicki to Cady. "That's very important. Don't touch anything unless I give you the signal. Karl is a powerful witch. The same wardings that keep me out might protect his most valuable treasures."

"So how do we steal things, if they're warded?" Nicki asked, matter-of-factly.

"We'll cross that bridge when we come to it," Renate replied.

Nicki and Cady got out of the carriage. The driver's assistant followed like a loyal servant, if a very well-armed servant. They stopped at the door to the duplex where Jasinski had his shop.

"Mr. Kovach chose me for the trip because I speak Polish," the driver's assistant said. "I'm Tomasz. I can handle the introduction to the landlady, and fend off questions while you ladies do what you need to do."

Nicki grinned. "I think you'll work out perfectly, Tomasz."

Tomasz knocked at the door to the landlady's side of the duplex. A worn-looking woman answered, wearing a faded dress, her gray hair tied up in a scarf. Tomasz offered a polite greeting in Polish, and made what Nicki guessed was a request to access Karl's shop. After what sounded like a heated back-and-forth, Tomasz presented the note from Mrs. Kozinski, and the landlady read it over, then nodded grudgingly and produced a key, which she tucked into Tomasz's hand, followed by a stern warning. Then she shut the door and Tomasz returned to where Nicki and Cady were standing.

"What was all that about?" Cady asked.

"Just convincing the landlady that we weren't with the police, and we didn't want to cause trouble," Tomasz replied. "She's worried about Jasinski, and even more worried about who is going to pay for his shop and apartment rental if he doesn't show up soon."

"If you've got the key, let's get going," Nicki said. "I don't like standing around where people can see."

Tomasz led the way to the shop door and slid the iron key into the lock. Karl Jasinski's shop had a small storefront with a grimy window and a sign that read 'Fortunes told, problems solved' in both English and Polish.

Inside, the small shop smelled of dust and stale air. In the front room, Jasinski sold candles of all colors, amulets of the saints, and bunches of dried herbs. Bottles of powders and vials of elixirs sat on shelves, gathering dust. In the back of the shop was a table covered with a cheap red cloth where Jasinski must have done his readings for clients. A tarot deck lay to one side. Adorning the walls were paintings of crowns, a large tree, a single eye, and an elaborately decorated egg. Blown eggs of every size, covered with symbols, filled one glass case.

"Why all the eggs?" Nicki asked, bending to peer into the case.

"They're *pisanka*," Tomasz replied. "Traditional Polish art. Also, powerful magical symbols, but most people just think they're pretty."

Nicki withdrew the oculus from its bag and cradled it in her hand. Slowly, she made a full circle, holding the orb out in front of her to give Renate as good a view as possible.

Cady moved in the opposite direction, peering through the glass cases, squinting at the writing on the labels for the vials and powders, and eyeing the papers that had been left on the counter.

"I can't make out anything from the books," Cady said, staring at a shelf containing close to a dozen old volumes. "They're all in Polish."

"*The Way of the Left Hand*," Tomasz translated one title. "*Path of Mists*." He paled and crossed himself. "Holy Mother protect us. This man was not just a fortune-teller. He was *koldun*."

"What does that mean?" Nicki asked. She moved to see better, bringing the oculus closer, and the orb glowed a golden yellow as she held it up to each of the books.

"*Koldun* have bad magic," Tomasz said, and his accent grew a little thicker with the telling. "They set curses, cause bad luck. Spoil things. Bad people."

"*Koldun* sounds like a Russian word," Nicki mused, having given the orb a look at the books, moving on when the golden light faded.

"Fine," Tomasz said nervously. "*Czarodziej*. Russian, Polish—bad news is bad news. For a Pole, he had a lot of Russian books. Do you think they're important?"

"Renate seemed to think so. What topics do they cover?" Cady asked.

"Mostly burial customs, from what I can make out," Tomasz replied.

"Thomasz, why don't you take the books out to the carriage and then come right back?" Nicki suggested.

Cady was down on her hands and knees, examining papers on the floor. "Hey Nicki—come over here!" Nicki followed the sound of her voice and found Cady teasing out some fallen papers from beneath the desk.

"Renate told us not to touch anything," Nicki warned.

Cady quirked an eyebrow. "That's rich, coming from you." She waved at the papers scattered across the floor. "If we can walk on them, they shouldn't kill us to touch them."

Nicki brought the oculus closer so that Renate could see the papers. Some were in English, others in Polish. About half of the papers were typewritten, and the others were filled with cramped, Cyrillic letters. The oculus began to glow again.

"Renate thinks you've found something," Nicki said. "Go ahead and gather those up. We need to move along."

Nicki moved past the desk to a shelf cluttered with objects, both practical and arcane. Candles and crystals, and a carved pointing stick that looked suspiciously like old bone—the jumble of objects looked like Jasinski had dumped out his valise, and maybe his pockets for good measure.

She muttered to herself as she tried to angle the oculus for a good view. When the orb began to glow once more, Nicki cursed under her breath in French.

"How am I supposed to know which one is important?" she asked the orb. Annoyed, she swept all of the knick-knacks into a cloth sack.

Tomasz had returned, and he was studying a cluster of family photographs. "See, he wasn't all bad," Nicki quipped. "He had a family."

Tomasz leaned forward for a better look, then took a step back as he drew in his breath sharply, cursing in Polish. "They're dead! All of them. Damn him! These are death photographs."

"Maybe he's just sentimental," Cady replied, making a pile of the spilled papers. "My aunt had pictures like that made when my cousin died." She shuddered. "Horrible custom, but it matters to some people."

Nicki had made a full circle around the shop's main room. The oculus had glowed golden on at least a dozen objects, but for the most part remained dull, even when Nicki ran it past the conjuring items Jasinski had obviously used when he gave readings for clients. She swept back the curtain that separated the front room of the shop from the small, cramped back office. A narrow, twisting set of steps led up to what she guessed was Jasinski's rented room above the shop. The late afternoon light was fading, but still sufficient to reveal most of the room's content. A desk took up most of the space. More papers and ledgers were piled on every flat surface.

"I'm going upstairs," Nicki called out, gathering her skirts with one hand while she held the oculus aloft with the other. The stairway was not much wider than her shoulders, and it turned twice before it got to the top, making the treads narrow and dangerous. Curiosity led her onwards; that and the hunch that whatever Jasinski prized, he would not keep it in such a public space as his shop.

"Nicki? Wait up!" she heard Cady call from behind her, but she kept climbing, drawn forward by the tingle of intuition.

The air grew stale as she climbed, with remnants of old cooking odors and cheap cigarettes. The room above Jasinski's shop was barely adequate. Faded chintz curtains screened the single, dirty window. Half-empty bottles of vodka and gin lined one windowsill. An ashtray filled with stubs sat on a scarred, cheap coffee table next to a threadbare chair and equally hard-used footstool. On the other side of the room, a metal-frame single bed was covered with a worn, stained quilt.

Nicki looked around with a mixture of pity and barely-contained curiosity. It was obvious that Jasinski had not been home for quite a while, as evidenced by the half-eaten, moldering remnants of food left on a plate.

"Nicki?" Cady's voice called again reaching the top of the steps as Nicki moved farther into the room for a better look. Books were stacked everywhere and Nicki took a step toward the rumpled bed, peering at the piles stacked on the floor beside it. A flannel nightshirt was thrown over the piles, and the unmade bed covers spilled across the bedframe, but as Nicki got closer, she realized the mess hid a square trunk.

Nicki grabbed a broomstick from the corner and used the handle to lift the bedclothes away from the books. As she did so, a small, leather-bound book and a drawstring pouch fell to the floor. When the pouch landed, a few carved stones spilled to the floor. The oculus glowed brightly and Nicki carefully scooped up the pouch, stones, and book and slid them into her bag.

"What are you doing?" Cady said, reaching the upstairs landing. "Make sure you use the orb!"

"We'll be fine," Nicki replied absently. She poked at the nightshirt until it fell to the far side of the bed, and then jabbed at the books, sweeping them out of their piles until she could make out the trunk.

"Now that's interesting," she murmured. She set the broom aside and pulled one of her long hatpins from her hair, sliding the oculus into her pouch without noticing that it had taken on a distinctly red glow.

Nicki knelt next to the trunk. The box was covered in smooth black leather, with a solid brass lock. Nicki reached for the lock, and drew back, feeling a quiver of hesitation. Drawing a deep breath and steeling her nerve, she poked the hatpin into the lock and began to feel for the mechanism.

"Nicki!" Cady pushed into the room behind her as Nicki fiddled with the hair pin, jiggering it left and right until she heard a *click*.

The lid flew back, slamming against the metal bed frame so loudly it sounded as if someone had hammered on a pan with a wooden mallet. As Nicki desperately scrambled backward, a miasma of cold, fetid air began to billow from the trunk. The oculus in Nicki's bag flared, glowing so brightly that a red light shone through the cloth, casting the small room in hellish shades.

Nicki screamed and threw one book after another at the specter, which was taking shape from the grave-cold fog. She got her feet under her, and dug out her derringer, squeezing off a shot to no effect.

"Cady! Get out of here. We've got trouble!"

As more of the fog poured from the trunk, the shape became more solid, growing in nightmarish proportions. Its narrow, elongated head was covered with matted, tangled hair, like a corpse pulled from the water. Red pinpoints of light glared where eyes should have been, and its jaw hinged like a snake, revealing sharp, serrated teeth.

Cady headed down the steps without being told twice. "Come on!" she urged. Nicki was backing toward the stairs, trying not to fall over the mess Jasinski had left behind, but the specter was growing fast, keeping its blood-red eyes fixed on its prey.

She was almost to the doorway when the revenant struck. Moving fast as a storm wind, the black-mist figure reached for Nicki with clawed hands that looked solid enough to grasp and tear. Nicki squealed and reached into her pouch, pulling out the oculus and thrusting it forward.

Blinding green light flared from the orb, lighting up the room like the headlight of a locomotive. The ghostly shape pulled back, giving Nicki the chance she needed to bolt down the stairs.

Cady was just a few steps down from her. "Nicki, what's going on—"

"Run!" Nicki shouted, clamoring down the steps with her skirts gathered in one hand, and her bag clutched in the other. She could feel freezing cold air stirring behind her, and the tomb-rot stench of the revenant was enough to make her gorge rise.

Nicki had no idea what Cady sensed or saw, but she flew down the steps, taking them as quickly as she dared. Cady made it to the bottom and was with Tomasz. Nicki, afraid to look over her shoulder, made the first turn in the stairway without missing a step, but on the second turn, her foot slipped, carrying her down the last three steps in a tumble of skirts and limbs.

The specter was right behind her; the back of Nicki's neck prickled, and every sense screamed a warning. Ghastly, insubstantial hands tore at the hem of her skirt. Nicki couldn't get to her feet fast enough. She rolled as soon as she hit the floor, trying to get out of the way.

Cady and Tomasz opened fire, but the bullets went right through the billowing darkness to lodge in the walls.

Tomasz shoved his gun into his belt and grabbed Nicki by one arm and began to drag her toward the door, pushing Cady ahead of him with the other hand. Nicki scrabbled to her feet and ran.

Nicki, Cady, and Tomasz spilled out of the doorway and onto the sidewalk, running for their lives. Two figures stepped up to block their path: Renate Thalberg and a black-clad man dressed in a priest's cassock, with dark hair and a dark beard. The carriage driver, one of Kovach's guards, stood beside them, a sawed-off shotgun leveled at the monster.

"Stay back!" the priest shouted.

Renate stood shoulder to shoulder with the priest, and her entire form was limned in a green glow. Light streamed from her hands, forming a gleaming cage of magical energy that surrounding the shifting black mist and trapped it as it billowed from the doorway. The black phantom surged against the force that contained it. Tomasz ran to stand next to the carriage driver, drawing his gun for want of anything else to do.

Tomasz and the carriage driver opened up with a barrage, but the shells and bullets streaked right through the black mist, lodging in the walls of Jasinski's shop. Muttering curses, they reloaded and fell back, unsure what to do in the face of a threat without a solid body.

Renate's hands moved and the power shifted, pushing back at the dark presence. The green glow intensified as her face tensed in concentration. As Renate swayed and chanted, the priest held up a golden box that looked to Nicki like a reliquary.

"Be gone!" he shouted at the phantom, and repeated the command in Polish. A searing blast of gold light flared from the box in the stranger's hands, tearing through the mist, rending it like an old shroud.

Yet as quickly as the phantom was torn to shreds it re-formed, a boiling, billowing mass of darkness. Bystanders who had stopped to see what was going on screamed and ran for cover as the hideous shape contorted in its green prison.

Cady's Peacemaker was still in her hand, but Tomasz shook his head. "Bullets aren't going to damage that thing. You two better get in the carriage."

"Not without Renate," Nicki snapped.

The phantom twisted and writhed, straining at Renate's prison. The dark-haired stranger lifted his voice in a new chant, raising the golden reliquary again as the darkness threatened to break loose.

Renate wielded the silver amulet she wore on a chain around her neck, a rectangle marked with runes, holding it up in front of her like a shield.

"Together!" the priest shouted, and light flared from their objects of power, blindingly bright, burning through the dark miasma with enough brilliance that it seemed as if the black mist itself were burning.

The phantom shrieked and twisted, fighting against the power, but the combined force was too much for it, and the creature dissolved, the light eating away at its edges, consuming it, until nothing remained. Gone for now, Nicki thought, but hardly likely that it was entirely destroyed.

Renate was trembling with exertion. The greenish glow no longer surrounded her, but she gripped the silver amulet as if she might never let it go. The priest was the first to speak.

"You're the absinthe witch." His voice was neutral, without judgment, but there was a sense of authority in his manner. Nicki took a good look at the man and realized that he was younger than she first thought, perhaps in his thirties.

Renate nodded. "And you're the demon-priest."

To Nicki's surprise, the priest laughed. "Is that what they call me? Sounds like *I'm* the demon instead of describing what I fight."

"Father Matija," Renate said, and the priest inclined his head in acknowledgement. "So it's true—the *Logonje* have returned."

Matija glanced around them. None of the bystanders had ventured from cover, though nervous faces watched from behind blinds and curtains at every house. "Yes," he said, "and with reason. There's much to discuss, but not here."

"Dare an Orthodox priest share a carriage with a witch and her helpers?" Renate asked.

Matija gave a wan half-smile. "As you might expect, I am a rather unorthodox Orthodox priest. So yes, and on the way I would like to know what brought you here and how it was the wraith was released."

Tomasz and the driver looked to Nicki for confirmation, and at her nod they climbed to their seat as the stranger opened the carriage door and stood to the side for the three women to enter. Nicki studied him as he climbed into the carriage and took his seat.

Father Matija was striking. A pity, given his vocation, Nicki thought. His dark hair was cut short, and his eyes had an intelligent glint to them. Matija's broad hands were calloused and muscular, as if the priest were no stranger to hard work—or perhaps weapons training.

"You show up in the oddest places," Renate observed, giving Matija an appraising look.

Matija chuckled. "One could say the same of you—all three of you." Nicki had the feeling that although she had never met Matija, he knew her and Cady on sight.

"You've been watching Jasinski's shop?" Renate asked.

Matija shrugged. "More like watching for dark energy. Where it's been active, we observe—and step in if there's a way we can help."

"So you know Jasinski's missing," Renate said.

"I'd heard that. And I've heard he had attracted notice before he vanished, claiming there were monsters loose in the city."

"Do you know who's behind the monsters?" Renate asked.

Matija regarded her for a moment before speaking. "The *Logonje* believe the monsters may have been freed accidentally; as much as greed and arrogance are truly 'accidents'. The question is, who now benefits from the damage done by the monsters?"

"The names Drogo Veles and Richard Thwaites keep coming up in certain circles," Renate replied.

Matija nodded. "I have heard the same, but proof and hearsay are two different things."

Renate turned to meet the priest's gaze. "If we brought you proof, would the *Logonje* take action?"

A hint of a smile played at Matija's lips. "That would depend on the nature of the proof. But it is a distinct possibility." He leaned forward to knock on the window, signaling the driver to let him out.

As the carriage slowed to a stop, Matija stood. "Please be sure to convey my best wishes, and my greetings, to your 'brother'." And with that, the priest stepped out of the carriage and out into the bustle of the downtown traffic.

"A new player—as if this whole thing weren't complicated enough," Cady muttered.

"Let's see what we can make of the things we took from the shop," Nicki replied. "We know Veles is tied up in this somehow, which means he stands to gain money or power—or both. I'm just not sure how. Yet."

"We must proceed with caution. They've already killed Thomas Desmet, and possibly Karl Jasinski, and they've made more than a few attempts on the family," Renate warned. "We need to connect those pieces soon, before anyone else dies. Including us."

Chapter NINETEEN

"YOU'RE CERTAIN HE'S drugged?" Drogo Veles peered cautiously at the captive. The prisoner was in his early forties, with shaggy dark hair, an untrimmed beard, and a pair of wire-rimmed glasses sitting askew on his face. The man was bound at the wrists and ankles, and again across the chest, tying him to the chair.

"My man got him with the dart two hours ago," Thwaites replied. "It's a hefty dose."

Veles circled the bound man. The prisoner hung against his bonds, apparently insensible. *It's a delicate thing, questioning another mage—especially a powerful one,* Veles thought. *Can't leave him with his powers, but take away the powers and one's not certain what remains of the mind.*

The prisoner was the Polish witch Karl Jasinski. What Veles wanted, *needed*, was locked inside Jasinski's mind and unlikely to be given up willingly. Yet if he dug too assertively, the precious knowledge about how to control—or banish—the *gessyan* might be lost completely.

"You've got magic. Why can't you just make him tell you what you want?" Thwaites asked, his tone mocking.

"As usual, it's not as easy as you assume," Veles replied, his voice a quiet growl. "It's a delicate thing to get information from another witch who doesn't give it willingly." He had no desire to elaborate. His 'partnership' with Thwaites was necessary, but hardly based on trust. Veles had not lived for so long by trusting others with knowledge about witches and their secrets. Even the drug he had given Thwaites to use against Jasinski was one Veles had long ago developed a tolerance for. Should

Thwaites decide to double-cross him, Veles would likely have no worse than a bad headache, rather than Jasinski's complete collapse.

Jasinski moaned. "He's coming around," Thwaites said. "Ask your questions."

Interrogating a witch of real power was a difficult undertaking, Veles knew. Mortal torture could compel a prisoner to provide answers for the sake of ending pain, but most of the time the answers were false, given just to stop the torment. Witches were even more complex to question. Leave them with their powers intact, and they would fight to the death rather than give up their secrets. Suppress their powers with charms and curses, and the questioning witch was in danger of damping his own magic to the point of uselessness.

Every attempt to bribe, flatter or scare Jasinski into cooperating had failed. Chasing his damned crate halfway around the world and pursuing Jasinski for weeks had come down to this: a man drugged nearly insensible, and a dark witch at the limits of his patience.

"What did you ship from Poland to Brand and Desmet?"

"Alekanovo stones and a book."

"Marcin of Krakow's book?" Veles pressed.

"Yes."

"Where is the crate?"

"Don't know."

"Did you arrange for it to go missing?" Veles asked.

"No." Jasinski's voice was faint, like a man jarred from a deep sleep who believes himself to still be dreaming.

"Did you send someone to take it?"

"No."

"Did you steal the crate from Brand and Desmet?"

"No."

"This is getting us nowhere," Thwaites fumed. He picked up a riding crop from where it was leaning against a crate and brought it down hard across Jasinski's face, opening cuts across his nose and cheek. "Tell us what you did with the crate!"

Veles used a flicker of magic, and the crop was torn from Thwaites's hand, flying through the air to land in his own outstretched palm. He broke the crop over his knee and dropped it. "I control this interrogation," he said, meeting Thwaites's gaze. "I will not warn you again."

"And it's coming along so beautifully," Thwaites retorted sullenly, but he did not make another move toward Jasinski.

Veles returned his attention to the prisoner. "What's in your apartment and store that's connected to the *gessyan*?"

It took Jasinski a moment to reply, as if his addled mind were searching for words. "Books. Papers. Drawings. Things."

"Can you use them to control the *gessyan*?" Veles pressed.

"No. Need the stones."

Veles cursed in Romanian. He began to pace. They had chosen to interrogate Jasinski in the Vesta Nine storage building where Tumblety and Brunrichter constructed their automatons and created their clockwork corpses. The air stank of decay and embalming fluid. Guards surrounding the perimeter of the building ensured that they would not be disturbed, and the wardings around the interrogation area contained Jasinski's power. The single overhead light did little more than intensify the shadows surrounding them. And though Veles had used his magic to make certain that nothing would trigger either the clockwork corpses or the automatons, yet he eyed their still, unnatural forms with suspicion.

"How much did you tell Thomas Desmet about the stones?" Veles asked. The drug mixture he had concocted was lethal in high dosages, and he had made a strong portion to assure Jasinski's compliance. The poison would give them a finite amount of time to question their prisoner, but make him more docile, stripping away most of his magic. It was a devil's bargain, in more ways than one.

Veles watched Jasinski closely. Every witch worth their salt had a death spell, a final curse to cheat an enemy of victory. Veles's own conjuration would send a city block up in flames. Other witches he had known took different approaches, all of them unpleasant and fatal to themselves and their captors. He did not want Jasinski to regain enough lucidity to use his.

"Enough. Enough that he knew how important it was. He waived the fee." Jasinski's voice was barely above a whisper. "Desmet knew the things in the crate were magic. Dangerous."

"Did you tell him about the *gessyan*? About Vesta Nine?"

"No. Just... bad spirits."

Thwaites moved to backhand Jasinski, but Veles's arm snapped out, stopping Thwaites before he could touch the drugged witch. "If you make another move to hit him, I will hurt you," Veles growled.

"We're not getting anywhere!" Thwaites snapped. "He's not so tough now."

"A drugged witch is unpredictable," Veles said with more patience than he felt. "Like a wounded dog. Ask him questions, he'll answer. Rough him up, and he may be able to summon up enough magic to incinerate you in self-defense."

Thwaites's eyes widened, and he stepped back, sulking. "What good are your drugs, then?"

"He hasn't incinerated you yet, has he?" Veles replied, then ignored Thwaites and turned back to Jasinski.

"How do I control the *gessyan*?" Veles asked. "How do I use the Russian stones and the witch's book?"

"You can't," Jasinski said, his voice drifting and unsteady. "Need the *Logonje*... priests. Holy magic..."

Veles felt his temper rising. "Tell me what I want to know. I can give you an easy death—or a hard one."

Jasinski straightened and for one terrifyingly coherent moment, his eyes were clear and his voice steady. "Go to Hell," he said, and muttered a word of power. He was dead before the breath left his body.

"What just happened?" Thwaites demanded. "Did you bugger this up?"

Without a backward glance, Veles clapped his hands and Thwaites was hurled across the room, slamming into the wall. He landed hard on his back, dirtying his bespoke Savile Row suit. Thwaites lay still, cursing a blue streak, as Veles moved forward cautiously and felt for a pulse.

"Damn," Veles muttered, although he had known Jasinski was dead before he tried. He laid a hand on the dead witch's forehead and reached out with his magic. Trying to read a dead man's mind was difficult, forbidden and dangerous.

Veles gasped, and tried to draw away. Jasinski's brain was an unreadable puddle of goo, mangled as if by a shotgun shell. But the witch's last spell drew Veles down, drowning him in the madness of a dead man's decomposing brain.

Veles struggled against the spell, but Jasinski had used all of his cunning. The Polish witch was even stronger than Veles had suspected. Tendrils of power lashed out, worming their way into Veles's defenses, burning skin and psyche, boring into his power. Veles cried out, sending a blast of magic to free himself as the dead witch's power launched a last, brute-force attack, a spell prepared in advance to trigger with the witch's last breath.

Jasinski had nothing to lose. The outlay of power to launch the spell had taken all his life force, his breath and body heat, the energy of his brain and heart. Everything was poured into a complex, deadly spell which forced Veles to call on his own magic to fight off the tendrils of power that burned him any time they slipped past his defenses, depleting his power.

He means to take me with him. He means to kill me.

Fighting Jasinski's spell was like fending off an army of octopi. Welts rose all over Veles' body as his life drained out of him with every painful blow of the tendrils. His skin was a mass of bloody sores. Blood ran from the open wounds and trickled down from his scalp. Distantly, he realized that Thwaites was screaming, but he had no time to deal with his panicked partner.

Worse, Veles knew the blood would draw the attention of the *gessyan* still in the depths of the Vesta Nine. He sensed that they were watching, and that if he failed to break free, they would surge up from the darkness to suck the marrow from his bones before tearing his spirit free of his wretched corpse.

Veles sent his will deep into the ground beneath his feet, drawing on the power of the earth. He willed that elemental force to geyser up through him, burning across sinew and veins, blasting from his palms into Jasinski's body. The blast ripped the corpse apart, shattering its rib cage, flaying the skin from the face, crushing bone.

For an awful instant, Veles felt the tendrils of the dead man's magic hold firm, until the power frayed and snapped with such force that Veles staggered back. He found himself in a defensive crouch, hands raised as if to fend off another attack, facing a savaged corpse tied with bloody bonds to a splintered chair.

Behind him, he heard he heard the slow, sarcastic applause of one man clapping. "Bravo!" Thwaites cried out. "Jolly good show. Encore!"

Were his power not utterly spent, Veles might have indulged himself in the luxury of blasting Thwaites with a bolt of energy, shutting the socialite up permanently.

"Shut the hell up and get rid of the body," he gasped.

"Me? Get a guard!" Thwaites snapped.

Veles rounded on him, snarling like a cornered beast. "Get rid of the damn body or I will turn you inside out and let you lie, gasping, while your ruptured lungs heave for breath."

Thwaites blanched. His lip rose in a sneer, but he grudgingly took one step and then another toward the bloody, mangled corpse. With a baleful glare toward Veles, Thwaites dragged the broken chair over to where Tumblety and Brunrichter left the unused 'bits' of their clockwork corpses. He pulled a straight razor from one pocket, snapped the blade open, and sliced down through Jasinski's bonds, letting the body fall onto the rotting, maggot-infested heap.

"Happy?" he snarled.

"No. I'm not *happy*," Veles replied venomously. "Jasinski is dead, and we don't have the Russian stones or the Polish witch's book. Desmet is meddling dangerously, and so is the Scottish detective. We have tourmaquartz left to mine, for buyers who are despots and arms dealers across two Continents. Men who will not look upon us kindly if we do not meet our obligations." He took a menacing step toward Thwaites.

"You think what I did to Jasinski was bad? If we fail to deliver, that's *nothing* compared to what our clients' witches will do to us.

How many times can you be tortured to death, resuscitated and killed again?" he asked, slowly advancing on Thwaites, who had the good sense to back away.

"Get a grip on yourself!" Thwaites ordered. "We'll deliver. The mining's gone on despite Desmet and his nosy friends. You said yourself, the deposit's almost completely exposed; that should make it easier to remove. Just another week or two, and we can cash in and leave this god-forsaken hole."

A shudder went through Veles from head to toe. He took a deep breath and relaxed his balled fists, forcing his jaw to unclench. "It's taken twice as long as it was supposed to. There'd better be no more problems."

"Not once my men kill the newest DSI spy," Thwaites replied. "We keep killing them, and they keep sending more. And we need to get rid of Jake Desmet and Rick Brand. That snoop Fletcher, too. They need to go—permanently."

"You tried and failed to do that with the sabotage at Brand and Desmet," Veles pointed out. "And your ham-handed attempt to kidnap Farber nearly destroyed the Tesla-Westinghouse building—and nearly killed him." He fixed Thwaites with a lethal glare. "I want Farber alive."

"It's not my fault!" Thwaites snapped. "We were going to pull Farber out before the bombs went off, but Desmet and his friends got there first." He gave Veles a self-satisfied look. "Although killing Farber would have still been better than letting Desmet have him."

"And you failed to kidnap *or* kill him," Veles pointed out. "Now he's missing, and so are most of his designs. I told you sending that spy to be his assistant would backfire."

"I still say it's time to make sure Jake Desmet and Rick Brand stop sticking their noses into our business—and their private investigator, too. They need to die," Thwaites argued.

Veles nodded. "Do it. It's taking all my power to keep the *gessyan* still in the mine from breaking loose—or attacking the miners. It's all coming down around us—and that will look like paradise compared with what our clients will do if we disappoint them. You'd better come through on this," he said, eyes narrowing.

"Don't have a fit," Thwaites said. "I'll take care of Desmet and his friends. We'll step up the mining. Tumblety and Brunrichter have more of their mechanical marvels to help."

"You'd better," Veles replied. "If I have to face our backers with a failure, I am offering up your squirming, toady body first."

Chapter TWENTY

"SORRY, ALL THE beds are full tonight. No vacancy." Dr. Zebulon Sheffield, New Pittsburgh coroner, chuckled at his own joke.

"I wasn't really looking for a room," Drostan Fletcher replied, patiently.

"Hey, did you hear this one? What's black and white and red all over?" Sheffield asked without looking up from the corpse he was cutting into.

"A newspaper."

"Nah. The bodies that came in here after the boiler explosion." He glanced up from his work. "Get it?"

Drostan sighed. "I get it. What happened?" He leaned against the wall; Sheffield would tell his story at his own pace.

"One of the boilers blew over at the processing plant. Vicious things, boilers. Hate them. In this case, one boiler went and set off another one. Big, industrial boilers. God. Boiling to death is an awful way to go."

Drostan didn't have much to add to that, so he stayed silent and tried not to cringe at the sound of the bone saw cutting through the dead man's ribs.

"Brought the guys in on the back of a truck," Sheffield said, working as he talked. "Nothing anyone could do for them. Skin peeled right off. Made it tough to identify the bodies."

"So why send them to you?"

Sheffield shrugged. "Too many for the locals and it's Company policy. Need a ruling on the deaths. When they get worried it gets all 'official' like. But most of the time the locals handle it... and there's talk that lately some of the bodies never make it out of the mines."

"And your ruling is?"

"Accident." An edge to Sheffield's voice told Drostan that there was more to the story.

"Except maybe not so much?"

Sheffield was quiet for a while. "You're not with the police?" he said finally.

"No."

"The mines or mills?"

"Not them, either. Private client."

Sheffield broke the rib cage open like he was cracking a lobster. Drostan looked away. "I don't doubt the *how*," Sheffield grunted. "But I'm a little iffy on the *why*."

"How come?"

"You know how they say things come in threes?" Sheffield said, going about his work like a knacker rendering a horse. "Well, lately seems these kinds of things have been coming in thirties. Boilers blowing up. Dead miners. And yesterday, a couple of people from a house over in Pulawski Way—carbon monoxide. Not to mention the unpleasantness over in Allegheny and down the Mon."

"How could those be connected?"

Sheffield shrugged. "No idea. That's the problem. Maybe they aren't. But I can't shake the feeling that it's not just coincidence." He gave a harsh laugh. "Then again, no one pays much attention to me. That's why I'm stuck down here in the basement with the stiffs."

Drostan weighed his words carefully. Sheffield was a good man, beneath the cynicism his work demanded. He was also one of the few people in an official position willing to help Drostan along with bits of information making him a resource to be handled carefully. And on occasion, he was a damn fine drinking companion. Plenty of reasons Drostan did not want to muck things up.

"I heard that lately there were more miners dead than usual," Drostan prompted.

"You ever hear that quote about life being 'solitary, poor, nasty, brutish, and short'?"

"Hobbes, isn't it?"

Sheffield nodded. "Yeah. Well that goes double for the poor fellas down in those mines. Gah, what a way to live! Down in the dark, constantly afraid of the roof caving in, working all hunched over. If they don't get crushed to death or fall down an elevator shaft, they get blown up by firedamp or suffocate from the blackdamp." Under the harsh tone, Drostan could hear anger, maybe at death itself.

"So what's different now?"

The coroner took long enough to reply that Drostan was not sure an answer was coming. "Look, if you tell anyone I said this, I'll deny it," he said, looking up long enough to fix Drostan with an angry stare. "Or I'll say I caught you sniffing ether and you were out of your head."

"I'm not planning to tell anyone," Drostan replied patiently.

"I think they're cutting more corners than usual, down in the mines," Sheffield finally said. "Greedy bastards. They want the last ounce of coal, so they take risks because, hell, it's not them or their sons down there.

"They chip away at the pillars that hold up the roof, and then act surprised when there's a cave-in, although any miner with a first-grade education could have seen it coming," he ranted. "They skimp on the fans and ventilation shafts, so the poor sons of bitches die from bad air. Not that anyone cares."

Drostan didn't question it. Immigrant labor was cheap, even with the occasional strikes. And after the Homestead Strikes, the Oligarchy had made sure their Pinkertons and private armies kept all but the most incendiary personalities in check.

"It's the way of the world," Drostan said with a shrug. "Not much different back in Manchester, or Newcastle. Some men die young and some men grow rich."

Sheffield grimaced. "Maybe. But there are... irregularities. And no one wants to hear about them. In fact, I've been officially ordered not to notice."

Drostan raised an eyebrow. "Oh?"

Sheffield wasn't the ambitious type. He had no political aspirations, no hunger to climb the social ladder. As far as Fletcher knew, the New Pittsburgh coroner had everything he wanted from life: a long-suffering wife, a tidy house in Bloomfield, and a large mutt that looked like a cross between a German shepherd and a wirehair pointer. The mutt, Benny, lay even now in the corner of the operatory, oblivious to their conversation. Sheffield had no clout and no reason to make waves. Which did not mean he had given up his conscience; he just kept it muted by common sense.

"The bodies that come in here don't always match the tally," Sheffield said. The late hour and the silence of the morgue made for a confessional atmosphere, helped along by the bucket of beer Drostan had brought before Sheffield had started on his 'patient'. "The mines have to release something to satisfy the press and the family, and a senator or two if too many people die close together and word gets out. But the reports don't have to include everything, if you know what I mean," he added bitterly. "They ship some of the bodies here, and I get pulled in to make it all 'legitimate'."

"Sometimes, there are too many pieces, or not enough," Sheffield went on. "That can happen, especially with airship crashes or industrial accidents. But the injuries I'm seeing don't match the kind of accident reported, or the sort you'd expect in a mine." He pushed his glasses up his nose with his wrist, before using his gloved hands to remove organs from the cadaver on the table.

"If miners die of blackdamp, it's bad air in the lungs. I wouldn't expect to see bodies that look like they'd been torn apart by wild animals. Maybe fingers torn up trying to dig out, that kind of thing. But if you could have seen them..."

"Which mines?" Drostan asked, trying not to sound too interested.

Sheffield worked a bit more on the body before he answered. "Mostly Vesta Nine—the big one, the one the bosses are so damn proud of."

"You think the bosses are covering something up?"

Sheffield gave a bitter laugh. "The mining bosses are always covering something up. Question is, what is it this time?" He shook his head. "For the number of bodies that have come through here, it's been quiet—too quiet. Like someone's got a lid on the situation. And before you ask, there's no one honest to report it to, even if I had proof."

"I heard that the survivors—when there are any—had some wild tales to tell," Drostan prompted.

Sheffield gave him a hard stare. "I should have known you never come in without a few cards up your sleeve, Drostan. But yeah. I heard a little of that myself, although the mine superintendents were quick to shut down the talk. Monsters. Huh."

"Rumor has it, some of those survivors—the ones with the interesting stories—ran into bad luck," Drostan replied. "Fell down the stairs, drowned in the river. Or just up and disappeared."

"I heard that, too." Sheffield sighed. "Don't doubt it." He paused, as if they both remembered that most of the police working across the street were on Richard Thwaites's take. "I'm not sure I'd blame what I've seen on monsters. But I do know that if it goes on too long, the miners won't stand for it. They won't stay cowed by the Pinkertons if there's something that scares them worse down below."

Just then, Benny raised his head and sniffed the air. He gave a low growl.

"Hush," Sheffield commanded. Benny gave him a mournful look and ducked his head.

"You think there's union trouble coming?"

Sheffield shrugged. "I hope not. Depends on how far the owners push this. Folks'll put up with a lot to earn a living, but when too many die, and the bosses don't care, people get their backs up."

Benny suddenly got to his feet, hackles raised. He gave a growl, then began to bark with more urgency than Drostan thought the old dog had left in him.

"You expecting company?" Drostan asked.

Sheffield tried to hush the dog, but this time, Benny refused to quiet down. "No, I'm not. Supposed to be a quiet night. And Benny knows the night guard and the regulars who have business here. He doesn't act like this."

Drostan had already drawn his gun. "Then maybe he knows something we don't."

The morgue had two entrances: the front door on Diamond Street across from the new, massive Pittsburgh Jail, and a back door for 'deliveries'. Benny stood facing the back door, lips pulled back in a snarl, back hunched, barking for all he was worth.

"Yeah," Sheffield said, glancing from Benny to Drostan's gun. "Maybe he does." He peeled off his heavy rubber gloves and grabbed a skull chisel and a nasty looking claw hammer. "Since when does anyone try to break into a morgue?"

When they want to hide the evidence, Drostan thought.

Bang. Something hard hit the wooden door hard. Not a knock; more like a battering ram.

Benny barked louder, transformed from a lazy family pet to a vicious guard dog.

Bang. Whatever hit the door was heavy, tipped in metal from the sound of it. "What are the odds some lost bloke saw your lights and decided to ask for directions?" Drostan quipped nervously.

"In a morgue?" Sheffield eyed the narrow windows, set high on the walls. He pushed a chair over to one of them and climbed up.

"Well?"

"Looks like three men, can't make out much more," Sheffield said.

The pounding at the door came louder and harder. Any sane person would think twice before trying to force entry into a room with a frenzied dog on the other side. But the pounding continued, each blow harder than the last, heedless of the warning.

"Can we get out the front way?" Drostan asked. "Doesn't matter what they want; at this hour of the night, it can't be good."

"The office staff usually lock that door when they close up around five," Sheffield replied. "I have a key to the back, but I lost the front door key a while ago. Meant to get a replacement." Sheffield went to the back door and tried the knob. "Locked."

"How long do you think that door is going to last?" Drostan asked. "Do you have any alarms in here? Any way to summon help?"

Sheffield just stared at him. "It's a morgue. My patients don't usually give me a hard time."

Crack. The sound of splintering wood made both men turn back to the door.

"Someone's awfully determined to get in here," Drostan said. "And they're going to succeed in a few minutes."

"We can slow them down, give ourselves some cover," Sheffield said. "Grab one end of the table."

Together, Drostan and Sheffield pushed the heavy autopsy cart in front of the door with the corpse still in place, chest splayed wide open.

"Help me with this," Sheffield said, gesturing toward two other carts. "If we turn them on their sides, we can get behind them. These are solid steel."

Drostan and Sheffield managed to get the two carts overturned just as the door gave way. The click and hum of gears accompanied a stench like an abattoir in the summer heat.

Three hideous creatures barreled through the doorway. Once, they might have been men. Now they were nightmares, animated by clockwork. Their skin was mottled, the color of deep bruises and spoiled meat. Clockwork mechanisms stiffly animated their joints, visible on jaws, fingers, wrists, and glimpsed beneath their tattered clothing. Benny's fierce barking trailed off into a frightened howl, and he bolted for the back room.

"What are those things?" Sheffield asked, eyes wide with fear.

"Nothing good," Drostan replied.

As one of the creatures raised his hand to strike, Drostan could see where it had been impaled by a splinter from the shattered door. *The clockwork corpses care nothing for pain or damage to themselves,* Drostan reminded himself. Another of the mechanized cadavers shoved aside the autopsy table blocking the doorway as if it were nothing.

"These tables aren't going to slow them down for long," Drostan muttered. "We're going to have to fight them."

"I'm a coroner, not a cop," Sheffield protested.

"You're going to be a dead coroner if we don't do something. Maybe if we raise enough of a racket, some of your jailer friends across the street will come to see what's going on."

Sheffield tightened his grip on his claw-hammer and bone saw. Drostan popped up from cover and squeezed off three shots in quick succession. The bullets struck their targets, driving the creatures back a pace. One of the clockwork cadavers was struck square in the chest, blowing a spray of dead flesh out the exit wound.

For a moment, the clockwork assassins halted. And then, with the relentless click and hum of the mechanisms that drove them, they renewed their advance, strange glass eyes oriented on Drostan and Sheffield.

Drostan got off three more shots. "I need to reload! Hold them off!" He ducked for the cover of a heavy autopsy table, and Sheffield stood, pale with terror, a white-knuckled grip on the tools in his hands.

"Get back!" Sheffield said, giving a warning swing with the hammer he used to open up the skulls of corpses. His bone saw rattled in the other hand. But the dead kept coming, the taut skin of their bloated faces registering neither anger nor fear.

Drostan stood and put a bullet through the forehead of the first clockwork monster. The creature's head snapped back and he reeled. Drostan fired again, and his bullet entered the eye socket of the second monster, shattering the glass eye and blowing away the back of the thing's skull, filling the morgue with the smell of gunpowder and formaldehyde. Drostan fired once more, and his bullet destroyed the third attacker's face, smashing the nose, flattening the cheekbones as the sinus cavities collapsed, and sending a shower of rotted skin, matted hair and decomposing brain matter to foul the operatory.

"They're not slowing down!" Sheffield shouted, his voice high with panic. The lead corpse was almost to the barricade. He swung with his hammer and winced when it hit with full force against the creature's outstretched right arm, shattering bone. The monster never slowed its steps, although its damaged arm hung at an unnatural angle, bent between the wrist and elbow.

"Use the claw!" Drostan shouted, squeezing off three more shots, targeting the zombies' eyes. He shot out the remaining glass eye of one of the creatures, and took the top off the head of the one whose nose his last shot had destroyed. For once, the monsters hesitated.

"I think you've stopped them!" Sheffield cried. Nearly in unison, the abominations slowly pivoted, seeming to focus on the sound of Sheffield's voice.

"They can still hear us," Drostan replied. "Separate. Take them on however you can. No one's riding to the rescue. We've got to do this ourselves."

One of the zombies remained oriented on Sheffield, but the other two had turned to focus on the sound of Drostan's voice.

"Damn," he muttered as the creatures walked mechanically into the table barrier. The table stopped their advance for only a moment; then the zombies clawed at it until they had dragged it out of the way.

Sheffield backed up against a table of morgue tools. Abandoning the bone saw as too cumbersome, the coroner grabbed a crowbar-like tool used for prying open rib cages. Armed with the hammer in one hand—claw-first—and the tine end of the crowbar in the other, he grimaced as he swung at his attacker with his full strength.

The crowbar dug into the dead flesh of the clockwork zombie's shoulder, opening a gash bone-deep. The hammer smashed against fragile finger bones, crushing them. Still the creature came.

"Go back to the devil who spawned you!" Sheffield shouted as he put his full strength into a swing that caught the zombie in the neck with the crowbar, ripping the head from the body. As the twitching corpse sank to the ground, Sheffield kept on pounding, sending chunks of rotten flesh flying.

Drostan backed up as far as he could go until he found himself up against a set of metal shelves. Bottles and jars clanked a warning as he jostled them.

No time to reload. He jammed his gun in his belt and reached behind him, grabbing whatever came to hand. He threw the first bottle behind the zombies, buying himself time as they paused at the sound. Drostan pelted the two approaching zombies with heavy glass jars filled with formaldehyde and discolored, gelatinous organs preserved for study.

"That's evidence!" Sheffield objected.

Drostan hurled jar after jar. Glass shattered, shards stuck out like porcupine quills, lodged in dead skin, and the stinking chemicals bathed the zombies, fouling the air so that Drostan thought he might reel from the smell. Still they came, undeterred.

Bits of clockwork zombies splattered the operatory's tiled walls and cement floor, covering every surface with decomposed flesh and organs. Drostan and Sheffield had backed up as far as they could go. One of the monsters lay twitching on the ground, headless, its body still bucking and jerking, hands scrabbling against the tile.

"Stay back!" Drostan shouted as he grabbed for a box of safety matches. Sure that it was better to act than debate consequences, he struck a match and tossed it at the formaldehyde-soaked mechanized corpses.

"Are you *nuts?*" Sheffield shouted.

The roar of flames cut off Drostan's response. The two creatures nearest them went up like torches, flailing and moaning, blundering around the room as the flames rose from their clothing and hair. One of them veered close enough for Sheffield to swing his crowbar again, knocking the flaming head from its shoulders. The severed head rolled, igniting the fluid on the floor, and the first downed clockwork burst into flames.

Drostan grabbed a set of rib cutters, long-handled jointed blades like pruning shears, and got them around the third zombie's neck. He jerked the handles together, severing the head from the shoulders.

Three decapitated clockwork corpses lay on the floor, flames guttering in the pools of chemical solution as the zombies shuddered and went still.

"Stay clear of them," Drostan said, choking on the noxious smoke. "We don't know if the bodies can still move."

He swung the rib cutters at two of the windows, shattering the glass to let in air and clear the heavy black smoke. He was heaving for breath between the smoke and the heavy smell of formaldehyde.

"Where the hell are the cops?" Sheffield demanded, looking around his ruined operatory. A fine layer of soot covered the formerly pristine white tiles. Puddles of foul liquid muddied the floor.

"Makes you wonder," Drostan said, toeing one of the cindered corpses out of the way with distaste.

"My morgue," Sheffield groaned, looking around at the wreckage. He shook his head. "It's going to take forever to put things back." He eyed the empty shelves, where Drostan had grabbed jars and bottles to hurl at the zombies. "And you've just compromised a dozen investigations."

Sheffield came around from behind the battered table and poked one of the charred zombies with his crowbar. It lay still, but he glared at it mistrustfully.

"Cover me," he said to Drostan. "I want to get a better look at those gears."

The attacker was headless, with a gunshot wound through its chest, and dead to start with, so the absurdity of Sheffield's request did not escape Drostan, but he bit back a remark and reloaded, leveling his gun at what remained of the clockwork corpse.

The clockwork joints were still visible, though scorched by the fire. Sheffield sat on his haunches, using the claw end of his skull hammer to pry the mechanism loose.

"Crude, but effective," he muttered. "What I'd really like to know is how they tied the gears in with the joints and muscles." He probed some more at the dead thing, heedless of the smell. "And I wonder, how were they being controlled?"

"I'm still wondering why all the noise and gunshots down here didn't have any guards heading down here at a run," Drostan said.

A nasty suspicion was forming in his mind, but before he could put his thoughts into words, a uniformed cop came to the door.

"You're late!" Sheffield snapped, rising to his feet. "Where the hell have you been? We were attacked!"

The cop glanced around the ruined morgue, paid scant attention to the charred bodies on the floor, and fixed his gaze on Drostan. His expression hardened. "I'm here to arrest one Drostan Fletcher, on suspicion of conspiracy."

Sheffield gaped. "Did you not hear a word I just said? Fletcher and I were attacked!"

The Oligarchy would have the means to create abominable machines like the clockwork zombies, Drostan thought as his suspicions grew. *They might have been afraid Sheffield knew something, too. That's why we didn't get any help.*

"I have a warrant for Fletcher's arrest," the cop said, and one hand fell to the butt of the gun in his holster. "I'd suggest you come along peacefully."

Drostan had not voiced his suspicions aloud, but he saw the skepticism in Sheffield's eyes change to anger. The cop took a step toward them, drawing his gun, and Drostan raised his hands in surrender. Sheffield slipped behind the cop. With one swift movement, he brought the blunt end of the skull hammer down in a glancing blow behind the cop's ear, and the man dropped like a stone.

"Get out of here, Drostan. Someone's setting you up." Sheffield said as he knelt by the fallen officer and checked for a pulse. "He'll be out for a while, but you need to hurry."

Before Drostan could make a move toward the door, they heard voices and the sound of running feet.

"Hide!" Sheffield hissed.

Drostan looked wildly around him, seeing nowhere in the chaos of the operatory to go. He took a step towards the back room. "Here," Sheffield said, stepping around the downed cop and the charred zombies to lead Drostan toward the body drawers.

"Get in," he ordered, yanking one of the slabs open. "It's cold, but there's air, and I'll let you out again once they're gone. Hurry!"

Drostan forced down his fear as he climbed onto the slab. The stone was cold, and the air coming from the bank of mortuary drawers was icy. Sheffield had once told him that the city bought a huge amount of block ice to keep the drawers chilled. Drostan had barely laid down when Sheffield shoved the drawer shut, sealing him in the dark.

Terror seized him. The drawer was slightly wider across than Drostan's shoulders and a little longer than he was tall, and there was about six inches of open space between his face and the ceiling. Claustrophobia made him desperate to sit up, stretch out, take in great lungfuls of breath. Rationality forced him to remain still, breathe shallowly and stay quiet.

Drostan could hear muffled voices on the other side of the drawer. Sheffield sounded like he was arguing with someone. Footsteps grew louder, and Drostan gripped his gun, unsure of just how well he could get off a shot if someone suddenly opened his drawer.

"We'd better have a look inside those drawers," an unfamiliar voice said.

"Suit yourselves," Sheffield replied. "That's where we keep the smallpox cases." There was a few seconds' silence, then, "Nasty thing, smallpox. Real easy to catch if you're not immune to it, like I am."

"Maybe... we can take your word for it that the drawers haven't been disturbed," the voice replied, sounding less certain than before.

To Drostan's relief, the steps receded. More muffled voices sounded in the distance, and some banging and scraping. He wondered whether Sheffield had gotten the cops to help him turn the tables back over and remove the charred remains. He heard a few more minutes of talking, then silence.

To keep himself from giving in to full-blown panic, Drostan forced himself to think through the case. At Catherine Desmet's request, he had drawn a map that showed the killer making its way up the Monongahela River from near Vestaburg toward larger communities—and more prey. He doubted it was a coincidence that Vestaburg was the closest town to the Vesta Nine mine.

The deaths along the rivers had been nobodies, unimportant to anyone in a position of power; the Night Hag had chosen victims unlikely to be mourned. Smart behavior for a predator, he thought. And if more miners than usual had died lately from problems with the mines, that was regrettable, but of no consequence to anyone important.

But Thomas Desmet had been somebody. Desmet hadn't been killed by the Night Hag, but he had been killed by magic. *We must be getting close*, he thought. *The more people are trying to kill us, the more likely it is that we're making someone nervous.*

Someone had sent the clockwork cadavers after him after he'd ignored the warning. Maybe that someone would have been happy to have Sheffield silenced as well. The cop had paid no attention to the headless, charred bodies and the war zone of the operatory, and focused solely on arresting Drostan—for conspiracy. Conspiracy to do what? Against whom? Drostan had no desire to give himself over to custody to find out.

Obviously someone in power thought he was dangerous. *What do I know that is so important?*

The morgue was silent. *What if the cops arrested Sheffield? What if he isn't coming back for me?*

Drostan's heart pounded, and he choked back a scream. He felt around the confines of the mortuary drawer. Steel on the sides and top, granite beneath him. He stretched, touching the front of the drawer with his toes. Drostan had no idea how much time had passed, but already the cold was beginning to make him shiver.

If I don't suffocate, or starve to death, I'll die of cold.

He thrust his hands against the top of the drawer, trying to push against the surface to slide the drawer out. The heavy granite slab beneath him did not move. No one had expected the drawer's occupant to need to leave.

Maybe hiding in a morgue might not have been a smart idea for someone able to see and hear ghosts.

Drostan could hear the buzz of dead voices. Most were heavy with the accents of their native languages: German, Polish, Hungarian, and Italian, though there were others. Nearly all were male.

Drostan focused his attention on the voices, if only to blunt his own claustrophobia; their stirring was unusual. Thankfully, the dead were silent most of the time. It seemed the appearance of the clockwork zombies and the imprisonment of a living man inside a body drawer was enough to rouse the spirits from their half-sleep.

"What do you know about clockwork corpses and the Night Hag?" Drostan asked in a whisper. "I can hear you. Tell me."

For a moment, the voices grew silent. Drostan was acutely aware that he was the stranger here, in the land of the dead. The spirits were deciding whether or not to trust him, even though they were beyond the reach of consequences. Or perhaps, he thought, fear of creatures like the Night Hag lasted even after death.

"There are things in the dark," a man's voice said, thick with a Welsh lilt. "Deep in the mines. Creatures that ought not be let loose."

"How did they get loose?" Drostan murmured.

"Dig, they told us," another man answered in an Irish brogue. "Deeper. Always deeper. For their coal. And now, for other things. To make them rich. And if we die, no matter. There are more where we came from. But now, what's gotten loose will kill them too, kill everyone."

"They said you died of bad air, blackdamp."

"They lied."

"What about the clockwork corpses?" The image of those mechanized abominations would haunt Drostan's sleep for years.

"Not all of us got out," a man with a Polish accent replied. "We were sent here. The lucky ones. They took some of the bodies. Don't know where. Maybe to experiment."

If the spirits of the mining dead had followed their corpses to the morgue, Drostan did not want to think about the ghosts of the clockwork zombies being aware enough to know what had happened to their human shells.

"What about the boilers that blew?" Drostan asked. Questioning the ghosts was helping him hang onto his sanity in the close, cold dark.

"Evil things are loose," replied a ghost, his consonants clipped and guttural, like his German native tongue. "They feed on death, on blood. And no one knows how to lock them up."

The ghosts seemed to lose interest in the conversation and gradually drew farther away. In the silence, Drostan was left alone with the darkness, and the walls of the mortuary drawer seemed to close in around him until he thought he might scream and begin to tear at the steel.

Just as Drostan thought he could not contain his panic any longer, footsteps sounded outside the drawers. The drawer jerked open, and light and air flooded in. Drostan blinked, trying to determine whether his savior was friend or foe, and he raised his pistol.

"Jesus, Drostan. Point that thing somewhere else," Sheffield said. "We need to get you out of here."

Drostan sat up, struggling against the irrational urge to suck in huge breaths of air, to run around the morgue stretching his arms and basking in the relative warmth of the room. "What happened?" he asked, hoping he sounded steadier than he felt.

"Couple more cops showed up. Didn't care at all about the zombies. I told them the clockwork guys hit their buddy," Sheffield added with a smirk. "Makes me think they might have been the ones that sent them." He sounded aggrieved. "If that's the case, I have a real bone to pick with them. Anyhow, all they wanted to know was where you were. Said you were dangerous. Said you were consorting with anarchists. Bunch of hornswoggle if I ever heard it. They picked up the other cop, who was still out cold, and left."

"I owe you," Drostan said, getting to his feet.

"You sure as hell do," Sheffield agreed. "I've already assaulted an officer and perjured myself on your behalf." He paused. "As far as the cops know, the zombies assaulted the officer—but you can bet they'll blame you for it. Which means you really need to get going. And know there's a warrant out for your arrest."

"Won't they be watching the door?" Drostan asked.

Sheffield shrugged. "Not if they believed me when I said you were already gone. After all, they searched the place. Lucky for you, they didn't want to take a risk opening the drawers. Most folks have an aversion to dead bodies—and communicable diseases." He grabbed his overcoat and hat from a peg on the wall. "Here. Take these. We're about the same height. Keep your head down, and they'll think you're me. If they ask, I'll tell them you stole them at gunpoint."

"Gee, thanks," Drostan said. "Dig me deeper, why don't you? And don't you think the cop will figure it had to be you that hit him when he comes 'round?"

Sheffield grinned. "Not if I hit him hard enough to scramble some gray matter. What are friends for?"

Drostan shouldered into the coat and took the hat. As he was leaving, Sheffield called out to him.

"Good luck, Drostan. Now get the hell out of here."

Drostan forced himself to step out into the night as if he had nothing to worry about. He stood tall and tried to walk with confidence, heading down the street toward the streetcar Sheffield usually took home. In case anyone was watching, he caught the streetcar, rode it several blocks, then hopped off, took another streetcar in a different direction, and then another.

While he rode the streetcars, he thought furiously, trying to come up with a plan. If someone in the Oligarchy had sent the clockwork zombies to kill him and the police to arrest him, then odds were good his rooming house was being watched. Drostan thought of contacting Finian, and dismissed the idea. It was a toss-up whether Finian would weigh friendship over duty, and Drostan did not want to make that wager unless he had run out of other options.

Then he remembered the pigeon. Agent Storm had left him a clockwork carrier pigeon, roosting outside his room at Mrs. Mueller's. If Drostan could get to the pigeon, he could warn Mitch and his partner about the clockwork zombies and the Oligarchy's involvement. Assuming that the federal agents weren't also in the Oligarchy's pocket.

Recovering the clockwork pigeon sounded better to Drostan than aimlessly riding the night trolleys. He took a different route across the Allegheny River than normal, to a stop he had never used before. That meant he had a dozen or more blocks to reach his rooming house, but no one who had been watching his movements would have anticipated him.

Allegheny's streets were quiet in the middle of the night; closer to dawn, they would bustle with mill workers coming off third shift. It had rained while Drostan was in the morgue, and the streets and sidewalks were wet, glistening in the light of the streetlamps.

Drostan walked with the stride of a busy man, someone who had every right to be where he was. He kept his collar up and his head down, just another weary workman anxious to go home. Drostan did not slow his pace as he neared the rooming house.

He passed the street by, with only a cursory glance as if it did not matter. He spotted two policemen in front of the house, and guessed that someone was also watching the rear.

Drostan headed for the river. It was quiet along the banks as the dark, swift water flowed past the sleeping city. With a hand on his revolver, Drostan feared little except the Oligarchy and the Night Hag. To his relief, neither seemed in evidence.

"I need your help," he murmured to the empty, trash-strewn shore. "I'm trying to find out who was behind your deaths, and someone's doing their best to stop me. Please," he said. "I need your help."

One by one, the ghosts of the riverbanks materialized. They formed a ring around him, and the hair on the back of Drostan's neck prickled. No matter how often he spoke with the dead, it struck him anew every time that although they had once been human, they were now something other. And that the longer they remained dead, the less connected they remained to the concerns of the living.

"What can we do? We're dead." The old woman looked at him with a defeated, weary gaze.

"I need a distraction," Drostan said. He knew that what he was proposing was a long shot, but getting that mechanical homing pigeon seemed his best shot at staying out of jail. "Two men are watching my room. I need to get something important from my window ledge and get away. That's all. Can you distract them long enough for me to do that?"

"You in trouble with the cops?" asked the ghost of a young man with sad eyes and the stocky build of a dock worker.

"Yeah," Drostan admitted. "I am. And it's all over the questions I was asking, trying to figure out what's going on and how all of you died."

The young man's ghost gave a half-smile. "I always enjoyed giving the cops a good chase. I'm in."

"I had my share of run-ins with the police," the ghost of an old vagrant replied. "I don't mind foxing them now. Serves them right."

Drostan did not pretend to know how ghosts traveled, but he sincerely hoped the revenants would keep their word. He worked his way up the narrow alleys of the Allegheny neighborhood, staying to the shadows.

He passed the alley where Ralf and his gang were playing cards. It had crossed his mind to ask Ralf and his band of delinquents for help, but Drostan knew the boys were usually in enough trouble with the police. They would make an easy target for reprisal, while the dead were beyond the law's long arm.

The two policemen were still patrolling in front of Mrs. Mueller's rooming house, walking back and forth under the glow of the streetlights. This section of Allegheny was usually safe, and Drostan had never seen officers stay in one place for so long if they were truly walking a beat. Neither man was Finian.

Drostan slipped down the dark side street that ran behind the rooming house. He did not see any police watching the back door, but the small yard had bushes and a shed, providing ample places to hide. He looked up at the dark window of his rented room. A bird perched on the windowsill, unremarkable at this distance. Pausing in the shadows, Drostan dug out a bit of paper from his pocket and a pencil stub.

Clockwork zombies. Big fish after me. Help? Riverside. It was all he had room to write on the bit of paper the clockwork pigeon could carry in its capsule. It crossed Drostan's mind that if Agent Storm was in league with the Oligarchy, he could be delivering himself into their hands. Hoping he was right about Mitch, he tucked the paper into a pocket and set about getting the pigeon.

He bent down and picked up a rock. Staying to the shadows, Drostan hurled the rock to the other side of the small yard, smacking lightly against the fence. No one emerged from the bushes, and so Drostan ventured out of the alley. He had requested the room at the corner because it afforded an easy way out, with a short drop from his window to the roof over the back door, and from there to the ground. Drostan had never intended to sneak in.

The hair at the back of his neck prickled, and he knew that the ghosts from the riverbanks had arrived. "If anyone comes around back, distract them," Drostan whispered, wondering just how much his ghostly informants could do.

Climbing up to the roof over the back door was enough of a challenge. Doing it silently so as not to rouse the police or the sleeping occupants of the house was even more difficult. Drostan dragged himself up onto the shingled surface, and eyed the distance to where the mechanical pigeon perched on his windowsill.

The sill was just a few inches higher than his outstretched arm. Drostan looked up, and saw Olivia the ghost girl watching him with concern. Drostan jumped, and missed the pigeon by an inch. He tried to land lightly, but the soft thump seemed to him to echo like cannon fire. Drostan sprang again, and this time his fingers brushed the metallic feet of the clockwork carrier pigeon, enough to jar it from its perch.

It fell, and Drostan lurched to catch it before the precious gears and mechanisms could tumble and break. As he lunged, just before the pigeon landed in his outstretched hands, he glimpsed Olivia's ghostly face in the glass.

She was shouting a warning.

A shot fired over Drostan's head, barely missing him, chewing into the clapboards of the rooming house. Had he been in his room, the bullet might have hit him as he lay in his bed.

"Drostan Fletcher! Come down with your hands up. You are under arrest." The voice announced itself from the shadows, but even now, Drostan could not see anyone lurking there.

This is what I get for having ghosts for bodyguards.

Clutching the clockwork pigeon close to his chest, Drostan dropped and rolled, tumbling from the pitched roof over the back door to land in a crouch in Mrs. Mueller's peony bushes.

A figure rose in the darkness across the yard. Drostan heard running feet coming from the other side of the house.

"He's out there!" a voice said. "I just can't get a bead on him."

"Better bring him in, or there'll be hell to pay," the second voice replied.

Just then, a blue orb floated out of the climbing roses. It stood still, as if waiting for the officers to notice it, and then began to zig-zag across the yard.

"D'ja see that?" the first man said.

A second, yellow orb drifted up from the hemlock bush by the side of the house. It hung at eye level, bobbing and weaving to make sure it was seen, then slowly and deliberately began to advance on where the two policemen stood.

"What the hell *is* that?" the second man said, and Drostan heard fear in his voice.

Overhead, the windowpane in Drostan's room began to rattle and bang so loudly that he expected to be showered with broken glass. The sound grew louder and louder, like someone slamming a fist against the glass, shaking the window frame. The officers' attention rose to the sound of the noise.

Framed in the window was the ghostly apparition of young woman in her twenties. Drostan recognised Olivia, and she was angry. She'd taken a shine to him, happy that he could see and hear her, lonely after all these years for company. Now he saw what she was capable of doing.

Olivia's hair streamed out around her; a blue glow suffused the room behind her, making it impossible for an observer to mistake her dead-white skin for a living person. Olivia's fists beat on the glass, and her lips drew back to reveal a feral expression.

The green and blue orbs began to fly across the small back yard, diving directly at the officers and making them duck. A sudden loud *rat-a-tat-tat* exploded in front of the officers, who dove for the ground with a shout.

Drostan held the clockwork pigeon to his chest with his left hand while his right held his pistol. He was edging his way out of the yard, staying close to the house and making a mental note to apologise to Mrs. Mueller about her garden. He took advantage of the distraction to make good his getaway.

A hand rested on his shoulder and he swung, finding his gun pointed at Ralf's nose.

“Saw you slink by earlier,” Ralf said. “Knew something was up when the police were waiting outside your place. My boys are throwing some fireworks at the coppers. Let’s get you out of here.”

Grateful for whatever help presented itself, Drostan followed Ralf’s lead. The young hooligan knew the neighborhood’s back alleys and hiding places much better than he could ever hope to.

More loud bangs split the night air. Lights were coming on up and down the street, as neighbors rolled up blinds and opened windows, wondering what was going on.

“Hey, you!” Drostan heard Mr. Mueller shouting at the cops in heavily accented English. “Get the hell out of my yard!”

Drostan ran, keeping pace with Ralf, and despite the dire circumstances, he chuckled, imagining the reception the two police officers were likely to receive if they tried to convince Mrs. Mueller that he was a dangerous criminal. They were going to get a tart piece of the landlady’s mind, along with a thwack of her broom. Mrs. Mueller would not take kindly to strangers disparaging one of her favorite lodgers.

With a silent thank-you to his ghostly protectors, Drostan followed Ralf through a warren of back streets and alleys barely wide enough for him to fit through sideways. Finally, they came to a deserted house many blocks away from the rooming house.

“All right, Fletcher,” Ralf said, ushering him into the parlor of the abandoned house. Heavy blankets covered the windows, hiding the light of a kerosene lamp. Inside, Drostan recognized half a dozen of Ralf’s gang. They relaxed when they saw their leader enter, flipping closed their switchblades and straight-razors and tucking their weapons back into belts and pockets. “We saved your ass. Now you owe us a good story—and a nice big wad of tobacco in the bargain.” He eyed Drostan dubiously. “And you can start by telling us why you’ve got a metal chicken.”

Drostan let out a chuckle. “Give me a moment to catch my breath, and I’ll tell you the best story you’ve ever heard.”

Chapter TWENTY-ONE

"AFTER ALL THAT, the thug knew next to nothing," Andreas Thalberg said.

"You glamoured them, and they still couldn't tell you anything?" Jake asked. He and Rick sat on a flocked velvet couch in the elegant parlor of the Thalberg home. Andreas had offered both of them fine scotch, while the deep red liquid in his snifter was something definitely other.

Just a few days had passed since the near-catastrophe at Brand and Desmet's headquarters. Kovach had brought the three would-be bombers to Andreas, hoping that the vampire-witch could use his considerable skills to pry loose information.

"They could not tell me what they did not know," Andreas replied. Had he needed to breathe, Jake got the feeling the centuries-old man would have sighed. "That isn't the same as having no information of value. It just required a different method of inquiry."

"You magicked them," Rick said.

Andreas gave an eloquent shrug. "I assumed you brought them to me for a reason. Was I mistaken?"

Rick was a little more squeamish when it came to vampire interrogation after his own personal encounter a few years earlier. Jake had long ago made peace with the idea that the world contained many strange and horrifying realities. "Of course not," Jake replied. "What did you find out?"

In the adjacent sitting room, Nicki, Cady, and Renate toiled over scraps of information that they had removed from Jasinski's apartment. They felt sure the items would yield something important with a little more investigation. The door had been closed, so they would not be distracted by the men's conversation in the next room, though from time to time, Jake heard excitedly raised voices or Nicki's curses in French.

Andreas paced in front of the fireplace. "Not surprisingly, they were told nothing except their task and the payment they could expect for doing the job. But there were bits of information they observed or overheard, things that meant nothing to them, that might prove quite valuable to us."

"Like?" Jake asked.

"Combining my magic with the glamouring, I was able to see what the miscreants witnessed, and come to my own conclusions. The man who hired them, someone they had never seen before, is in the employ of Drogo Veles."

Rick gave a low whistle. "That's not good."

Andreas shook his head. "It is never a good thing to draw the interest of a powerful dark witch."

"Veles's name keeps popping up," Jake added. "Along with Richard Thwaites."

"Why is someone as high and mighty as Drogo Veles hiring thugs? Doesn't seem like his style. Doesn't he have his own people for that kind of thing?" Rick wondered.

Andreas nodded. "Both men are quite well staffed when it comes to private soldiers, and Thwaites has a number of police on his payroll. But those are men they've trained, fighters with special skills. In this case, I suspect Veles needed someone disposable."

"He expected the false plumbers to get caught or killed in the blast," Jake said.

"Exactly. But it's difficult to screen out everything someone may see or hear. And that's where we hit gold. Or coal, as the case may be."

"Let me guess," Jake said. "This has something to do with Vesta Nine."

"Yes." Andreas resumed his pacing, and Jake found it interesting to note how many mortal mannerisms a man of Andreas's considerable age still retained. "All three men came from the tenements in Vestaburg, the company housing of the mining firm."

"Not an unlikely place to hire muscle desperate to make a little money on the side," Rick observed.

"Granted. But while the men were waiting for their contact, they saw what was going on around them, although they paid it no heed. My magic showed me what they saw. And one of the things they saw was a large delivery wagon with a huge wooden crate on the back."

"A big concern like Vesta Nine must get all kinds of shipments," Jake said. "Drilling equipment, replacement parts, that sort of thing."

"True—but from Tesla-Westinghouse?" Andreas replied. "The crate, covered by a tarpaulin, was brought in at night. When the driver stopped to get access to the area inside the fence, wind caught the tarp and blew it back enough for the name on the crate to show. It was meaningless to the saboteurs, but interesting, I think, to us."

"Adam told me some of his shipments to the Department of Supernatural Investigations went missing—and for some of Tesla-Westinghouse's other patrons, too," Rick confirmed.

"And we heard the same from Mitch Storm," Jake added. He took a sip of his scotch. It was excellent, smooth, and smoky, and he wondered, given Andreas's great age, just how old his collection of wine, cognac, and whiskey was. "I'm still trying to figure out whether Storm and his partner are allies, or liabilities."

Andreas sipped the blood in his goblet. "If the enemy of your enemy is your friend, then for now, in this, they are allies. I've heard better things of Storm and Drangosavich than of the Department as a whole. Still," he allowed, "I would not trust them fully, or tell them anything beyond what they need to know."

Rick nodded. "We interrupted an attempt to kidnap Adam, then a bombing attempt at Tesla-Westinghouse, when we went back to steal Adam's equipment *for* him before someone could steal it *from* him. I wonder if the bombing was meant to cover up someone else's robbery and we got in the way."

"I believe that's likely," Andreas agreed. "And while we have no idea what was in the crate the false plumbers saw, I'm glad you got your friend out of harm's way. I wouldn't like to see someone with Adam Farber's talents come under the control of Drogo Veles."

Jake repressed a shiver. "Makes you wonder what was in the box, doesn't it?"

"It could have been a steam generator, or an electrical gadget for the mine elevators," Rick mused. "But if it was a legitimate delivery, why hide it under a tarp and show up in the middle of the night?"

"I can ask Adam if he's aware of any projects for the Vesta mines," Rick said. "And whether anything he might have left stashed away at Tesla-Westinghouse would have any normal connection to that business."

Andreas nodded. "There was one more interesting observation. While the wagon was waiting to enter the complex, the gate opened and a very expensive carriage came through—one with a crest with a red falcon. It's owned by Mr. Richard Thwaites."

"There he is again. Thwaites is pure Oligarchy blue-blood," Rick said. "So is he part of an Oligarchy plot, or is this something he's cooked up on his own?"

"Veles isn't Oligarchy," Jake replied. "He'd disdain something so mortal. The Oligarchy is small potatoes to someone like him, unless he can use them to gain him greater power."

"So what's in it for him?" Rick mused. "Veles isn't the type to share power; he likes to call the shots himself. Thwaites may be a lightweight compared to his daddy, but the man has an ego the size of his bank account."

"You'll get the chance to observe for yourself," Andreas pointed out. "The reception for Mr. Carnegie's new exhibit at his museum is tomorrow night." He glanced at the black armband Jake wore. "It's the kind of thing propriety forgives you for attending, even if you're in mourning. Just don't look like you're having a good time."

Jake sighed. "It's been such a whirlwind since Father died, I've hardly had a chance to adjust to the new order of things. I highly doubt most of what I've done since the funeral counts as proper mourning etiquette."

Andreas's eyes darkened with old memories. His gaze flickered to an oil painting of a dark-haired woman in a gown at least eighty years out of date. "Grief waits," he said quietly. He seemed to pull himself out of his thoughts. "Your father will be best mourned when he is well-avenged, and the threat to your family and business is ended."

Just then, the doors to the sitting room flew open. Nicki stood in the doorway, face flushed and eyes alight with triumph. "You've got to see this!"

Rick, Jake, and Andreas dutifully followed Nicki into the parlor. Cady and Renate had cleared everything from one of the large tables. Renate had gathered the elements of a ritual on a piece of pristine white linen. Four thick white pillar candles anchored the corners of the linen. A wide silver bowl sat in the middle. The room smelled of sage.

Next to the ritual space on the table was a crystal absinthe decanter and two crystal glasses, as well as Renate's silver pentacle spoon. To the other side lay several small carved stones, a yellowed map and several pages that looked as if they had been torn from a diary.

Cady pointed to an old map. "From what we've been able to translate from the journal Nicki found, Jasinski seemed to be obsessed with Alekanovo, a remote mountain section of Russia—and a name that was on Thomas Desmet's list, if you recall. We found sketches Jasinski made, notes he jotted to himself, and it always came back to the same thing: a large stone and several smaller stones with symbols carved into them."

"Symbols like these," Nicki said, holding one of the small stones aloft. "We managed to translate some of his Polish notes, but the symbols had us stumped until Renate realized that they weren't in Russian; they're in a magical language."

"Once I had the region identified, I did some digging in the Russian books we have at the university," Cady continued. "Turns out that about fifty years ago, Alekanovo had some of Russia's deepest mines, and then in just one year, the mines the Czar had poured so much effort into building were closed and tens of thousands of workers vanished."

"Vanished?" Jake said. "You mean they abandoned the mining towns?"

Cady shook her head. "No. I mean that the people disappeared—and so did the crews sent in to find out what happened." She gave a triumphant smile, proud of her research. "Jasinski had interviewed people from near that area. They told stories of hungry spirits and night creatures prowling the towns and the deep mines. Most of the stories involved finding people and livestock torn apart and partly eaten, or dragged into the depths."

"Like the Night Hag attacks," Rick said, and Cady nodded.

"I don't think it's an accident that Jasinski disappeared not long after he returned home from making contact with scholars in the Alekanovo region," Renate said. "Throughout his notes, Jasinski talked about the 'Dark Ones' and the 'Deep Wraiths'. Several times, he calls them *gessyan.*" She paused. "*Gessyan* seems to be a term that covers a lot of territory—the Night Hag, wraiths, malicious ghosts, monsters, terrible shadow dogs... you get the idea. It's something of a supernatural catch-all term for bad things."

"His notes also refer to pages in Marcin's book," Nicki said. She looked at Jake. "Like Marcin of Krakow—the mystic Dr. Nils told you about, and another name on Uncle Thomas's list."

"Except that we didn't find the book anywhere in Jasinski's apartment," Cady added.

"We think the large stone had some kind of instructions carved onto it, maybe a way to control *gessyan*," Renate continued. "I can tell that it's been used in the presence of strong magic, but I'm not sure yet whether the big stone has power itself. The smaller stones might have been amulets or talismans. And Marcin's book could have been the instructions on how to use the stones." She paused, eyes bright.

"What if Jasinski had gathered the small stones himself, but he needed help getting the bigger stone with the remaining inscription?" Renate postulated. "So he asked your father to acquire the stone and ship it and Marcin's book through Brand and Desmet?"

Jake thought through the implications. "But that's still not a reason for Veles and Thwaites to kill my father, whether they actually planned to release the *gessyan* or letting them out was an accident."

"If the *gessyan's* release was the fault of Thwaites and Veles, intentional or not, they'd want to cover that up," Rick said, thinking aloud. "Maybe *especially* if it was an accident and they didn't know how to control the spirits. Maybe they got wind of Jasinski's shipment, and wanted to beat him to it, and Thomas was in the wrong place at the wrong time when they tried to steal it." He frowned. "They might have been worried that Jasinski told Thomas something they didn't want anyone else to know. And they're still trying to kill *us* in case he told us, too."

Renate nodded. "That's our theory."

Rick frowned. "It's got to have been an accident that the *gessyan* got out. What would Veles and Thwaites gain from having spirits like that loose? The ghosts would be a danger to them and their people, and the killings have attracted too much attention." He shook his head. "There's got to be something much more valuable than coal that made them sink their money into the Vesta Nine mine and risk unleashing the *gessyan*. Something really big that they were afraid Thomas could somehow ruin for them. I think we're missing something."

"I agree," Andreas said.

"It also doesn't explain how Jasinski became involved, or where he got the money to pay Father for the shipment," Jake said.

"But we know more than we did before," Renate replied. "And now, I'm going to see what I can coax out of the stones to see if we're right."

Renate stepped forward to the table where Jasinski's stones and her ritual elements were set out, as the others found seats. No matter how many times Jake saw Renate work her absinthe magic, it always intrigued him.

A circular braided rug lay beneath the table. The weave of the rug held the protective wardings and bounded the ritual space. Renate chanted quietly, and Jake strained to hear the words, but they seemed to slip away from him, as if they were not meant for his ears.

Renate took the crystal pitcher of absinthe, and she laid the silver pentacle spoon across one of the glasses. As she chanted, she poured a thin stream of absinthe over the silver pentacle and into the glass. The green waterfall of liquor had an inner light, touched by Renate's magic. As the absinthe flowed into an intricately etched glass, the patterns in the crystal glowed.

Renate took the second glass and let a few drops of water fall over the pentacle and into the absinthe, forming a smoky louche. She removed the pentacle and lifted the cup to the four points of the compass in blessing. Then she took the small carved stones and placed them in the silver bowl, poured some of the absinthe from the glass over the stones, then drank what remained of the consecrated liquid.

Sparkling green embers flashed and flickered in the air within the warded circle, like fireflies. Renate took a deep breath, and stared down into the bowl at the smooth, rune-scratched rocks which now glowed with their own, magical fire.

She began to speak in a language Jake thought sounded like Russian. Her voice took on the measured cadence of an incantation. Renate bent over the bowl, blew across it, and made a gesture with her hands.

Fiery letters danced above the bowl, rearranging themselves from arcane runes to Cyrillic Russian under the force of Renate's will and magic. Then the runes disappeared and an image took their place. It was small, as if glimpsed across a vast distance, and Jake leaned forward for a better look.

Hulking, dark creatures lumbered across wind-driven snow that stretched for as far as the eye could see. A torchlit army of villagers stood to oppose the creatures, armed with scythes and butcher's knives, rakes, and homemade pikes. Standing on a slight ridge above the villagers were four figures, and beside them was an elliptical black stone about knee-high and two handsbreadths wide. The figures were dressed in furs from head to toe, but it was clear that they were human, which the creatures definitely were not.

The creatures surged forward, moving at an alarming pace through the deep snow. The villagers raised their weapons. Although the villagers outnumbered the enemy, in the first few moments of battle it was clear the advantage went to the dark creatures—tall, misshapen things with impossibly long arms, clawed hands, and toothy, lantern-jawed maws. Yet as the villagers battled, Jake's attention shifted to the four fur-clad figures and the black standing stone.

Each of the figures held something aloft, but the image was too small for Jake to make out the details. The air around them was distorted, like heat from a sidewalk on a scorching day, making the image waver and shift. In a sudden burst, the distortion swept down the hillside, leaving the fighting villagers untouched, to break over the creatures like a storm surge. It glimmered on the snow with the iridescence of a soap bubble, yet it knocked the creatures back, tumbling them like leaves in the wind.

The translucent, shimmering force wavered, glistening in the harsh winter sun, growing more solid as it began to turn and twist in the air. Flashes of light flickered inside the churning power, until a wall of cold white light stood between the creatures and the villagers. The white light enveloped the creatures, flashed blindingly bright, and then both the white fire and the creatures were gone.

RENATE DREW A deep breath and let her chant slow as she thanked the powers that sustained her magic. The image disappeared as her hands fell to her sides, and the green embers that flickered and danced above the liquid's surface winked out.

"What did we just see?" Jake asked, looking at the items on the ritual table with a mix of fear and wonder.

Renate gave a tired smile. She dismissed her wards, and the energy seemed to drain from her. Andreas was beside her before anyone else could blink, catching her before she sank, exhausted, to a nearby chair.

"We saw the past," Renate replied, sounding as if the vision had taken everything out of her. "We saw what the stones remembered."

"Did those stones do that? The fiery wall of death stuff?" Rick asked, staring at the silver bowl as if it might explode.

Renate shook her head. Cady had already gone to the kitchen to fetch her a glass of water, which Renate accepted gratefully. She drank it, and some color gradually came back to her face.

"Not by themselves," she replied. "These smaller pieces were amulets, focus stones, a way for witches, or mages, or shamans—whatever you prefer—to fix their will and gather their power." She paused. "And I'd bet that Father Matija and his *Logonje* know more about this whole thing than they're telling. After all, he is a *Russian* Orthodox priest."

"Did the people in that vision get their power from the big stone, then?" Nicki asked.

"Not exactly," Renate replied, taking another sip of water. "Some of the magic came from the witches. But the big stone may well have stored magic for them, and it was likely their *inukshuk*, their totem—and their way of recording history. Odds are good that the Alekanovo witches may not only have stored power in the large stone, but also engraved information on it to protect the village—and maybe to preserve instructions for the future."

"If they had the information, why did people disappear at Alekanovo fifty years ago?" Rick asked.

Renate gave a tired shrug. "Maybe they lost their witches. Maybe they forgot what the stone meant. You saw the images—the last time the creatures rose was a very long time ago."

"Marcin of Krakow bound the *gessyan* in Poland in the fourteen hundreds. They show up again in Russia a lifetime ago," Rick said. "Someone—witches, priests, whoever—bound them at Alekanovo. So how did they get here?"

"Hodekin said they not only lived in the deep places, they could move through the Earth's core," Jake replied. "The distances would be a lot smaller if you could go *through* the earth instead of *over* it. Maybe they know when someone opens a weak point somewhere. Then they show up until the opening gets sealed again."

“Which means the secret to fighting the *gessyan* lies with the Alekanovo stone—and Marcin’s book,” Cady said. “What if we aren’t able to find them? What if Veles has already destroyed them?”

“Then you had better say your prayers,” Andreas replied. “Because we will be facing those dark creatures on our own.”

Chapter TWENTY-TWO

"I NEVER REALIZED that a museum could make such a grand place for a reception." Rick Brand said under his breath. He and Jake stood shoulder to shoulder in their tuxedos, watching the well-dressed crowd ebb and flow in the massive sculpture hall of the new Carnegie Museum on Fifth Avenue. A string quartet played chamber music in one corner. Waiters in formal attire passed out silver platters of delicacies and flutes of champagne, while in the corner, bartenders served up stiffer drinks.

"It's a brilliant idea," Jake replied, taking a sip of an excellent scotch from the Carnegie cellars. "No strangers trooping through your private spaces. No missing flatware when they all go home. And it advertises his pet project. There's a reason the man is insanely wealthy."

Andrew Carnegie stood at the far end of the huge room, chatting with Thomas Mellon and George Westinghouse. New Pittsburgh's upper crust were on prominent display, decked out in evening attire. By comparison, Rick and Jake were small fry. Dr. Nils had added them to the guest list, and now Nils's prominent role within the museum had him glad-handing donors and working the crowd, although he had acknowledged them with a nod when they entered. Jake looked around at the guests, but did not see Andreas Thalberg, and he wondered if the vampire would put in an appearance.

Per Carnegie's new-found obsession with philanthropy, representatives of his favorite causes were also present, including the administrators from the huge new library that bore his name, and several scholarly men Jake suspected had something to do with the technical school Carnegie was planning to open.

"There he is." Jake nodded in the direction of a tall, slim man talking with Henry Clay Frick. Drogo Veles looked more like an Eastern European nobleman than a centuries-old dark witch. He chatted with Frick, utterly at ease among the wealthy and powerful. Then again, Jake thought, Veles's magic probably gave him far more power than mere money or prestige.

"Brand. Desmet. Didn't think you'd be here, what with the circumstances and all." Richard Thwaites was suddenly in front of them, a gin and tonic in one hand and a canapé in the other.

"Business goes on," Rick replied noncommittally. Both he and Jake wore the black arm bands mourning etiquette required. Rick clapped Thwaites on the shoulder, and as he drew his hand away, managed to tip the button-sized listening device Adam Farber had created under the socialite's collar without being noticed.

"Quite." Thwaites tossed the canapé into his mouth and followed it up with a slug of his gin and tonic. "Such a loss. And a caution."

Jake felt his blood rise. "I'm not sure I take your meaning," he said, steel in his voice.

Thwaites managed to look bored, as if the conversation did not merit his full attention. "Put all your eggs in one basket, that's what Mr. Carnegie always says," Thwaites replied. "Your father got involved in things that didn't concern him. Now he's gone. There's a lesson to be learned there."

"Is that a threat?" Jake said, bristling.

For all that Thwaites sold himself as an errant playboy, Jake glimpsed both malice and intelligence in his steady gaze. "It's what you make of it," he said, tossing back the rest of his drink. "But don't say I didn't warn you." At that, he ambled off in search of a bartender.

Rick laid a restraining hand on Jake's arm as Jake took a half-step to follow. "Let him go," Rick cautioned. "It's likely the gin talking." He dropped his voice to a whisper. "We'll see what Nicki picks up on the receiver from that microphone."

"He threatened us," Jake retorted.

"Maybe. Richard Thwaites couldn't fight his way out of a paper bag, but he does have some very dangerous associates."

Coincidentally or not, at that moment Drogo Veles chanced to turn around, caught Jake's eye, and inclined his head in acknowledgement.

"I want to know what Thwaites and Veles had to do with my father's murder," Jake said, his voice barely restrained.

Rick nodded. "So do I. But this isn't the time or the place. Accost them here, and you'll accomplish nothing except getting yourself thrown out, and lose half our business to boot. Destroy their game, and you've struck a blow for your father."

Jake took a deep breath, willing his fists to relax. Raised voices near the door rose above the murmur of conversation and the sedate music.

"I'll thank you to take your hands off me!" A man's voice with a distinct Irish accent rang out. "I've got business here."

Heads turned to see the altercation. Jake recognized the speaker—'Dynamite' Danny Maguire, the Irish immigrant-turned-construction magnate and councilman whose wealth and solid pro-union views made him a thorn in the side to New Pittsburgh's elite.

Maguire looked like he would be more at home unloading crates on a dock than hobnobbing with the well-to-do. He was a little taller than average and solidly built, although the belly straining at the pearl buttons of his tuxedo shirt testified to his ability to enjoy his newly comfortable life. Red-haired with a temper to match, Maguire bustled in as if he owned the room.

One of Carnegie's security men trailed him, and Maguire wheeled on the man. "Don't you have something better to do than harass guests? Don't make trouble for me, and I won't make any for you." Maguire turned back toward the scandalized socialites and grinned. "Don't stop on account of me. Carry on."

Maguire had one of Carnegie's elegant invitations in his hand, though whether or not it was genuine was another question. As a second security man edged toward Maguire, Jake spotted Clayton Price, one of Carnegie's more respectable enforcers, heading toward the union man with the expression of a pained maître d'. Around the room, guests whispered to each other, and Jake wondered how many were taking bets that Maguire would end up tossed out on his ear before the evening was over.

Jake glanced away from the altercation, and caught a glimpse of a figure moving off to his left, through a darkened section of the museum that was roped off to visitors. He thought for a moment that it was Drogo Veles, but when he looked back toward the reception, Veles was standing with two of the city's most notable financiers.

"Something's going on," Jake said. "Let's go."

He caught Rick up on what he'd seen as they wound carefully through the crowd, doing their best to avoid conversation while trying not to look as if they were hurrying. Maguire provided a convenient distraction, as he struck up a loud conversation with William Flinn and Christopher Magee. The two political bosses were the closest thing New Pittsburgh had to an Oligarchy counterweight, and even men like Andrew Carnegie were obliged to handle them gently or face public unpleasantness. Jake suppressed a smile; Andreas had put Maguire up to the stunt, to create a distraction.

When Jake and Rick reached one side of the huge main exhibit area, Jake looked both ways to make certain that the exit did not have a watchful guard in attendance. Then they slipped into the shadowed room on the other side of the rope.

The Carnegie Museum was a massive temple to knowledge. Built of huge, gray blocks of stone and rising three stories high, it was an imposing structure, and equally impressive on the inside. Marble staircases, parquet stone floors, and stained glass skylights in the Tiffany style gave the museum the gravitas of a shrine. But now, the cavernous rooms were shadowed, and what light filtered in through the windows was cold and gray and did little to dispel the darkness.

The hulking shadow of a dinosaur skeleton made Jake shiver as he passed. The bones of other long-dead beasts filled one of the chambers: Irish elk, mastodons, mammoths, ancient horses and saber-toothed cats. In the next room, taxidermied animals watched balefully through glassy eyes as Jake slipped silently past the exhibits, including one of the museum's most notable displays, a huge glass case showing a lion attacking a traveler on camelback.

Jake glimpsed motion ahead. He signaled for Rick to pause in the doorway to the next room, just in time to see a tall figure slip through the glass cases and dioramas and down a stairwell reserved for museum staff. Jake glanced around trying to get his bearings in the near-dark. He had visited the museum fairly often with Dr. Nils, and taken the back passageways more than once.

The stairwell was lit only by a few ghostly light bulbs hanging far overhead. They reached the bottom, and Jake carefully opened the door. This section of the museum was off-limits to regular visitors. It housed the offices of the museum curator and the staff, several classrooms for special programs, and a large receiving and storage area where items not on exhibit were kept until the curators could ready them for display.

"It can't be Veles," Rick murmured. "We saw him standing in the reception at the same time you saw the shadow man."

Jake nodded. "But I'm betting a witch as powerful as Veles could come up with something."

Rick looked uncertain. "So is what we're chasing real or not?"

"At least as real, I wager, as those ghosts you ran into behind Tesla-Westinghouse," Jake cautioned.

The museum offices were closed for the evening, doors shut and lights out. Jake paused, waiting long enough to allow his quarry to get to the far end of the corridor before venturing out from the doorway. He had brought one of Adam's latest toys with him, a pocket-sized electric torch. He hoped he would not have to use it, sure that it would make them an easy target. To his relief, the long basement corridor was dimly lit by two flickering Edison bulbs dangling from the ceiling on long cords.

The dark figure passed the room where collections not currently on display resided on endless rows of metal shelves. Perhaps it was a trick of the dim light, but Jake was certain he could see through the shadowy man. From Rick's unsettled expression, Jake guessed his partner had observed the same thing.

The figure slipped inside the next room, passing right through the closed door. Jake and Rick followed at a prudent distance, and Jake opened the door slowly, praying that the hinges would not squeak.

Jake remembered the storage room being filled with wooden crates and cardboard boxes bound with metal straps. It was the museum's receiving room, where acquisitions were temporarily stored until Nils and the curators could tag and document the rare treasures as part of the official collection. And now that he had followed the shadowy man to the room, a suspicion began to build in the back of Jake's mind.

Jake paused, watching the figure move on. It struck him that the bulbs overhead did not illuminate the figure's face, even when it passed directly beneath them, and that his footsteps made no sound, even though the intruder was not moving stealthily.

The prowler moved quickly among the boxes, examining the labels, searching for something. Jake and Rick tracked him from a few aisles away, one on either side of the apparition, staying low to remain out of sight. Jake expected the intruder to find what he was looking for and snatch it, but the dark figure never touched anything, going around objects that blocked his path rather than moving things out of the way.

Jake ducked behind a stack of crates to hide. The top crate rocked back and forth at the movement, and the prowler's head whipped around, staring straight toward Jake's hiding place.

The intruder had no face.

In a heartbeat, the creature vanished. Jake's hand fell to the derringer in the pocket of his tuxedo jacket, though what his gun could do against a creature raised by a witch of Veles's strength, he had no idea. He tensed, expecting the prowler to suddenly appear in front of him, materializing as quickly as he had disappeared. Jake's sixth sense sounded a warning, and he followed his intuition, moving as far as he dared to find a new hiding place.

The lights went out.

Jake stood completely still, flattened against the crates. He dared not use his electric torch, and in the darkness, he could not see where Rick was hiding. The room suddenly grew cold, as if an arctic wind had swept through. Silvery ripples reflected on the walls, like mercury shimmering in the light.

Jake shifted enough to see the door. Three fluid, silver creatures hovered in the doorway. They glided into the room, rising up so that they could see down the long aisles.

An ear-splitting screech echoed from the room's stone walls, and one of the silver creatures streaked toward Jake. A second ghost headed into the center of the room, while the third peeled off to the left, heading for Rick, who gave a startled yelp. Jake ran, no longer fearing to flick the switch on his electric torch, sending a bobbing, erratic beam in front of him.

"What's your plan?" Rick yelled as he tried to keep an eye on the silver ghost behind him while he dodged between the crates.

"Get to the back door in one piece!" Jake replied.

"That's it?"

"You've got something better?"

In response, Rick wheeled, took up a shooting stance, and aimed at the silver ghost that was gaining on him. The shot echoed in the receiving room, and the bullet passed right through the specter, lodging in a wooden crate. Muttering curses under his breath, Rick sprinted for the door.

"That's likely to bring the security guards down here," Jake said, ducking as one of the ghosts swooped low enough to slash at him.

"At least we've got a fighting chance against the living," Rick replied as he ran headlong toward the doors.

Jake felt like a cow herded down the chute at the slaughterhouse. The crates were stacked waist high, and the long, straight aisles made a perfect killing zone. At the far end of the room was an exit and the delivery doors, but they might have been half a league away for all the good they did Jake.

The silver ghost dove at Jake, and he threw himself to the floor. Long, silver tendrils scraped across his back, leaving bloody scratches.

"Hey you!" Rick yelled at the ghost, trying to draw it off. "Over here!" The ghost paused, giving Jake a chance to scramble to his feet, then hurtled towards Rick.

"Damn!" Rick muttered, leaping over a low stack of crates.

Jake's heart sank as he realized that two of the ghostly creatures were heading toward him faster than he could run, cutting him off from the door. He and Rick were too far in to go back, but not far enough to make it to the other side before the silver ghosts caught up with them.

The ghosts rushed toward Jake, and he threw himself over the wooden crates, landing badly. He heard seams rip on his tuxedo and wondered if he hadn't cracked a rib in the process. Not stopping to look behind him, he ran down the aisle, fixed on the far wall and the exit. Rick was running the same obstacle course, his face pale with fear.

If that door is locked and there isn't a way to open it, we're dead.

The ghosts came at him again, and Jake careened into a row of boxes, sending them to the floor and falling head-over-heels behind them. He was past the middle of the room, only a few rows from the exit. The ghosts were growing closer by the second. Jake managed to climb over another set of boxes, and then another, but he was tiring and the ghosts seemed willing to wait for an easy kill. He could hear Rick running nearby, breathing hard.

Jake's arm ached, and he was shivering from the sudden cold. The light in his electric torch flickered, and Jake shook it, desperate to see where he was going. He kept running, but the torch flickered on and off, until finally dying.

"Why did you do that?" Rick demanded from the next aisle.

"I didn't!" Jake shot back. "Keep running!"

The ghosts struck. Three silvery, nightmarish figures, faceless, glowing like moonlight, rushed toward them. Jake blundered away, tripping over boxes, throwing crates over, stumbling and falling and regaining his feet. No matter how fast he ran, the ghosts gained on him, and Jake knew he would not reach the exit in time.

He tried to hurdle the next row of crates, only to bring them crashing down around him. He barked his shin, sending pain streaking up his leg. The silver ghosts were nearly on him.

As the creatures swooped in for the kill with an ear-splitting shriek, a bright light flared from one of the boxes Jake had broken open with his fall, sending an iridescent cone of power rippling out to meet the attack.

Jake did his best to flatten himself against the wreckage as two forces far beyond his understanding met in battle. The shimmering force that he had seen in Renate's vision now hovered protectively over him, holding the silver ghosts at bay. Colors, pure and intense, glistened and shimmered, strong enough to stand against the assault of the three angry ghosts. Rick stared at the iridescent dome in wide-eyed wonder.

The glittering power swelled, and fire alarms began to go off all over the museum, tripped by the wall of energy. The silver creatures made one final, desperate assault and then disappeared as quickly as they had come.

The lights flickered back on. Jake struggled to his feet, wincing from his bruised ribs. Rick staggered, looking equally battered. Jake took a step and stumbled, limping from a turned ankle.

"Come on!" Rick said, getting under Jake's shoulder to help him. "We've got to get out of here."

Jake grimaced as he looked out over the destruction the battle with the silver ghosts had wrought. Alarms blared, and he knew that the building would be evacuated as a precaution. Firefighters might show up at any moment, making it awkward to explain why he was in an off-limits area.

But before they went anywhere, Jake was determined to find the source of their unexpected protector. He turned around, dropping to his knees to begin sifting through the damaged crates that littered the floor.

"What are you waiting for? Security's going to be here any second, and I don't fancy explaining this to old man Carnegie!" Rick urged.

"Got it!" he said triumphantly. The piece of broken wood he lifted to the light had a shipping label stamped by Polish and US Customs, and the address clearly read 'Mr. Thomas Desmet, Brand and Desmet, Smallman Street.' A glance at the boxes nearby showed two other Brand and Desmet crates, correctly delivered to the museum. *Could it be as simple as a delivery error?* Jake wondered, and guessed that the answer was yes. A second look at the markings revealed that the crates had been delivered earlier that day. *Wrong destination and late—we've got to talk to our people.*

He would ponder how Jasinski's shipment got sent to the Carnegie Museum later. Now Jake pawed through the wreckage, looking for the Alekanovo stone and Marcin of Krakow's book. Rick knelt next to him and helped with the search, digging quickly, fearing discovery at any moment. And there, swaddled in crumpled newspapers and old rags, lay a black elliptical stone the length of his arm, carved with runes, and an old, leather-bound book.

"Grab them and go!" Rick's tone verged on frantic. He hefted the stone, while Jake held the book and hobbled toward the door.

At the doorway, Jake hesitated; the dim light of the acquisitions room would leave them perfectly silhouetted should an assassin be ready to target them as they stepped into the night.

"Stand to the side," Jake hissed. "Just in case." Rick flattened himself to one side of the door and pulled the lock while Jake grabbed the handle and yanked the door open, shielding himself behind it.

A shot fired, splintering the doorframe next to Rick's head, and they dove for cover. Jake dropped to the ground, protecting the book, while Rick curled around the Alekanovo stone. The stone had been effective against hostile magic, but Jake did not want to rely on it against bullets.

More shots pinged against the huge foundation stones. Raised voices sounded, and in the distance, Jake heard the ringing of police alarms. Three men climbed the loading dock to stand in front of Jake and Rick, shielding them and firing into the night toward the attackers. When the answering gunfire ceased, one of the three headed for the door.

"Jake? Rick?" a familiar voice called.

"We're here," Jake replied, rising from where he had taken shelter from the shots. Rick got up and dusted himself off before reaching down to grab the precious Alekanovo stone.

"Come on," Kovach hissed. "Maguire's men are covering us. Get to the carriage!"

Kovach and his men escorted them from the dock to the street and into waiting carriages. Kovach shoved Jake into the coach. Rick followed a moment later, falling onto his elbows to protect the Alekanovo stone he clutched against his chest. The door slammed shut, and Kovach swung up beside Charles as the carriage jolted forward. Shots fired behind them, answered in kind by Kovach's men.

Jake and Rick managed to take their seats, still clutching the stone and Marcin's book. By the glow of the passing streetlights, Jake made out Rick sitting across from him. To his surprise, 'Dynamite' Danny Maguire was in the other seat, sitting next to Nicki, who had a headset on and waved impatiently for them to be quiet.

"Looks like you've had a busy evening," Maguire said.

"Those were your guys, with the guns?"

Maguire nodded. "Seemed neighborly, seeing how someone was trying to take you out." He leaned forward. "I hear you've been asking around about the Vesta Nine."

Jake's heart had finally begun to slow and he could breathe without gasping. "Yeah. I think there's bad stuff going on down there, and whatever it is had something to do with my father's murder."

Maguire raised an eyebrow. "Murder, is it? That's not what the obituary said."

"Don't believe everything you read in the paper," Rick replied.

"All right then, here's something you might find interesting," Maguire said, leaning back against the plush seats. "You're right about something funny going on over at Vesta Nine. I hear things, you know? A whole lot of men are dying down there. Lots more than usual, and not in the usual ways. Some just disappear. Others get... eaten."

"By what?" Rick asked.

Gessyan. Jake thought to himself, letting Rick fish for what Maguire might know.

Maguire shrugged. "Oh, there are a lot of bogeyman stories, about Night Hags and monsters, but no one really knows. And that's the problem. Something got loose down there, and they don't know how to bottle it back up again. Don't want to miss mining any of their precious coal—if that's what they're really mining," he said with a sneer. "The mine bosses are still sending men into the hole, and now the men have had enough of it. They're more scared of what's down there than they are of their bosses, and word on the street says it's all going to come to a head soon."

"Strikes?" Jake asked. The bloody Homestead Strikes were still in recent memory. He had no desire to see that bloodshed repeated.

Maguire nodded. "Aye. Maybe worse. This could go very badly. Riots. Shootings. I hear tell that the Oligarchy wants none of it. They're stuck between a rock and a hard place. They can't afford to let the miners get away with a strike, but they've got no belly for another Homestead. Bad for business, and for their reputation."

"Back up a minute," Rick said, holding up a hand. "What do you mean, 'if that's what they're really mining'?"

Maguire gave a canny smile. "Because I've heard tell that what they're pulling out of the deepest reaches of the mine isn't coal. It's a weird greenish stone, but no one says what it is and the miners who go that deep don't live long enough to tell tales."

"Greenish crystal—like quartz but sort of glows?" Rick asked. He kept his voice calm, but Jake could see the excitement in his eyes. Maguire nodded.

"Yeah, sounds right," Maguire confirmed.

"But why tell us?" Jake asked.

"Because I heard you've been nosing around, asking questions. And I know you've got connections you don't like to talk about," Maguire said, with a raised eyebrow. He might have been fishing, but Jake was pretty sure Maguire meant the Thalbergs, or Jasinski, or both. "And I think somehow, this might have something to do with Mr. Desmet's death, and the problems you've been having over at Brand and Desmet."

"Go on," Jake prompted.

"I've heard something else. I've been told that down in the deepest places, where no sane man would go no matter what you promised to pay him, the mine bosses have been using the dead to work the shafts." Maguire leaned forward. "Mechanical men, made from dead bodies. I've heard it directly from the men who saw them—before they turned up dead themselves. They swore that men they knew, men whose wakes they'd attended, showed up with clockwork pieces embedded in their flesh, working deep in the mines."

Just then, an ear-splitting squeal burst from Nicki's headset, and she tore the device off, flinging it across the carriage in a burst of gutter French. Jake grabbed the headphones and switched them off, silencing the painful noise.

"*Mon Dieu*!" Nicki swore. "I thought my head would explode!"

"What happened?" Rick asked.

"I was listening through the device you planted on Richard Thwaites," Nicki replied. "I could hear everything he said, until the stupid microphone nearly deafened me!"

Jake sighed. "I suspect either Thwaites or Veles found the listening device. Did you get anything good?"

Nicki rolled her eyes dramatically. "Not much. Richard Thwaites likes the sound of his own voice. But there was a comment, right before he tried to scramble my brains with that noise, that might be important. A man's voice—thick accent, I bet it was Veles—said that Thwaites needs to be patient. The 'problem' will be dealt with, and the pay-off would be worth the aggravation. 'Just a few more days', he said."

"So whatever Veles and Thwaites are up to, we need to move fast, or we'll lose them," Jake said.

Rick looked at Maguire. "You want a chance to score a hit against the Oligarchy? Here it is. Are you in?"

A malicious smile spread across Danny Maguire's face. "Oh, yeah. I live for this kind of thing. I'm in—and so are my men."

Chapter TWENTY-THREE

INSIDE THE VAST complex that was the Vesta Nine coal mine, Drostan Fletcher did his best to be invisible. He had a dark woolen cap pulled down over his red hair, and he wore a black sweater and pants over sturdy work boots equipped with steel toes strong enough to break bone.

Jacob and Mitch had insisted on coming with him. They made it through the fence together, before Jacob veered off with an ironic salute, while Mitch headed to the mine offices. Jacob was wearing a strange set of goggles and the uniform of a Vesta Nine miner, and he carried a counterfeit union card, in case he needed identification. Hans the clockwork man was with him, also dressed as a miner. Jacob intended to infiltrate the mine and record evidence of what he found with Adam Farber's special goggles, with Hans along as back-up.

Jacob headed for the mine entrance, intending to lose himself in the crowd heading for third shift. Dangerous as Drostan's own mission would be, he did not envy Jacob his job.

Jake Desmet had sent Drostan to scout the area, see what he could learn in the storage buildings topside, and discover any weakness they could use to their advantage. Drostan had asked Mitch and Jacob to act as back-up, happy not to be going underground himself. While Jacob and Hans went below, Drostan poked around the warehouses and Mitch headed into the mine office to see what he could learn from their files.

Drostan was used to reconnaissance. Watching and waiting were the meat and drink of a private investigator. Now, he relied on his skills learned in the British Army in the Sudan; stealth, observation, and if it came down to it, hand-to-hand combat. Desmet had supplied Drostan with a map, and several unusual gadgets that Drostan eyed with suspicion. All the same, he was grateful for the light of the electric torch, filtered through a black scarf to dim its beam.

All he had to do now was get in and out alive.

Vesta Nine was a huge, sprawling complex of buildings and railroad spurs. Getting inside the fence had been surprisingly simple. Drostan's wire cutters made a neat break and he left a small gadget of Farber's behind to help him locate the exit on his way out of the complex. Inside, he paused in the shadows, observing the pattern of the guard patrols and watching where the miners came and went. It did not take long for him to note that Vesta Nine's guards were exceptionally well-armed, unusual for a coal mine.

A good lock pick got Drostan into the first storage building. The guards, Drostan noticed, walked past but did not enter. Inside, he found mining equipment—drill bits, and various mechanical odds and ends of no interest to him. The second building was equally mundane. But in the third building, Drostan found rows of crates stacked shoulder high, and toward the front, three large boxes gave him one of the answers he had come looking to find.

"'Tesla-Westinghouse: Deliver to Adam Farber,'" he murmured, staring at the shipping labels on the three crates. He withdrew a small crowbar from his pack and jimmied open the top of the first box. Inside lay cardboard boxes full of clockwork gears of varying sizes. A second box held a variety of metal rods and pins. The third crate contained a baffling array of rubber hoses, springs, and flexible tubing. He replaced the lids carefully as a worrisome idea began to form in his mind. The stolen items weren't something normal miners might need, but if Mitch Storm was right about Tumblety and Brunrichter being part of the Vesta Nine situation, the pieces might be something the resurrectionist doctors would want. He dropped one of Adam's listening and tracking devices into the space between the stacked boxes and moved on.

A cold breeze stirred and Drostan dropped to a crouch, gun in hand. He heard no footsteps, but every instinct told him that he was not alone. Something skittered past in the shadows with a faint clicking sound that sent shivers down his spine. A few moments later, the chill in the air faded and the sound receded. Only then did he realize he had been holding his breath.

Drostan straightened, glanced around to assure himself that he was alone, and made a cautious exit. He had moved towards the back of the Vesta Nine complex and, from here, could see the huge hulking buildings, the tipples and the pit heads along with the structures housing the entrances to the shafts down into Vesta Nine's depths. Electric lights lit the shaft entrances and the doors to the other buildings, and widely spaced lamps dotted the night along the railroad lines that carried cars filled with coal out to market.

A guard came around the corner of the nearest building and Drostan crouched, sure he had been seen. But the man was more intent on his cigarette than on security, and he ambled past the high grass where Drostan hid in the shadows. When Drostan's heartbeat finally slowed again, he made his way to the next storage building and picked the lock.

Sidelined mine cars, lengths of replacement rail, rope, chain, and lumber filled the huge building. Drostan saw more of the same in the next building. Which left the last storehouse, the one farthest away from the rest of the mining operations.

Drostan picked the lock and entered the building through a side door that appeared to have been unused for some time. He hesitated. Instinct warned him to run but he ignored it, and slipped further into the building.

Something low to the ground and not entirely solid tripped him, sending him sprawling. An overpowering stench made him want to retch. He fumbled for his electric torch and flicked it on, careful to shutter the light through his fingers.

A partially decomposed human head stared back at him.

Drostan swallowed back a yelp. The body was in the latter stages of decomposition, split open like a ripe fruit, rippling with the thousands of maggots feasting on the putrefying flesh. He tried to remind himself that he had seen far worse in Her Majesty's Service, men he had known well reduced to worm fodder. The thought did not blunt the revulsion, but it did help Drostan get a rein on his emotions as he backed away.

From the clothing, he guessed the body was male, a little shorter than he was. The cut of his clothes told him it was someone either newly immigrated or who returned frequently to Europe. A glint of silver caught the light, and Drostan shifted for a better view.

Around the corpse's neck was a silver pentacle.

Drostan let out a breath that hissed through his teeth. New Pittsburgh had a secretive magical community. Symbols like pentacles were not openly worn, certainly not unless the person was a devout practitioner willing to bear the consequences of exposure. And in the close-knit neighborhoods of recent immigrants, tales and the fear of witches were real and strong.

He was willing to bet the dead man was the missing witch, Karl Jasinski. And since a powerful witch would usually be difficult to kill, Drostan's money was on Drogo Veles as the murderer. *Want to bet that Jasinski heard about the Night Hag, went poking his nose in, and got more than he expected?*

Drostan's hands were shaking as he pulled out another of Adam's locators and tucked it near the body, shuddering as something sticky brushed his fingers. With a sigh, he murmured a few words of blessing, the least he could do for a human being who had not come to a good end. Then he turned his attention to the rest of the warehouse, and felt as if he had tumbled into Hell.

Six other corpses lay on big blocks of ice set upon sawdust. They looked fresh, a day or two old at most. Four stainless steel surgical tables were lined up beneath large operatory lights. On the tables, Drostan saw more well-preserved corpses, and near them, a large vat of embalming fluid. Drostan felt his gorge rise as his light played over the modifications that had been made to the cadavers. Bits of metal had been sunk into the flesh of knees and elbows, wrists and jaws. Glass eyes glittered in sightless sockets.

He looked up, unsurprised to see a crowd of ghosts hovering nearby. They hung back, watching him. Many of them bore the evidence of horrific burns and crushed bones. Some of them glared at Drostan with accusing looks, as if to challenge him to do something about their deaths.

Missing people. Missing bodies. Missing crates of equipment a genius inventor had used to build his prototype mechanical *werkmen*. This was where the clockwork zombies had come from, the ones who had attacked him at the morgue. They'd tried to get to him before he could learn anything from Sheffield, tried to keep him from putting the pieces together.

Mitch was right about Tumblety and Brunrichter being back, Drostan thought. He'd seen their abominations before. *What a ghastly way to create workers that don't tell secrets.*

His electric torch flickered past the autopsy tables, and shone on four pale faces. Four dead men, standing at attention, pale as moonlight. Glass eyes reflected the light of Drostan's torch. Clockwork gears shone against dead skin at jaw and wrist, though the rest of the bodies were covered in workman's clothing. These were the finished products of the nightmare tinkerer.

With a click and a hum, the clockwork corpses woke up. An unearthly red light pulsed in their eyes, which fixed on Drostan, and the creatures took a shuddering step toward him.

Drostan turned and ran. But before he could reach the side door through which he had entered, the overhead lights over the autopsy tables at the front of the building blazed on. He dropped to the floor, trying to stay in the shadows at the back of the laboratory, and found himself lying next to Jasinski's corpse, between the decaying body and the wall. So very close to the side door, but unlikely he could make it out without being spotted.

When the lights went on, the clockwork hum stopped.

Two men entered the building from the front door, walking towards him, one with brown trousers and the other with black pants that were a bit too short for his height.

"What's this?" one man exclaimed, seeing the clockwork corpses out of line. He had the burr of Drostan's native Scotland in his voice. "Something's set them off again." Drostan's heart sank as he recognized Francis Tumblety's voice.

He'd had the misfortune of running into them before. Francis Tumblety, quack doctor, charlatan soothsayer, and one-time suspect in the Jack the Ripper murders, was the man in the brown trousers. Adolph Brunrichter, vivisectionist, disgraced physician and convicted felon, was the other fiend.

Just a year ago, Drostan had helped Mitch Storm and Jacob Drangosavich blow up a house with both Tumblety and Brunrichter inside. He had hoped that was the end of them, though both men had a reputation for being hard to kill.

"Go have a look around," Brunrichter said in a thick German accent.

The first man walked toward the darkness that shrouded the rear of the building. He played his light around the corners of the lab and the stacks of wooden crates. Drostan froze, trying to flatten himself beside the corpse, holding his breath as the light touched on the body beside him briefly before moving on.

"Probably just rats," the first man said, turning back.

"Veles wants twenty more of these before the end of the month," Tumblety said.

"Veles can kiss my ass. *Werkmen* can't be built that fast. He'll have to wait," Brunrichter replied.

"The miners are scared." Tumblety's voice was arrogant, and the man was quite likely insane. The last time Drostan had seen Tumblety, the mad doctor had sported a ridiculous moustache and affected epaulettes and brass buttons on his coat like a military officer. Drostan did not dare raise his head to see whether Tumblety's wardrobe had improved.

"And Veles thinks they will be less scared when they see more of these?" Brunrichter replied. "Right now, they have legends of the Night Hag to explain the monsters in the dark. Do you think that, given the choice between two nightmares, they'll prefer walking dead men to deadly shadows?"

"Word is they're scared enough to go on strike."

"Let them. They can be replaced. Veles has enough enslaved to handle the tourmaquartz processing. He only needs the living men to mine the coal. There are more where they came from."

"If they strike, we'll have fewer bodies to choose from to replace the clockwork corpses. Veles will want more, and he'll want them fast, and he won't be happy." Brunrichter grunted. "I never promised Herr Veles enough clockwork miners to dig all his precious crystals. I only promised enough to go to the deep places. That was our bargain."

"And if more *gessyan* escape?" Tumblety challenged. "Bad enough that the Night Hag and the wraiths have gotten out. Other things, too. We don't need any more monsters running about. People are talking. Even Thwaites won't be able to keep the police away forever, if the murders continue."

"Veles set spells. It's kept the rest of the *gessyan* in their place," Brunrichter replied.

"What if the spells don't hold?" Tumblety argued. "I told you it was a mistake for him to kill the other witch. Thwaites said that the witch had a plan to stop the *gessyan*, put them back where they came from. Now what? All those deaths along the rivers, they're attracting too much attention. Sooner or later, someone's going to come looking around here."

"Like that Scottish detective?" Brunrichter said contemptuously. "After what happened at the morgue, no one will listen to him. Thwaites said he fixed it with the cops."

"I don't like it," Tumblety replied petulantly.

"Gah. You worry too much. Herr Veles is a powerful *Zauberer.* He'll take care of it."

"If he's so powerful, why hasn't he sent the *gessyan* back where they came from? And why'd he need that Polish witch?" Tumblety said. "Maybe he doesn't *want* the spirits to go away. Maybe he's got a plan he hasn't told anyone about."

"These new bodies appear to be usable," Tumblety replied. "I would have liked to see some bigger men, heavier boned. Easier to sink the mechanisms in when the bones are strong." He walked over to one of the bodies. "This one will be tricky. Young and strong, but slightly built."

"I've talked to Veles about the possibility of pre-selecting our corpses," Brunrichter said. "Identify the workers with the right body types, and then make them available to us. Cuts down on waste."

Drostan felt his stomach tighten at the casual discussion of murder.

"Let's check the other shipments," Tumblety said. "I think the new embalming fluid should be strong enough to overcome the extremity failure we've seen. I can adjust the mix."

"I want to get started in the morning," Brunrichter warned. "The bodies are fresh. Good if your fluid is here, but we begin with or without it."

The lights were switched off and Drostan heard the two men shut and lock the door behind them. He remained where he was long enough to assure himself that Brunrichter and Tumblety would not hear him leave by the side door.

In the darkness, he heard footsteps. Drostan had his gun out as he reached for the door. A hand came down heavily on his shoulder, and he turned to meet the open, staring glass eyes of one of the clockwork corpses barely visible in the low light.

Choking back a cry, Drostan fired at close range into the mechanical zombie's chest. The suppressor deadened the noise, but it still seemed to echo in the cavernous warehouse. He knew he could not kill a dead man, but the shot sent the creature stumbling backwards, giving Drostan enough room to squeeze through the door and make it outside. He quickly locked the door behind him.

He had no idea whether the zombies would try to follow through the door, but he knew he could not hold them off by himself. Taking that shot was risky. Drostan flattened himself against the side of the building, willing his body to stop shaking, listening for signs of pursuit.

Bam. Bam. Bam. Heavy fists pounded against the door behind him. The zombies might not be able to open the padlocked door, but they could pound away at it until the door either broke or someone came to investigate. Drostan heard voices, coming closer. He did not wait to see who they belonged to, but set off as fast as he dared, staying in the shadows, eyeing the dark stretches between buildings where he might be spotted.

A guard reached the spot where the clockwork corpses were pounding on the door and blew an ear-splitting blast on his whistle. Drostan melted into the shadows. More guards joined the first at the building Drostan had just left. The door to Tumblety and Brunrichter's hellish laboratory flew open, guards screaming as the clockwork zombies pushed their way out.

The guards' screams would bring more security men; Drostan's chance to escape was fading fast. Drostan ran toward the hole in the fence where he had entered—he didn't need Farber's locater, in the end—only to find three more clockwork zombies between him and the fence. He eyed the distance to his bicycle on the other side of the fence. The zombies would be on him before he could make it.

Drostan heard the rhythmic scrape of wheels on rails and looked up. Cars loaded with coal were heading out of the Vesta Nine compound. He glanced at the zombies, then at the train cars, and began to sprint. The zombies could not change direction quickly, but his movement attracted the attention of the human guards. A shot hit the ground near Drostan's feet.

"Hey you! Stop!"

Drostan kept running. Glancing back, he saw the clockwork zombies heading his way with a terrifying singleness of purpose. *If I survive this, I'm charging George Brand double.*

As a teenager back in Scotland, Drostan had occasionally hopped freight trains. That was a long time ago, when he was younger and faster. The coal cars were slowly accelerating, and Drostan knew that if he did not catch up soon, he would never be able to jump onboard.

More shots, one of them nearly grazing Drostan's left shoulder. He swore under his breath, pivoted, and squeezed off three shots; two hit the zombies, knocking one flat on its ass and forcing another back several steps. The third shot went just shy of the pursuing guards, since Drostan had no desire to have blood on his hands this evening.

Drostan thanked the stars for his long legs and ran after the last coal car. The zombies were close behind. He jumped, and his hands caught the back of the last car, just as cold, strong hands clamped onto his leg, nearly pulling him free. The train was accelerating, and Drostan felt as if he were flying off the end of it like a flag.

A shot zinged off the side of the car, sending up a shower of sparks. Drostan let the train's momentum swing his body from side to side, the zombie on his ankle flailing behind him. One of the zombie's legs tore off, when its left foot caught in the railroad ties. The right leg ripped away a moment later. The torso swayed crazily, and the zombie began to climb, hand-over-hand, up Drostan's leg.

Holding on for all he was worth, Drostan swung himself to the right just as they passed a light post. The pole caught the zombie in the chest with enough force that it nearly tore Drostan from his hold on the car. The blow shattered bone, and ripped the undead creature's torso away, leaving two severed arms clinging as tightly as before.

With a monumental effort, Drostan heaved himself into the coal car and began kicking at the zombie hands, not resting until he had broken both limbs free and pitched them overboard. Only then did he lean back on the hard bed of coal and draw a deep, shuddering sigh of relief.

We've got the missing links. We know what happened to Jasinski, and we've confirmation on the tourmaquartz—those 'precious crystals'. With luck, Jacob and Hans would turn up more evidence, and Mitch would find something of value in the records. A 'simple' murder investigation had become a dangerous conspiracy, and until it was finished, Drostan was in the crosshairs.

Chapter TWENTY-FOUR

JAKE, NICKI, AND Rick dropped off 'Dynamite' Danny Maguire at a corner where a hansom cab was waiting. When they were alone, Jake slumped in his seat, still clutching Marcin of Krakow's book.

"Want to talk about it?" Nicki asked.

Jake shook his head. "No. There were monsters."

Nicki nodded, as if that answered everything. "All right. You're both here," Nicki said. "You've got the book, and the Alekanovo stone. So how did they end up at the Carnegie?"

Jake sat up, cradling the book. "Good question. It could be an innocent mistake."

Rick snorted. "Yeah. Sure."

Jake shrugged. "It wouldn't be the first time a box went awry, and we do a lot of work for the museum."

"Maybe," Rick admitted grudgingly. "At least it kept it away from Veles and Thwaites."

"What's the plan?" Nicki asked.

"We take the stone and the book back to Andreas and Renate, and hope to high heaven that they can figure out a way to use them to stop the *gessyan*—and get some justice for Father by shutting down Veles and Thwaites," Jake replied. "We'd never be able to make a case against them for Father's death in court—and that's not even counting Thwaites's influence with the judges," he added. "So we'll have to take the matter into our own hands."

"Think we'll hear from Fletcher tomorrow?" Rick asked.

Jake checked his pocket watch. "Probably. Here's hoping he found something noteworthy out at Vesta Nine."

The carriage lurched, throwing them from their seats. Charles, with Kovach riding shotgun, was taking them at ever-increasing speeds through the dark, empty streets of New Pittsburgh.

"What the hell?" Jake muttered, climbing back to his seat with an arm around the book, while Rick held on tightly, keeping the precious Alekanovo stone safe in his lap. Kovach banged three times on the window between the carriage and the driver, a warning that something was wrong. Nicki muttered under her breath in street French, her derringer already in hand.

Jake and Rick peered from the carriage's windows. The wide expanse of Fifth Avenue lay dark and empty. Maybe too dark.

"Am I imagining things, or are the shadows... wrong?" Jake said.

Rick frowned, staring into the darkness. "Now that you mention it, they seem to be following us."

Rick peeled off his jacket and nestled the Alekanovo stone in it, laying it carefully on the floor of the carriage. Jake did the same with Marcin of Krakow's book and drew his gun, although what use it would be against shadows he did not know.

Outside, the streetlights seemed to struggle just to cast a pale glow. By the time the carriage passed each light, the last was already lost in utter blackness. The night was unnaturally quiet. And then, in the darkness, Jake saw movement.

"Something's out there," he said, watching the shadows for another glimpse.

"I saw it," Rick agreed. "Don't know what it is, but it's fast."

"Not 'it'. Them. Whatever's out there, there's a lot of them."

Charles urged the horses to greater speed. Jake and Rick grappled for a hold as the carriage jolted over the paving stones.

Something heavy struck the carriage from the side and Jake heard the report of Kovach's rifle. Another thud, the sound of a body striking the coach, and now Jake could hear the scrabble of claws very close at hand.

Kovach fired again, and an infernal cry rent the night air. A body fell away from the carriage, and its wheels jolted as the coach rolled over the attacker.

"What in Hell are those things?" Rick asked, staring out the window.

They were huge black dogs the size of lions. Red-eyed, frothing at the mouth, the creatures snarled and howled, displaying powerful jaws filled with stained, pointed teeth.

"Hell hounds," Jake replied. "Another type of *gessyan*. Something Veles probably called up. I think that he knows we found Jasinski's shipment."

"*Mon Dieu*," Nicki said. "In France, they are called *rongeurs d'os*, 'bone crushers'. They draw their power from the dead." Fifth Avenue was close to both the Minserville and German cemeteries. "We need to get away from the graveyards!"

Jake flinched as Kovach's rifle fired three times in quick succession. One of the black hounds fell from the side of the carriage, only to be replaced by another, sinking its claws deep into the carriage frame.

"Steel plates or not, it's not going to be long before those things either rip the carriage to pieces or go after Kovach and the horses; and even with their armor, I don't like their chances," Rick said. "Got a plan?"

Veles sent his shadow-double looking for the Alekanovo stone and Marcin's book at the museum. He knows I saw him and he's got to suspect I found what he was looking for, Jake thought. *The alarms bought me time; Veles couldn't go after me in the confusion. But he knew we had to head home eventually. And when we did—*

"Behind you!" Rick shouted as one of the black hounds ripped away a corner of the carriage.

Jake dove to the other side, and the three of them opened fire. The bullets tore into the hell hound's massive body, knocking it away. With a heavy impact and the scrabbling of claws, another monster took the place of the first. Jake planted a bullet square in its maw.

"This isn't going well," Nicki said.

"Keep shooting," Jake snapped. "Cover me."

The night air had grown unseasonably cold, and through the hole in the carriage, Jake could hear the hell hounds howling. The carriage lurched violently from side to side, and Jake heard the panicked squeal of the horses. He pressed a button, and a panel slid back to reveal the Gatling gun protruding from its bullet-proof glass bubble.

Rick squeezed off more shots to keep the hell hounds away and Nicki kept watch while Jake got into position. His seat swiveled, allowing him to lay down covering fire in a smooth sweep. The shots echoed, tearing into asphalt and ripping through the creatures' bodies. He cheered as a dozen of the monstrous predators were torn apart under the Gatling gun's firepower.

The victory was short-lived. Jake's Gatling gun could keep the hounds away from the back of the carriage, but could do nothing to keep the creatures from circling around to block their progress, or to hedge them in from the sides.

The carriage came to an abrupt halt in the middle of the street as an iridescent curtain of shimmering energy sprang up out of nowhere, surrounding them in a glittering barrier, before it swept out toward the hell hounds with the force of a tidal wave.

"What's going on?" Rick said. "Why the hell are we stopping?"

"Off hand, I'd say it's because we've got new players," Jake replied. Rick bent down to see out through the glass bubble. Two figures dressed in long black cassocks had stepped from the shadows on the right.

"We've got two more over here," Nicki called out, watching from the carriage window to the left.

"Damn. Friend or foe?" Jake asked.

"That all depends on what they do next," Rick replied.

Both of the black-clad men had their arms upraised. Energy crackled from their outstretched palms, gathering for another salvo. The hounds had been driven back, but they could not or would not admit defeat, and Jake could see them readying for another assault.

"What the bloody hell is going on with that stone?" Rick asked.

Jake turned to look at where the Alekanovo stone lay on the coach floor. The runes carved into the black surface glowed with an inner fire and Jake felt a hum in the air, like the charge just before a lightning strike.

A pillar of light burst from the stone, streaming through the runes. It shone from the coach windows, from the bubble of the gunner's mount, and from the hole the hound had torn, blindingly bright. Jake threw up an arm to shield his eyes, while Nicki and Rick fell back, covering their faces.

The Alekanovo stone's fiery light erupted into the night sky and joined with the iridescent curtain of power raised by the four black-robed strangers. The energy swelled, too bright to watch, and then sent a powerful shockwave out from the circle, sweeping aside the hounds and the shadows with a blazing, scouring tide. To Jake, it felt as if the universe had gathered its breath and released it in a mighty blast.

Silence and darkness returned. Jake blinked, his vision still clouded. Rick righted himself and climbed back into his seat. Nicki smoothed her hair back with a shaking hand.

"Out of the frying pan..." Jake muttered as he saw two of the four dark-clad men moving toward the carriage. He reached for the controls to the Gatling gun, fearing the worst, but sparks flew as he touched the metal, and he jerked his hand back reflexively.

"We did not come to harm you," one of the men said. "The hell hounds are gone. They will not trouble you again tonight."

"Who are you?" Jake shouted.

"We are the *Logonje*," said a dark-haired, bearded man in his early thirties. "I'm Father Matija. Andreas Thalberg feared for you and sent us to bring you back safely." He looked at Nicki. "I believe your friend can vouch for us. We have met before."

Nicki nodded. "He's the one I told you about, the one who helped Renate keep that thing at Jasinski's apartment from coming after us."

"You carry a precious cargo," Matija said. "Drive on, and we will make sure you reach your destination safely."

At that, the four men stepped back from the road, and Charles urged the horses on. Jake stayed close to the Gatling gun.

"Renate and Matija knew each other, even before he showed up at Jasinski's apartment," Nicki said as the carriage drew away and the four priests faded into the darkness.

"I certainly appreciate the help, but I'm not sure that I'm ready to trust them just yet," Jake replied. He retracted the Gatling gun and took his seat. "Then again, I'm not surprised the Thalbergs have called in reinforcements."

"Reinforcements?" Rick mused. "Or allies? I can't quite imagine Father Matija and his priests working *for* Andreas Thalberg, although if the threat was great enough, they might work *with* him."

"Just as he worked with Renate," Nicki added.

Jake shrugged. "I guess we'll see. For the moment, if someone isn't shooting at us or trying to rip our heads off, that's good enough for me."

When they arrived back at the Desmet house, Catherine was waiting for them in the kitchen. Mrs. Jones already had a kettle boiling and a first aid kit on the table. She tended to Jake's cuts and bruises and wrapped his badly bruised and scraped shin while Catherine poured tea. Jake, Nicki, and Rick took turns recounting what had occurred at the museum, while Catherine listened intently. The set of her mouth and her grip on the fine tea cup gave evidence of her anger and fear.

"I'm just glad that you're all back safely," Catherine said when they had finished their tale. "And there was a message from Renate while you were out. She had a vision of danger—she was insistent that I pass along a warning."

"Spot on, as usual," Nicki replied, tossing off her tea and looking for some gin to replace it. "Did she say anything else?"

"Only that she thinks it wise for us to gather the whole group tomorrow night. By then, Drostan should have a report for us, and we may know more from Cady and the others as well." Catherine fussed with one of the pins that held her hair in place, a sure sign she was upset.

"I do wish this whole matter were settled," she said. "Bad enough what's happened so far, but the longer this goes on, the worse it gets."

"It's turned out to be a lot bigger than just avenging Father's death," Jake said. "But we're in too far to change our minds now.

I just hope we can stay a step ahead of the people chasing us until we can figure out how to bring them down, once and for all."

THE NEXT EVENING, an unlikely group gathered at the Desmet house. Three of the *Logonje* priests stood watch in the shadows across the street. Inside, Jake, Nicki, and Rick spoke quietly with Andreas and Renate, while Cady and Catherine Desmet chatted about books as they waited for everyone to assemble. Father Matija stood to one side, talking in low tones with Drostan Fletcher. Though he couldn't see him, Jake was sure that Wilfred lingered nearby, on hand to provide support in nearly any situation.

Kovach and Charles kept watch near the door. "I can't protect you if everyone and his brother can just walk on in," he muttered.

"If everyone's here, let's get started," Catherine said, calling the group to attention. "I thought it would be best if we could all hear what's new together."

"Then let us get some scotch to settle our nerves, and we'll fill you in," Jake said.

He and Rick laid the Alekanovo stone and Marcin's book on the table. Nicki dropped the ruined listening device next to them. Cady sidled up to the book, eyeing it with a scholar's curiosity. Renate and Andreas circled the stone, and Jake wondered if they were testing it with their magic, sensing its strength.

"I don't really know how that thing works," Jake warned, "but the last two times it's been around strong magic, it exploded. So if you're going to poke at it with your powers, let's not do it in the parlor."

Andreas's expression changed, the nearest thing to a smile Jake had ever seen on the vampire's face, then he and Renate retreated to a respectful distance. Jake poured a scotch for himself and one each for Rick and Nicki, and then settled into the big, upholstered chair that had been his father's favorite.

"The next time I complain about a black tie reception being boring, I hope someone reminds me of what it's like to be exciting," Jake began. The group listened intently to the recap Jake, Rick, and Nicki gave of the events at the reception and afterwards, ending with the perilous drive home.

Drostan recounted what had transpired at the Vesta Nine, his tale leaving everyone looking queasy. "I took liberties in asking Mitch Storm and his partner for help," Drostan said, "I've worked with them before, and they're good at what they do. Jacob and Hans haven't reported back yet, but Mitch confirmed that the Department suspected Veles and Thwaites were mining something other than coal."

"Tourmaquartz," Rick replied. "Enough to make Veles and Thwaites even more powerful and wealthy. They can sell it for a fortune to arms dealers and despots in hot spots around the world and literally bring down kingdoms."

"At least we know what happened to Karl Jasinski," Renate said. "No one deserves that kind of an end."

"And we know who was after the crate Jasinski asked Father to smuggle out of Poland, and what was in the crate," Jake said, feeling the loss anew. "As well as who was responsible for his murder."

"We've also got a pretty good answer to the killings along the rivers," Drostan said. "Once the *gessyan* are free, they gravitate to where they can feed the best, and spread out so there aren't too many predators in one place. Mitch and I are speculating that Veles might not be able to control the *gessyan* or bottle them back up, but he might be able to work some kind of magic to keep them from eating all the miners. So the Night Hag followed the rivers, and the hell hounds moved toward the old cemeteries, as did the wraiths."

"Everything we've found out also explains Thwaites's involvement, and the Oligarchy connection," Rick said after a moment to consider what Drostan reported. "Veles contributed his magic, Thwaites brought his political connections to make sure they weren't disturbed, and they both walk away with a fortune—and the power to change the destiny of nations. Breaking the miners' union, if it came to that, would seem like a bonus."

"Mitch and Jacob are not officially with the Department on this project," Drostan said, and filled the others in on what he had learned from the agents. "They wanted another shot at Tumblety and Brunrichter, and those abominations they create. But if the Department has Vesta Nine under observation, it's possible they could raid the place, and things could get complicated."

"The clockwork corpses are only part of the problem," Andreas reminded them. "There's still the matter of the *gessyan*, both the spirits that have gotten loose as well as those still in the mines. Until they're overpowered and the gateway is sealed, people will continue to die. Apparently, Veles can't keep them contained and Jasinski didn't have the stone and the book to help him succeed. So it's up to us to bottle them back up." He looked toward Drostan. "If the Department were to attack the mine without magic, I fear it would be a slaughter."

"Veles and Thwaites probably have plans to make a quick getaway if they need to," Rick added. "The tourmaquartz deposit is probably fairly small, given how rare it is. There's no telling when they'll decide they've gotten it all. "

"In which case, we need to move quickly," Matija added. "Because more *gessyan* are likely to escape if a binding is not made soon."

"And how do we do that?" Rick demanded.

"Carefully," Renate replied without a hint of humor. "Andreas and I will work with Father Matija and his priests to deal with the *gessyan,* including the Night Hag—and make sure none of the other spirits escape."

"Then we destroy the deep levels," Andreas replied. "Jacob and his clockwork man are likely to confirm what I suspect—that the only workers at those depths are dead men and automatons. No one else can withstand either the conditions or the presence of the *gessyan*."

Jake nodded. "That's why Veles and Thwaites would have called in the mad scientist team. Automatons aren't just cheap labor; they're workers who will never breathe a word about what they see—and miners who can't be killed because they're already dead." He paused. "We could see what help Eban Hodekin might be."

Rick shivered. "I'd rather not, if it's all the same to you."

Jake shrugged. "I didn't say we had to have him over for dinner. But kobolds know the mines. He could be valuable."

Rick fixed Jake with a pointed stare. "'Know the mines'?" he repeated incredulously. "In half the tales I've heard, they're the ones who bring the ceiling down on the miners, or who lure them into dead-end tunnels where the air is bad."

"It depends on who's telling the tale," Andreas said, bringing a halt to the argument. "In this case, I would say that caution is advised, though we should not rule out help where it can be found. We may yet have need of Hodekin."

"Suppose we *can* shut down Vesta Nine," Rick said. "Thwaites and Veles have a lot of influence. Won't they just dig down and across from one of the other mines?"

"Maybe," Andreas admitted. "But none of the other mines are nearly as deep as Vesta Nine, so it will take a while to reach that level again. Tourmaquartz is rare, so there's no guarantee they'd find more of it. If they start up again, we'll know how to counter it. And perhaps the *gessyan* are more than Veles wants to deal with, if he has a choice." He paused. "I don't think freeing them was part of a master plan, although Veles made the most of the panic as a diversion. And I'm sure he would love to control them if he could. He is very much an opportunist."

"Blowing up the deep shafts sounds like something that would be right up Adam's alley," Rick said, and Jake heard a glimmer of glee in his friend's voice. Rick shared Adam's sheer joy in making things go boom.

"Even Veles would be hard pressed to stop a mine fire," Andreas said. "Magic is better suited for starting such things than for putting them out."

"How likely is it that the Oligarchy will retaliate?" Catherine mused. "After all, Thwaites is one of their number. Drogo Veles may or may not be a bona fide member, but he certainly has influence over them, and I don't doubt many of them owe him favors. Consider Mr. Fletcher's experience with the police; he may not be the only one at risk."

"With men like Maguire gaining political power, the Oligarchy can't afford to move too openly, or too heavy-handedly," Matija replied. "Neither can Drogo Veles. It will remain, as it has been, a shadow war, with forces on both sides working just beyond the light."

"And the federal agents?" Rick asked. "What do we do about them?"

"We need all the help we can get," Jake replied. "Drostan already has the connection. If Jacob makes it out of the mine alive, his information will be essential for our attack." He grinned. "They don't have to know everything. And even if Mitch and his partner are operating on their own, having them involved might camouflage our role in all this."

"I agree."

Everyone turned to look at Catherine. She raised her chin, and her expression was defiant. "This has gone beyond Thomas's murder. There have been far too many deaths. It needs to end. And we're going to make sure that it does."

Chapter TWENTY-FIVE

"I'm going crazy down here." Adam Farber set aside his wrench and flopped down into a chair. "And I need more coffee."

Jake and Rick surveyed the clutter in the basement that had become Adam's secret hideout. Coffee rings stained every table and countertop. Adam had rigged up a small coal oil stove to do his cooking and boil water for coffee. Jake and Rick made sure that food, coffee, ice for the ice box and the materials Adam needed for his work were delivered regularly and with appropriate stealth. And for once, Adam had the utter quiet that he so often claimed to crave; but it appeared to make him even twitchier than usual.

"You won't have to stay here by yourself much longer," Rick said. "And look, we brought you a whole box of the equipment you wanted."

Adam gave a long, dramatic sigh. "Thanks. But I really am going a little nuts down here. It's not even that I miss people, most of the time. In fact, there's a lot I don't miss about being in the old lab. No one interrupts me. No one pulls me away to talk to people who think they're even more important than they are. It's just—"

"A little lonely?" Jake finished for him.

Adam nodded, and reached over to grab a half-empty coffee cup, downing the cold contents in a gulp. "Now and then."

"Well, if it's any help, you've also had a pass on having to deal with all the questions about how, exactly, the lab managed to blow up," Rick said. "Local police, federal agents; from what I hear, the place has been crawling with cops since they got the fire out."

Adam winced. "How badly was the building damaged?"

Jake gave him a sidelong glance. "Not as badly as the last time you burned it down. Doesn't appear that the men who set the bombs really knew what they were doing." He grinned. "Luckily, from what we've heard, the damage was mainly in the back and on the loading dock, so they don't have to rebuild the upper floors—this time. I think they reinforced the walls after the last incident."

"Yeah, yeah. Make one mistake and no one lets you live it down," Adam replied. "I'd been working on the power source for one of my projects, and I got the pressure gauge wrong—"

"Speaking of power sources," Rick said, "Have you had a chance to work on a smaller version of that weapon you used at the cemetery?"

Adam brightened. "You mean the energy ray?"

"Yep."

Adam jumped up and began moving through the erstwhile lab excitedly, gathering up papers and various pieces of equipment, which he dumped on the table nearest to where Jake and Rick sat.

"I've been working on it a lot lately. Trying to stabilize the beam, get the energy levels more precise."

"We could also use that force gun you showed me," Rick added. "Maybe even the disruptor."

"Really?" Adam said. "That would almost make up for being stuck down here. We don't happen to be blowing up the people who blew up my lab, do we?"

"The man's bright," Rick said to Jake, raising an eyebrow. "That's why they gave him a lab coat. Quick on the uptake."

Adam gave Rick a withering look. "Jealous," he sniffed, but the corners of his mouth turned up in a smile. "So, fill me in."

It took a while for them to bring Adam up to speed. When they finished, Adam sat back in his chair, tented his fingers, and closed his eyes, thinking.

"All right," he said. "So Veles and Thwaites were after the tourmaquartz all along. The *gessyan* were an accident, but Veles used the confusion to keep people from looking too closely at what they were really doing at the mine. Jasinski got in their way and knew too much. And Jasinski's involvement ended up getting your dad killed, and having Veles and Thwaites go after all of us—right?"

"That's what we think," Rick said.

Adam smiled, but this time, it was a cool, calculating expression. "And they're the ones trying to hurt you and Rick? Well then. I guess I don't have any qualms about blowing them up."

Adam rocked his chair back and forth. "You know, for Veles and Thwaites it's not just the money. Tourmaquartz is power. Right now, there are only a few handfuls of the crystals in circulation. But if someone found more of it—that could change the balance of power. Weapons, locomotion devices, all powered by tourmaquartz." He glanced from Rick to Jake in utter seriousness. "Whoever controls the tourmaquartz controls the world."

They sat in silence, thinking about that for a moment. "What have you been working on down here?" Jake finally asked.

"I thought you'd never ask. I told you I fine-tuned Mr. Tesla's ray. Managed to get the source box smaller, more portable. The one we tried out in the cemetery needed to be hauled in a wagon. What I've got now is light enough to go up in an airship."

"Have you tested it?" Jake said, and Adam fixed him with a withering look.

"Do you see scorch marks? No. But it should work. The calculations are right."

Jake did not mention that, given the power he had seen in the cemetery, relying on calculations alone did not make him feel extremely confident, especially if he might be going up in an airship with the weapon. "That sounds perfect," he said, although the sidelong glance he got from Rick told him his friend had the same reservations.

"Right," Adam said. "Cullen loves it. He stops by to visit between runs. Been working on some new defenses for the *Allegheny Princess*; airship armor. Gonna need it, with the company you've been keeping. You know, Rick, you'd be up on all of this if you spent more time here."

"Once we're through this and no one is trying to kill me, I'd be happy to work on some of these with you," Rick replied.

"I also improved the range on the wrist telegraph I gave Mitch and Jacob," Adam said. "Used to only be good for about a mile between the sender and receiver. I managed to boost the signal, so it should go two miles at least. Jacob has a pair of my gadget glasses; I think it's what he's using to have Hans look around the deeper levels at the mine."

Adam walked over to another table, with the look of a proud father. "And these are the next generation of my listening devices. The range on the one I gave you was only a few hundred feet. These will go between an airship and the ground—within limits." He moved around the table to hold up a small box. "Know what this is?"

When Jake and Rick shook their heads, Adam grinned. "A camera. Easy to conceal. Nowhere near as big as those boxy monstrosities the photographers use. Think of what you could get with this on an airship! Or, for that matter, how easy it would be to conceal it if you had to get in and out of a place without being noticed." His smile widened. "I think Mitch and Jacob will pay a premium for it, don't you? Maybe even throw in some beer."

"Make sure you keep some of the good stuff for us and I'll buy you all the beer you can drink!" Rick said. "And speaking of Agents Storm and Drangosavich, do you really believe the story they gave Drostan, that they've been put on probation and they're working rogue?"

Usually, Adam was circumspect about what he said. Jake was hoping that the time alone in a basement, on the heels of an attempt on his life, might make him a little more willing to share information.

"It wouldn't be the first time," Adam said. "Mitch blows stuff up almost as much as I do. He just blows up enough of the right stuff that they slap his wrist and then bring him back into the fold." He downed another cup of coffee. "Those two men your private investigator saw, Tumblety and Brunrichter—they're trouble. Mitch and Jacob tangled with them—and their clockwork corpses—before. So did Drostan. And when the mad doctors got away, I think it made Mitch angry."

"So Mitch and Jacob intended to inflict some payback on the mad docs, and stumbled onto something bigger—and messier—than they bargained for?" Rick asked.

Adam nodded. "And that puts them in a tough place. In case you hadn't noticed, Mitch Storm doesn't play by anyone's rules but his own. That keeps him and his partner alive, but if he and Jacob get caught by the Department compromising an investigation—"

"They'll bust him down to private and send him out to clean the stables," Rick finished.

"Bingo," Adam replied. He paused, then forged ahead. "Mitch has been trying to protect you. He and Jacob have always played fair with me. I think you should trust him—cautiously."

"Why cautiously?" Jake asked.

Adam grimaced. "Because you're exactly the kind of people the Department wants to have up its sleeve. Think about it. You and Rick go in and out of different countries all the time. You bring big boxes of stuff with you. You work for wealthy, powerful people, some of whom might be a little shady. You acquire interesting objects, with questionable provenance. In other words, you'd be the perfect spies. And they would love to recruit you."

"No," Jake and Rick said in unison.

"We work for ourselves," Jake added

"The Department's been after both our fathers for a while," Rick said. "They refused. Father told me that while he would assist them when he agreed with their cause, joining them 'officially' was a slippery slope and we wouldn't like the outcome… or the rules."

Adam held up a hand. "Don't shoot the messenger. I'm just telling you how Mitch Storm thinks. On the other hand," he said, a crafty expression stealing across his face, "guys like Mitch and Jacob are good friends to have if you're in a jam. So a few favors done and returned could be valuable—if you hear what I'm saying."

"Just make sure you bring all your good ideas to the meeting tonight," Rick said.

Adam looked from Rick to Jake and back again. "Given how many people are trying to kill us, should we really be going to the Desmet house?"

Jake shrugged. "Where would you feel safer? Andreas and Renate are going to reinforce the wardings, and I believe Father Matija has some precautions he intends to take as well. There isn't anywhere that's truly safe, and it allows Mother to keep to the polite fiction of remaining in mourning seclusion."

"After everything that's happened, she's still concerned about etiquette?" Rick asked.

"Oh, hell no," Jake replied. "But Henry's obsessed with what the neighbors think. Someone sent him a wire after the last incident, and since he's still miffed about being shot, he decided the whole thing must have been my fault." He grimaced. "We just don't want to annoy him enough that he decides he has to come home."

Chapter TWENTY-SIX

"IT'S DEFINITELY TOURMAQUARTZ." Jacob Drangosavich paced the floor of the Desmet home as he gave his report. He looked haggard and there was a spreading bruise on one side of his face.

"You're sure?" Adam Farber said.

Mitch Storm nodded soberly. For once, he showed none of his usual cockiness. His eyes had the hard glint of a man who had seen more than his share of action. "We'd heard the Department was concerned that a tourmaquartz deposit had been found and not properly reported."

"And you two really didn't know that the tourmaquartz was in Vesta Nine before this?" Jake asked with suspicion.

Mitch shook his head. "Honest. We wanted to bring down Tumblety and Brunrichter. But the more we learned about how Veles and Thwaites were handling everything, the more our suspicions grew, because they've taken risks that don't add up if all they're getting is coal."

"Hans and I got into the mine without a hitch," Jacob said. "I stayed on the upper levels and kept an ear out for what the miners were saying—helps to speak their languages," he added. "Hans went deeper. That's how I got the rest of the information." He glared at them. "At a cost, I'd add. Hans volunteered to stay behind, be our man on the inside. We have to get him out."

"Here's what we know, thanks to Hans," Jacob continued. "There are hundreds of men on three shifts down in that mine, on the coal-only levels. Those miners don't go to the deepest levels. They're terrified of what goes on down there—with good reason. The deeper you go, the more likely you are to encounter the 'monsters'—that's where most of the 'accidents' have happened. But the talk is that the attacks have been happening closer and closer to the surface.

"As you descend, there are... what I'd call *secure* levels. The first level below the regular coal mining is pretty much slave labor. Shackles, manacles—it's clear they plan to work the blighters to death before replacing them." Jacob paused, as if the horror of what he had seen would not leave him.

"On the next level down, it's the clockwork zombies," he continued. "They're more advanced than what Tumblety and Brunrichter came up with the last time. They can be set to perform specific tasks.

"The deepest levels are *werkmen*, not many of them but enough. I'm guessing that since they couldn't recruit or kidnap Adam into working for them, Veles and Thwaites had their engineers take apart one of the *werkmen* who'd gone missing from the Department and figured out how it works." He stopped to take a drink of water.

"They're the ones who are pulling out most of the tourmaquartz. The workers on the other secure levels process it, and then send it up in sealed containers under guard. The guys on the upper levels don't know what's really going on, and they don't want to know. They just move the boxes, and try to forget anything they see. When I asked, they clammed up tighter than a drum. They told me that if I wanted to see daylight again, I should stop asking questions and keep my nose out of it."

"How much tourmaquartz are we talking about?" Adam asked, leaning forward. "Even the smallest shards of it are enough to run some of my most powerful designs."

"That's just it," Mitch said. "We're not sure. Since the tourmaquartz comes up in sealed containers, we aren't sure how much of it there is. But there's very little tourmaquartz to be had now, so it doesn't take a lot to double, even triple the supply. And it would still be more valuable than diamonds."

"I don't really want to see Drogo Veles wield more power than he already does," Andreas replied.

"I think we're agreed on that point," Mitch agreed.

"I've gone over the papers Agent Storm took from the mine office," Cady said. "Between what he found and what we got from Jasinski's apartment, the other few names on Thomas Desmet's list were witches who were helping Jasinski—and according to Agent Storm, they're all dead."

"Some of the documents I found indicate potential buyers for the tourmaquartz," Mitch added. "And Jacob and I spotted at least two of the Department's operatives among the security men. So we've got to expect that once all hell breaks loose, the Department is likely to show up and take all the credit."

"They can have the credit," Rick muttered. "We just want to be well away from there when they come tromping around."

"Exactly," Jake replied. He looked around at the unlikely crowd. Jake, Rick, and Nicki sat on one side of the room, along with Cady and Adam. Renate stood with Andreas near the front. Mitch and Jacob leaned against the wall on the other side of the room. Miska Kovach and Drostan Fletcher were in the back, along with Father Matija and Cullan Adair. Catherine sat in her favorite armchair, knitting.

"The *Logonje* will go with you," Father Matija said. "Karl Jasinski came to me with questions about Marcin of Krakow and Alekanovo. But he never told me he was seeking the artifacts, or that he'd found them. I warned him away from the situation, told him to let us handle it." He sighed. "Unfortunately, he did not listen."

"The vision I saw. Those were your priests at Alekanovo," Renate said, turning to meet Matija's gaze.

"Not 'my' priests, since that happened many years ago. But members of my order. *Logonje*. Priests who use magic to protect the flock."

"I believe that now that we have the Alekanovo stones and Marcin of Krakow's book, Renate and I can work with the *Logonje* to pull the Night Hag and the other *gessyan* back into the deep places and seal them there," Andreas said.

"Adam, Cady, Nicki, and I will be overhead in the *Allegheny Princess*," Cullan said. "If Adam's new toys work—"

"They will," Adam said confidently.

Cullan gave him a skeptical look. "If they work," he repeated, "you'll have air support, and those whiz-bang new transmitters he came up with should let Jake and Rick talk to us from the ground."

"The miners won't say anything on their own, but there's strength in numbers, especially if the union is behind it. Danny Maguire will gin up a riot outside the gates," Jake added. "He says the miners are itching for a walk-out, and he can bring some of the other union men along for support. With luck, that means fewer men in the mines to worry about."

"Hans and I will get the rest of the miners out," Jacob said. "We'll save anyone we can from the lower levels."

"My men will cover you," Kovach said. "We'll have your backs while you do what you need to do." He grinned. "And I won't mind trying out a few of Adam's new guns. Not if they make big holes in things."

"Mitch and I—and a couple of Kovach's men—will go after Brunrichter and Tumblety," Drostan replied. "And while we're at it, we'll make sure as many of those clockwork zombies as possible go up in flames."

"Jake and I will give the signal once the mine is clear for Cullan and the *Princess* to seal up the entrance," Rick said. "I'll be going below with Miska and Jacob and the *Logonje*. That way I can help Jacob plant the charges and I can drop the Maxwell box down the elevator shaft to help call the—"

"I thought we had agreed that I was going to go," Jake interrupted.

Rick raised an eyebrow. "We need you up top, coordinating everyone else. You know no one ever listens to me," he said with his most rakish, deprecating smile. "And you've got the biggest stake in this. Thomas was your father."

"You're going to have all the fun," Jake protested.

"Dynamite. Angry ghosts. Murderous *werkmen* and clockwork zombies," Rick said. "Believe me, I'd rather let you go into the mine. Next time, you can have the honors. But this time, I'm going, and Miska agrees with me."

Jake glanced over at Kovach, who nodded. "Sorry, Jake. I'm going to have to side with Rick on this, much as it pains me. We need you on the surface, calling the shots."

"I wish none of you had to go in," Catherine replied, looking up from her knitting, looking worried. "There have been enough people hurt and killed. Don't take more chances than you have to," she said, and leveled a gaze at Rick and Jake that they both understood well. Jake knew that if it were remotely possible, Catherine would have insisted on going herself.

"You beefed up that ghost box?" Kovach asked, looking from Rick to Adam. "It put on a show at that old building, but this mine is going to take the heavy-duty version."

Adam grinned. "Oh, it'll work. I made several adjustments. It'll take care of calling in the ghosts; the rest of you just have to seal them up."

Just then, a knock came at the kitchen door. "I'll get it," Jake said, and before Wilfred or anyone else could gainsay him, he headed to the back. When he returned, Eban Hodekin was beside him.

"Don't," Jake said warningly with a glance toward Kovach, who had already moved for his gun. "I invited him."

"He shouldn't be here." Kovach's voice was a low rumble.

Hodekin regarded him evenly. "I have no grievance against you, boy. Best you leave it that way." In the parlor light, the kobold was even uglier than he had appeared at the Edgar Thomson Works. He reminded Jake of the drawings of trolls and gnomes he had seen in children's picture books. Although most of Jake's co-conspirators regarded Hodekin warily, Andreas and Renate appeared only mildly curious.

"Mr. Hodekin has agreed to help," Jake said.

Jacob gave Hodekin a suspicious look. "Can we trust him?"

Hodekin laughed, a sharp, unpleasant sound. "You don't have a lot of choice, son. Even your warlocks can't do what I can do."

"Which is?" Kovach did not bother veiling the mistrust in his voice.

"If you value the lives of the miners, I can get them out faster than any alarm," Hodekin said. "They'll run, they will, when they hear the knockers." Jake had heard stories of knockers, spirits whose tapping deep inside mines was a dire warning of a collapse about to happen. He had also heard tales where the knockers' intentions were much less altruistic; Kovach had good reason for concern.

"It's a big mine for you to do that all yourself," Jacob said, and it was impossible to tell from his flat tone whether he was in favor of the idea or not.

"I won't be alone," Hodekin replied. "Call them what you will—bluecaps, coblynau or bucca—there are many of my kind in the mine. They've done what they could to harry the men who dug too deep, get them out of there. A rockslide here, a cave-in there, but it's not like the old days. Too many iron tools, too many machines. Nobody heeds the warnings anymore." He looked from Jacob to Kovach. "They'll listen to my call and you'll have naught to fear from them. They're angry at the *gessyan* for attacking some of our own. Don't worry. They'll be hungry for a chance to strike back."

Kovach grabbed Jake's arm. "You can't trust a kobold. They're dangerous."

Hodekin gave a hideous smile. "Aye. That we are. You're wise to be careful. But think on this: which would you rather? To have me with you, or to have my kind against you? Reckon before you answer. There's more than *gessyan* and ghosts in the dark down there."

"I don't see how we have a choice," Jake replied. "We don't need something else down there trying to kill us. There're enough creatures out for blood as it is."

"I don't have to like it," Kovach replied sullenly. Hodekin's unpleasant grin broadened.

"I'll get myself in, and get myself out," Hodekin continued. "Leave that to me. You just send the *gessyan* back down, and we'll be waiting for them."

"And when the dynamite goes off?" Kovach asked.

Hodekin raised a misshapen shoulder. "We're creatures of the rock, boy. We'll like it better when it's quiet."

Jake looked from Kovach's scowling face to Jacob, who looked thoughtful but not opposed, and then to Renate and Andreas, who nodded.

"One more detail," Mitch said. "You do know that the house is being watched, right? How are we supposed to get out of here without being nabbed—or worse—by whoever's out there?"

"Not to worry," Andreas said smoothly. "My men have taken care of it." Jake remembered the dark-clad vampires who had 'taken care' of the attack in Braddock, and could not repress a shudder.

"All right, then," Jake said. "Sounds like we have a plan."

"Get some sleep," Rick said. "Tomorrow's going to be a busy day."

Chapter TWENTY-SEVEN

THE MOOD OF the crowd in front of Vesta Nine's gates was ugly and had grown steadily worse all day. Hundreds of miners shouted and gestured, while a line of guards and Pinkerton men secured the gates. Even from a distance, Jake could hear Danny Maguire's booming voice challenging the miners to speak up for themselves, a tactic that would probably gain him more votes in the next election.

"Good. No one's getting in for the next shift," Jake said, peering through a spyglass for a better view of the chaos at the gate. At that moment, a klaxon started shrieking from the mouth of the mine. Alarms began to sound all over the complex

"Sounds like Jacob and Hans are in position," Rick added.

Jake hid in the deeper shadows between the storage buildings near the mine. As the alarms blared, miners began to stream from the mine's entrances. Covered in coal dust, talking in a babble of languages and accents, the miners rushed toward the gates held shut by the Pinkerton men and mine guards. Now the guards were caught in the middle of hundreds of irate miners. The fence around the compound was beginning to bow as men pushed against it and climbed over it.

The guards rallied to the front of the complex, shoring up the barriers and shouting at the miners to restore order. Shots fired into the air were returned by the striking workers outside the gates, and in the distance, Jake could hear sirens. *Won't be long before the cops show up,* he thought.

Fortunately, Maguire had already thought of that. Flaming roadblocks and rubble piled high on the roads leading into the mine would stymie wagons and carriages, slowing the arrival of the police. Reporters with notepads and cameras had been invited to witness the strike by Maguire, who never missed a trick when it came to getting his name in the paper and made certain the reporters were present before blocking the roads. Having an audience seemed to fuel Maguire's rhetoric, which was as incendiary as the magnesium flashes of the photographers.

"That about does it," Jake said, dusting the dirt from his hands. He and his team were in the railyard, and he took a moment to look over the results of their work. Piles of heavy wooden railroad ties and overturned coal cars blocked the trestles and tracks.

"No one's getting in or out this way," Rick replied.

"All right," Jake said. "Everybody—listen up! Rick, Miska, Renate—check your ear pieces. We want to make sure everyone can hear me once we get to the mine entrance, because there's going to be a lot going on." He tested the newfangled headset that Adam had refined for them, and after a few tries, everyone indicated that they could hear him.

"Rick, Miska, Father Matija, and the *Logonje*—head inside the mine. If Hodekin keeps his word, he'll meet you inside, and so will Jacob and Hans," Jake said. "Drostan and some of Miska's guards went with Mitch to take care of Tumblety and Brunrichter. Andreas and Renate—stick with me. We'll hold the mine entrance and be in place to trap the *gessyan*."

He paused for a moment to listen to a message on his ear piece. "That was Nicki," he said to the witches. "Cullan's got the *Allegheny Princess* heading our way."

Andreas and Renate had the small carved stones, the Alekanovo stone, and Marcin of Krakow's book. Once they reached the mine's entrance, they would ready the ritual to seal the *gessyan* back in the deep places for all time. Jake glanced up, scanning the night sky. Overhead, amid the clouds that hid the moon, the *Allegheny Princess* was ready to supply back-up. It was a good plan, and a solid strategy. And yet Jake's skin prickled and the hair on the back of his neck rose in warning. His gut was tight, a feeling he had learned to depend on.

"Are you in position?" Nicki's voice was scratchy in Jake's earpiece.

"Yeah. What can you see?" Jake knew Nicki was training the airship's telescope on the mine as Cullan maneuvered into position.

"There's a fight at the gate. Looks like Maguire got plenty of turn-out. You want us to take a shot—" Her voice broke up on the next sentence.

"Don't shoot!" Jake whispered. "Not yet!"

"I said, did you want us to take a shot at locating Thwaites?" Nicki's voice came through, clearly enough that he could hear her irritation.

"Yeah," Jake replied. "Try to keep an eye out for him *and* Veles. I don't think this is going to be a walk in the park."

"That's what makes it so much fun," Nicki replied.

Jake toggled the switch on his transmitter. "Flatfoot," he said. "What's going on?"

"Getting into position now," Fletcher whispered. "Tell you more later."

"Good enough." He toggled again. "Hey, Partner, talk to me. Where are you?"

"Heading down," Rick replied. "Between the riot and the tommyknockers, the mine's clear of workers—on the normal levels. Don't be surprised if you can't reach us, we're going deep."

"Just check in when you can," Jake ordered. "Too damn many moving parts to this plan," he muttered.

Rick started to reply, but the transmitter suddenly hissed static and the connection was lost. *Adam meant his contraption to carry sound through the air, not through solid rock,* Jake thought. *Let's just hope that with all the back-up, Rick doesn't need to call for help.*

Andreas and Renate were talking in hushed tones off to one side. From their gestures, Jake guessed they were arguing about where best to set up the ritual. Father Matija and the *Logonje* had gone into the mine with Rick, but they would be back, hopefully, in time for the big finale.

Let's hope we know what we're doing, Jake thought. *Or we'll be kicking off a bloodbath New Pittsburgh will never forget.*

Chapter TWENTY-EIGHT

DROSTAN FLETCHER LED the way to the vivisectionists' lair. Mitch followed, with Kovach's guards bringing up the rear.

Drostan was armed with a shotgun as well as his service revolver and combat knife; his pockets were heavy with ammunition. Mitch had a revolver holstered at his belt beside another wicked knife. In his hand was a shotgun, and a rifle was slung on a strap over his shoulder. Kovach's guards were equally well-armed.

The storage shed was quiet. Kovach's men circled the building, watching the doors. Two of Kovach's men carried a lightweight Gatling gun, which they quickly got into place. Mitch and two of the guards were armed with extra firepower and as many Ketchum grenades as they could carry. Kovach's last two men carried a pair of Adam's latest experimental weapons: canisters of kerosene equipped with a hose, spray nozzle, and air jet.

"I see they've replaced the lock," Fletcher said.

"Looks like a whole new door," Mitch said.

He bent to the lock with a thin piece of metal; it opened with a quiet click. Mitch swung the door carefully open, and then he and Drostan fell back, happy to let Kovach's sharpshooters take the fore.

"Damn!" one of the soldiers swore, choking at the stench that met them: a slaughterhouse in summer, thick with the scent of blood and offal. The clockwork zombies were already heading towards them.

"Take them down!" Mitch shouted as he fired his shotgun into the clockwork cadavers. His shot blew apart one of the zombie's chests, exposing a rib cage packed with straw and horsehair.

"Legs and heads, people, legs and heads!" Drostan yelled, firing, sending a spray of foul-smelling flesh into the air. Even lacking its head and with a huge hole in its chest, the clockwork zombie staggered onwards until Drostan's next shot blew through its steel-jointed knees.

"Stay clear of the arms!" Drostan shouted. "Just because they're down doesn't mean they're harmless!"

Kovach's men fired in volleys, every second man firing while those in between reloaded. The two men with the flamethrowers switched to their shotguns, unwilling to risk setting the building afire while they were still so close to it.

The zombies spilled through the doorway, forcing them back.

"Let the Gatling have a go at it!" Drostan yelled.

Kovach's men moved back and the Gatling gun lay down a deadly barrage. The clockwork zombies exploded, torsos and limbs flying. The men with flamethrowers incinerated the twitching mechanized corpses, filling the air with the smell of roasted, putrid meat.

A rifle shot cracked through the air and one of the men running the Gatling gun crumpled to the ground.

Mitch ducked for cover and leveled his rifle, aided by a pair of Adam's nightsight goggles. He pulled the trigger, dropping one sniper, but an answering shot hit close to his shoulder, forcing him to drop to the ground for a moment.

A shot smacked into the dirt beside Drostan. He dove behind a pile of broken crates and brought his revolver up, sighting on the shadowy forms he glimpsed by the faint moonlight. He returned fire, his targets made easier to hit by the light of the burning corpses.

"Mine guards. I'll handle them," Mitch yelled. "Then I'll circle back to meet you here."

Kovach's men gave the others enough cover so they could pull the fallen gunner out of the line of fire and finish off the clockwork zombies with the flamethrowers. Mitch melted into the darkness. A moment later, there was a loud bang and a flare of white light as two Ketchum grenades exploded one after another. Several rifle shots sounded in quick succession, then there was silence.

"Is that all of them?" Mitch seemed to appear out of nowhere, with Adam's goggles pushed onto the top of his head.

Fletcher shrugged. "We'll know if more people shoot at us."

Mitch glanced behind him. "I got at least two of them, might have wounded a third, and the grenades were more than they had the belly for."

Cautiously, two of Kovach's men edged toward the doorway. When no zombies appeared out of the darkness, the men made their way inside, guns leveled and ready. The electric lights buzzed into life, illuminating the laboratory.

Fletcher had warned them what to expect, but he doubted that their worst nightmares could have prepared them for the sight. Five fresh corpses lay on operatory gurneys, partially dissected. Metal gleamed from the joints of corpses where steel pins had been inserted and some of the clockwork mechanism installed. Drostan eyed the piles of crates and equipment, wondering if the two vivisectionists were hiding somewhere within.

"Look at those... *things*," one of their bodyguards murmured, and Drostan wondered if the man was about to throw up. The smell of embalming fluid and formaldehyde was heavy in the air.

"Spread out!" Kovach ordered. "Rogers, you guard that door. I want Tumblety and Brunrichter found and captured."

"Stay sharp," Drostan warned. "We don't know if there are any other nasty surprises."

One of Kovach's men remained outside with their wounded comrade, manning the Gatling gun. Two more moved together through the building, while Rogers guarded the door and another man kept watch at the corner of the building.

"Surgical instruments, bottles of ether, lots of formaldehyde—looks like these guys were planning to build an army," one of Kovach's men said as he used a crowbar to rip the lid off a crate.

"Here's one of the Tesla-Westinghouse crates," Mitch noted. The lid had been pried off, exposing gears, wires and tubes, along with a variety of lab equipment.

"Get it to the door, and we'll load it on the sledge," Drostan said. Mitch had shown up with a steam-powered velocipede, yet another of Adam's creations, along with a wheeled metal trailer. They hoped to get out of the complex with the stolen equipment in the ensuing chaos, exiting through a cut in the back fence where a delivery wagon would be waiting on a side road. Maguire's men had blocked the roads, but Drostan had scouted an abandoned logging trail where the wagon could hide until the situation cooled off.

"Got another Tesla-Westinghouse crate," another of their bodyguards confirmed, noting the shipping label.

"Here's one of the Department's crates," Mitch said.

"Let's load them up," Drostan ordered. "We've got plenty of other work to do tonight. Nice of them to move the crates. They were in the other building earlier."

Two of Kovach's men bent to heft a crate between them. Mitch and Jacob did the same. But as soon as they lifted the boxes, the hum of gears sounded from the back of the warehouse, as four more clockwork zombies surged to their feet.

Drostan swore under his breath as he brought up his shotgun and took the head off one of the nearest cadavers.

"Fire!" Mitch shouted. A barrage of bullets flew at the clockwork zombies, thudding through their decaying bodies and lodging in the brick walls behind them. Shotgun blasts tore through the zombies' chests, blew through shoulders to send arms flying, but they still kept coming.

One of the zombies fell when a blast took out his metal-hinged knees, yet on he came, dragging himself along with his hands.

One of the bodyguard's guns clicked empty and he grabbed a crowbar from where it lay between the rows of crates. He swung the heavy iron bar back and forth, hitting the dead men with the sound of ripe melons breaking open. Another swung his empty gun at the zombie closing in on him, but the creature was faster than he expected, and it grabbed his wrist, effortlessly breaking bones. The man screamed as the monstrosity closed its geared hand around his neck, snapping his spine. Mitch turned his weapon on the zombie, blasting it into oblivion.

"These guys don't know when to quit," Drostan muttered, as the last clockwork zombie crashed through a stack of crates, single-minded in his pursuit.

"Tumblety and Brunrichter aren't here," Mitch yelled. "You can bet they'd be running if they were."

"Let's get the crates and get out of here!" Drostan shouted. He and Mitch fired on the last zombie as Rogers and another of Kovach's men got the lab equipment clear. The smell of gunpowder now overlay the embalming fluid and rotten meat.

As soon as the last of the crates were out, everyone fell back to the doorway, wary of any new clockwork zombies showing up. Kovach's men loaded the crates onto the steambike's wagon, and two of their bodyguards went roaring off toward the road with their reclaimed treasure.

"Burn it!" Mitch shouted.

Kovach's men outside had refilled the kerosene fire guns, and they turned their nozzles on the doorway. With a *whoosh*, torrents of fire engulfed the mechanized corpses and the crates behind them.

"Get back!" Mitch yelled, although Drostan and the others needed no prompting.

"When the fire hits that embalming fluid—" Drostan began.

An explosion and the roar of flames drowned out what he was going to say. The building went up like dynamite, sending a hail of shattered brick that pelted them as they ran.

"We've got trouble!" One of the bodyguards was watching the shadows, and now, illuminated by the burning building, he could make out shapes moving towards them.

"We weren't exactly having a picnic before!" Drostan snapped.

"*Werkmen*—heading our way! And I don't think they're ours."

Kovach's guards swung the Gatling gun around on its mounting. Staccato blasts of gunfire clanged against metal. But as Drostan peered at the new enemy, something about them seemed all wrong. These opponents moved more naturally than *werkman*, and flinched when shots hit them.

"They're not *werkmen*," Mitch yelled. "They're men wearing metal armor!" The shots set the armored men back a step or two, but still they advanced, as the bullets bounced off their chests and creased the metal plates covering their arms and legs.

"Armor makes them slower," Drostan shouted. "Switch up your positions—and aim for the head!" He aimed his shotgun and fired, hitting one of the armored men square in the face. The force was too much for the metal helmet and the man fell backward with a crash.

With an explosion that rocked the ground, the building collapsed and the earth around it opened up into a giant hole into the tunnels beneath it.

"Get away from the building! It's going under!" Drostan shouted.

The whole building slid into the depths with a thunderous roar. Some of the armored men could not move quickly enough to avoid the ground vanishing beneath their feet. Screaming in panic, they fell and were carried away with the tide of brick and rubble.

"It's a sinkhole!" Mitch yelled, as the mouth of the crater continued to expand. "Run!" The bodyguards manning the Gatling gun had to stop their fire to haul the gun away from the crater as ground that had been firm moments before disappeared into the abyss.

More armored men advanced, trapping Drostan and the others between them and the crater. Drostan, Mitch, and Kovach's guards scrambled for cover as they blasted away at the new attackers.

Kovach's man with the crowbar managed to circle around behind the armored men, getting in several bone-crushing blows before his attackers could turn to face the new threat.

The roar of an engine came from the tree line. The guard riding the steam velocipede had dropped off his load and was now circling back towards them. "Watch out!" the man shouted. He pressed a button on the handlebars of the steambike and there was a flash and a whoosh as a Ketchum grenade shot from the front of the bike and exploded amid the advancing men in a flare of blinding light.

Four of the armored attackers were sent into the air, chunks of metal raining down on Jake and the others.

Stealth had been compromised long ago, Drostan knew, but as grenade after grenade exploded, he still expected the Pinkertons to descend on them in full force. A glance toward the mine's gates explained why that had not happened.

The crowd at the gates had become a riot, with the Pinkertons and the mine guards outnumbered despite their guns and clubs. Long abused without recourse, the miners vented their frustration with rocks and boards, wading into the fray fearlessly. Some of the miners had pistols, and returned fire when the guards shot into the crowd.

"I think the Pinkertons have their hands full," Mitch observed.

Movement in the shadows and the sound of horses' hooves caught Drostan's attention. In the light of the fires that ranged all around the gaping sinkhole, Drostan could see a black carriage headed pell-mell for the rear gates. And on the back and side of the carriage were crests showing a crimson falcon.

"Someone's getting away!" Mitch shouted.

"Not yet." Drostan toggled the transmitter on his lapel. "Airship—can you hear me?"

"I thought you weren't going to make a scene?" Nicki snapped. "Flyboy had to make us all airsick to avoid that fireball you sent up!"

"Sorry, sorry," Drostan muttered. "Look, I need to talk to Wunderkind—"

"I'm here," Adam's voice cut in.

"Someone's trying to escape; may be Brunrichter and Tumblety," Drostan said. "They're too far away from us, and we've got hostile fire between here and there. Can you do something to stop them—preferably without killing them?"

"We're on it," Adam replied.

"Don't you dare leave me out of this!" Nicki interrupted. "You need me to locate the targets!"

"I wouldn't dream of leaving you out," Drostan replied.

The *Allegheny Princess* loomed large in the sky, following the speeding carriage. A bolt of man-made lightning streaked down, burning into the grass a few yards ahead of the carriage, sending the horses rearing in panic, kicking up clods of dirt and a fine shower of toasted grass.

When Drostan's eyes had adjusted once more to the darkness, he saw that Farber's lightning had carved a rough circle around the carriage, leaving it stranded on its own little island.

"What do you think?" Adam chortled, proud of himself. "And that's only at half-power!"

"I think you're a dangerous man," Drostan replied. "Great job. We'll be in touch."

Smoke hung over the mining complex. The air was sharp with the smell of burnt wiring, scorched metal and roasted zombie. The Gatling gun's muzzle glowed red. Between gunfire and Ketchum grenades, the armored men lay in a tangle of broken bodies and twisted metal. Behind them, the fire around the crater where the warehouse had once stood was burning itself out.

"Let's get back to the mine entrance," Drostan ordered. "Jake will need our help." He pitched in with Mitch and Kovach's guards to carry what remained of their equipment and weapons.

"What now?" Drostan asked as he trudged back to where Jake stood guard at the mouth of the Vesta Nine. "We took care of the mad doctors, and there won't be any more zombies—at least, not from that direction."

"Good work," Jake said.

"How can I help?" Drostan asked.

Jake eyed him thoughtfully. "You see ghosts, right?"

Drostan hesitated, then nodded. "Yeah."

"What do you see now, here?"

Drostan took a deep breath and focused his concentration. Finding ghosts at the mine was not difficult; not being overwhelmed by their numbers was the challenge. "I see lots of dead men," Drostan said. "Miners. All the hullaballoo brought them out, but they've got no reason to run away—except..."

"Except what?" Jake pressed.

"They're afraid of the *gessyan*," Drostan said. "They hide from them."

"Can you tell them what we're doing? Get them on our side?" Jake asked. "We're going to need all the help we can get."

Drostan nodded. "I can try. Not sure what they can do, but I'll tell them." After a moment, he turned back to Jake. "Done."

Another transmission through the earpiece startled Jake. It was from Kovach's second-in-command. "The men are in position, sir. Locked and loaded."

Jake peered toward the angry mob at the gates. "Anything changed out front?"

"Negative. Looks like a big brawl from here."

"Good," Jake replied with a smile. "Let me know if anything changes, and make sure no one gets past your line."

"Affirmative, sir."

Jake turned back toward the mine to find Renate walking toward him. Andreas was maneuvering the biggest of the Alekanovo stones into place. "It took a little debate," Renate said, with a smile that suggested 'argument' would be more accurate, "but Andreas and I think we've determined the most powerful positioning of the Russian stones."

"The more you can prepare now, the faster we can act once Rick and the others come out," Jake said. "Anything you can do in advance, do it. We can't count on having time to do more than react when the explosions start."

Renate nodded. "I figured as much. We're planning to have all the wardings set so all we have to do is activate them. At least," she added, "that's the plan. And you know what they say."

"Nothing ever goes as planned," Jake said. "I know. But let's hope that just this once, it doesn't apply to us."

Jake was restless, and the burden of being the point man for the night's activities weighed heavy on him. *This is for you, Father,* he thought. He might not have been able to get the kind of evidence necessary to convict Veles or Thwaites in a court of law for Thomas Desmet's murder, but he could make it expensive for them, and warn them off troubling Brand and Desmet's people in the future. It wasn't enough. Not nearly enough. But it would have to do.

The earpiece gave a shrill squeal that nearly deafened him. "What's going on down there?" Nicki asked. "Have the men come out of the mine yet?"

"Not yet," Jake replied. "See anything from up there?"

In the distance, Jake heard gunfire, both small arms and the *rat-a-tat-tat* of Gatling guns.

"There's a firefight going on, behind a building," Nicki replied. "We're high enough I can't see which side is winning. Looks like it's getting out of hand at the gates. People are waving burning torches around and firing rifles. Better stay clear."

"Got my hands full where I am," Jake said. "Have you spotted any 'company'?"

"*Non*," Nicki replied. "And my friend continues to read the telegrams. They're very interesting tonight." That meant Cady was code-breaking the encrypted messages from the Department, and between Veles and Thwaites. They had already agreed that since their transmissions between the ground and the airship might be intercepted, no names would be used.

"Anything?" Jake asked.

"Nothing we can't handle." There was a commotion that drowned out a few words. "Gotta go." The transmission clicked off.

Now we wait for Rick and the others to get back so we can seal up the Night Hag and her gessyan *friends—for good*, he thought.

Chapter TWENTY-NINE

"WE'VE GOT TO get the rest of those men out before we lure the *gessyan* back in." Rick adjusted the straps on the combined gas mask and night-vision goggles that Adam Farber had created. He glanced at the others—Kovach, Father Matija, and the *Logonje* priests—and decided that they all looked like creatures from a nightmare with their faces covered by the gear.

The real nightmares lay ahead of them, in the depths of Vesta Nine.

"Jacob and Hans are down below," Kovach said. "The deepest two levels are being mined by *werkmen* or clockwork zombies. That's where the tourmaquartz is—and likely there are natural shafts going even deeper, to where the *gessyan* were before they got loose. We're not going that far. The level above those has been using slave labor. Jacob and Hans are going to need some help freeing the slaves from their manacles and sending them back up in the elevators. That's where Rick and I come in."

"And what would you have us do?" Matija asked. Matija and his fellow priests were dressed in long black cassocks, covered by black leather baldrics with a variety of pockets and scabbards for cavalry sabers.

Kovach met the priest's gaze. "Hold back the dark, Father. Those *things* are down there, and they may decide they want fresh meat."

Kovach and Rick each carried one of Farber's new force guns. Their night vision goggles would help them move through the darkness, and they came prepared with several of Adam's electric torches and miners' lamps, just to be on the safe side. Rick was armed with a revolver and a knife, as well as the Maxwell box and the remote trigger Adam had rigged just for this operation. Kovach had a shotgun and a revolver, as well as a rifle slung over his shoulder. Rick was certain that Kovach had other, concealed weapons on him, as well as the sack of explosives he carried with disconcerting nonchalance. He caught a glint of silver at the neckline of Kovach's shirt, and knew that he'd been sure to wear his saint's medal this night.

"Time's a-wasting. Let's get moving," Rick said.

Thanks to the knockers and the alarms, miners and guards had already cleared out, making it easy for Rick and the others to enter at ground level. Even through the masks, the air smelled of coal dust, sweat, lamp oil, and damp dirt. Kovach led the way to one of the cage elevators that took men deep into the shaft. Rick did not let himself think about the almost bottomless drop into the darkness as he and the others shuffled into the square metal cage.

"On the way back up, we can pack the elevator like they do for the shifts," Kovach said. "Each of these cages can hold at least thirty men—more if they're skinny. You can move practically a whole shift with one load—we hope."

The clank of chains and the rumble of gears made Rick's stomach clench. *We're hanging over a drop that goes most of the way to China, with monsters at the bottom. No reason to be nervous.*

An oil lamp burned on each level of the mine, and Rick counted them as they made their descent. Most miners wore a lamp attached to their hats, and even that was risky due to bad air, what miners called 'firedamp'. The explosions that occurred when an open lamp flame hit a pocket of firedamp had killed hundreds of miners. Even worse was the blackdamp, poisonous air that seeped up from the depths of the Earth. What with bad air, tunnel collapses and frequent accidents, mining was already dangerous without having to worry about immortal, bloodthirsty monsters lurking in the dark.

"Almost there." Kovach's voice seemed loud in the darkness. With all but the slaves and *werkmen* gone, the shaft was eerily quiet. Beyond the single lamp on each level, tunnels stretched into impenetrable darkness. The priests had begun to quietly chant, and Rick found himself envying Kovach the protective medal he wore.

The air was stuffy and breathing seemed more difficult. The deeper they went, the more every one of Rick's instincts screamed for him to run while he still had the chance. *What does it feel like for someone who actually has magic, like Matija?* he wondered.

The clanking slowed and they reached the final landing. The elevator hung suspended over the abyss, and a six-inch gap separated them from the tunnel. Rick resolutely did not look down as they disembarked. He tried to stretch, only to nearly hit his head on the rough ceiling.

"There's a reason a lot of miners are short," Kovach said with a chuckle.

Deep below them, the sounds of steel on rock carried up through the elevator shaft, a constant clink and thump as clockwork creatures worked in conditions untenable for the human slaves. Near the elevator, Rick spotted two metal boxes the size of lunch pails. One of them was locked, but the other's lid was open, revealing handfuls of opaque greenish crystals. Rick and Kovach exchanged a glance, before filling their satchels and pockets with as many of the crystals as they could.

Down the long, dark tunnel, a dim yellow light bobbed closer. Kovach raised his shotgun, while Rick reached for his revolver. Matija and the priests each drew a golden relic from inside their cassocks, ready for the worst.

"Glad you're here." Jacob emerged from the darkness. "Hans and I have most of the slaves out of their shackles, but they're a sorry lot. We can save their lives, but I fear they'll be fit for nowhere except Dix Mountain."

Rick and the others followed Jacob down the tunnel. The darkness seemed to have physical weight, pressing in on them from all sides. Rock enclosed them like the walls of a tomb, and the warm, fetid air stank of unwashed bodies and urine. Rick had never been claustrophobic, but now he had to consciously fight the urge to flee in panic.

Jacob led them into a chamber off the tunnel. The ceiling was low enough that Rick had to duck. The enormous weight being held up by the support pillars—all those levels above them—did not bear dwelling on, not if he wanted to stay sane. The dim glow of oil lanterns and miner's lamps dispelled enough of the gloom that they could push their nightvision goggles up on their foreheads.

Rick could make out the shadowy forms of pale, half-starved wretches in the dim light. Hollow-cheeked, painfully thin, filthy and unshaven, the enslaved miners stared at Rick and the others with deadened gazes, as if the concept of rescue had long ago been abandoned. On the nearest slaves, Rick could see dark ulcers on their ankles where manacles had kept them at their job.

"Rick and Kovach—start getting them into the elevator," Jacob said. "Hans and I will free the last of them. Father Matija—I'd be obliged if you and your companions would make sure we don't get surprised by things that go bump in the night."

Matija nodded, and said something in his native tongue before he and the other priests spread out, two of them lining up watchfully on either side of the elevator, focused on the pit below, and the others moving toward the tunnel to stand sentry against the blackness that seemed to stretch on to infinity.

"Come on folks, time to go," Kovach said as he and Rick moved toward the ragged miners. The men shuffled slowly towards the elevator as though too weary to comprehend freedom. Rick saw the same anger in Kovach's eyes that he felt himself: at Thwaites, at Veles, and at the mine bosses who must have known and kept their silence.

"Move all the way to the back," Rick urged, trying not to retch at the smell of the slaves. "It'll be tight, but we want to get everyone in one run." The miners stumbled their way toward the elevator, and Rick cajoled them inside as Kovach kept the line moving.

The elevator cage had three levels. When they had ridden down, they had done so in the top-most tier. When that section was so full that Rick could not fit in another of the emaciated men, Jacob closed and latched the door, then worked the lift controls to bring the second section to the level of the tunnel floor.

Loading the first group had gone without a hitch, though much slower than Rick would have liked. But as the first of the new group shambled toward the elevator, the man in front stumbled, falling across the gap between the tunnel floor and the cage just as the car suddenly lurched up.

Rick dove to catch the miner, and found himself badly off balance. He grabbed the man's bony wrist, crying out as he started to pitch forward. The miner hung half-in and half-out of the elevator, held only by Rick's grip on his wrist. Rick had one foot on the tunnel floor, one on the elevator's steel platform, and a death grip on the wire cage, tight enough to draw blood.

For a moment, Rick stared straight down into the abyss. The rocks that had been jarred loose by the miner's tumble fell in silence, so far down he would not hear them hit bottom. The terrified miner scrabbled to climb into the elevator, making the whole contraption swing farther away from solid ground. The man's frantic movements strained Rick's grasp on his wrist, and made the wire cut deeper into his other hand as he struggled to keep them from falling to their deaths.

If the fall doesn't kill us, the gessyan *will eat us,* he thought, fighting down a surge of panic.

"Gotcha!" Kovach said as he grabbed Rick by the coat and pulled him back to safety. The dangling slave lurched into the elevator, and Rick let go of the cage, looking ruefully at his damaged hand.

"Wrap that up," Kovach said, producing a linen bandage from one of his pockets. "Make sure you clean it when we get out of here. You don't want to get lockjaw." Rick wrapped his hand, trying to ignore the pain.

"They smell blood." Father Matija paused in his chant. "Better hurry. They're coming." Rick did not need to ask who the priest meant.

"The rest of you! Get moving!" Kovach ordered the vacant-eyed miners, who resumed their shuffle toward the elevator. Jacob and Hans herded the slaves from the back, weapons at the ready in case any surprises emerged from the tunnels.

As the last of the wretched miners crouched and scuttled their way into the elevator, there was room for just one more passenger. Jacob climbed inside. Hans grabbed a hold of the outside with his metal hands to ride along. "I'll take them up to the surface and make sure they get clear," Jacob said. "Then I'll come back down to get you. Be ready—I don't think it's healthy to stick around down here," he added, nodding down the dark shaft toward where the *gessyan* and the mad doctors' creations ruled the shadows.

The elevator began to clank its way to the top. Rick could not tear his gaze away from the empty stares of the enslaved miners. *Do they realize we came to set them free?* he wondered. *Or are they too far gone to know what's going on?*

Rick unpacked a metal box and a coiled rope of twisted steel from his pack. He flipped a switch and Adam's Maxwell box hummed to life. It was bigger than its predecessor, and had been altered by Adam to allow for a remote trigger, linked to a small winding gadget that would crank up the power to the highest level. With luck, that would call the *gessyan* that had escaped back to the mines and imprison them along with the spirits that had not fled the deep places. Rick and the others would be well clear by the time that happened. He secured the box to the steel rope through a metal loop, then drove a stake into the rock near the ledge and eased the Maxwell box down into the abyss. He let out the last of the rope, then straightened, still staring into the pit.

Kovach jostled his arm. "Come on, let's set those charges."

From the elevator shaft, they heard the sound of a clanking chain. "That's awfully fast for Jacob to be on his way back down," Rick said.

A metal arm clamped onto the rock and red eyes in a brass skull rose into sight, as a *werkman* hauled himself over the lip of the pit.

"We've got trouble!" Kovach shouted, leveling his force weapon and blowing a hole in the mechanical man's head. The automaton staggered before regaining its balance and continuing the attack. Another *werkman* had appeared at the edge of the shaft, eyes glowing.

Father Matija hefted a large rock and hurled it at the nearest *werkman*. The heavy stone put a deep dent into the *werkman*'s chest. A second priest pitched a fist-sized rock like a baseball, hard enough he could have qualified for a spot on one of the teams at Exposition Park. The rock slammed into the *werkman*'s head with enough force to give a living man a concussion. The damaged metal man continued forward, gears protesting and eyes flickering.

"We'll hold them!" Kovach shouted. "Go plant the charges!"

Rick shouldered the equipment and headed into the large chamber where the slave workers had been mining. The smell was overpowering and Rick kicked angrily at the discarded shackles that lay all across the floor. He sized up the area. Tourmaquartz wasn't mined on this level, but the raw ore was brought up from where *werkmen* and the clockwork zombies mined it in the depths below, for the slaves to process before sending it for shipment.

On one side of the room was a mine car filled with tourmaquartz ore, brought up from the levels below for processing by the slaves. Picks and pickaxes were strewn across the floor. It did not escape Rick's notice that the effort required to turn a mine car full of large rocks into a lunch pail of slivers and marble-sized pieces would have been enormous.

Rick dug into his satchel for the bundles of dynamite fortified by Adam Farber with Sprengel explosives. He placed them all around the mine car and whistled under his breath as he set the detonator.

"When this blows, they're going to hear the explosion for miles," he muttered. "Probably rattle dishes all the way out in Homestead."

A noise in the tunnel behind the mine car made Rick freeze. Shuffling footsteps, headed his way. Cursing under his breath, Rick backed away from the tunnel. He had almost made it to the far side of the chamber when three clockwork zombies burst from the darkness, moving fast.

"Oh, shit." Shooting the clockwork zombies was out, not with the tourmaquartz and the explosives so close. Rick grabbed a pickax with his right hand, and snatched up a pair of manacles from the floor with his injured left hand.

"You looking for me?" he said, though he doubted the mechanized corpses could understand him. Taunting them made him feel a little braver, though his palms were clammy and his body tingled with adrenaline.

One of the zombies came at him from the right, while the other two circled around. Rick swung the pickax at the nearest creature, sinking the point into its back. Ribs tore loose as he jerked the ax free, and foul-smelling ichor oozed from the gaping wound. The zombie struggled forward, slowed but on its feet.

The second clockwork creature attacked from the left. Rick gripped one end of the manacle and swung the chain, lashing out at the zombie. He bit back a cry as the chain bit into his makeshift bandage, straining the cut in his palm. The chain and manacles slashed down through the dead man's face, smashing its nose and ripping lose a flap of mottled skin.

For a moment, the second zombie was blinded by the ichor gushing into its mechanical eyes. The last creature, in the middle of the three, made its move, rushing Rick with its arms outstretched, hands twisted into claws.

Rick brought the ax down with his full strength, snapping through the zombie's forearms like tinder. He winged the ichor-stained manacle at the zombie on his right, snaring one of its wrists with the chain. With a jerk, he pulled the creature off its feet and brought the pickax down through the clockwork zombie's head.

Strong hands grabbed his shoulders from behind. Rick twisted, glad his coat allowed for some wiggle room. He freed his knife with his left hand, and drove it back through his coat, into the belly of the creature, then wheeled, bringing the pickax down through the zombie's hunched shoulders into its chest.

Two down, one to go, and some volatile explosives ready to go boom. Rick grabbed another set of shackles from the floor, swung them round and round overhead and let them fly like a bolas. The chains wheeled through the air, slamming into the last zombie's head and wrapping around with such force that one of the metal cuffs sank through the rotting flesh and lodged in the creature's forehead.

Rick heard more footsteps headed up the passageway behind the mine car, but had no desire to wait around. He grabbed another set of shackles, ignoring the pain in his left hand, and took the pickax with him as he headed for the elevator tunnel.

Sounds of battle echoed down the corridor. Jacob's shotgun sounded and Rick winced, wondering whether a stray spark or shot would blow them sky high.

He rejoined the others to find Hans and Jacob fighting three more of the clockwork zombies that had emerged from one of the side tunnels, while Kovach fought off a battered *werkman*. Hans's extra strength from his own mechanical enhancements made him an even match for the zombie he battled, though as a living man, Hans could still be injured, while the zombie wouldn't slow down until he was destroyed. Jacob fired the force gun and took the second zombie through the knees, then brought the butt of his gun down hard on the creature's skull, smashing it open like a rotten pumpkin.

Rick took the third zombie, wheeling the manacles overhead and sending them in a tangle around the legs of the monster, which fell with a dull thud. The pickax finished him off. Kovach leveled his next shot at the *werkman*'s ankles, blowing him off his feet and onto his back where the metal man struggled like an overturned turtle. Kovach leveled the force gun at each of the machine's hinged joints, until all that remained were smoking bits of severed metal and a metallic torso that finally lay still.

Two more zombies clawed their way up over the lip of the abyss. Out of the corner of his eye, Rick saw shadows flowing along the tunnel's walls as dark shapes skittered across the rock. Eban Hodekin and two more creatures like him dropped from the ceiling, planting themselves between Rick and the zombies.

Hodekin was fast. He and the other kobolds launched themselves at the clockwork zombies. Rick had thought the mechanical monstrosities were strong, but they were no match for the kobolds. Hodekin ripped one zombie's head from its shoulders with his bare hands, and made it look easy. In seconds, the kobolds had torn the zombies limb from limb with their bony fingers and razor-sharp teeth. Then without a word, Hodekin and the others dragged the mangled zombies into a narrow crack in the rock wall. The sound of smacking lips and crunching bones gave Rick no doubt as to what had befallen the clockwork cadavers. With effort, he kept his gorge from rising.

Only then did Rick realize why Matija and the *Logonje* priests had not come to their rescue. What looked like thick black smoke roiled up from the depths of the shaft. It was the same inky, unnatural darkness that had followed their carriage, stinking like an old tomb, and Rick knew that these were the *gessyan*, come to feast on their souls.

Matija and his priests raised their relics as they chanted, casting an iridescent curtain of light between them and the *gessyan*.

"We've got to get back up that shaft!" Jacob said. He looked at Rick. "Can't you use your box? Isn't it supposed to call the *gessyan* down to where it is?"

Rick met his gaze levelly. "Not until we're out. Not unless you want to meet the Night Hag on your way up."

"Get into the elevator," Matija yelled over his shoulder as the priests continued to chant.

"No offense, Father, but I'm not sure my faith is that strong," Jacob replied, eying the billowing darkness.

"Then you'll have to make do," Matija replied. "There's only one way out of here."

"And we'd better hurry," Rick replied. "The detonators have been set."

According to the plan, Matija and the *Logonje* were not supposed to unleash the full power of their magic against the *gessyan* until right before the explosions, when they and the others were out of the mine. Rick had no desire to see whether or not the consuming white light that the priests could summon would set off the tourmaquartz early.

Matija's voice rose to a sharp command, and the iridescent light flared. The glare was painful after the near-darkness of the mine, and Rick was blinded for a few seconds. When his vision returned, he saw that the curtain of light had become a floor, forcing the angry shadows down below the elevator, temporarily capping the deep shaft.

"Go!" Matija commanded.

Jacob had brought the elevator down so that the top tier was level with the ground. Rick dove in head first, sliding across the metal floor. Hans followed, then Matija and the priests, still chanting, relics limned with a golden glow. Kovach squeezed in next, and Jacob came last, slamming the door behind him.

"Hang on," Jacob said. "We're taking the express." He jammed the lever forward, and the elevator moved at its top speed, ballast rattling past. The cage suddenly jerked as something grabbed it from below.

Jacob pressed close to the wire screen and let out a tirade in Croatian that Rick didn't need translation to understand. "Damn zombie," Jacob finished. He turned to Kovach. "Anchor me."

Kovach barely had a chance to grab Jacob's belt before the cage door slid open and Jacob leaned out, his head only inches from the sides of the shaft. He shot three times, and Rick glimpsed something falling away beneath them. Kovach hauled Jacob back in and the door slammed shut.

"I hope we're close," Matija said, and his voice sounded like he was straining against a heavy weight.

"Ground level, coming right up," Jacob replied.

As soon as the car came level with the ground, Jacob had the door open. He and Kovach stood guard as Matija and the priests scrambled out, followed by Rick and Hans. "Coming out, don't shoot!" Rick yelled into the transmitter to Jake. "And make damned sure our patron is ready, because all hell's about to break loose." And with that, he activated the trigger on the Maxwell box.

Chapter THIRTY

"You made it!" Jake said, relief rushing over him as he saw Rick and the others emerge, covered in coal dust and spattered with blood and ichor.

"The charges are planted," Rick said wearily. "Enough dynamite to blow a hole through to China as soon as Father Matija gives the signal." Jacob set down a locked metal box. Rick caught Jake's gaze and patted the bulging pockets of his coat. Jake gave a slight smile and nodded.

Tourmaquartz, Jake thought. *A king's ransom in a coal hod.*

Before anyone could answer, a bone-chilling howl came from inside the mine entrance. The temperature plummeted until Jake could see his breath. Dozens of ghosts rose from the depths of the mine. Behind them came the same huge, black, dog-like *gessyan* that had pursued Jake's carriage in the city; Veles's hell hounds, summoned to do their master's bidding.

"Here we go again," Kovach sighed, shouldering his shotgun and taking aim as the men behind him scrambled to ready the Gatling gun.

Terrified screams rose from the crowd of rioters and guards at the front gate. Men climbed the metal fence, bringing it down with their weight and the pressure of the surging mob behind them, and those that did not move quickly enough were trampled underfoot. Miners and Pinkertons ran away as fast as they could, stumbling into each other in their panic.

Gunfire echoed as Kovach and the others turned their weapons on the ghosts and demon dogs bounding toward them. The ghosts were the mine dead, raised by malevolent magic to serve those whose negligence had caused their deaths. Crushed in cave-ins, suffocated in tunnels by bad air, or lost to their deaths down near-bottomless mine shafts, their bodies had never been recovered. Bullets did nothing to stop the ghosts, but the hell hounds stumbled and fell when they were hit, though they got back up and renewed their charge. One of the hounds came at Jake, claws and teeth bared. Jake dove to the side as Rick locked and loaded, blowing the hell hound's head away.

"Thanks!" Jake said, then wheeled and fired as another hound launched itself at Rick. In and around the hell hounds, the malevolent spirits howled and keened, with long fingers that ripped cloth and left deep, bloody scratches.

"Do something!" Rick shouted, dodging the hell hound, which moved unnaturally fast. The demon dog had him in one leap, grasping him by the shirt, and Rick wrestled with the creature to keep its large, sharp teeth away from his throat.

Jake raised his gun and aimed.

"It's too close! You'll hit me—"

Bang. A bullet grazed Rick's ear and hit the hound in the head, splitting open its skull and covering Rick with stinking goo. Jake grinned. "Got him!" he cried before turning to pick off another hell hound. Amid the hounds, Jake saw a new threat: pale dead figures moving almost faster than he could follow.

"Hold your fire!" Andreas shouted. "They're my men."

Vampires, Jake thought. These newcomers were as pale as the ghosts they attacked. Moving with supernatural speed, Andreas's brood launched themselves at the hell hounds.

One of the demon dogs leapt into the air, lunging toward Jake. Before he could throw himself out of the way, a vampire tackled the hound, and by the time the two hit the ground, the hell hound's head had been torn from its neck. Mitch stood his ground, taking his shots as if the hell hounds were targets on a firing range, hitting more than he missed.

Jake and Rick stood back to back, conserving their fast-dwindling ammunition until they were certain of a killing shot. Andreas and his brood never gave them the opportunity. The battle was over as suddenly as it had begun, and the vampires sauntered away from a ground strewn with the dismembered bodies of the hell hounds as the ghosts drew back, no longer keen to attack.

"Shouldn't your Maxwell box have gone off by now?" Jake shouted. "I thought it was supposed to be pulling the *gessyan* back into the mine, not letting them out to fight us!"

"I activated it a few minutes ago; I think it just kicked in," Rick said. "Look behind you!" Jake turned to see shadows sweeping toward them, blotting out the streetlamps as they passed.

"We've got *gessyan*!" Drostan shouted, knowing from experience his gun was no match for the cold darkness, wondering what the vampires could do against the new threat.

"Get out of the way!" Jake ordered. "Let them pass! They're being called by the Maxwell box." Rick and the others were happy to comply, though Andreas remained beside the Russian stones, and Renate drew back with the other mortals.

Summoned by the Maxwell box, the many *gessyan* that had escaped the depths of Vesta Nine streaked across the night sky, an ice-cold maelstrom of dark energy and malevolence. Wraiths and hell hounds followed the call. Revenants small and large followed in their wake and Jake realized that he had underestimated just what Veles had unleashed on New Pittsburgh. 'Hell with the lid off', someone had once called New Pittsburgh, and tonight it was truer than ever before.

"What's going on down there?" Nicki's voice was loud in Jake's earpiece. "The clouds rolled in and we can't see!"

"Not now!" he hissed.

"Don't you 'not now' me! We're up here to pull your chestnuts out of the fire!"

"*Gessyan*. Ghosts. Hell hounds. Feel better?" Jake ignored the response as he and the others retreated behind Andreas and the mages. Andreas and Renate were ready to finish the night's work. As Jake stared at them, both witches were limned in faint light, their power made visible. In the moment before Andreas and Renate loosed their magic, it occurred to Jake that he had never seen exactly what they could really do.

Renate and Andreas had erected the Alekanovo stone between them, and the runes carved into its smooth, black surface had begun to glow with power. As Andreas stepped forward to hold the *gessyan* at bay, Renate and the *Logonje* priests held up the small carved stones Nicki had taken from Jasinski's apartment, while Matija readied Marcin of Krakow's book, the tome for which so many people had died.

Cold blue energy flared from Andreas's open palms, rushing toward the shadows like a storm surge. His power swept out in an arc, rolling back the darkness, and as the energy touched the wraiths, they shrieked and writhed, fleeing before the consuming wave of power, vanishing into the blackness that spawned them.

"Pretty impressive," Rick murmured.

An unnatural silence settled over the area, and the street lamps overhead dimmed. Drogo Veles stood at the mine entrance.

"Go home." Veles's voice carried above the howl of the *gessyan*.

"Not until we're done," Andreas replied as Jake and the others stood their ground.

"You are meddling in my business."

"Like Thomas Desmet? Is that why you had him killed?" Andreas said. "Your 'business' set monsters loose on the city and abominations loose in the mine. It ends now."

"The *gessyan* were a fortunate accident," Veles replied with a cold, terrifying half-smile. "We hadn't planned to free them, but once they were loose, it helped to keep attention... elsewhere."

"So you could mine the tourmaquartz," Andreas supplied.

Veles nodded. He regarded Andreas coldly. "You have overstepped the mark. I am not a patient man."

"Neither am I," Andreas replied, and a wave of the same blue energy that had driven back the *gessyan* blasted toward Veles.

Veles brought his hands up and around in a gesture of warding, and the blue arc flared away without touching him. A second fluid gesture shot a torrent of fire back at Andreas as Renate and Father Matija stepped up beside him. Jake and the others fell back, and Jake and Kovach held their force guns impatiently, unable to get off a clear shot.

The three mages moved in concert. Andreas threw his hands up, palms open, and a translucent wall of energy blocked the fire, which spread out along the barrier in a golden glow.

The instant the fire was spent, Andreas dropped the shield. Renate was limned in a green haze, and she gestured, sending a milky cloud of sparkling particles toward Veles as he summoned more fire. The cloud absorbed the fire, breaking it into glowing embers that flickered and winked out.

The seconds of delay Renate bought them were all Father Matija needed as he lifted a golden reliquary from the folds of his cassock and held it aloft in one hand, holding Marcin of Krakow's book in the other. A bolt of blue lightning crackled from the relic as Matija began to chant. The lightning forked once, then twice, then again, sending eight streams of blue energy that sizzled all around Veles, striking his shield in multiple places. The energy shield wavered and flared as Veles fought against the onslaught. Abruptly, the shield vanished. Six of the lightning bolts had been absorbed by the shield. The other two touched down near enough to Veles to singe the hem of his well-pressed trousers and char the dirt around his boots.

"To hell with this," Jake muttered. He and Kovach already had Adam's force guns shouldered. They squeezed the triggers just as the last of the lightning spent itself, and a cone of iridescent power caught Veles by surprise, knocking him backwards. Mitch lobbed a Ketchum grenade toward Veles, just for good measure. It exploded with a bright flash. When they could see again, Veles had vanished.

"Huh. Science," Kovach said with an approving nod, patting the gun for a job well done.

"Don't be too sure," Renate replied. "Veles left because it suited him." Her eyes widened as she looked over Jake's shoulder, toward the mine entrance. "And I think I know why."

Rick was looking in the opposite direction, toward the river, his eyes wide with terror. "Trouble!" he yelled.

Jake felt a cold shiver run down his back—his sixth sense was serving him well tonight—and turned to see a sight out of a nightmare. A hunched figure in a tattered, shroud-like dress descended from the sky. Gnarled, bony hands outstretched to grasp and rend, she plummeted toward them, eyes glowing a hellish red. Behind her swirled a black cloud of distorted, nightmare figures.

Nocnitsa. The Night Hag. And with her, more *gessyan.* Between Adam's Maxwell box and the spells Andreas and Renate wove, the *gessyan* were returning, and with them, the most fearsome monster of them all. A bone-chilling cry, somewhere between a raptor's shriek and a deranged keening, drowned out even the gunfire.

"Andreas! Renate! Incoming!" Jake shouted.

"She's fighting the power of the Maxwell box," Father Matija shouted.

"I was afraid of that," Rick said.

"Get that thing into the mine!" Jake shouted to Andreas and the mages.

"More trouble," Rick yelled. "Guards—headed this way."

Kovach and Jake blasted the biggest, baddest *gessyan* of them all with their force guns. The iridescent wall of energy passed right through the specter. The Night Hag's form wavered, but did not dissipate. The Night Hag gave a predator's howl that made Jake's skin crawl.

Matija's priests stepped away from where they had shielded the Alekanovo stone from Veles's attack. Matija had handed off Marcin of Krakow's book to Renate and Andreas and now held his relic aloft, bathed in the golden glow of its power. Renate held Marcin's book, and as she and Andreas read aloud from its pages, the runes of the Alekanovo stone began to glow brighter and brighter. The two of them held up two of the small, carved rune stones, as did Matija and his priests. The priests murmured a chant as they lifted the stones and their golden relics. The four relics were lit by an inner light, surrounded by an otherworldly nimbus, and the stones' carvings glowed with uncanny energy.

The roiling cloud of *gessyan* screeched and roared, fighting the call to return to the depths of the mine. Bony fingers, tooth-filled maws and long, sharp claws reached out from the dark miasma of spirits. The Night Hag darted forward. She grew more solid with every passing second, her long, muscular arms, tearing at whatever she could reach with her bony fingers and vicious claws. A swipe of her sharp talons ripped at Rick's jacket and he gave a cry of utter terror as he struggled to get loose.

Mitch dove to grab Rick by the wrist, hauling him out of the way. Jake shoved the force gun into the Night Hag's maw. "Eat this," he said, pulling the trigger.

The force gun that had no effect when *Nocnitsa* was a disembodied spirit now sent its expanding energy into the physical form of the Night Hag. Andreas and Renate followed up with a blast of greenish-blue lightning aimed at the Night Hag and the rest of the *gessyan* spirits, as Mitch and Rick fell to the ground, trying to get out of the way.

The Night Hag screamed again, but this time, it was a howl of pain as the magic and the force gun's energy ripped her to bits. The other spirits tried to escape, struggling against the inexorable pull of the Maxwell box and Father Matija's incantation, as the Alekanovo stone's inscriptions grew brighter and brighter. The *gessyan* were hauled, screaming, into the pit, and along with them, the writhing remains of the Night Hag.

"Watch out!" Mitch yelled. "Guards, from the south!" Out of the corner of his eye, Jake saw a dozen guards running toward them.

Before Jake and Kovach could react, a hail of bullets from out of the sky dug up the ground in between the guards and Jake's companions. Two short bursts of gunfire from overhead sprayed dirt and rocks in every direction, drawing a very clear line and daring the mine guards to cross it. Apparently, their pay did not include being shot at by airships. The guards scattered, shouting obscenities as they withdrew.

"Are you trying to kill us?" Jake called into his headset.

"No, of course I wasn't trying to kill you," Nicki replied calmly. "How was I supposed to know you'd seen them coming? Don't be ungrateful. They ran away, didn't they?"

"Why did Flyboy let you have the guns? Who's in charge up there?"

"Don't you yell at me! And don't even try that—just because he's the pilot doesn't make him the boss of me!" Nicki retorted before cutting out.

"Now!" Jake shouted, and in unison, he and Kovach trained their force guns on the mouth of Vesta Nine. The Alekanovo stone sent out a blinding flare of white light, joined by the iridescent power surging from the *Logonje*'s relics. The high-pitched whine of the force guns and the chants reached a deafening crescendo, forcing the last of the hellish cloud of *gessyan* back into the maw of the mine.

Jake toggled the transmitter on his collar. "Hey up there! We need that beam now!"

"You couldn't give us a little more warning—" Nicki replied.

"Now!"

"He's doing it. He's doing it. Hold your horses!" The transmission cut for a moment, then: "There's something you need to know—"

"Now, dammit!" Jake yelled. Nicki muttered a curse in French and the transmission clicked off.

A column of white, consuming fire burned toward Vesta Nine from the heavens like the wrath of an angry god. The air smelled of ozone and burning dirt as the fire struck deep into the shaft, igniting the coal, sending a pulse of super-heated energy into the bowels of the cursed mine, collapsing the rock and blocking the entrance. From deep within Vesta Nine came a roar as Rick set off his charges. The ground shook beneath their feet, and the mouth of the mine shuddered. Rocks fell and the timbers holding up the opening split with a crack like thunder.

It also set off the tourmaquartz.

The blast was deafening, and the explosion's shock wave lifted the rearmost guards and miners, who had not yet escaped the compound, off their feet, throwing them several yards. Jake, Rick, and the others had tucked themselves into tight balls on the ground, covering their heads with their arms. Flying rocks pelted them like a hail of bullets. A suffocating cloud of coal dust rose like a new wraith over the deep crater, and as the deep levels began to collapse, the land around the mine's mouth shuddered, then crumbled and fell into oblivion.

When Jake dared raise his head, Vesta Nine was gone. And when he looked skyward, so was the *Allegheny Princess*.

Jake was about to toggle his transmitter when Mitch Storm grabbed him by the arm. "You've got to get out of here—now!"

"I don't—"

"You really don't want to be here when they land," Jacob added drily, and pointed toward the sky. Moving like ghosts against the clouds, Jake could barely make out the shapes of two black airships.

"Remain where you are. This is the United States Government," a voice blared from afar.

"Friends of yours?" Rick asked as Mitch and Jacob hustled them toward the rear of the mining compound and the unmarked carriage where Charles the *werkman* waited.

"Not at the moment," Mitch replied. "I spotted a couple of the Department spies early on, and knocked them cold so they couldn't report on the irregularities. So right now, I'm in no hurry to see them myself."

"They've been watching this place for a while, but I'm a little surprised they're quite so late to the party. And they won't be happy to lose whatever tourmaquartz might have still been mined, so it's time for your team to grab your stuff and disappear." Jacob pointedly nudged the locked metal box with this boot.

"Get out of here. Go home. Stay low. Make sure all of you have an alibi and people to back it up," Mitch said.

"Go!" Mitch said, nearly pushing Renate after Jake and Rick. "Stick to the plan, get to the carriages and stay on the back roads as long as you can. Don't look suspicious."

"Yeah," Jake replied. "We'll be real casual."

Mitch fixed him with a glance. "Trust me. You do not want to go to Western Penitentiary. Get out of here."

"What about you two?" Rick asked suspiciously.

Mitch gave a lopsided grin. "We're going back to get Tumblety and Brunrichter out of their carriage and haul their sorry asses over to district headquarters to get ourselves off suspension. It won't surprise anyone if Jacob and I show up somewhere we aren't supposed to be."

"No," Jacob replied with a long-suffering sigh. "It really won't."

Chapter

THIRTY-ONE

THE *ALLEGHENY PRINCESS* ghosted through the night. In the moonlight, most of the countryside below was quiet, and the river was a dark ribbon. On the ground beneath the airship, the Vesta Nine mine was a mass of large, shadowy buildings. The gloom was pierced by a few security lights which did little to push back the darkness.

"We're in position," Nicki said into Adam Farber's gadget. Adam himself was down in the bowels of the airship, babying the modifications he had just finished like a proud papa.

"We're not the only ones transmitting," Cady warned, sitting at a device with a pair of headphones over her ears, scribbling on a pad of paper.

"What are they saying?" Nicki asked.

Cady shook her head. "It's in code. And not the same DSI code I broke last week."

"Maybe it's not DSI sending it. Maybe it's someone else."

"I'm on it," Cady said with a fierce grin. She had a small difference engine, built for code-breaking by Farber, a mechanical wonder no larger than a suitcase. "Calculating."

"What?" Nicki asked, seemingly to no one. She pressed the earpiece to her head with one hand and held the microphone closer to her mouth. "Can't hear you. Speak up!"

"Tell Jake to hurry it up," Cullan Adair said. "I doubt we're going to be alone up here for long, and I've got no desire to play cat-and-mouse with a Department zeppelin."

"Yeah. What can you see?" Jake said, his voice scratchy and barely audible.

Nicki muttered a curse in French and set aside the headphones, moving over to a spyglass on a swivel-mounted pedestal. "How can we back Jake up if we don't know what's going on?" she fussed.

"I've got the first word!" Cady cheered. "I think."

Nicki returned and put the headphones back on. "There's a fight at the gate. Looks like Maguire got plenty of turn-out. You want us to take a shot at locating Thwaites?"

"If it keeps the police from getting to the mine, it's all good," Cullan said, looking up from where he was quietly consulting with two of his bridge crew.

"Don't shoot!" Jake responded. "Not yet!"

Nicki looked to Cullen with a glare and raised her eyebrows. "I said, did you want us to take a shot at locating Thwaites?"

"Yeah, try to keep an eye out for him *and* Veles. I don't think this is going to be a walk in the park."

"That's what makes it so much fun!" Nicki said with a wink to Cullen.

The deck of the *Allegheny Princess* had panoramic, bulletproof windows on three sides. Nicki stood with her nose pressed up against the glass, desperately trying to peer down on the land directly below them. More than once, she wished that she could open a window and lean out for a better view. "I can't see properly," she fretted. "I keep seeing flashes of gunfire, but I can't tell who's shooting who."

"Whom," Cady corrected absently. "Who's shooting *whom*."

"You knew what I meant," Nicki replied. "I need to get a better view." The metal trap door in the floor of the deck caught her eye. Cullan had shown her where it led, and now she pounced on it with a cry of triumph. "Yes!" she said, yanking the door open and, before anyone could stop her, jumping feet first into the three-foot-deep well of the gunnery mount.

"Ms. LeClercq! I must insist you come out of there. It's dangerous!" Cullan said, striding over. Cady gave a snort.

"No one's shooting at us," Nicki said, giving a dismissive wave of her hand, as if sending away a bothersome waiter. "But I can see so much better down here!" The gunnery mount was a cage of steel and bulletproof glass, with a Gatling gun that could move along a track together with the gunner's seat. The mount gave nearly perfect visibility, enabling Nicki to see the whole Vesta Nine complex below. She could also feel the vibration of the *Allegheny Princess's* motors and the rush of the wind. It was heady and terrifying and she loved it.

As Nicki watched, a pattern of rapid flashes, like large angry fireflies, lit the night. A few moments later, long fiery lashes streamed from a source hidden in the darkness. "*Mon Dieu*!" Nicki exclaimed, her eyes widening. "What is that?"

Cullan peered through the bridge's windows. "Off hand, I'd say someone's making use of those fire-throwers Farber came up with."

"There's a fight by the main gate and another by one of the buildings." Nicki reported. "Oh! They're firing the Gatlings again!" The clouds shifted, and for a moment the moon shone down.

A huge fireball shot into the air from where the flame throwers were being used. Cullan pulled the ship sharply starboard, throwing Nicki into the glass and causing many of the crew to cry out in alarm as they avoided the flames.

"Airship—can you hear me?" Drostan called through the headset.

"I thought you weren't going to make a scene!" Nicky snapped as she picked herself up. "Flyboy had to make us all airsick to avoid that fireball you sent up.

"Sorry, sorry. Look, I need to talk to Wunderkind—"

Adam's voice cut in. "I'm here."

"Someone's trying to escape, may be Brunrichter and Tumblety," Drostan said. "They're too far away from us, and we've got hostile fire between here and there. Can you do something to stop them—preferably without killing them?"

"We're on it," Adam replied.

"Don't you dare leave me out of this!" Nicki interrupted. "You need me to locate the targets!"

"I wouldn't dream of leaving you out," Drostan replied.

Nicki turned and shouted. "Cullan! Someone's getting away! There's a carriage heading for the rear of the complex."

"Changing course," Cullan replied, and from her perch beneath the *Allegheny Princess*, Nicki had a front-row seat as the scenery slid past and the airship banked and turned.

She gulped, resolving not to be airsick, and closing her eyes for a moment until the ship had changed course. It helped that it was dark outside, making the long drop to the land below less obvious. After a moment, she peered down through the rounded glass, trying to get a clearer view.

"Definitely making for the railroad cars," she shouted to Cullan.

"Hang onto your hoopskirts," Cullan said, and a high-pitched whine filled the bridge. Nicki covered her ears as the wine grew shrill, and then a bolt as bright as lightning sizzled from a metal rod beneath the airship, forward of Nicki's position and just a few feet lower.

She jumped with a squeal, and the smell of ozone filled the air. Nicki blinked rapidly, the image of the bright bolt imprinted on her retinas. After a moment, she could see clearly again.

"How about some warning, *s'il vous plaît*!"

"Sorry," Cullan replied, although she could have sworn he was laughing.

"What do you think?" Adam voice said over the headset. "And that's only at half-power!"

"I think you're a dangerous man," Drostan responded, his voice almost drowned out by static. "Great job. We'll be in touch."

"I've got more of the message!" Cady yelled. "And I think it's from Thwaites!"

"Keep at it," Nicki encouraged. "We've got to figure out what he's up to." She peered down into the darkness, and could barely make out the shape of the carriage she had spied a few moments before. Cullan's Tesla ray had carved a swath into the ground around the carriage, effectively stranding it on a little island within a still-burning moat of scorched, melted dirt.

"What's going on down there?" she asked, after an endless, tense few minutes. "Have the men come out of the mine yet?"

—

"Not yet," Jake replied. "See anything from up there?"

"There's a firefight going on, behind a storage building. We're high enough I can't see which side is winning. Looks like it's getting out of hand at the gates. People are waving burning torches around and firing rifles. Better stay clear," Nicki reported.

"Got my hands full where I am. Have you spotted any company?"

"*Non*, and my friend continues to read the telegrams. They're very interesting tonight."

"Anything?" Jake asked.

"Nothing we can't handle." Nicki said and startled as something caught her eye. "Gotta go."

A streak of translucent gray streamed past the glass and steel bubble. Nicki stared at it, then blinked again, sure the brightness of the Tesla ray was playing havoc with her vision. A second gray streak wafted past, then more. Nicki slid her seat around its track, staring out into the night, and saw a stream of ghostly forms rising from the countryside, gliding along the river, some even pouring in from the direction of the lights of New Pittsburgh.

Nicki crossed herself. "*Spectres*," she murmured. "That Maxwell box Adam and Rick talked about—it really works! They're calling in the spirits, the *gessyan*! There must be hundreds of them!"

Another tense wait followed. Nicki looked toward the ground to check on their team, but found it hard to see through the clouds.

"What's going on down there?" Nicki yelled. "The clouds rolled in and we can't see!"

"Not now!" Jake responded.

"Don't you not now me! We're up here to pull your chestnuts out of the fire!"

"*Gessyan*. Ghosts. Hell hounds. Feel better?" Jake snapped.

"*Imbécile!* What do you think is surrounding us? *Mon Dieu*!"

Above her, on the bridge, she heard Cady, Cullan and the airmen exclaim as the skies around them filled with the ancient creatures that had been sealed away for so long in the depths of the Earth. Now the air around the *Allegheny Princess* was thick with the smoky, uncertain forms. Nicki held her breath as the beings floated past her in a silent stream, terrified that they might pay attention to her or to the airship. After them came the hell hounds that had chased her carriage, huge black ghost dogs impossibly loping across the night sky, slavering and snapping, yellow eyes filled with madness, teeth bared as they, too, struggled against the inexorable magic that drew them back into the abyss.

One of the creatures slid across the curved glass and steel of Nicki's bubble. The *gessyan* turned, like a dog scenting a rabbit, and its dark, empty eyes met Nicki's. She squealed as the beast's maw opened wide, like he meant to swallow her and the entire gunnery mount, and her hands closed around the controls to the Gatling gun, squeezing off several shots.

"What the hell are you doing!" Cullan shouted.

Cady dove for the hole in the floor. "Catch!" she shouted, tossing something to Nicki. Nicki snatched it out of the air instinctively, and held it up. A bright, golden light flared from the small, cold stone in her hand. The *gessyan* shrieked and fell away and the rest of the spirits drew back, giving the *Allegheny Princess* a wide margin.

"It's one of the Alekanovo stones we got from Jasinski's apartment," Cady said. "I found it in my pocket. Keep it—you might need it again."

"I've got to get into position," Cullan said. "Jake's going to need us soon."

Cady went back to her code-breaking machine. "I've got it!" she yelled a few minutes later. "Thwaites is meeting a buyer for the tourmaquartz at midnight outside Exposition Park."

"You've got to let Catherine know," Nicki said. "She'll get Miska's men to do something about it."

"Exactly what I was thinking," Cady agreed with a grin that made it clear how much she was enjoying the adventure. Her dark chestnut hair was caught back in a chignon, and she and Nicki had both opted for bicycling bloomers and simple shirtwaists, outfits much more suitable for activity and less restrictive, should they need to move quickly. A moment later, Nicki heard the tapping of the telegraph key as Cady sent her message to the private telegraph Wilfred monitored back at the Desmet house.

"Something really strange is happening at the mine entrance," Nicki yelled to the others. "There are some weird colored lights and stuff that doesn't look normal."

"Magic," Cady shouted back. "Want to bet Andreas and Veles are battling it out?"

"Dear God! There are guards coming at them from behind!" Before Cullan or Cady had a chance to react, Nicki slid her chair into position, gripped the handles of the Gatling gun and fired off a long warning rattle of gunfire, aiming at the open area between the mine mouth and the running team of guards. The gunfire was deafening, and the vibration of the gun rattled Nicki's bones and made her teeth chatter.

"Are you crazy?" Cullan shouted, stalking over to the hole in the deck. "Get out of there right now!"

Nicki muttered something unflattering in French that made Cady giggle. "Not until we're done," she said.

Just then, the headset squealed. Jake was shouting loudly enough for everyone to hear.

"No, of course I wasn't trying to kill you," Nicki replied calmly. "How was I supposed to know you'd seen them coming? Don't be ungrateful. They ran away, didn't they?"

"Why did Flyboy let you have the guns? Who's in charge up there?" he demanded.

"Don't you yell at me! And don't even try that—just because he's the pilot doesn't make him the boss of me!"

"Oh, my God! What is that thing?" Cady's voice rang out across the bridge. Nicki released the transmitter and stared through her glass bubble at something that appeared to have come straight from one of Grimm's fairy tales.

A hunchbacked old woman flew through the air like a witch from a child's nightmare. Her gnarled hands had long fingers and sharp nails, and her skin was pulled tightly over sharp cheekbones and a jutting chin. Her mouth was open, filled with jagged teeth, and her eyes glowed red in the darkness.

"The Night Hag!" Nicki exclaimed. She sent a hail of bullets through the creature, to no avail. The *gessyan* twisted and writhed, fighting the power that summoned it back to the deep places, to the depths where she and the rest of the *gessyan* would be bound once more.

Nicki caught her breath as the black wraiths followed the Night Hag like a swarm of vampire bats, black winged and deadly, their shroud-like figures blotting out the stars.

"It's working!" Cady exulted. "The Alekanovo stone and Marcin's book—they're working! The *gessyan* are returning to the mine!"

Nicky's headset filled with static "…need that beam now!" Jake's voice broke through.

"You couldn't give us a little more warning?" Nicki yelled. "Cullan! Adam! Jake said he needs us to fire the beam."

"Now!" Jake shouted.

Nicki stood up and yelled to Cullan. "He says, fire at the mine. Now!" To Jake: "He's doing it. He's doing it. Hold your horses!"

"We've got trouble!" Cady sang out. "Just picked up a Department telegraph. Good thing they don't know I can read them. They've got airships on the way. We've got to get out of here!"

"There's something you need to know—" Nicki started.

"Now, dammit!" Jake's voice sounded followed by a burst of static.

An explosion echoed beneath them as a fireball rose from what had been the Vesta Nine mine. Cullan sent the *Allegheny Princess* upward at an alarming rate of ascent, leaving Nicki's stomach feeling as if it had dropped into her shoes. She clung to the gun handles, careful not to press the trigger, feeling lightheaded from the sudden change in altitude.

In a dizzying sweep, Cullan brought the airship down and back into position.

The now-familiar whine of the Tesla ray warming up grew to a deafening crescendo. This time, forewarned, Nicki covered her ears, squeezing her eyes shut. The ray cut loose, so bright that it shone even through Nicki's closed eyes, turning the world red for an instant.

The ray hit the mine's main entrance.

"Everyone brace!" Cullan shouted. The *Allegheny Princess* shot up into the sky with a lurch. The shockwave from the explosion struck and nearly threw them all from their seats. The ship bobbed like cork on the ocean waves.

"Go, go, go!" Cady shouted at Cullan. "Those Department ships will be here any moment!"

"Too late." Cullan's voice was tight. "Two black airships sighted, at ten o'clock and two o'clock. Evasive action!" he shouted to his bridge crew. "Get us away!"

A barrage of gunfire erupted from the closer of the two airships. Bullets zinged past Nicki's bubble, narrowly missing the *Allegheny Princess*. The blast was deafening, and a second round sent a bullet into the reinforced glass of the gunner's mount, shattering one small panel.

"*Baise-moi*!" Nicki muttered. She gripped the controls of the Gatling gun, slid her chair into position, and opened fire.

A hail of bullets streamed toward the Department airship as Nicki circled back and forth along the chair's track, laying down covering fire.

"Are you trying to get us all a one-way ticket to Western Penitentiary?" Cullan shouted. "Those are *government* agents!"

"I'm not hitting them, I'm warning them! Fly, dammit!"

"In for a penny, in for a pound," Cullan grumbled, and activated the Tesla ray one more time. He aimed it between the *Allegheny Princess* and the pursuing ships, to dissuade them from coming closer. Nicki heard the machinery whine, closed her eyes, and squeezed the trigger on the Gatling guns, sending out a spray of bullets. Just for good measure, Adam dispatched two of his unmanned hover-saucers, the same ones that had proved so valuable in the fight above the Atlantic. As the black airships drew back, the hover saucers pursued them, sending out bursts of gunfire that forced the government craft to keep their distance.

"Oh, my!" Cady exclaimed. "I've never heard anyone telegraph those kinds of words before! They didn't even bother with code."

"I don't care if they're angry," Cullan replied between gritted teeth. "I care that they don't catch us!" He barked orders to the rest of his bridge crew, who scurried to do his bidding.

"Won't they recognize the name on our airship?" Cady asked. "They'll know who we are?"

"I changed the registration number on the stern and painted over the name," Cullan snapped. "Honestly, it's not like this is the first time we've done this sort of thing. Give me a little credit!"

"It's working!" Nicki yelled. "They're falling back!"

"They're not giving up," Cullan shouted back. "They're maneuvering, trying to box us in."

"Shall I shoot them again?" Nicki asked.

"No!" Cullan replied. "Wait. Yes—dammit!" He swore under his breath. "We are so screwed."

"Wunderkind!" Nicki shouted into the transmitter. "We need ideas!"

"Well I haven't tested it in anything like this but… against an airship it might work without any permanent damage," Adam replied.

"We're listening. Be quick—we don't have much time." Cullan snapped.

"I brought the disrupter. I use it in the lab to shut down experiments in an emergency. If we aimed it from the turret, it shouldn't affect the *Princess* but would shut down another airship, or at least make their systems stall for a few minutes. They won't fall from the sky or anything— just hang there, dead in the water, so to speak." He paused. "I'll be up in a minute." It seemed like he was on the bridge before the transmitter went silent, carrying something that looked like a cross between a rifle and a steam-powered canon.

Nicki grinned. "You're a genius. That's perfect. The men in the other airships are just doing their jobs; we don't really want to hurt them, just give us time to get away."

She moved to offer Adam her seat in the gunner's mount, but he shook his head. "Actually, it would be better for you to shoot it," he said. "You're a much better shot than I am. Just pretend it's a rifle. The effect spreads like a cone. We'll just have to hope we're close enough and it's strong enough," Adam said as he handed the odd contraption to Nicki.

She positioned the device on top of the gun controls, steadied it, and squeezed off a shot as soon as Cullan brought the first Department ship in range. The pursuing ship's running lights went dark and its engines fell silent. It careened slightly to one side, and Cullan put on a burst of speed.

"Second airship at twelve o'clock!" Cullan yelled.

"They're at the wrong angle. I can't get a good shot without hitting part of our ship!" Nicki shouted back.

In response, the *Allegheny Princess* suddenly descended, so quickly that Nicki felt her seat drop out from beneath her for a moment. She yelped, holding tightly to the disrupter and narrowly avoiding hitting her head on the low ceiling of the bubble. Cullan swung the *Princess* around, then climbed rapidly, so that she was now coming up on the Department airship from below and behind.

Nicki aimed and fired. Again her aim was true and the second Department ship went dark. Cullan angled them away sharply.

Only then did Nicki realize that Jake was shouting. At first, she made out a few curse words, and exclamations of complete and utter consternation. After a moment, Jake's verbal torrent slowed, and the words became more coherent.

"If you can hear me, get out of there! We'll meet you. It's done. Go!" he urged.

"You heard the man," Nicki said, scanning the horizon for any more of the black Department airships. "Let's go home."

Chapter THIRTY-TWO

"WELL, WHAT DO you know about that?" Nicki mused aloud in the parlor of the Desmet home. She set aside the newspaper and looked to Catherine and Jake. "They're calling it the Great Vesta Strike of 1898, and by all accounts, everyone says it will be one for the record books." She chuckled. "Amazing how people can just un-see the supernatural things they can't explain. There's not a word anywhere about killer ghosts or hell hounds. Imagine that!"

"Good thing we were nowhere nearby," Jake replied, leaning back in his chair. Days later, he was still sore, and all the scotch in the world was not going to erase the nightmares.

"I wager Richard Thwaites wishes he hadn't been in town," Nicki said.

"Imagine getting caught in the middle of a deal with such disreputable buyers—and by the Department, no less," Cady added.

"That's something we won't be reading about. But the muckraking reporter who ran so many articles on the Night Hag murders and the 'Totems and Idols' exhibit at the museum did manage to get a solid scoop on some real criminal activity," Nicki continued. "Seems he was a friend of Ida Tarbell's, and when Miss Tarbell visited Aunt Catherine—while we were off doing everything else—she happened to meet him, and she had the clout to get the reporter's story taken seriously. What with all those charred bodies at the mine, and documents suggesting Thwaites had those unsavory Tumblety and Brunrichter characters on a hidden payroll and records of payoffs to the police..."

"Don't forget the miners picketing his house and the feeding frenzy of reporters and photographers that kept him pinned inside, until the government filed their unlawful mining charges," Catherine said with dubious innocence, as she reached up to secure the hairpins in her chignon.

"You put Ida Tarbell onto Thwaites, didn't you?" Jake said, unsure whether to be proud or horrified.

The ghost of a smile touched Catherine's lips. "What are old friends for?" she replied with a sidelong glance at Wilfred. The butler's expression was utterly unreadable. "I just dropped a few hints, and passed along some typed notes recalling some of Thwaites's scandalous behavior, things everyone in our circles knew but no one said aloud."

"Aren't you worried someone will trace it back to you?" Rick asked.

Catherine chuckled. "Hardly. Thwaites was a bully and a womanizer; if every jilted suitor and wronged young lady's father were asked to stand in line for a shot at him, the queue would go around the block. It's just that the gossip hadn't traveled outside of certain social circles."

George and Rick occupied two of the other parlor chairs, and like Jake, they each had a glass of fine scotch to celebrate the occasion. The bottle of expensive scotch sat on a side table, a gift from Adam Farber, in thanks both for his new secret lab and for the stash of tourmaquartz Jake and Rick had managed to grab just before they had fled the mining compound.

"Veles and the Oligarchy really hung Thwaites out to dry, didn't they?" Rick said, swirling the amber liquid in his glass. "The gossip rags have made a hash of his reputation, the photos are there for all to see, and now that the government has pressed charges, odds are he'll be occupying a cell at Western Penitentiary for a very long time."

"Everyone's talking about it," Nicki said. "Poor boy. I suspect his career prospects have dimmed—not to mention his marriage prospects."

"Tesla-Westinghouse and their clients are beside themselves now that Adam Farber turned up alive," Rick noted. "Seems they also found a trail of paperwork implicating Adam's supervisor and that shady assistant in Thwaites's schemes. And if the Department saw or suspects anything about the Tesla ray incident at the mine, well, they're not saying."

Jake took a sip of his scotch and let it burn down his throat before he replied. "Actually, Adam filed a police report as soon as he got back to the Castle. Said he went through the rubble and found that several of his experimental machines had been stolen."

"Imagine that," Catherine remarked with a sly smile, not looking up from her needlepoint.

"Oh, and Dr. Nils sent word to the office that his staff found a couple more Brand and Desmet boxes that were delivered to the museum by mistake... all from the Krakow-to-Paris run," Jake said, shaking his head.

"Did Cullen get the *Allegheny Princess* patched up?" George asked.

"Oh, yeah," Rick replied. "Good as new. After all, the *Princess* is his baby. If he hadn't been able to outrun those Department airships, I think he would have rammed them."

"*Mon Dieu*!" Nicki exclaimed, fanning herself with exaggerated horror. "I thought we were goners."

"Danny Maguire sure came out smelling like a rose," George observed, pointing to the newspaper Nicki had discarded. News of the mine disaster had dominated headlines for days, and speculation about the cause of the blast fueled rumors each more fantastic than the last.

George picked up the paper and pointed to a large photograph of 'Dynamite' Danny Maguire, with a headline proclaiming him 'New Pittsburgh's Little Giant'.

"Seems like Maguire is getting credit for setting the Pinkerton boys back on their heels," George continued. "He's won a blow for labor, and folks are predicting it might take him to the governor's mansion—maybe even the White House."

"Wouldn't hurt to have friends in high places," Rick noted with a hint of a smile. The deep scratches inflicted by the *gessyan*'s attack were healing well, thanks to Renate's magic.

"Certainly might be good for business," Jake added. "Changing the subject a bit, did you read Drostan Fletcher's final report?"

George nodded. "The carriage was empty when Mitch and Jacob went back for Tumblety and Brunrichter. They never did find them, and Drostan guessed that the two mad doctors must have fled on foot." He sighed. "On a brighter note, with the mine destroyed, the river murders and the rest of the monster sightings have stopped."

"Sad they didn't find Tumblety or Brunrichter," Rick said with a sigh. "I imagine Mitch is steamed about that. He figured they would be his trump card with the Department."

Jake walked to the window. Despite the triumph at the mine, he had not been able to shake a feeling of melancholy. Nicki slipped up beside him. "You're thinking about your father," she said.

He nodded. "I guess we got justice for him—sort of," he said. "Thwaites is going to jail—not for arranging Father's murder, but it's punishment all the same. Veles lost lots of money on the deal, and a high-society business partner, and came out looking like a fool. That's some kind of payback." He sighed. "Neither one is very satisfying."

Rick joined them and put his arm on Jake's shoulder in silent support. Nicki looked at Jake, and for once all mirth was gone from her expression. "It won't be, Jake," she said. "Your father is gone, and revenge can't bring him back. But the men who were behind it paid a price. It's not fair, or satisfying—but sometimes, it's all you get."

"I suppose you're right," Jake said after a moment.

"But you never know what opportunities tomorrow will bring... and we are a creative bunch," Rick said, letting Nicki steer them back to where the others were still regaling one another with details from the big fight.

Wilfred appeared a few minutes later holding a clockwork pigeon. "Excuse me," he said, "but this flew into the kitchen a few minutes ago and refuses to leave."

Rick and Jake exchanged glances. "Mitch," they said in unison.

Jake rose and took the mechanical carrier pigeon out of Wilfred's hands, placing it on the writing desk and looking the bird over for a message capsule. Inside was a small note. *Press button by tail feathers,* it read in cramped handwriting.

"Next he'll want you to pull its finger—" Rick abruptly fell silent, remembering that ladies were present, but Catherine chuckled quietly and Nicki just grinned.

Jake found the button and pressed it, then stood back.

"Glad you got out," a scratchy Edison cylinder recording of Mitch Storm's voice said. "That was close. Wanted to tell you, all's good with the Department. They already had spies in the mine and think Veles and Thwaites blew it to cover their trail. They were thrilled to catch Thwaites in the middle of a deal and nab the crystals he was selling. The offer to work with you still stands. Drostan knows how to find us. Oh, and we won't tell about the *other* crystals. You owe us one."

The recording stopped and smoke began to seep from the hinges and joints of the mechanical pigeon. It began to rock back and forth violently. Then with a muffled thump, the metal bird ballooned to the size a turkey and fell to pieces, leaving nothing but a smoking pile of twisted tin.

"I guess Mitch got the last word," Jake said, staring at the ruined mechanical bird.

"Not exactly," Wilfred said from the doorway. "We've just received a telegram from your brother Henry in New York." Henry had retreated to New York for an extended convalescence after his injury in the gunfight at the cemetery.

"Henry? I'd nearly forgotten about him—and I was enjoying that," Jake said. Catherine gave him a reproving glance, but the half-smile suggested that she did not altogether disagree.

"What does he say?" Catherine asked.

Wilfred cleared his throat uncomfortably. "Shall I summarize, or read it word for word?" He paused. "It is a bit... intemperate."

"I'll spare you," Jake said, walking over and taking the telegram from Wilfred's hands. He read it over, and shook his head. "Oh, this is classic," he said, barely containing a laugh.

"Come on—share it with the rest of us!" Rick urged.

Jake sighed. "You asked for it. Here it is: 'Deal with Thwaites fell through. Stop. Is this your fault? Stop. Your office says paperwork is late because of plumbers. Stop. I knew it was a mistake to put you in charge.'"

"Stop!" Nicki begged. "Please—stop!" She was laughing so hard that tears ran down her cheeks. Catherine hid her laughter behind her needlepoint.

"Perhaps we shouldn't tell Henry about the new project," George said, wiping a tear from his eye as he chuckled.

Jake frowned. "Project?"

George nodded. "Andreas Thalberg was most impressed with the three of you. He wants to send you out to bring back a very delicate acquisition..."

"Fabulous!" Nicki said, clapping her hands. "I can have my trunk packed in an hour."

"Here we go again," Rick said with an exaggerated sigh, downing the last of his scotch.

"Tell Cullan to get the *Allegheny Princess* ready," Jake said. "We're good to go."

EPILOGUE

Drogo Veles leaned against the railing of the steamship. The Atlantic Ocean stretched to the horizon, dark and ominous in the moonlight. Far away from New Pittsburgh, but not yet far enough.

Idiots. All of them, idiots. Getting a ticket to England at the last moment had not been difficult, especially not with his large number of useful acquaintances, most of whom owed the dark witch some type of personal debt. He moved quickly enough that he was well on his way before the Department of Supernatural Investigations could have the government looking for him.

A private airship took him to New York, and an ocean liner seemed the most discreet way to leave the country. After that, a false name and a falsified passport did the rest. The ship's captain had once asked Veles's help in destroying a rival's business. Veles had supplied the magic necessary, and the captain found himself forever entangled. He was one of many who discovered, too late, that money is the least costly way to pay for what one wants.

A man in a sailor's coat walked up to the railing near Veles, leaned against it and casually rolled a cigarette. He took a deep draw and released it, with an air of satisfaction. "Message sent," he said.

"Good," Veles said, casually handling over a folded bill, easily a week's salary. "I may have a few more messages before we reach port."

"Fine by me."

"Was there a response?" Veles asked.

The sailor nodded. His manner told Veles the man was no stranger to deals done under the table. "Nightshade. Stop. Fell minus two. Stop. Passage arranged. Stop."

Veles met the man's gaze. "Not a word to anyone," he said, extending a flicker of magic to assure his will would be done. "Cross your heart and hope to die."

The sailor gave him a wary look, as if on some level he realized he had just been placed under a geas. "Sure, guv. Whatever you say." With that, he sauntered away, and Veles leaned against the rail once more, sure that the man would have no memory of their encounter, and a deep aversion to ever speaking of him to anyone.

The telegram had been most informative, for one who knew the code. *Mandrake Club, ten p.m.* the first part said. The Mandrake was one of London's many prestigious members-only clubs, though one regarded by most people to be mere fiction. Veles knew for a fact that the club was very real, and its membership of powerful practitioners made sure its existence and whereabouts remained quiet.

'Passage arranged' was clear enough, though only Veles and his patron knew where. An ambitious Hungarian noble had beseeched Veles to help him with some thorny business dealings. The man had been very happy to find his invitation suddenly accepted, even on short notice.

Far enough away that New Pittsburgh might as well not exist, Veles thought. *Close enough to Krakow for me to see if Marcin left anything else of value behind.*

He was sanguine about the loss of Vesta Nine. *Just business,* he thought with a shrug. *Something that imbecile Thwaites never grasped. Though perhaps, as things turned out, I should thank him for taking the fall on this with our buyers. Not to mention that this will drive the price of tourmaquartz sky high on the black market.*

Vesta Nine's collapse—and the sudden interest by the U.S. government in its investors—sent a shock wave through the rogues' gallery of arms dealers and petty despots who had sought tourmaquartz for their own purposes. The clients awaiting tourmaquartz shipments from the mine's most recent production were likely to be ruined financially and investigated to boot. Veles smiled coldly. *No real harm done there—to me. They were dangerous dabblers. I've almost done the world a service by destroying their fortunes.*

A newspaper headline in New York read: 'New Pittsburgh Society Son Defrauds Investors'. A deliciously unflattering photograph of Richard Thwaites accompanied the article, which was likely spoonfed to editors from the Department's lackeys. *Drivel about the mine being a fraud and rumors of a silver vein gone dry. Enough to satisfy the rabble, and cover the Oligarchy's patrician asses.* Still, Veles took a measure of cold amusement at Thwaites's fall from grace. *Dear Richard was so very certain that he was cheating me out of my fair share by having his name on all the documents,* Veles thought with a satisfied sigh. *His kind never realize their role until too late. That makes them remarkably useful.*

Before he left New Pittsburgh, Veles had arranged transportation for Francis Tumblety and Adolph Brunrichter to Canada, their silence purchased with a generous stipend and sealed with magic. *A bit more work, and their creations will sell to the highest bidders.* Veles thought. *A worthwhile investment, and easy enough to dispose of if they become difficult.*

His assets had always been safely stored in banks across the Continent under a variety of assumed names, usually in gold and diamonds—easy to liquidate, hard to trace. He had wired all but a pittance of his holdings in New Pittsburgh to London at the first hint that DSI was interested in Vesta Nine, and the money had been moved through a series of shell accounts since then, enough to confound government accountants should they come looking.

Several safety deposit boxes spread among the best banks in Europe held something more valuable: tourmaquartz. Veles had skimmed his portion of the mine's production off the top and moved it out of the country early. Thwaites had been none the wiser, too busy spending his portion to support his opulent mode of living. *That's the problem when you're so busy flaunting your wealth that you don't have time to watch the books,* Veles thought.

A few matters, however, remained unsettled and the thought of that soured Veles's mood. Andreas and Renate Thalberg were old enemies and a known quantity. They had co-existed thus far by agreeing to leave each other alone unless forced into confrontation. He could abide their continued survival. The *Logonje* were beyond Veles's ability to destroy, but he had been working around them for so long that he accepted their interference as a force of nature. Jake Desmet and Rick Brand, on the other hand, had caused entirely too much trouble. They were bad for business, and likely to pop up again, unwanted and at the worst possible time. They needed to be eliminated.

There was time, Veles knew, to figure out the particulars of where, when and how. He had already tried a straightforward curse, only to have his magic turned aside by Andreas's protections. But there were other, equally dangerous ways to solve the problem.

Andreas warded for the obvious: death spells, magical attack. Veles thought. *Here's one that puts the odds in my favor, one even Andreas can't repel.* It was an old curse, and a powerful one, known to many cultures for its subtle, deadly potency. *Jake Desmet and Rick Brand,* Veles said, summoning his power and forming his curse. *May you live in interesting times.*

Authors' Note

PITTSBURGH, PENNSYLVANIA IS a real place, but we have embellished, a bit, around the edges. We grew up in small towns a few hours north of Pittsburgh, went to college near the city, and lived in a suburb of Pittsburgh for ten years. Two of our children were born in Pittsburgh, and we worked for Pittsburgh-based companies. We visit the area frequently, since we still have close family living nearby. It's one of our favorite cities, and we always enjoy a visit to the 'Burgh'.

In the late 1800s, Pittsburgh really was the nation's industrial epicenter, quite deserving of a steampunk legacy, since steam powered the factories of legendary industrialists like Andrew Carnegie and Henry Clay Frick. In the Gilded Age, Pittsburgh was also home to more than its share of Robber Barons, men whose inventiveness shaped our modern world and whose rapacity and desire to live large were breathtaking, even by today's standards. And in case you wondered, history reports that Nikola Tesla and George Westinghouse did work together for a time... what if they had taken their partnership further? Thereon hangs a tale.

New Pittsburgh is a fictional construct. While many of the places mentioned in *Iron and Blood* (and some of the historical figures) are real, we've also invented people, places and things and taken liberties with key events to create a raw-around-the-edges Gilded Age true to the city's frontier heritage. Historians may notice that we've fudged a few details here and there. Please forgive us in the name of entertainment.

Our co-authorship grew out of working closely on many books together over the years, brainstorming plot elements, passing revisions back and forth, collaborating on ideas to get past writers' block. That grew from looking for typos and continuity issues into full collaboration, and although the steampunk series is the first to bear both our names, it's the fact that we work together full time on the books that has made it possible to write three series, bring out monthly ebook short stories and contribute to anthologies. We are thrilled to find that a life partnership has developed into a creative partnership as well.

You might want to check out the rest of our epic and urban fantasy books, the *Deadly Curiosities* series, *The Chronicles of the* Necromancer series, the *Fallen Kings Cycle*, and the *Ascendant Kingdoms Saga*. We also bring out a new short story every month on Kindle/Kobo/Nook in the *Jonmarc Vahanian Adventures* and the *Deadly Curiosities Adventures* and coming in 2015, the *Storm and Fury Adventures* (featuring more from Mitch and Jacob, the *Sturm und Drang* boys as their boss calls them).

If you've enjoyed *Iron and Blood*, look for the short stories featuring the further adventures of Mitch and Jacob featured in several Steampunk anthologies including *Dreams of Steel 5*, *The Weird Wild West* and *Clockwork Universe: Steampunk vs. Aliens*. You can find details on our website, at www.JakeDesmet.com. Please also find us on Twitter @GailZMartin and @LNMartinAuthor, on Facebook.com/WinterKingdoms, on Goodreads.com/GailZMartin, and we post free excerpts of our books on Wattpad.com/GailZMartin.

Thank you for reading!

Acknowledgements

So many people take part in making a book a reality. Thank you to Ben Smith, Jon Oliver, David Moore, Lydia Gittins and all the other wonderful people at Solaris Books. Thanks especially to our agent, Ethan Ellenberg, for believing in and championing this concept early on. Also, thanks to our wonderful cover artist, Michael Komarck, whose art may look familiar to readers from the first three books of the *Chronicles of the Necromancer* series. Many thanks as well to all our writer and convention friends for their support and camaraderie. We also owe thanks to the bloggers, book reviewers, genre websites, booksellers, and convention runners who make it possible for us to get our work into the hands of readers. And of course, we owe a debt of gratitude to our readers, because your continued enthusiasm for these stories makes it possible for us to spin more tales. Thank you.

GAIL Z. MARTIN'S
THE CHRONICLES OF THE NECROMANCER

BOOK ONE

THE SUMMONER

ISBN: 978 1 84416 468 4 • £7.99/$7.99

The world of Prince Martris Drayke is thrown into sudden chaos when his brother murders their father and seizes the throne. Forced to flee, with only a handful of loyal friends to support him, Martris must seek retribution and restore his father's honour. But if the living are arrayed against him, Martris must learn to harness his burgeoning magical powers to call on different sets of allies: the ranks of the dead.

The Summoner is an epic, engrossing tale of loss and revenge, of life and afterlife – and the thin line between them.

"Attractive characters and an imaginative setting."

– David Drake, author of *The Lord of the Isles*

BOOK TWO

THE BLOOD KING

ISBN: 978 1 84416 531 5 • £7.99/$7.99

Having narrowly escaped being murdered by his evil brother, Jared, Prince Martris Drayke must take control of his magical abilities to summon the dead, and gather an army big enough to claim back the throne of his dead father.

But it isn't merely Jared that Tris must combat. The dark mage, Foor Arontala, has schemes to cause an inbalance in the currents of magic and raise the Obsidian King...

"A fantasy adventure with whole-hearted passion."

– Sandy Auden, *SFX*

GAIL Z. MARTIN'S
THE CHRONICLES OF THE NECROMANCER

BOOK THREE

DARK HAVEN

ISBN: (UK) 978 1 84416 708 1 • £7.99
ISBN: (US) 978 1 84416 598 8 • $7.99

The kingdom of Margolan lies in ruin. Martris Drayke, the new king, must rebuild his country in the aftermath of battle, while a new war looms on the horizon. Meanwhile Jonmarc Vahanian is now the Lord of Dark Haven, and there is defiance from the vampires of the *Vayash Moru* at the prospect of a mortal leader.

But can he earn their trust, and at what cost?

"A fast-paced tale laced with plenty of action."

– SF Site

BOOK FOUR

DARK LADY'S CHOSEN

ISBN: (UK) 978 1 84416 830 9 • £7.99
ISBN: (US) 978 1 84416 831 6 • $7.99

Treachery and blood magic threaten King Martris Drayke's hold on the throne he risked everything to win. As the battle against a traitor lord comes to its final days, war, plague and betrayal bring Margolan to the brink of destruction. Civil war looms in Isencroft. And in Dark Haven, Lord Jonmarc Vahanian has bargained his soul for vengeance as he leads the *vayash moru* against a dangerous rogue who would usher in a future drenched in blood.

"Just when you think you know where things are heading, Martin pulls another ace from her sleeve."

– A. J. Hartley, author of *The Mask of Atraeus*

Merchant, industrialist and explorer Trassan Kressind has an audacious plan – combining the might of magic and iron in the heart of a great ship to navigate an uncrossed ocean, seeking the city of the extinct Morfaan to uncover the secrets of their lost sciences.

Ambition runs strongly in the Kressind family, and for each of Trassan's siblings fate beckons. Soldier Rel is banished to a vital frontier, bureaucrat Garten balances responsibility with family loyalty, sister Katriona is determined to carve herself a place in a world of men, outcast Guis struggles to contain the energies of his soul, while priest Aarin dabbles in forbidden sorcery.

The world is in turmoil as new money brings new power, and the old social order crumbles. And as mankind's arts grow stronger, a terror from the ancient past awakens...

This highly original fantasy depicts a unique world, where tired gods walk industrial streets and the tide's rise and fall is extreme enough to swamp continents. Magic collides with science to create a rich backdrop for intrigue and adventure in the opening book of this epic saga.

Eveline Duchen is a thief and con-artist, surviving day by day on the streets of London, where the glittering spires of progress rise on the straining backs of the poor and disenfranchised. Where the Folk, the otherworldly children of fairy tales and legends, have all but withdrawn from the smoke of the furnaces and the clamour of iron.

Caught in an act of deception by the implacable Mr Holmforth, Evvie is offered a stark choice: transportation to the colonies, or an education – and utter commitment to Her Majesty's Service – at Miss Cairngrim's harsh school for female spies.

But on the decadent streets of Shanghai, where the corruption of the Empire is laid bare, Holmforth is about to make a devil's bargain, and Eveline's choices could change the future of two worlds...